3/28/08

To Madelyn McDaniel

Good reading

Paul Scott Martin

THE SEARCH FOR

SOONER SILVER

The Adventures
of The Blacktail Kids

Paul Scott Martin

The Blacktail Kids

The Blacktail Kids' Motto:
Honesty, Decency, Sharing, Courage and Caring

Printed by The Hardesty Press, Inc - Tulsa Oklahoma

Edited by Mary Lou Martin and Connie Tacker
Animal Illustrations by Mary Lou Martin
Situational Illustrations by Janet Fadler Davie
Perryman Ranch photo by Barbara Fadler
Interior and Cover Design by Millie Hardesty York

Maps: Rainfall, County, Highways and River/Lakes Maps Courtesy of United States Geological Survey, the National Atlas.

Aquifer Map Courtesy of the Oklahoma Water Resources Board.

ISBN: 978-1-60530-054-2

This work is dedicated to my mother, Mary Lou Martin of Tulsa, whose enthusiasm for Oklahoma's fascinating history and geography gave me the motivation I needed to write this work. Thanks Mom.

Special thanks to my sister Connie Tacker for all of her help in completing this book.

I would also like to thank Karan Stubbs of Bixby ISD and Laura Wilson of Jenks ISD for taking time to review the manuscript and offering many helpful suggestions.

THE BRIDGE

Amy gazed excitedly out the window as the last of Paris, Texas disappeared behind her. The flashing rays of a late spring dusk splashed the land in a beautiful reddish orange. Curled on either side of her were J.J. and Angel, the black stray dogs she had found only last winter in Arkansas.

"Mom, how much farther to Oklahoma?" Amy asked impatiently as she lightly tugged on Angel's ears and playfully pulled at J.J.'s front paws.

"Almost there, baby," Linda replied as she surveyed the floral carpet of blues, reds, yellows and purples now ablaze in the height of spring's brilliance. "Twenty miles and we'll cross the Red River. From then on it's Oklahoma."

"Hear that, girls," Amy chirped as the dogs came to attention. "We're getting close. Why do they call it the Red?"

"See the red dirt all around?" advised her mother. "When that dirt gets into the water it gives it a reddish tint, especially after a rain."

"Is the Red a big river?" questioned Amy, as she watched U.S. 271 cut through to the north.

"You bet," answered Linda "and critically important to the history of this region."

"How so?" countered Amy.

"See this highway," her mother explained. "In the old days roads like this simply didn't exist. If you wanted to travel you had two choices; use the Indian trails or travel by boat. The boats were a lot easier and you could carry more supplies and trade goods. That was important for the early traders and explorers. In fact you'll see that Oklahoma has lots of rivers and all of them were the highways of their time. In many ways the history of this country is the history of its rivers."

"Neat," beamed Amy, happy to have learned something new. "It's nice to travel easy," she laughed.

"Oh, it wasn't easy," countered her mother. "The Red's always been tough; tough and dangerous. Many a ship got stuck on the sandbars and I mean stuck for good. And in the days of the great cattle drives from Texas to the north the Red was one place the cowboys feared. Fast currents and quicksand took many a drover to his last roundup."

"Last roundup?" she puzzled, not knowing exactly what her mother meant.

"That's cowboy talk for heaven," explained her father Jack who had been itching to get in a word.

"And don't forget that the Red has always been an important boundary," he added. "In the early days the Red was the dividing line between Spanish Texas

1

and French Louisiana, then the Republic of Texas and American Louisiana, and now the states of Texas and Oklahoma."

"What's Oklahoma like?" Amy quizzed away.

"Pretty," replied her mother, "and always changing. Whatever kind of country you like, you can find in Oklahoma. It has broad rivers, shimmering lakes, clear mountain streams, pine covered mountains and rolling hills, thick prairie grasslands and dense forests, wheat filled flatlands and high plateaus. Oklahoma has just about everything. You'll see it all before we're through."

"And it has an incredibly interesting history," added her father. Amy smiled as she studied the map her parents had given her and then told the dogs they were in for a really good time.

"Where did the name Oklahoma come from?" quizzed Amy. "It's kind of strange."

"It's a Choctaw Indian word," answered her father. "It means 'Land of the Redman'."

"Why do they call it that?" questioned Amy.

"Because of al¹ the Indian peoples that live here," Jack answered, "some sixty different tribes. In fact a long time ago Oklahoma was called 'Indian Territory'."

"Did only Indians live there?" Amy quizzed.

"Oh, no," countered her father. "Europeans began coming to Oklahoma centuries ago."

"When did they change the name?" Amy asked.

"One hundred years ago," Jack replied," in 1907 when Oklahoma became a state. That's one of the reasons we chose to vacation here. We wanted you to see what a centennial celebration looks like."

"What's that word?" Amy blubbered.

"Centennial," interjected her mother. "It means one hundred years."

"Oh," stammered Amy as Angel grinned and J.J. seemed to snicker a little as she pawed Amy's arm.

"You didn't know that word either," she sniffed at the dogs, certain they knew exactly what the people were talking about. Linda laughed and told Amy that maybe the dogs had a better vocabulary than she did.

"I wish little Max was with us too," Amy moaned. "Why did we have to leave him at the vet's?"

"Badger Max," Linda chuckled referring to his nickname.

"He had to have his operation now that he's old enough and we thought it would be a good time to do it. Besides two dogs on one trip is enough."

J.J. pouted, a little insulted at the thought that they might be any trouble.

"What was the operation for," questioned Amy.

"So he can't make puppies," Linda replied.
You know the rules; too many homeless animals as it is. We don't want to make the problem worse."

"But if he made puppies we could keep them," argued Amy. "They wouldn't be homeless."

"That's true," her mother replied. "But we can only have so many dogs. What if we found another stray that needed a home but couldn't keep it because we already had too many? Then what would happen to it?"

"Oh, I see what you mean," nodded Amy as she thought about finding J.J. and Angel starving and freezing the year before. "If we'd have had too many pets last year we wouldn't have these two now."

"Exactly," confirmed Linda. "And wouldn't that be terrible?"

"It sure would," Amy agreed as she nuzzled the girls who both seemed to nod in agreement.

Amy thought about her mother's words as she played with the dogs. The Russells had found the two starving strays last winter at Blanchard Springs Caverns in Arkansas. They were nicknamed the Blacktail Kids because of their black tails. The older by two years, J.J. was incredibly strong, smart, and tough. Now filled out after months of good food and rest she was nearly seventy pounds of solid muscle. Mostly black with skirts of rust on her flanks, her short, stubby tail was always in motion. Her trim, healthy coat gleamed in the sunlight. Her little sister Angel was everything J.J. was not. Shy and much smaller at forty pounds, she always looked to J.J. for protection. Her long black fur finished in a fluffy tail that nearly reached the ground. Dashes of white marked her chest and feet. Both had piercing dark brown eyes.

After being abandoned by a bad owner in East Texas, she and J.J. had traveled much of the country searching for the Golden Bone of Happiness. What they found instead was the first good home they had ever had. Now happy and content with their new family in Houston, they would sneak into the study late at night to look at maps of the places they had seen while on their journey.

They were lucky that the Russells were the ones to find them. Mr. Russell was a NASA scientist, working at the Houston Space Center. Mrs. Russell took care of Amy, wrote children's stories for magazines, and did volunteer work for the local animal shelter. Five year old blonde Amy was already an accomplished reader who had developed a deep interest in U.S. history and geography. She was always studying maps and often wondered why she so often found them open on the floor instead of folded and on the shelf. On their way home to Houston after finding the girls, the Russells came upon policemen and humane society workers loading numerous dogs into a van. Their owner had neglected them terribly and was being taken to jail on charges of animal cruelty. One cute little lab caught Mrs. Russell's eye and she insisted on taking him home. They named him Max after the dog that had first started the Kids on their quest for the Golden Bone. But it wasn't long before little Max had a nickname of his own; the badger, given to him because he loved to dig more than he wanted to eat. Neither Amy nor the dogs had ever seen Oklahoma before and were eagerly looking forward to the trip.

"Looks like a storm's coming in from the west," Jack warned. "Look at those clouds."

"Just a few miles to the bridge," Linda offered.

"Hugo, Oklahoma straight ahead," squeaked Amy as she read the road sign.

"Very good," praised her mother. "Not bad reading for a five year old."

Amy beamed at the praise, certain her hard book work was paying off. J.J. gave her a paw pat of congratulations while Angel offered a wide grin.

Jack Russell's face betrayed concern as he looked to the west.

"Hope we can make it before the storm hits," he worried. "Could be a bad one," he added, nervously watching the tidal wave of dark boiling quickly toward them.

"Sure looks like it, " agreed a concerned Linda. "Look at the wind whipping the trees."

Amy and the dogs shuddered as great gusts of wicked wind sawed and snapped like twigs the stout branches of pecan and oak and elm that lined the roadway borders and sent them crashing to the ground. Dark leaves of spring filled the air in a heavy snow of green. It seemed more like autumn as they sailed the currents before finally finding ground. A deafening thunder pierced the windy howl as the first bolts painted carbon black skies in razor-cut tails of blinding white. Mile by mile the storm steadily swallowed the land.

The dogs huddled close to Amy as she covered and comforted them. Angel shook hard with each explosion. The car swayed and rocked with each gust. The rain drops came; first just a dusting of one then two then ten, each hitting with a muddy splat as it knifed through the churning air. Then, in an instant, the thunderheads emptied their bulging holds and a thick gruel of rain, hail, dust, grass and trash poured sideways and down to choke the tattered land below.

Jack Russell slowed the car to a crawl, his vision checked by the squall to but a few foggy, fearful feet ahead. Suddenly the grey steel girders of the Red River bridge appeared dimly on each side.

"Welcome to Oklahoma," he advised as a splitting trumpet of thunder announced their arrival.

Amy and the girls drew still closer as Mr. Russell inched his way forward, far too concerned with the weather to explain a geographic fact to Amy. He had intended to point out to her that the state of Oklahoma began at water's edge on the south bank. In most cases where rivers mark state boundaries, the dividing line is in the middle of the stream.

Danger hid just behind a low river ridge to the north. Unseen by Mr. Russell, powerful fronts of warm and cold began to collide. Strong winds from the south, west and north met and meshed in a twisting ring of frightful, deadly power. For an instant the winds calmed, their strength sucked in by the new threat rising just ahead.

"Tornado! Linda shrieked. "Get off the bridge!"

But it was too late. In an instant the funnel appeared and with bullet speed shot straight for the tressel. Like a rumbling train the air groaned with roaring thumps and thuds as the whirling mass of black and grey exploded through the bridge in a fury of ruin. The center section crashed into a river brimming full and rushing fast in a flood of reddish brown. With it fell the car. At the last instant Jack Russell lowered the windows hoping to provide one chance for escape. He knew a sealed car caught underwater was a deathtrap. Ever so briefly the car floated as he yelled for his wife to grab Amy and pull her up front. Amy shouted that she couldn't leave the dogs but Linda latched onto an arm and jerked her forward. Then she climbed to the back and quickly pushed first J.J. and then Angel out the window and into the swirling current which quickly swept the dogs downstream. Only a few feet apart with J.J. in the lead, both fought to stay afloat. Choking in panic, Angel cried out to her sister as they neared a sharp bend in the river. The change of course slowed the current just enough for the dogs to gain some control. In a bark barely audible through the whining winds, J.J. yelled to Angel.

"Swim to the bank!" she shouted as she paddled furiously for the sand but ten feet away.

Angel obeyed and with every last ounce of strength she could muster fought mightily to reach its safety. J.J.'s front legs finally found solid earth and with one last supreme effort of will she pulled herself to shore. Ahead Angel was still struggling to free herself from the powerful pull of the raging river. In a desperate lunge she hurled herself toward an inch-thick tree trunk rising just above the water. She hit the limb with such force that it nearly snapped. Now with a solid anchor she moved down the sapling the last few feet to water's edge. Once firmly grounded, she quickly turned back to look for her sister. Just down the bank J.J. was moving toward her as swiftly as fatigue would allow. When they met they nuzzled each other in relief and then collapsed to the ground, heaving in exhaustion. After a few minutes they rose to look out over the swollen Red that had almost killed them. Near the bank floated a large stuffed bear. It was Amy's.

"Maybe they got out," Angel whimpered still struggling to catch her breath "We did."

"Maybe," agreed J.J. with a wheeze. "Let's go upstream and look."

Drained by exhaustion the girls slowly worked their way up the river's north bank. Though black overhead, to the west a carpet of deep sky blue was spilling slowly eastward. Soon the sun's twilight rays broke through, drenching the Red River Valley in dazzling splashes of yellow orange. The air was strangely still. Not a leaf blew. With each minute the waters retreated and the current slowed to a gentle crawl. The mighty Red was now back in her banks.

As the kids closed in on the bridge they found it alive with activity. Police and emergency workers of all kinds fanned out on both ends of the structure, most of which was still standing. In the water near the middle they could see the tops of three vehicles, one of them their own. Tow trucks and ambulances were standing by, while men in rowboats were anchored near the cars and attaching long towlines to them. Hiding behind a bush near the shore the kids watched all. One by one the tow trucks pulled the cars to the Oklahoma bank where the ambulance crews waited. It seemed there were no survivors.

"I don't think they made it," Angel sobbed as she choked back tears and collapsed to the ground.

J.J. tried to speak but the words wouldn't come. All she could do was lay a paw on Angel's shoulder and stare at the bridge.

Angel rose and began to run toward the car but J.J. stopped her.

"No, Angel," she warned sternly. "We can't let them see us. They'll take us to the pound and we don't have anyone who will come for us," she finished, remembering that the Russells had no relatives.

Angel flashed back to what seemed like so long ago when she and J.J. had been caught and taken to a dog pound in New Jersey. She remembered how close to the end they had come there.

"You're right," agreed Angel. "But what do we do?"

"I don't know," J.J. shrugged. "But we'll think of something. We've been through tough times before and we've made it. We'll come through this, too. I know it's hard to imagine but something good will come from it. I know it."

"I hope you're right," sighed Angel as she rubbed up to J.J.'s side.

The day's last light faded quickly as the sun's crown inched down in the west. The dogs could hear the people talking. One said that the tornado was rated an EF-5, the most powerful measured. The girls watched as one by one the emergency vehicles pulled onto the highway and vanished south into Texas or north into Oklahoma. As the black of night chased away the dusk's last blues and yellows the kids sought shelter in a dense cluster of oaks just a few hundred feet away.

"We'll get some rest and then decide what to do in the morning," J.J. counseled.

"Okay," whimpered Angel.

Together they turned to take one last look at the bridge and then dragged themselves into the woods. They found a nice thick bed of cool, damp leaves at the base of a rocky ledge and curled up together. J.J. gave Angel one last pat of comfort as her little sister yawned and sank quickly into an exhausted slumber. Then she stared deeply into the dark woods and worried about what the days ahead would bring.

Well after midnight Angel's eyes gently fluttered. Shaking her head slightly she gazed dreamily into a night blessedly bathed in the soft yellow light of a bright full moon painted amber. Though grieving deeply, she found a kind of peace in the stillness of the woods. The echoing chirps, croaks, buzzes and blasts of a thousand creatures eased her despair. She studied J.J., still fast asleep, and thought about how strong she had always been; how mentally tough. J.J. was always the one to protect her; always the one to give her confidence when she could find none on her own; always the one determined never to give up; to fight on no matter how bad the situation seemed. She vowed that she would make herself the equal of her sister in character if not in physical strength, and together they would find a new home. With that pledge she rested her white whiskered chin on J.J.'s faintly heaving side and found soothing shelter in sleep once more.

"Time to get up," whispered J.J. as she gave Angel a little nudge.

"It's still dark," Angel protested.

"I know," J.J. agreed, "but I think it's near dawn," she added as she noted just the slightest brightening in the eastern sky. "Did you sleep well?"

"Not bad," answered Angel, not telling her sister about awakening earlier. "What are we going to do now?"

"I'm not sure," J.J. confessed, " but let's find some water and think about it for a while."

"I think there's a creek just over there," Angel noted as she pointed toward a stand of cottonwoods. "I can hear the water."

"I think you're right," commended J.J. "Let's go see."

Together they plodded through the dewy dampness and, just as Angel had reckoned, there was a narrow draw of clean, cool water trickling ever so slowly back toward the Red.

Parched throats dampened, they ambled back to their hideout and sat down to talk. Just as J.J. was about to speak they felt the rush of a cool breeze blowing out of the woods just above their ledge. Then they heard the crack of crunching leaves moving slowly toward them.

"Something's coming," J.J. warned as she poked her head over the rocks and looked into the trees.

"What is it?" whispered the little one as she joined her sister. "What's that light?"

"Don't know," murmured J.J. as she watched an oval of brightness approach them.

"Let's run," Angel bleated.

"No," J.J. countered. "Keep quiet and be still. It'll probably pass right by."

The Kids were confused by the light. It certainly wasn't sunlight as the horizon was still nearly black and it wasn't anything like a flashlight. And it was heading straight for them.

They huddled together below the ridge and tried not to make a sound as the beam drew closer. Then they heard a slight shuffle of feet just above them and their little hole began to brighten. Knowing they had been spotted, J.J. let out a vicious growl. But the light did not move. As their eyes adjusted to the new brightness they could see a woman looking down on them. She held no beacon.

The illumination came from the cloud that surrounded her. Tall with copper skin and deep black eyes, she wore a finely tooled, fringed buckskin dress that fell to mid-calf. The front and sleeves were covered in delicate patterns of beadwork; white and yellow and red. Soft moccasins cushioned her feet. Her hair was stunningly beautiful; the most refined the dogs had ever seen. Worn loose and falling to her waist, the thick but silky strands of darkest black glistened even in the pre-dawn dark. She moved with exquisite grace, her soft hands gently waving in the cocoon of light that framed her.

She said nothing for a moment, only motioned for the girls to sit. As they obeyed she edged slightly toward them and pointed to the thin sliver of silvery light trying hard to break through night's last darkness.

"A new day comes for you," she advised in a kind but firm voice. "Each new day means the start of a new life. Begin today to build that new life. Find the Sooner Silver and you'll find a new home."

"What's the Sooner Silver?" Angel questioned, not the least bit afraid but quite puzzled.

"You'll know soon enough," she advised.

"Where do we find it?" quizzed J.J.

"Ask the animals. They know all. And do exactly as they tell you," she warned. "Take this," she added as she handed them a simple leather pouch. "Remember, you must not lose it."

"What is it?" Angel asked as she accepted the offering and shared it with J.J.

But the Indian woman did not answer. Slowly she began to back away as the dogs raised up to watch her. Just as she reached a stand of trees the air around her flared white. The dogs gulped as the woman seemed to take the form of a large white animal and in an instant vanished down a narrow trail. The girls saw nothing more, but heard the heavy beats of giant hooves pounding the forest floor. Then all was quiet.

For a moment the dogs just stood looking into the woods as the day's first rays shone down. Stunned, they looked at each other for answers.

"Where did she go?" squeaked Angel.

"I don't know," replied J.J. with a shake of her head. "She just disappeared."

"How did she turn color like that?" pondered the little one.

"It looked like she turned into a big animal," J.J. "A really big animal."

"It was probably just the light," reasoned Angel.

"Probably so," agreed J.J., still convinced she saw what she saw. "What's in the pouch?"

"Let's see," chirped Angel as she opened the leather bag. "Nice pouch," she added as she pulled out its contents.

"Sure is," affirmed J.J.

"I wonder what this is?" queried Angel as she pulled out a pointed object about three inches long.

"It's an arrowhead," advised J.J. as she studied the point and the sharp edges. "It looks like silver."

"What's an arrowhead?" Angel quizzed.

"Don't you remember some of the books we've looked through?" J.J. stated. "Arrows were what they used for hunting before they had guns."

"Oh, ya," affirmed Angel, embarrassed that she hadn't remembered.

"Remember what she said," J.J. warned. "We have to be careful with this. Let's tie it to your neck," she counseled as she knotted the long leather strings into a loop and slid it over Angel's head.

"What now," Angel asked.

"Talk to the animals. That's what she said to do," reckoned J.J. "And let's look for some breakfast," she added.

"Ya," nodded Angel, now remembering how hungry she was. "Which animals," she quizzed.

"Don't know," J.J. shrugged as she surveyed the woods. "But I'll bet there are plenty of them out here to talk to."

Angel just nodded in agreement.

THE BADGER, THE BEAVER, AND THE BEAR

The kids had been in this situation before. In their earlier journey they quickly learned the art of survival. Food and water were always their first concerns. In eastern Oklahoma water was usually no problem. Some parts of this region received nearly sixty inches of rain a year, keeping the many streams and lakes full and the countryside green. But finding food was a challenge wherever they were.

"I guess we should try the highway," J.J. reasoned. "Maybe we'll find some food at a roadside park or something."

"Good a place as any to look," Angel agreed. "Let's head north along the road."

The girls took another look at U.S. 271 and were grateful that the highway's flanks were heavily lined with pine and oak. They could easily stay out of sight until they came to a place that might offer something to eat. A sign indicated that they were not far from the city of Hugo. They soon came upon a little park but found no food. But next to a trash can they did find a large, sturdy, zippered tan canvas bag with two stout handle-straps at its top.

"We'll take this with us," J.J. stated. "I can slip my front legs through the straps and mount it on my back. It'll be good for carrying things."

"Ya," confirmed the little one. "That's a great pack. Now if we can just find something to put in it."

J.J. laughed in agreement as they continued up the road toward Hugo. Just on the south side of town they came to the back of a small barbecue stand.

"Boy does that smell good," Angel sighed. Just as she had finished her sentence the back door opened and a man came out with several plastic bags and placed them on a barrel. Then he went back inside.

"Let's check that out," J.J. ordered. "You stay here out of sight and I'll go sniff those bags."

"Be careful and be fast," warned Angel, knowing that her sister would be in sight of several people standing outside.

Without another word J.J. made a dash to the bags and quickly put her powerful nose to work. The aroma told her it was meat. She grabbed one bag with her mouth and then made a beeline for Angel. Luckily the people outside had their backs turned and did not see her.

"Smells like good stuff," she smiled.

"What about the other one?" Angel asked.

"Let's try for it, too," J.J. counseled. "We need all the food we can get."

11

"I'll go," Angel offered.

"No, Let me," J.J. countered. "This stuff's pretty heavy and I'm bigger. Put that sack in our new bag."

"Okay," obeyed Angel as she opened the top and placed the meat inside.

J.J. took another look and saw no one watching. Quickly she once again made a sprint for the sack sitting on the barrel. When but a few feet away the door opened and out came a man. J.J. didn't hesitate but quickly latched onto to the white plastic and sped away. The man yelled and kicked at her but it was too late. The treasure was hers. She quickly ran to Angel hiding in the shrubs.

"Good work," Angel praised. "I thought sure that guy would get you."

"I almost stopped," admitted J.J. "But I was too close to give up. I thought I could beat him to the punch."

"You did, but just barely," Angel teased. "Now let's get out of here."

The dogs found a nice quiet spot just a few hundred feet away; a nice grassy clearing enclosed by a grove of oaks. Alongside ran a rock bottomed, clear running creek brimming with minnows darting in and out of the thick green moss.

"This is a good place," Angel said as they both laid out in the shade. "Open the bag. I'm starving."

J.J. pulled a plastic sack from their bag and opened it. The sweet smell of freshly cooked beef and pork filled the air as she and Angel both pulled out thick, juicy ribs and began to gnaw away.

"I can't believe they were throwing this away," J.J. marveled as thick drops of sauce ran off her chin.

"Me either," confirmed Angel as she rolled her tongue all around her mouth. "But I'm sure glad they were. What do we do now?"

"Well let's finish eating and then take a little nap. After that we'll think about it," J.J. suggested.

A cool early morning had melted into a hot afternoon in their walk to Hugo. All of a sudden they were tired. They finished their meals and then returned the sack to their bag.

"This should hold us for a while," J.J. reasoned.

" Should," replied Angel. "There's a lot of meat in there."

After zipping up the bag they went to the creek, drank deeply, and washed their paws and muzzles. They then returned to their shady spot and stretched out on the sweet spring grass. A gentle breeze blew in from the west to cool them. In but seconds both were fast asleep.

The dogs rested until late afternoon when J.J. was awakened by a faint scratching sound coming from behind a fallen log near the creek bank. She softly poked Angel to alertness and then rose to her feet. Angel stretched her legs and did the same.

"Hear that noise?" J.J. questioned.

"Ya," confirmed the little one. "Wonder what it is?"

Together they marched to the log and looked over its broad, rotting trunk. Behind it, digging furiously in the damp earth, was a kind of creature they had never seen before. A few feet long with thick, light brown fur, it kicked up piles of dirt with each scoop of its clawed paws. Deep streaks of white ran up his pointed nose, between his eyes and around his ears

"What are you doing?" Angel asked as the critter looked up.

"Digging a hole," he replied in an annoyed voice.

"What for?" Angel continued.

"Because I'm a badger," he spat. "That's what we do."

"We've never seen one of you before," J.J. admitted. "But we do have a little brother named Badger. His real name is Max but he digs so much that our family started calling him the little badger and the name just stuck."

"Digs a lot, huh," the critter queried.

"That's about all he does," responded Angel.

"Sounds like a first rate dog," the badger commended.

"He is," replied Angel with a sob, thinking about how much she missed him.

"Why isn't he with you?" the badger asked.

"He's back in Houston," J.J. explained, telling the critter about the trip they were on and the tornado that had ruined it.

"That's too bad," the badger sympathized. "I heard that twister all the way up here."

"Didn't hit you though, huh? J.J. asked.

"Nope, missed us," the critter answered. "That's the nature of those things. You never know what they'll do or where they'll go."

"Oh, I forgot my manners," J.J. stated. "My name's J.J. and this is my little sister Angel. Do you have a name?"

"Make it Billy," the badger replied.

"Billy Badger," Angel grinned.

"What are you two going to do," Billy asked. "You're a long way from Houston."

Angel told him the story about the Indian woman and what she had told them to do. She then recited the long story about the Golden Bone and how everything had worked out just right because they did exactly as they were supposed to.

"We don't know this country at all," Angel confessed. "Have you ever heard of Sooner Silver?"

"Oh, ya," Billy affirmed. "I heard about it early this morning. It came over the people radio."

"Really," both dogs asked in unison as their eyes brightened.

"Yup," he continued. "There was a guy fishing upstream where the creek is deeper and he had his truck radio going. I was hiding in one of my holes just a few feet away. It seems the thieves stole the whole Sooner Silver Collection from a bank in Idabell."

"A silver collection," Angel quizzed.

"Ya," answered Billy. "It belonged to an old Oklahoma family; one that's been here since way back when the state was still a territory. It had just about everything in it. French and Spanish silver coins going back to the days when Oklahoma was part of Louisiana; American silver dollars, some minted in 1907; finely crafted vases and plates, one with the seal of the King of Spain; arrow heads and lance tips; rings and necklaces; the whole works. It's worth millions in people money. It was on display as part of the Oklahoma centennial celebration. The collection was supposed to be exhibited all over the state this year. But I guess now a lot of folks will miss it. Too bad."

"Who took it?" J.J. probed.

"They don't know," the badger shrugged. "But I'll bet they've got the police looking everywhere. And now you two as well."

"Oh, look Billy," J.J. bubbled as she pulled the pouch from her neck and opened it. "I forgot. Look what we have." Billy examined the silver arrowhead and was obviously impressed.

"Looks like you've got a big job on your hands. Better not lose this," he counseled. "It's big medicine; a lot of power. It'll help you everywhere you go."

"Oh we won't," promised Angel. "That's one thing she made clear. We don't want her mad at us."

"Probably Choctaw," Billy added. "You're in their country now."

"Our family said there were lots of Indian people in Oklahoma," J.J. stated. "Do you know how many?"

"Dozens and dozens," the badger answered. "I suspect you'll get to see a lot of them before you're through. In fact I reckon you'll know more about Oklahoma than any dogs alive."

"There's a lot to know, isn't there," J.J. quipped.

"Whole lot," the badger snapped. "So much the human mind can't hold it all. No trouble for badgers, though," he added with a grin.

"Dogs, either," J.J puffed.

"Do you think we have a long way to go?" Angel questioned.

"I think so," Billy replied. "You better get going."

"What should we do first,?" J.J. pondered.

"We don't even know where to start," Angel added with a whine.

"Well," Billy reasoned. "Like so many jobs in life you have to start at the bottom and work your way up."

"What does that mean?" J.J. questioned.

"Oh, nothing," the badger smiled. "It just kind of means you have to start at the beginning; the scene of the crime; in Idabell."

"Do we keep going north?" Angel asked. "What's up that way?"

"No," the badger counseled. "Up north is Antlers. Nice town but Idabell is east; straight down that road," he finished as he pointed just beyond the trees to U.S. 70, one of Oklahoma's main east-west corridors. "Check things out in Idabell and then head north toward the Ouachita and find the beaver. He might be able to help you from there."

"The what?" J.J. choked.

"The Ouachita," the badger stated again. "It's a nice forest; awfully pretty country. You'll like it."

"Thanks, Billy," Angel chirped. "I'm sorry you couldn't have met little Max. You would have liked him."

"I'll bet I would have," the badger replied. "Maybe you'll find him again and you can bring him to me."

"Do you think so," the little one bubbled.

"Could happen," Billy assured her. "Just remember: Labor Omnia Vincit."

"What!" the Kids blurted in unison cocking their heads.

It's the Oklahoma state motto: Labor Conquers All Things," the badger explained. "It comes from an old language called Latin and means that if you throw everything you have into a task then most of the time things work out like you want 'em to."

"Good advice," J.J. stated. "We'll remember it."

"Well, got to go now," Billy finished. "Good luck to you."

"And to you," the girls countered. In an instant the badger disappeared into the thick underbrush while the Kids turned to get their food sack. To the west the sun's top half draped the trees in soft, sweet orange.

"Must be about six or so," J.J. reasoned as she noted the sun's location.

"About," Angel agreed. "Good time to walk. It's starting to feel like summer."

"Sure is," J.J. replied, remembering how in their earlier adventure they had often traveled at night during the summer heat. "Let's get a drink and then get going."

"Sounds good," Angel said with a quick nod of her head.

The Kids took a good slurp from the creek and then ambled to the highway. Then, staying just out of sight behind the treeline, they headed east toward Idabell. Just as the sun's lamp began to flicker out behind them they looked to the north and saw a large body of water. A road sign identified it as the southern tail of Lake Hugo, a part of Hugo Lake State Park. The lake was fed by the waters of the Kiamichi River, a body that rose in the high country and drained south into the mighty Red. The Kids stopped for a drink and, as they crossed the river, a cool breeze began to blow in from the north.

"Boy that feels good," exclaimed Angel as the wind rustled her long, black fur.

"Sure does," seconded J.J. as she turned her snout into the wind. "Let's stop for a few minutes and have a quick bite. I'm getting a little hungry."

"Me, too," seconded Angel as they nestled in under a large pecan tree about ten feet from the river's bank. "I'll help you take off the pack."

J.J. slid out of the backpack, opened it, and pulled out a food sack. From it she took two meaty ribs and gave one to her little sister.

"Chow down," she laughed as Angel grabbed the morsel.

"I hope we can find food like this all the time," Angel squeaked as she gnawed the last meat off the bone.

"Don't count on it," J.J. advised. "You remember the last time. Sometimes we were lucky and sometimes we weren't. We can't take anything for granted. We always have to look way ahead and be prepared."

"I know," Angel coughed as the last of her meal went down. "Look at the moon," she added as she looked into the eastern sky.

"Pretty, yellow and full," J.J. observed as the lunar light drifted down on them. "It's almost like the daytime."

"Close," Angel agreed. "We can see by it. That's enough."

"Sure can," J.J. confirmed. "Finished?"

"Yup," affirmed Angel with a smile.

J.J. opened the bag and began to stuff the food sack back in when she noticed a piece of folded paper down at the bottom and pulled it out.

"I wonder what this is?" she questioned as she showed it to the little one.

"Open it," Angel commanded as she moved closer to get a better look.

"Looks like a map," gushed J.J. as she moved the paper into better light.

"Sure does," affirmed Angel, "a map of Oklahoma."

The Kids quickly focused in the soft light on an outline map of the state and its heading; *The Sooner State.*

"Not much detail but it does show some roads and cities," J.J. commented. "I wonder why they call it the Sooner State?" she speculated.

"Don't know," confessed Angel. "Sooner State, Sooner Silver, Sooner everything. We'll find out though," she added. "And look at those squiggly lines," she observed as she ran a paw down one. "I'll bet they're rivers."

"Think so," agreed J.J. "This one right here must be the one we're on; the Kiamichi. "Let's mark it."

"With what?" Angel asked. "We don't have a pencil."

"Oh, ya," J.J. huffed. "Well, remember the name and we'll find something to write with along the way. Do you think you can remember how to spell that," she finished with a chuckle.

"I'll try," shrugged Angel, "but you'll have to help me. That's a lot of word for just one dog to remember."

"Okay," J.J. hooted. "But don't forget you're always our official speller."

Angel just grinned, folded the map, and placed it in a pocket on the pack's outside. Then they were off once more.

Shortly before dawn they came to a small town; Fort Towson.

"Tired?" J.J. asked.

"A little," Angel admitted. "You?"

"I could stand a rest," J.J. replied. "Let's hide in that clump of trees over there."

J.J. had noticed a nice stand of sweetgums just behind a large, one story building.

"I think that's a school," Angel observed as she squinted through the night's last darkness.

"Maybe we can find a pencil there."

"Ya," brightened J.J. as she remembered they needed something to write with.

"And some water."

"Let's look for a water bottle, too," suggested Angel, "just in case we need it."

"Good idea," commended J.J. "This country's well watered but it never hurts to be on the safe side."

The Kids approached the circle of trees and found a good place between two large bushes. Here Angel helped J.J. remove the pack and then they began to scout the area behind the school. They soon found an outdoor water tap near the base of the back wall and J.J. turned it on. They each took turns lapping up the cool liquid and then, after closing the spigot, began to explore the area. Near a back door they found several small, empty plastic bottles and took two back to the faucet to fill. Then, as the morning dawn peeked over the eastern sky, they sniffed around some more. School had just let out for the summer and the trash cans were full.

"Good, pencils," Angel stated, "and some pens, too," she finished as she pulled several from a can.

"Look at this," J.J. gushed in excitement. "Books and maps."

"Oh, great," chirped Angel as she rushed to her sister's side.

"History of Oklahoma; another outline map; a road atlas; good stuff," J.J. beamed.

"Anything about this town?" Angel queried.

"Probably in the history book," J.J. reckoned. "Let's go back to the trees and look."

The Kids skipped back to their hideout with their water, pens and pencils, maps, and book. When settled J.J. opened the book and soon found a reference for Fort Towson.

"What's it say?" Angel asked enthusiastically.

"Interesting place," she stated as Angel looked on. "The town was named for a U.S. Army post built near here way back in the 1820's. During the Civil War the Confederates captured it and it was here that the last Confederate general, Stand Watie, surrendered to Union forces in 1865."

"Stand Watie?" Angel questioned.

"Uh huh. A Cherokee. It says he led many of the Indian troops who sided with the south," J.J. explained as she read on.

"Hard to believe that war got all the way out here," Angel quipped, remembering how they had seen Fort Sumter on the Atlantic coast the summer before.

"Must have been a big war," J.J. reckoned as Angel nodded in agreement.

"I wonder if all of Oklahoma fought with the south?" Angel quizzed.

"Maybe this book will tell us," J.J reasoned.

"There was another town here once, too," J.J. continued. "Doaksville. It was an important meeting place for the Choctaws."

"What happened to it," Angel asked.

"It became part of the new town, Fort Towson," J.J. answered as she finished reading the passage.

"Neat," Angel beamed. "We're going to learn a lot here."

"I think so," J.J. stated. "But right now we have to get moving. We want to cover some ground before it gets too hot. Let's grab a bite and then load up."

Angel opened the pack, pulled out a food sack, and withdrew several pieces of meat. They ate quickly. After returning to the water faucet and drinking their fill, they ambled to the trees, strapped the pack on J.J., and surveyed the area.

Their earlier travels had taught them that towns could mean trouble and they tried to avoid them whenever possible.

"We'll have to skirt the town," J.J. advised as she studied the morning traffic growing heavier in the now bright morning. "We'll pick up the highway on the east side."

"Makes sense," Angel agreed. "We'll just circle a little to the south."

The Kids quickly scampered from their hideout to a small pasture just to the south of the school. From there they found a narrow trail that took them far to the east of the town and then back to near the highway. Trees and brush along the roadway's southern flank gave them fine cover and they walked until late morning. All along the way they spotted police cars, some patrolling the highway and others manning roadblocks and searching cars.

"I guess they're looking for the Sooner Silver," Angel reckoned.

"Must be," J.J. answered.

"If they can't find it, how can we?" Angel moaned.

"We'll find it," J.J. replied with certainty. "I know we will."

"I just wanted to hear you say that," Angel chirped with a wide grin. "It makes me feel better."

J.J. said nothing, only gave Angel a broad smile and led on. Near noon she suggested that they find a place to rest during the afternoon. They soon found a nice shady spot in a pecan grove near a large, mossy stock tank. A few cows grazed nearby while others stood knee deep in the cool water and drank. In the pasture's far corner one piebald horse chewed lazily on thick, high chutes of lush green grass as the Kids settled in for a drink, a meal, and a nap.

"How are we doing on food?" J.J. questioned as she opened the pack and pulled out a bag.

"This one's about empty," she answered, "but we still have plenty in the other; plenty for now at least."

"Well let's keep the empty sack. We might need it," J.J. cautioned.

"Good idea," commended the little one as she began to eat.

Each wolfed down a healthy ration of beef and then shuffled to the tank for a drink. Both waded in chest deep and drank their fill as the cows on the other side looked on.

"The water feels so good," Angel squeaked as she moved farther out and began to paddle around.

"Sure does," clucked J.J. as she did the same. "Now let's go rest and maybe read the book a little."

"Okay," Angel answered.

And let's don't forget to mark the map. You do remember how to spell Kiamichi, don't you?" she finished with a sniffing grin.

"Let's check that road atlas we found," countered J.J. It might do the work for us."

"Ah, let's not cheat," giggled the little one.

J.J. laughed as they reached the tank's edge, returned to dry ground, and shook themselves dry. Together they walked slowly to their spot among the trees and picked a nice, soft pile of wet, cool leaves to settle in. Angel grabbed the pack in her mouth, drew it to her, and pulled out the book and the maps as well as a pencil. J.J. first opened the outline map and began to hunt for their location.

"We must be about here," she reasoned as Angel looked on. "And that must be Kiamichi and Lake Hugo right back here," she continued as she pointed back to the west and traced the squiggly river line with her paw. "Why don't you mark it?" she chuckled, testing her little sister's memory.

"Let's spell it together," Angel cracked. "Ready, go!" Together the girls spoke letter to letter as Angel wrote: K-I-A-M-I-C-H-I.

"We both got it," Angel giggled. "Pretty good for two Texas mutts."

"Not bad at all," J.J. ribbed as she gave Angel a quick, soft, poke in the side. "Let's check it against the atlas and then look at the book."

Angel opened the road map and confirmed their spelling, then grabbed the history book and pawed through several sections. J.J. looked on over her shoulder. Then Angel returned to the first and began to read.

"It says that Oklahoma was home to many Indian tribes for thousands of years before the Europeans came," she quoted. "They lived off the rich land and in a few places built big towns. They even had trading networks that covered much of what's now the United States. They think the first Europeans to visit might have been the Vikings over a thousand years ago."

"Who were the Vikings?" J.J. stammered.

"Let's see," Angel mumbled. "Oh, here's something. They were a seafaring people from far northern Europe. They built great ships and traveled all over."

"Oh, neat," grinned J.J.

"Anyway," Angel continued, the Spanish came next. A conquistador named Coronado crossed far western Oklahoma in 1541. That same year a man named Hernando De Soto entered the state in the east, near the Arkansas River."

"What were they were looking for?" J.J. mused.

"Golden cities," Angel advised as she read another paragraph.

"Wonder if they ever found one?" questioned J.J.

"Don't know," answered Angel. "It doesn't say anything about it in the book so I'll bet they didn't."

"Next came another Spaniard, Juan de Oñate in the early 1600's. Like Coronado he went through western Oklahoma," Angel finished.

"Guess he was looking for gold, too," J.J. reasoned.

"Probably," Angel agreed.

"Anyway," she continued, "the French came next. First a man named LaSalle explored much of the Mississippi and claimed the land west of the river, including Oklahoma, for France. But it doesn't sound like he ever set foot here himself. That was in 1682. Then around 1718 two more Frenchmen traveled here,

St. Denis and Bernard de la Harpe. St. Denis explored the Red way upstream and eventually got all the way to Santa Fe in what's now New Mexico. La Harpe went up the Red as well, but he also explored some of the other rivers like the Arkansas and the Grand. All along the way both he and St. Denis made trading agreements with the Indian tribes and wanted to do the same with the Spanish settlements in New Mexico."

"Remember what Linda said," J.J. interrupted, "about how the explorers used the rivers as a highway system. It sounds like the French were good at that. I can't wait to see some of these other rivers."

"Well we've already seen the Arkansas," Angel reminded her. "But that was in Arkansas. I didn't know that river was in Oklahoma, too."

"I didn't either," confessed J.J. "I wonder where? Up north, maybe?"

"Probably," reasoned Angel.

"Where does the Red go?" asked J.J. "Does the book say?"

"Ya, right here," answered Angel. "It goes all the way to the Mississippi; same for the Arkansas. The Kids had seen much of the Mississippi on their earlier adventure. They had never forgotten the sight of that magnificent, mile-wide body of muddy grey and green.

"So you have a water highway all the way to the Mississippi, J.J. reckoned.

"Even farther than that," Angel stated. "Think about it. Remember how the other big rivers like the Ohio emptied into the Mississippi? That means that men in boats could travel from way far north and east and eventually get to Oklahoma by water."

"That's right!" commended J.J. as she slapped herself on the head. "That's good thinking."

"And we've found out how much floating beats walking," Angel added with a laugh as she thought about the boat rides they had caught before. "They must have figured that out, too."

"Must have," J.J. grinned. "Let me read some."

Angel handed J.J. the book and nestled in close to read along.

"It says that the French traders kept coming, lots of them, especially after the founding of New Orleans in 1718," J.J. read as she reminded Angel of the city's location near the mouth of the Gulf of Mexico.

"I remember," Angel assured her. "I guess a lot of the goods the French traded for went down river to New Orleans and then on to Europe."

"You're probably right," J.J. replied. "And then traders brought French goods through the city and then up to the people in Oklahoma."

"Makes sense," Angel responded with a nod of certainty. "Read on."

"In the 1750's and 60's there was a big war between the British, the French, the Spanish, and a whole bunch of Indian tribes. It seems like everyone wanted to control the rivers and trade routes. The British and their allies won and as part of the peace treaty, the Treaty of Paris, the French had to cede Louisiana to Spain." J.J. read.

"I wonder if that means the state of Louisiana today?" Angel questioned.

"That and a whole lot more," J.J. replied as she read on. "Look at the map," she instructed as together they looked at a map of the huge expanse of land that came to be known as Louisiana.

"Here's Oklahoma," Angel gushed as she pointed to a spot on the map. "I guess they didn't call it Oklahoma back then, though."

"Guess not," J.J. answered. "Want to hold the book now?"

"Ya, my turn again," Angel squeaked. Angel took the book and continued reading.

"It says that the Spanish held the territory until around 1800 when the French got it back; actually it sounds more like they took it back. Anyway, Napoleon now ruled France and needed money to fight his wars in Europe. U.S. envoys were talking to him about buying New Orleans and he surprised them by offering to sell all of Louisiana. The Americans knew a good deal when they saw one and snapped it up. So in 1803 all of Louisiana including Oklahoma became United States territory."

"Quite a story," commented J.J. "I guess that's enough for now. We need to get some rest."

"You're right," Angel chirped, "but I could read on all day. This is interesting. I'll bet the badger didn't know all this."

"Well maybe the beaver will," J.J. joked. "Remember we have to find him next. Now put the book back and lets have a nap."

"Okay," Angel obeyed as she shut it and folded the maps and carefully returned them to the backpack."

The thick canopy of spring green high in the arching trees sheltered the Kids from the burning sun as they curled up to sleep. A mild but cooling breeze blew in from the north to challenge the heat. They found peace in the sounds of chirping birds, softly mooing cattle, and gently rustling leaves excited by the prairie wind. Deep soothing slumber soon swept them into that vital world of refreshment.

Angel awoke first. As she shook her head and looked to the west she could see the sun fighting but losing its daily battle with night. She rose stiffly and shook each leg to work out the kinks of inactivity. Then she gave her sister a gentle nudge. With a deep yawn J.J. sprung to alertness.

"Time to move," the little one prompted.

J.J. gave a mighty shake that sent a host of last winter's leaves flying through the early evening breeze.

"Let's have a drink and then load up," she advised.

Together they trotted down to the tank and drank deeply as an old cow watched with little interest. Then they returned to fetch the backpack and plot their course.

"We'll just stay to the south of the road," J.J. reasoned. "There's plenty of good cover."

"Makes sense," seconded Angel. "I wonder if we can get to Idabell tonight?"

"Might," replied her sister. "Let's try anyway."

"The police are still out," commented J.J. as she noticed two patrol cars just down the road. "They must still be looking for the loot."

"We'll beat them to it," Angel puffed. "They'd have probably already found it if they had a good dog working for them," she added with a laugh.

J.J. just smiled in agreement.

For several hours the Kids plodded the highway's edge as they moved east. Soon a set of headlights splashed a road sign but a few feet ahead.

"Idabell, five miles," J.J. gushed as she read aloud.

"Oh, boy," Angel chirped. "Almost there."

In a few moments they came to a narrow creek where they stopped to drink and snatch a moments rest. In the distance they could see a small shack outlined in the moon's full brilliance. Though the rundown house looked empty, they could see a small light inside what looked to be a small shed next to an old corral.

"Want to check it out?" J.J. asked as she turned to Angel.

"Might be some food there," Angel reasoned. "Let's go see."

The Kids crouched low and cautiously approached the old shack. As they neared they could see the outlines of two men leaning against the back of a shiny white van parked halfway inside the crumbling shed. Just behind the van was an official looking vehicle with a logo on the side. Soon they were close enough to hear the men who were quietly talking.

The Kids studied the men closely in the dim light. One was fairly tall and thin

with a full head of hair on his hatless head. He wore what looked to be a business suit which seemed out of place in this rural location. He had a habit of chopping his hand through the air with each sentence. The other was short and quite round. Circling his waist was a wide leather belt clasped by a big silver buckle. He wore jeans and boots and a broad beamed hat.

"The cops are all over the main roads," the short one advised. "But I just came down the old cut-off and didn't see a soul. You can take that all the way to Broken Bow."

"They probably figured we'd try to get far away," the tall man stated. "They'll never think of looking right under their noses."

"That's what I thought, too," the short man huffed. "We'll lay low for a few weeks. You just keep that stuff tucked away safe in that van and when the time is right we'll move it out west. I know a good place to hide it. After all this blows over I know where we can sell it. There's a guy down in Dallas who likes this kind of stuff and he's not real particular about where it comes from."

"How long do you figure we'll have to wait?" the taller one questioned.

"Six months or so," came the answer. "Let's don't get itchy. It's way too hot to move right now."

"How much do you think we can get for it?" the van man asked.

"I reckon at least a million, maybe two," the fat one replied.

"Not bad," the thin man chortled with a shifty smirk.

Angel could hear J.J.'s heart racing in excitement right along with her own. She started to speak but J.J. shushed her with a paw to her lips. As they watched the heavy man entered his car, started the engine, and then drove off lights out. The logo on the car's side read "County Commissioner".

Then the tall man cranked up his van and backed out of the shed. On the van's side was a large advertising sign: Rob Silver-Antique Treasures. He quickly wheeled in the opposite direction down the narrow dirt trail and soon disappeared.

"They took the silver!" Angel shouted. "They're the ones!"

"Sure sounds like it," J.J. seconded. "At least now we know who to look for."

"Who would have guessed it!" a stunned Angel exclaimed, "a county commissioner?"

"Ya," snapped J.J. "It is kind of hard to believe. For a minute there I thought we were back in Texas."

Angel doubled up with laughter and slapped the ground as her sister smiled widely.

"Now what do we do?" Angel bubbled. "Should we try to follow the van's tracks?"

"Oh, no," J.J. cautioned. "Remember the rules. We have to do just what the animals tell us. We still go to Idabell and then north to find the beaver. Besides we have no idea where he'll go and we can't go as fast as a van."

"They were going out west, remember?" Angel reminder her sister.

"Ya but Oklahoma's an awfully big place and out west could be just about anywhere," J.J. advised. "Besides, they didn't say exactly when they'd go there. But if we follow the rules we'll find them sooner or later."

"You're right," Angel admitted. "Let's get to Idabell."

The Kids quickly covered the last five miles to Idabell and entered the town around 4: 00 A.M. They moved quietly in the shadows of a town still asleep and soon came to the bank where the Sooner Silver had been on display.

"I wonder how they were able to rob the place without getting caught?" Angel pondered. "Looks like that would have been hard to do."

"You'd think so," J.J. agreed. "They must have had a good plan."

"Well. we learned a long time ago that to do something big you have to plan it out," replied Angel.

"And then stick to that plan," added J.J., "no matter what."

"Yup," nodded Angel. "What now?"

"We have to get out of town before dawn," counseled J.J. I wonder which way we should go."

"There are some signs over there," Angel stated as she looked over the intersection where the bank was located. "Let's check them out."

"Good idea," commended J.J. as together they skipped to the row of directional markers clustered together at one corner.

"Broken Bow and then the Ouachita straight up this road," Angel squeaked. "Still U.S. 70 she added as she studied the road which now took a sharp turn to the north. "Oh, and look at this," she continued. "It says that the area around Idabell is the lowest point in Oklahoma; less than 300 feet above sea level."

"I wonder what the highest is?" J.J. questioned.

"Don't know," Angel answered with a shrug. "Maybe we'll find it later."

"Hope so," J.J. said. "Say didn't the robbers say something about Broken Bow?"

"Sure did," Angel affirmed. "It's where the short guy told him to go."

"Well let's keep our eyes open in case we spot him," J.J. counseled. "If we can find a way to get him away from that van we can get the Sooner Silver,"

"Ya," chirped Angel, "and then we'll find a new home."

"A new home," sighed J.J. "Sounds good."

Quickly the Kids turned north and moved back out into open country. As the sun's crown peeked over the eastern horizon they stopped in a cornfield for a brief rest. Hiding between rows reaching high for the sky, J.J. scratched at the dirt beneath her. "Looks like good farm country," she stated as she pawed the rusty rich soil of the Red River Valley.

"Must be," confirmed the little one as she dug down a few inches. "Look at all the corn. It's everywhere." she added as she looked over the countryside.

"I wonder what else they grow here?"J.J. queried.

"Probably a lot of stuff," Angel mused. "Have you ever noticed how often you see good farmland near rivers?" she continued as she thought about some of the other rivers they had seen.

"Never thought of it," admitted J.J. "But now that I look back on it you're right."

"Must be a reason for it," quipped the little one.

"Must be," affirmed J.J. "Want a bite?"

"Ya," replied Angel. "I almost forgot about food."

Angel helped J.J. drop the pack and together they pulled out a food sack. The meat was now starting to run low as they noticed the second sack was not nearly as full as the first.

"We need to keep our eyes out for more food," J.J. counseled. "This meat won't last much longer."

"We'll find something," Angel promised as she finished her meal and looked up at the sun now wholly outlined in blue and fully risen in the eastern sky.

"Gonna be a hot one," she continued as she looked skyward once more.

"They'll all be hot from now on," J.J. stated. "I think summer just chased the spring away."

"Happens fast, doesn't it," Angel remarked.

"Every year," J.J. added.

The Kids loaded up their gear and continued marching north. Soon they came to a broad stream which a sign identified as the Little River and another as the Little River Wildlife Refuge.

"Another river," bubbled Angel.

"Ya," said J.J., "and this one's easier to spell than Kiamichi."

"A lot easier," Angel laughed. "Even you could remember how to spell this one."

J.J. chuckled at the ribbing and then turned somber again.

"Should we try to cross the bridge?" she wondered aloud as from behind a tree they watched the heavy traffic crossing the narrow span.

"I don't know," Angel whined. "Maybe we should wait for night."

"I'd hate to lose a whole day," countered J.J. noting that it was barely midmorning.

"Maybe we should go downstream and look for a place to ford," Angel reasoned.

"That's a good idea," J.J. commended. "Let's go downstream."

For over an hour the Kids worked their way down the south bank of the Little River. Finally they came to a spot where the water narrowed. Here the thick trunk of a newly fallen cypress nearly spanned the stream.

"We can cross on that," J.J. stated as she studied the timber bridge. "But we have to be careful," she added. "We can't let the pack get wet. It would ruin our book and maps."

"I'll go first" Angel offered.

"Okay," approved J.J.

Angel stepped up on the log and began to slowly work her way across, following the log to its end just a few feet from the opposite side. Here the water was shallow and she had no trouble slithering up the bank to dry land.

"Nothing to it," she advised her sister.

J.J. said nothing as she quickly mounted the cypress and in seconds joined Angel on the northern side of the Little.

"Feet are wet but the rest of us is dry," she chuckled. "Let's take a break."

"This is a pretty place," Angel said as she studied the thick woods all around her. "It's kind of spooky, though; too quiet."

"I know," J.J. quipped, "not a car to be heard."

"Look," Angel squeaked as she pointed through the bushes and trees. "That looks like a little pond; might be a good place to rest."

"Ya," said J.J. as she locked in on Angel's line of sight. "Let's check it out."

The Kids poked through the thick growth and came to the pond's south bank. To the west they could see the shallow creek that fed it and to the east a small dam blocking its flow toward the river.

"Beaver dam?" J.J. questioned.

"Could be," Angel chirped as she thought back to others they had seen before.

"Maybe this is where we meet one."

"Might," answered J.J. "But let's not worry about it now. If there's a beaver around and he wants to talk he'll come out. Let's have a drink and a little lunch. Help me with the pack."

Angel assisted J.J. in removing the backpack and then they drank deeply from the cool, clear pond. After a bite to eat they stretched out along the damp bank and quickly fell asleep.

J.J. awoke with a start as a loud splat from but a few feet away rang in her ears. She quickly wheeled toward the water as Angel cleared the cobwebs and snapped to attention.

"A beaver's alarm clock," the critter snickered as he eyed the two dogs and slapped his wood-hard tail on the water once more. "I though it was about time you got up."

"We thought you might be around," spat J.J., annoyed at the rude way in which the beaver had introduced himself.

"We noticed your dam," Angel added as she carefully studied the large animal with its sleek, thick brown fur and piercing, coal-black eyes.

"It's one of my better efforts," the beaver answered as he looked back at his handiwork. "What brings you two here?" he asked in a more serious tone.

The Kids told him their story as the beaver listened intently.

"Was that Billy Badger who sent you this way?" the critter asked.

"Yup," J.J. replied. "You must know him."

"Oh, ya," the beaver answered. "I used to live over on the Kiamichi. I saw old Billy all the time. How's he doin'?"

"Seems to be just fine," responded Angel.

"Good," barked the beaver. "Oh, I'm Bobby by the way. And you?"

"I'm Angel and this is my sister J.J.," the little one offered. "Tell us about this place."

"The refuge?" he questioned.

"Uh, huh," Angel affirmed.

"Great place," the beaver started. "It's about the last bottomland hardwood forest left in southeastern Oklahoma; about 15,000 acres worth. They set it aside to keep the people out and give the animals a good place to stay. We've got about every kind of critter here you can think of; possums, raccoons, beavers, and a whole lot of different ducks and other birds. Trees, too," he went on. "That was a cypress trunk you crossed the river on."

"You saw us?" questioned J.J.

"Oh, sure," the beaver chuckled. "I had you spotted way down river. I started to say something when you got here but you looked so tired I figured I'd let you rest awhile."

"Thanks for that," praised the little one.

"Anyway," he went on, "we've got hickory and oak, sweetgum and walnut and pine. The whole works."

"Does the Little go into the Red?" J.J. asked.

"Oh, ya," Bobby informed them, "but way over in Arkansas."

The Kids told the beaver about their maps and the book they'd found at the school. J.J. produced the outline map and showed him how they marked it.

"We found a good atlas at the school but we still mark this map just for fun," she informed him."

"Good practice," Bobby barked, quite impressed when he saw Angel write "Little River" on the squiggly line that represented the river.

They also told him how they tried to read a little of the book at every stop and then asked him if he knew much about the history of this area.

"Oh, boy," the beaver smiled with his massive front teeth, "don't get me started on that."

"We want to know," Angel insisted.

"Okay," replied Bobby as he patted a webbed foot on the ground. "What do you want to know?"

"We read up to the Louisiana Purchase and how Oklahoma was part of that," Angel stated. "What happened next?"

"Well I guess the important thing was the creation of Indian Territory. That's the name the United States gave to this land. Washington decided to set it aside as a place to move most of the Indian peoples then living east of the Mississippi River," Bobby stated. "There were a lot of tribes involved but the big ones were the Cherokees, Choctaws, Chickasaws, Creeks, and Seminoles. They were called the Five Civilized Tribes and came from the South; Georgia, the Carolinas, Alabama, Mississippi, and Florida," the beaver continued.

"Why did the government want them to leave?" J.J. questioned with a puzzled look.

"They had a lot of good land and the whites wanted it," Bobby explained.

"Doesn't sound right," Angel huffed.

"It wasn't," Bobby confirmed. "A whole lot of them died trying to get here. The Cherokees called it the 'Trail of Tears'."

"That's sad," J.J. sniffed. "Wanting land doesn't seem like a good enough reason for all that."

"Wouldn't seem like it," the beaver agreed with a slap of his mighty tail. "But that's why the migration from Europe happened. Sure many of the early explorers were looking for gold; there's a gold lust in all of us. But even more came for land. Europe was full up and if you wanted your own dirt you had to go someplace else; and this was it."

"Why was land so important?" Angel asked.

"In those days land was everything," Bobby went on. "You have to remember that back then most people, probably about 90%, made their living off the land; not like today where most live and work in the cities. Life depended on what you could grow on the land or what you could take from it. In fact, when you think about it, the history of the world is the history of one people taking land from another. It's been going on since the beginning of time and it'll probably never stop," he added with a sigh.

"Had many of those Indian people ever been here before?" J.J. queried.

"Oh, sure," the beaver confirmed. "They'd been coming here to hunt and trade for hundreds of years. They knew it well."

"Billy the badger said we were in Choctaw country now," Angel recounted.

"Yup," Bobby confirmed. "Choctaws here, Chickasaws to the west, Creeks and then Cherokees to the north, and Seminoles west of them. Later on other tribes like the Cheyenne, Comanche, Kiowa, Arapaho and Apache settled farther west."

"We got this from a Choctaw," Angel squeaked as she showed the beaver the pouch with the silver arrowhead. "At least Billy the badger said so."

"Hmm," said Bobby as he looked over the arrowhead. "Best keep this safe."

"We will," Angel promised. "We know not to lose it no matter what."

"Good," was all the beaver said, but his expression left the Kids no doubt he knew its importance.

"Were the Indian tribes a lot alike?" J.J. asked, starting another line of questions.

"Oh, no," Bobby countered shaking his head. "Different as night and day; different languages, different customs, different ways of living. Some were great farmers and grew lots of corn and grains. Others raised cotton on big plantations. Still others like the plains tribes lived off wild game, especially the buffalo."

"Buffalo?" questioned Angel. "What's that?"

"Bison," the beaver replied. "Big, big meaty animals. They provided just about everything the people needed; meat for food, hides for clothing and shelter, bones for tools, the whole works."

"We've never seen one of those," J.J. admitted.

"You will when you get out west," Bobby counseled.

"Do you think we'll get that far?" Angel questioned.

"I have a feeling you will," the beaver answered with a gleam in his eye.

"Are there beavers out west?" J.J. asked.

"Not as many as around here," Bobby answered. "We like a lot of water. But there are some along the rivers; the Cimarron and Canadian, and of course the Beaver."

"Beaver River?" Angel chirped. "They named a river after you?"

"Not just a river," the beaver explained with obvious pride, "but a whole county."s

"Pretty good," beamed J.J. "Beaver County."

"That's not all," Bobby went on. "Just north of here is Beavers Bend State Park. It's in the Ouachita. See how popular we are."

"The Ouachita," Angel bubbled. "That's where the badger told us to go. How far is it?"

"Not far," Bobby replied. "Just up the road. Whole different kind of country, though."

"Oh, I forgot," J.J. asked. "What do you know about the Civil War?"

"Not as much as the bear," the beaver answered honestly. "Why don't you talk to him when you get to the high country."

"Do you think we can find him?" Angel questioned.

"Sure," Bobby answered." Just tell him I sent you. Now you had better get going. It's getting late."

"Thanks for the information," the Kids said in unison. "If we see any other beavers we'll say hello for you."

"You do that," the beaver grinned as he quickly disappeared under the water.

"Smart critter," Angel noted.

"Sure was," J.J. agreed. "Now help me with the pack and we'll head back to the road."

After a drink at the pond the Kids turned back upstream on the north side of the Little. To the west the fiery sun had nearly burned out. Just a few orange streamers still fought to escape the grip of the conquering darkness. Soon they could see headlights and they knew the highway was just ahead. Once there they turned north along the eastern side and began working their way toward the town of Broken Bow. Near midnight they reached the southern edge of the city and stopped to rest and plot their course.

"Should we risk going through town?" J.J. asked Angel who was looking ahead at the city lights.

"Ya, but let's wait awhile," Angel responded.

"Right," seconded J.J. "Let's give it another hour and let the traffic die down some more."

"Oh, and let's keep our eyes open for that van. Remember they said something about Broken Bow," Angel reminded her sister.

"I almost forgot," admitted J.J. with a shake of her head.

The Kids nestled under a broad oak just off the highway and watched the traffic while they had a little snack.

"Meat's running low," commented J.J. as she looked into the food bag. "We'll have to find some more food pretty soon."

"Maybe we can scrounge up something in town," Angel offered.

"Probably can," J.J. answered with a nod of agreement. "Traffic's light. Are you ready to go?"

"Looks good," replied Angel.

After helping J.J. with the backpack the Kids cautiously moved north into town. For safety's sake they quickly veered off onto a side street that ran parallel to the main highway. All was quiet.

"Looks like a nice little town," Angel commented as she and her sister cut through the shadows.

"Seems to be," J.J. seconded with a look of approval. "See a white van anywhere," she added with a laugh.

"Not yet," Angel chuckled. "The guy's probably hiding. He must know we're after him."

"The great canine detectives," J.J. howled. "If he only knew how much trouble he was in."

"We should have business cards," Angel joked.

Both Kids doubled over in laughter as they plopped down near a side yard hedgerow that lined a low chain link fence. As they fought for control a deep but soft growl came out of the shrubbery. Quick as lightning the Kids sobered up and whirled around in the direction of the sound.

"Shh," warned the voice. "You'll wake everybody up."

"Who are you?" J.J. demanded as she peered through the greenery at the bright set of eyes carefully studying them.

"I'm Dixie," the chocolate lab answered. "And you?"

"I'm J.J. and this is my little sister Angel," J.J. replied.

"Do you live around here?" Dixie asked.

"No, we're from Texas," J.J. answered as Angel edged in closer to get a better look.

"What are you doing way up here?" the lab questioned with a curious cock of her head.

"It's kind of a long story," J.J. responded.

"We're looking for the Sooner Silver," Angel added.

"Ahh," Dixie woofed with a smile. "I heard about that."

"You have," Angel asked in excitement.

"You bet," the lab answered. "That's about all anyone's talking about."

"The police haven't found it yet?" J.J. asked anxiously.

"Nope," Dixie replied. "And it's sure got everybody tied up in knots. The governor even sent a special detective squad out here but so far nobody's turned up a thing. Stay right there and I'll come out. This sounds like fun."

The big lab walked quickly to the side yard gate, balanced one paw on the gatepost, and with a flick of the other undid the latch that kept it shut. Then she skipped down the hedgerow to the Kids and pawed the ground in greeting. The Kids returned the salute and then all three sat down to talk. They explained to Dixie their situation and how they came to be in Broken Bow.

"Where do you go next?" the lab asked.

"Bobby the beaver down on Little River told us to go up to his park in the Ouachitas and talk to the bear," J.J. answered.

"Old Bobby, huh," Dixie grinned.

"Do you know him?" Angel asked.

"Oh, sure," the lab replied with a smile. "I chased him through the water two or three times. Never could catch him though; really didn't want to. It was just fun trying. He thinks everything in this state's named after him."

"There's quite a lot that bears his name," J.J. reminded her with a laugh. "Oh, I forgot. How come they call you Dixie?

"After the war a lot of southerners moved to this part of Oklahoma so it came to be known as Little Dixie," the lab explained. "So they just named me after that."

"You mean the Civil War?" Angel asked.

"Oh ya," Dixie affirmed.

"The beaver said the bear knows a lot about that war," J.J. stated. "We saw where it all started; a place called Fort Sumter in South Carolina.

"When was that?" Dixie questioned, rather embarrassed about her gaps in knowledge.

"Way back in the 1860's," J.J. answered. "1861 to be exact."

" I need to read up on that," the lab confessed. "If you get back this way let me know what you found out about it."

"Okay," Angel promised. "Oh, we're almost out of food. Do you think you could help us?" she continued as she showed Dixie the near empty food sacks.

"Let me have a sack," the lab offered. "I can get you some nuggets out of the can."

Dixie took a sack and then retreated back inside the fence. As the Kids watched she quietly tipped over the trash can, spilling an ample supply of nuggets onto the ground. Then she scooped it all into a sack and took it to the Kids.

"Thanks a lot," J.J. praised. "This will hold us for a while."

"Should we stay on this street to get through town?" Angel asked.

"Yup," answered the lab. It goes straight through town and then winds back to the highway on the far north side. Then you're just a short skip to the mountains."

"The Ouachitas?" J.J. questioned.

"That's right," Dixie confirmed. "You'll like it up there; pretty country. And maybe you can find that bear."

"We'll find him," Angel responded with confidence. "Thanks for helping us."

"My pleasure," Dixie said. "Good luck to you."

"And to you," the Kids replied together.

Dixie retreated back to her yard and the Kids continued up the street. Well before dawn they reached the highway intersection on the northern edge of town.

"A new road," J.J. commented as she saw that U.S. 70 now turned sharply east.

"Yup," confirmed the little one. "259 north to the Ouachitas."

After stopping for a drink and a short rest they lumbered on, watching as the first flickers of yellowy orange began to filter in from the east. The new dawn always excited them. They never tired of the beautiful sight of a new day rising. By morning's first full light they could see their objective in the distant north.

"Look!" exclaimed Angel, as she pointed to the towering green hills just ahead.

"A whole new country," J.J. gushed as she studied the rocky heights thick with pine. "Dixie was right. This does look nice."

Gripped by the excitement of discovery they quickly covered the last few miles that separated the hills from the flat valley lands behind them. On the first rise they stopped in a grove of pine to study the layout.

"Walking's going to be tougher now," J.J. reasoned as she surveyed the seemingly endless chain of highlands that lay ahead.

"Pretty means rugged," Angel added with a sigh. "It always makes travel harder."

"Sure seems that way," J.J. agreed. "Wish we could catch a ride through these hills."

"That would be nice," affirmed Angel as she thought back on their other travels and the times they had managed to snag a lift of some kind.

"Look at all the pine trees," Angel observed as she changed course.

"I guess the pine belt comes all the way out here," J.J. reasoned as she recalled the great pine forests they had seen in the deep East Texas and the rest of the South.

"Must," seconded Angel. "It's hard to believe that it stretches all the way from the Atlantic to Oklahoma. "That's a lot of wood."

"I'll bet you lumbering is big business here," J.J. reckoned.

"Probably so," quipped the little one as she rose to her feet. "Ready to go?"

"Sure," replied J.J. "We have time to cover a lot of ground before the heat sets in."

All morning the Kids trudged through the timbered hills of the lower Ouachita National Forest, a designation given to much of this region.

"I wonder why they call it a National Forest," Angel pondered.

"I was thinking the same thing," J.J. responded. "Maybe we can find a sign that tells us."

"It must mean something special," Angel reckoned as she looked at J.J. who gave a nod of agreement.

For another hour the Kids worked their way north until they came to a road cutting in from the east. A sign told them that that was the route to Beavers Bend State Park and Lake Broken Bow.

"We have to check this out," J.J. commanded.

"The beaver would never forgive us if we didn't," laughed Angel.

J.J. chuckled at the thought and then motioned for Angel to follow her into the trees along the south side of the road. Soon the road veered back to the north. Though exhausted from the trek through the hilly country they were excited by the prospect of finding something new; something the beaver had told them about. Soon J.J. stopped and peered intently through the thick stands of pine.

"Look!" she almost shouted. "I can see the lake."

"Ya," exclaimed the little one. "It looks like a nice one," she finished as she studied the deep blue breaking through the forest green.

"That looks like the dam just ahead," stated J.J. "Let's head for it."

Angel fell in just behind as J.J. led their way to the dam. A sign told them that Lake Broken Bow was fed by the waters of the Mountain Fork River which flowed west out of the Arkansas high country. Just below the dam four fishermen tried their luck in the clear rushing waters. After sneaking down to the river for a drink, the Kids cautiously crossed the road and headed for the shoreline. Here they staked out a nice shrub-covered spot behind a rocky crest, gathered up a thick bed of rusty-brown pine needles, and sat to watch and rest.

"Look at the boats," Angel bubbled as she pointed at several craft shooting through the glistening blue water.

"Looks like fun, doesn't it," J.J. remarked, "especially on a hot day like this one."

"Sure does," Angel affirmed as she imagined the cool spray from a zipping boat hitting her face and wetting her muzzle. "Hungry?" she asked.

"I could stand a bite," J.J. answered, realizing she still carried the backpack.

"Help me get this off."

Angel held the straps while J.J. slipped out and then opened the pack. She pulled out the bag with the last of the meat and emptied it, giving her sister a little more because of her greater size.

"That's the last of it," she moaned. "It sure was good."

"We'll get more," J.J. assured her. "But for now we still have plenty of nuggets. That will hold us for a bit."

The sun's reflection off the lake's glistening blue painted a picture of calm; a canvas of blue framed in the summer green of the surrounding hills. With stomachs full and eyelids heavy, the Kids laid out for a well earned rest.

Late afternoon brought arousal once more. Angel was the first to rise. After shaking her furry face to clear the haze of slumber, she gave her sister a gentle poke. "Time to get up," she softly spoke as she straightened her legs and arched her back.

"Okay," yawned J.J. as she twisted her back several times on the soft pine bed beneath her. "What time is it?"

"Looks to be about five," Angel reckoned as she took a reading of the western sun. "Let's get some water."

Together they plodded down the steep rise to the water below and drank deeply.

"How are the water bottles?" J.J. asked.

"Full," answered the little one. "We've barely touched them."

"Good," J.J. replied as they climbed back to their perch and prepared to leave.

"I guess we go back to the highway," Angel reasoned as she helped her sister secure the backpack.

"No," argued J.J. "Let's just follow the shoreline. The lake looks to go north just like the road and it won't be as risky."

"Good thinking," praised Angel. "And let's not forget about the bear. We have a better chance of finding him in the woods than on a highway."

"That's right," confirmed J.J. "I almost forgot about him. Let's go."

Through the late afternoon and early evening the Kids hugged the rugged shoreline of Lake Broken Bow as they plodded north. As the last faint glows of orange colored the western sky they came to its end and stopped for a rest on the left bank of the Mountain Fork River. Through the trees but a short distance away they could see headlights.

"Must be 259," J.J. reckoned. "I wonder if we're still in the Ouachitas?"

"Hard to say," Angel reasoned. "The land looks pretty much the same."

"Let's look at one of the maps," J.J. ordered. "Maybe we can get some idea what's ahead."

Angel helped J.J. remove the pack and from it she pulled the map. As she studied she noted that just ahead the Mountain Fork took a sharp turn east.

"We'll have to get back on the highway if we want to keep going north," the little one advised, "unless we want to take the back country."

"No," reasoned J.J. as she pursed her lips and surveyed their surroundings. "The road's the way to go."

"Guess so," agreed Angel with a nod. "Let's take a break and eat and then we'll go on."

Angel broke out a food bag and the dogs quickly crunched down several pawfuls of nuggets. "It's getting harder to see," she observed as she finished her meal. "The moon's not out like it has been."

"Nope," said J.J. as she looked up at the shrunken orb that but days ago had been full and bright.

"It's time like this I wish I was a cat," she chuckled as she thought about the superior night vision of the feline.

"Ya," laughed the little one. "But we don't do so bad. We can still see better than people.'"

"That's true," seconded J.J. as she crunched her last morsel.

J.J. placed the food sack back in the pack while Angel folded the map and put it away. They quickly covered the ground to the highway and then stopped to read the signs.

'Leaving Ouachita National Forest', the marker read.

"No bear," moaned Angel as they stopped to think.

"Nope," sighed J.J.

"What do we do now?" Angel squeaked.

"Let's keep going," J.J. ordered. "The beaver just said the bear was in the Ouachita. Maybe the National Forest is just a part of the whole thing."

"You're right," stated Angel who quickly moved alongside her sister.

Soon from their trail some twenty yards off the highway they spotted another set of signs at a highway intersection.

"Look!" shouted Angel. "The Ouachita National Forest again; straight ahead."

"There must be two of them," J.J. reasoned. "And look at this one," she added as she read 'Kiamichi Mountains'. "I can't wait until daylight to see them."

"There's that word again," Angel joked. "Bet you've forgotten how to spell it."

"If I can spell Ouachita I can spell Kiamichi," J.J. laughed.

"I guess the river must come out of these mountains and flow back south," Angel mused.

"Must," agreed J.J. "I wonder if they named the mountains for the river or the river for the mountains?"

Angel just grinned and together they started walking north again. The Kids plodded on until nearly dawn before stopping just outside the small town of Big Cedar. Here they found a nice quiet spot in a pine grove just out of sight, off the road. A tiny spring at the base of a crest filled a rock bottomed basin with sweet, cool water and the Kids drank their fill.

"I'm beat," Angel admitted as she stretched her weary frame over the cool dirt.

"Same here," confessed J.J. as she plopped down beside her. "We'll stay here for an hour or so."

"Do you want to take off the pack?" Angel asked.

"Good idea," J.J. answered as she rose along with the little one who helped her out of it.

"We forgot to read the book yesterday," Angel reminded her sister. "Let's be sure and read some after we stop for the afternoon."

"Okay," affirmed J.J. "I guess we were too busy talking to the beaver."

"Ya," giggled the little one. "He did bend our ears. I wonder if all beavers talk that much."

"He probably asked the same question about us," J.J. chuckled.

Angel just grinned and rolled over to face the north. The morning light had just now broken the plane of night and in the distance she could see the mountain outlines.

"Mountains and hills as far as I can see," she commented. "I guess the Kiamichis are a part of the Ouachitas."

"Must be," agreed J.J. who was looking north as well. "Sure are pretty."

"Sure are," seconded the little one. "I wonder how far they go?"

"I imagine we'll find out sooner or later," she quipped. "Now go to sleep for a while."

Angel did as ordered and J.J. quickly followed her lead. An hour later the harsh bellow of a semi's horn shattered the morning's soft stillness and the Kids jumped to attention.

"Time to go," J.J. commanded as she stretched her front legs. "Let's have a drink and then load up."

She then led Angel back to the little spring where they drank deeply of the pure mountain water. After loading the pack they were off once more.

Walking the mountain roads tested the Kids to their limits, both mentally and physically. Unlike the flatlands far to the south, the steep grades and narrow shoulders made cover scarce. In some places they had but a few feet between the road and the sheered rock side of a mountain cut. The sun cooked hotter with each hour. Summer was here. Still they went on, staying on the wider west side. Near noon they reach the intersection of State Highway 1; the Talimena Scenic Trail. Here, amongst a sparse patch of stubby oaks, they stopped for a badly needed rest.

"I don't see any water," J.J. stated as she took a hard look around. "It's a good thing we have our bottles."

Angel unzipped the pack, pulled out a bottle, twisted off the cap with her teeth, and passed it to J.J. who took a giant gulp. Then she took it and did the same. When quenched she replaced the cap and returned the bottle to the pack.

"There's not enough shade here," J.J. worried. "Let's take a look and see if there's a better place to camp."

"What about down there?" Angel asked as she motioned to a high stand of pine but a few hundred yards down a grassy slope on the road's north side.

"Looks better than this," J.J. affirmed."

Together they stumbled down the steep decline and soon reached the trees.

"Much better," Angel squeaked as she looked around for signs of water.

"Sure is," agreed J.J. already working to remove the pack as Angel tugged on its straps.

After taking yet another drink they sprawled out on the soft mix of needles and a soil of sandy red. Both Kids touched the sacred pouch for good luck and sweet dreams and then wilted away in sleep. Only the summer bugs buzzing broke the silence.

Late afternoon brought them to alertness once more. Each dog rose on wobbly legs and shook hard to sweep away slumber's cobwebs. Now far to the west, the new summer sun shot streamers of heat through the green hills and deep valleys. After taking refreshment from a water bottle, they settled in to decide their next move.

"This bottle's empty," Angel sighed. "Do you see water anywhere?"

"Nope," confessed J.J. as she looked hard all around. "The other's still full. That'll hold us until we find more."

"I hope so," Angel replied. "Let's look at the book," she added as her thoughts turned away from trouble.

"Good idea," gushed J.J. as she pulled the text from the pack.

"You read," she ordered as she opened it to the bookmark and handed it to her sister.

"It seems there are a lot of mountains in this region," Angel began. "The Ouachitas, the Kiamichi, the Winding Stair, the Jack Fork, and the Sansbois. And", she hesitated for just a minute to study the map on the page, "I think we're right here," she finished as she pointed to a spot.

"That's what the sign said," J.J. confirmed as she read 'Talimena Drive' aloud.

"It says that this road stretches from Mena, Arkansas in the east to Talihina, Oklahoma in the west."

"Hmm," mused J.J. "I guess they took the name Talimena from Talihina, Oklahoma and Mena, Arkansas. That was pretty smart."

"Must have," agreed Angel. "It says that the road is just full of pretty sites and interesting historical spots."

"Really?" chimed J.J. "Maybe we should take this road instead of going on north. What do you think?"

"That would be a good idea," cracked a gravelly voice right behind them.

A startled J.J. whirled around in a fighting stance and let out a loud snarl while Angel fell in behind her. But their new company only laughed as he flopped down hard on the ground before them. In an instant the Kids relaxed, knowing that this huge creature would do them no harm.

"You're the bear," Angel squealed in excitement.

"Boomer Bear at your service," he affirmed.

"We've been looking for you," J.J. confessed. "The beaver told us to find you."

"Bobby the beaver," the bear chuckled. "Is he still hiding out down on the Little."

"Yup," Angel replied. "At least he was just a few days ago."

"Are you from those parts?" Boomer asked, wondering why the beaver had sent them all the way up here to look for him.

"No, we're from Texas," J.J. answered as she settled back down.

"Texas!" the bear exclaimed. "You're a long way from home."

"We don't have a home anymore," Angel stated, "and we won't have another one until we find the Sooner Silver."

The Kids now told their new friend the entire story. He listened with deep interest and then gave a knowing nod.

"That's bad luck," Boomer responded sympathetically. "But you never know what good things can come from the bad."

"I hope you're right," J.J. replied as Angel nodded in agreement. "Have you heard anything about the silver?" she added.

"Oh, sure," Boomer confirmed. "The story's all over the woods. But I can't tell you where it is. I wish I knew myself."

The Kids gave a dejected look but then perked up again.

"Oh, would you like some water," Angel offered, embarrassed at having forgotten her manners.

"No, thanks," the bear declined, "I just had a good drink over at Horse Thief Spring."

"Where's that?" Angel asked as she thought about their one empty bottle.

"Not far down this road," Boomer answered as he pointed his nose to the west.

"Are there a lot of other bears around here?" Angel quizzed, wondering if they would see more along the way.

"A lot more than there used to be," Boomer quipped. "In fact, back around a hundred years ago there wasn't a bear to be found in all of the state."

"What happened?" J.J. asked with wonder.

"People ran us off," the bear answered. "They figured we were in the way of what they were trying to do. Later they realized they'd made a big mistake; that we were an important part of the whole system. So little by little they started bringing us back. We're doing pretty well now."

"That's good," Angel squeaked.

"The beaver said you knew a lot about the Civil War," J.J. stated, eager to hear what the bear had to say.

"Well that was a pretty complicated affair," Boomer sighed. "This much I know for sure. That war hit this region hard, both during and after."

"Really rough, huh," J.J. nodded.

"Yup," the bear went on. "It tore this area apart; wrecked the economy."

"From what we've heard and read so far, Oklahoma was divided. Some went with the north; some with the south," J.J. stated, adding that she and Angel had been at Fort Towson earlier.

"That's true," Boomer confirmed. "It split the tribes here and led to a lot of bitterness that lasted for years. And of course a lot of the Indians lost everything they'd worked so hard to build over the years. It was total chaos. Guerrilla raiders swarmed all over the state; some for the north and some for the south. They called themselves soldiers but they were just bandits looking for easy pickings. They stole about everything they could and destroyed the rest."

"Sounds bad," J.J. grimaced.

"It was," the bear went on. "But these folks were a plucky bunch and over time they built it back even better than before."

"Were there any big battles fought here?" Angel questioned as she thought back to seeing Fort Sumter.

"Quite a few," Boomer replied. "Honey Springs was a big one. That's not far from here; just north a little ways. And Boggy Depot over around Atoka; and Perryville at McAlester; and a bunch more; dozens in fact. You'll probably see some more as you go along."

"Do you know why they fought it?" Angel asked, still confused by it all.

"Whoa!", the bear bellowed with a shake of his head. "That's a question I wish I could answer. A lot of people try to make it sound simple but I don't think it was. To this day folks still argue about it. You'd better read a book on the subject; make that about fifty books; and then you probably still won't understand it."

The Kids could only laugh at what seemed to be the impossible task Boomer had assigned them. They were impressed by his knowledge of the subject and the enthusiasm he showed in talking about it. And he wasn't finished.

"Of course the war changed things a bunch," he continued. "As I'm sure you know by now this land was supposed to be set aside for just the Indian tribes. But after it ended there was a lot of pressure to open some of the territory to whites. Now the government in Washington was a little miffed that so many of the Indians here went with the Confederacy and wanted to teach them a lesson. So they decided to take what they called surplus lands, whatever that meant, and let some whites have it. It was all part of the revenge process that happened in every southern state in one form or another. It was called 'Re-construction' and really made healing the war wounds a whole lot harder."

"We met a dog named Dixie in Broken Bow. She said that a lot of southerners came to this part of Oklahoma after the war," J.J. informed the bear.

"That's right," he acknowledged. "There lives had been destroyed and they were looking for a place to make a fresh start. Oklahoma was it. In some ways it's not much different from what you two are doing now."

"I guess that's right," Angel chirped as J.J. shook her head in agreement.

"Why do they call you Boomer? J.J. asked, putting the history lesson aside for the moment.

"Never heard of Boomer Sooner?" the bear chided them.

"No," admitted the Kids in unison.

"That's the fight song for the University of Oklahoma," he laughed.

"Where's that?" Angel asked. "Is it near here?"

"Nope, it's way to the west," the bear answered. "Probably be awhile before you get there."

"Do you think we'll have to go that far?" J.J. questioned.

"Might," Boomer answered. "You'll just have to follow your orders and see what happens."

"Where should we go from here?" Angel quizzed. "Do you have any ideas?"

"Well, if you're looking for thieves, Robbers Cave would be a good place to look," the bear advised.

"Where's that?" Angel inquired.

"Just follow this road west all the way to the state park. Then see if you can find Lucky,"Boomer answered. "He'll put you on the right track."

"Lucky," J.J. questioned.

"Lucky the Loon," Boomer chuckled. "Listen to what he has to say. People think he's crazy but he's really pretty smart."

"We'll do it," Angel promised. "Thanks for all the advice."

"And the education," J.J. added.

"My pleasure," the black bear said as he shot the Kids a broad smile.

In a flash the giant critter skittered far down the slope and quickly disappeared in the valley brush below. The Kids were shocked to see something that big move so quickly and smoothly. After a drink they began to load up, putting the water bottle and book back in the pack. Then in their now well rehearsed ritual J.J. slipped the pack over her shoulders while Angel tightened the straps. A skip up the slope to the road and they were headed west into an early evening sun now turned crimson.

"I wonder what gives the sun that reddish color?" J.J. pondered as they walked the Talimena.

"Dust in the air," Angel explained. "I heard Linda talk about it once."

"Oh," J.J. quipped. "Sure makes for a nice sky."

"Yup," Angel acknowledged, "and it's staying up a little later each day."

"That's good," J.J. stated. "It means we can see longer and cover more ground."

The Talimena Trail was one of the most interesting roads the Kids had ever traveled. Each mile or so brought them to another scenic overlook; a place where a driver could pull off the road and admire the scenery. Site names such as Sunset Point, Big Cedar, and Shawnee dotted the highway. In a short time they reached Horse Thief Spring where the bear had told them they could find water. A beautifully constructed, split level roadside park surrounded the trickling spring which flowed out of the hillside. Here the Kids filled their empty bottles and found two more in the trash which they rinsed and filled. They also found a fresh half a pack of hot dogs that a picnicker had left behind. After two days of nuggets the aroma of meat made them drool. They drank their fill, devoured two franks apiece, then struck out once more down the Talimena.

Near nine they reached the Choctaw Vista where they stopped for a needed rest. The sun's last rays cloaked the valleys and hills in a soft, peaceful orange. As the Kids watched the surrender of day to night, they noticed a sign that told them the Talimena State Park was just ahead.

"Might be a good place to put in for a while," J.J. commented as she read the sign.

"Could be," the little one agreed. "Let's have a little water and then get going."

After a quick drink the Kids set out down 271 and soon came to the park entrance. They slipped through the gate and quietly tiptoed past the headquarters building. In the day's last glows they could see a small but tidy place with numerous camping spots. No one was there.

"Looks like we have it all to ourselves," Angel observed.

"That's good," J.J. replied. "We can find a nice quiet corner and not have to worry about being seen."

"Maybe we should stay here until dawn," Angel suggested.

"Ya, we could use a full night's sleep," J.J. answered, realizing that the long marches of the past several days and nights had tired them out.

"That looks good over there," Angel stated as she pointed to a clump of bushes just behind a far campsite.

"Sure does," responded J.J.
And I believe that's a water faucet right next to the grill."

"Great," chirped Angel as she began to move down the trail.

Together the Kids reached the spot and unloaded their gear. Then they helped themselves to a tasty meal of hot dogs and nuggets, washed down with cool water from the nearby faucet. After returning the food bag to the pack, they stretched out to watch the sparkling stars as they pierced the clear night sky. A stiff, steady breeze kicked up from the north and wrapped them in a blanket of coolness. Sleep soon swept them.

THE LOON AND THE LONGHORN

Dawn breaks early in June. By 5:00 A.M. the first splash of a new day's light had already rimmed the ring of darkness. The Kids woke as one. With a yawn and a stretch they quickly skipped to the faucet and rinsed out sleep's dryness. Then they returned to their spot for a bite of breakfast. Stomachs full they packed and talked.

"What do we do now?" J.J. quizzed.

"I don't know," the little one squeaked. "Just stay on this road?"

"Might as well," shrugged J.J.

As they looked back toward the park entrance they could see a light on in the headquarters building. Soon a large, flatbed truck roared through the gate and stopped near the door. A man dropped from the cab and entered the building.

"We'd better get going," J.J. counseled. "Things are starting to stir."

Quickly the Kids trotted along the edge of the camp road and came to within twenty yards of the building. Suddenly the door flew open and two men emerged; the driver and a park attendant. The dogs, wary of being seen, skittered behind a bush and watched.

"Where are you headed, Sam," the attendant asked.

"Up to Robbers Cave," the driver answered. "Got to take up this load."

The Kids quickly looked at each other and then scanned the truck bed. Large barrels that looked like trash containers lined the outer edges while cardboard boxes filled in the middle. At the rear of the bed was a two-feet deep black metal lift anchored halfway between truck bed and ground. A large logo on the driver's side door read 'State of Oklahoma-Parks'.

"That would be a great place to hide if we could get on the bed," J.J. spoke excitedly as she continued her watch.

"If those men would only go back inside for just a minute," Angel bleated.

"Well, better get going," the driver huffed as he moved toward the cab.

"See you this afternoon," the attendant replied as he disappeared into the building.

The driver, a large man in jeans, boots, khaki shirt and baseball cap stopped for a minute to examine his load. He then removed his cap and pulled a handkerchief from his back pants pocket to wipe his brow. Suddenly a shrieking sound pierced the air and a large, duck like bird shot through the early morning air. In a brilliantly executed strike, the bird snatched the cap from the man's hand and flew to the ground about fifty feet away. The startled driver stood frozen for a moment but then began running toward the bird which stood fast as the man approached.

"Now's our chance!" J.J. hollered softly. "Let's go!"

At full speed the Kids shot for the back of the truck. J.J. led and glided easily up onto the lift. Angel followed only inches behind. But the three feet from the lift to the bed was not a jump but a straight up climb. J.J. extended her long body upward, planted her front paws hard on the bed, and pulled with all her might. But the pack and the steep angle held her down.

"I have to grab that cable. Give me a push," she ordered the little one who immediately positioned herself under her sister and shoved upward. Angel's extra lift was all J.J. needed. With one mighty tug she managed to anchor first one front leg and then the other on one of the cables strung across the back to secure the cargo. That was the advantage she needed to bring her back legs to the truck bed and pull herself all the way up and over. She quickly looked around the side of the truck to see that the bird, cap in beak, was still toying with the man. With each of his advances it skittered just far enough away to elude his grasp. Now it was the smaller Angel's turn to climb. At fullest extent her front paws barely touched the truck bed.

"I don't think I can do this," she whined. "It's too high."

"Sure you can," J.J. encouraged her. "Spring as high as you can and I'll grab you."

Angel crouched low for a second to get extra lift and then, front legs fully extended , shot straight up. J.J., secure behind the cable, grabbed a leg high near the shoulder and pulled hard. Angel grabbed the cable, getting just enough of her body over it to keep her from falling back. Then with another giant tug J.J. brought all of Angel aboard. Quickly J.J. peeked through the cargo and could see that the bird was watching the truck. Then, just as quickly as it had come, it dropped the cap and flew off with a chilling shriek. J.J. motioned to Angel to follow and the two scurried between two rows of boxes. Crouching low, the Kids could see nothing from their hideout, but they clearly heard the man return to the truck and climb into the cab.

"Crazy bird," the driver muttered as he cranked up the engine, pulled out of the park, and accelerated down the highway.

J.J. and Angel could only giggle at the sight of the bird teasing the driver and smile at their own good fortune.

"It's almost like he was trying to help us," Angel remarked.

"Sure seemed like it," J.J. concurred. "Anyway, we sure got lucky."

The Kids then gave a quick glance around them and realized that this truck was ideal for sightseeing. The heavy containers which lined each side of the bed were spaced about a foot apart, hiding the Kids but allowing them a clear line of sight through the slatted wooden side rails. The boxes, many piled high against the cab's back window, blocked the driver's rear view of the truck bed.

"This is great," Angel gushed. "We can see everything and no one can see us."

"Fantastic," J.J. hooted.

Soon the truck slowed to a crawl as it approached a stop sign just outside the town of Talihina. The Kids ducked for cover, fearing that the driver might stop to check his load. When he sped up once more they reemerged, just in time to see a large bird tracking the truck's movements. As they watched it circled behind them and zeroed in on the truck bed. In one fluid motion it shot down from the sky and landed noisily on a box right next to the dogs. Shocked, the Kids could only stare at the newcomer. They soon realized that it was the same critter that had stolen the driver's cap and given them the distraction they needed to steal their ride.

"Howdy," the duck-like creature addressed them. "How's the ride?"s

"Great," Angel replied, still stunned by the bird's antics.

"You're the one who took the cap, aren't you?" J.J. quizzed.

"Yup," the bird admitted. "You looked like you could use some help."

"We did," Angel chirped. "You were watching us?"

"Oh, ya," the bird confirmed. "I know all about you. Boomer told me everything."

"You're Lucky!" the Kids exclaimed in unison.

"Sure am," the bird acknowledged. "Lucky the Loon."

"That was a great show," J.J. praised with a wide smile. "Welcome aboard."

"Thanks," he grinned.

"I don't think we've ever seen a loon before," Angel confessed, thinking that, except for the pointed beak, he looked pretty much like a duck.

"You probably have," the loon countered. "Plenty of loons down in Texas. That's where I hear you're from."

"That's right," both Kids answered.

The Kids studied his dark head and black and white crosshatched feathers "Did Boomer tell you we're looking for the Sooner Silver?"

"Uh, huh," the bird answered. "He told me to show you the way to Robbers Cave. You might find a clue there."

"That's where this truck's going," J.J. informed him. "We heard the driver say so."

"Great," the loon cackled. "That makes things easy. See why they call me Lucky."

"Wouldn't it be easier for you to just fly?" Angel asked with a puzzled look.

"Why waste the energy. I may be crazy but I'm not stupid," the loon laughed as he cut loose with his eerie cry.

"No offense, but you sure make a funny sound," J.J. grinned as she thought back

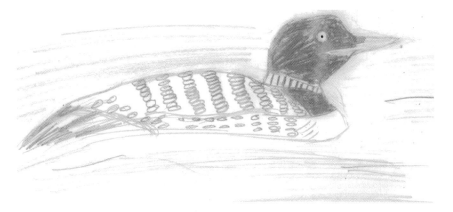

to the bird's shrieks.

"Ever heard the expression 'Crazy as a loon'," the bird chuckled. "That's where it comes from; scares everybody to death."

The Kids were having fun with their good-natured new friend. They sensed he could tell them a lot of things they wanted to know.

"Are there a lot of different birds in Oklahoma?" Angel asked.

"You bet," Lucky almost shouted. "If you like to birdwatch this is the place to be; thousands of species. Of course the loons are the most important," he sniffed as he lifted his beak to the air and puffed out his chest. "Looks like we're coming into Talihina," the loon added as he took a quick look ahead.

"Talihina?" Angel asked as she and J.J. crowded in behind the bird to see the town.

"Yup. That's the Choctaw word for railroad," Lucky informed them. "Oh, good," he continued, "looks like he's taking the long way. I can show you some interesting places."

"Great," the Kids gushed with eagerness.

The truck turned to the southwest following the lower leg of the scenic trail down Highway 271. Soon they once again saw the Kiamichi River as it skirted the road's south side. They passed through the little town of Albion which the loon informed them was the ancient name for England. Next came the hamlet of Kiamichi followed by Tuskahoma.

"Tuskahoma means 'Red Warrior' in Choctaw," the bird explained. "And right up there is the Choctaw Council House."

"What a pretty building!" J.J. exclaimed as she and Angel surveyed the magnificent red brick structure. "I wonder how old it is?"

"Built in 1884," Lucky answered. "They still use it today."

"What's up ahead?" Angel asked.

"We'll probably hang a right up here at Highway 2 and head north," Lucky replied. "That's the way to Robbers Cave. We'll pass over Sardis Lake on the way. That's where I stay when I'm in Oklahoma."

"You don't live here all the time?" J.J. questioned.

"Oh, no," the bird responded. "Loons come south in winter and go north in summer. A lot of Oklahoma birds are like that; 'migratory' is the word they use. I'm way late getting back as it is. All my buddies took off a long time ago. I'm just kind of slow sometimes," he finished with a laugh.

The Kids grinned at the old bird's laziness as the truck pulled up to the State Highway 2 intersection. Just as the old bird expected the driver cut north.

"What's that way?" Angel questioned as she looked to the south.

"Clayton," answered the bird. "Nice town; got a park and a lake."

"Sure are a lot of parks in Oklahoma," J.J. commented.

"And nice ones," Angel added, quite impressed by what she had seen so far.

Soon the truck touched the southern tip of Sardis Lake and the three looked over the broad expanse of blue that spread to the west.

"Well folks, I guess this is where I leave you," Lucky spoke sadly. "I've got to gather my stuff and head north."

"You're not coming with us to the cave," cried Angel, distressed to lose their good and helpful friend so soon.

"Nope," the old bird replied. "But this road takes you straight to Robbers Cave. You won't have any trouble."

"We were kind of hoping you'd stay with us awhile," J.J. stated as she pawed the truck bed.

"I really wish I could, but it's awfully late in the year for me to be here," Lucky lamented.

"What should we do next?" Angel asked, a slight bit of anxiety in her voice.

"After you leave the cave head back east; toward Poteau. Try to find the longhorn along the way. She knows a lot. Maybe she can help you," the loon advised. "Now I can't tell you where to find the silver. But I do know that if you use your heads and refuse to quit then everything will work out for you," Lucky added with a flap of his wings and a twist of his sharp beak.

"We never quit," the Kids both assured him.

"That's the spirit," the old bird chuckled. "You two would have made good loons."

With that the bird cranked his wings and in an instant was soaring out over the waters of Sardis Lake. The Kids watched in sadness as soon their new, now old, friend was but a shadow on the far horizon.

"We never even had a chance to thank him," Angel moaned as she settled back down on the bed.

"I think he knows how much we appreciate what he did," J.J. reckoned. "Some things don't have to be spoken."

Just after midmorning the truck crossed U.S. Highway 271 at Wilburton. A sign indicated that Robbers Cave was just a few miles ahead.

"Almost there," J.J. stated. "Let's get ready."

"We'll have to be careful," Angel warned as she thought about how they might get off the truck. "We don't want anyone to see us."

"You're right," J.J. affirmed. "Let's get off at the first chance."

The Kids quickly passed from the front of the bed to near the rear, hoping that at some point the truck would slow down enough for them to make a quick jump down to the lift and then to the ground. As the driver approached the park he began to slow, then turned onto a park road and came to a stop in front of a gate.

"Now might be our chance," J.J. whispered as she heard the truck's door open. "Get ready." J.J. watched through a slit as the driver, back turned to the Kids, stomped toward the gate and began to open it.

"Go!" shouted J.J. as softly as she could.

As one the Kids hopped to the ground and quickly scampered to a low bank of dense brush but ten feet away. As they looked back they could see the driver closing the gate behind him.

"Good work," praised J.J. "He never had a clue."

"Where do we go now?" Angel questioned, confused by her new surroundings.

"We'll stay here for a while," reasoned J.J. "This is good cover. Let's have a drink and a bite and get a little rest. Then we'll do some exploring."

After a quenching drink from a water bottle, the Kids broke out the pack of hot dogs and the sack of nuggets and sat down to an early lunch.

"Only two franks left," sighed Angel as she studied the bag.

"We're still okay on nuggets," J.J. stated as she poked the sack with her paw, "at least for a few more days."

"This looks like a big park," Angel observed as she looked around. "Maybe we'll find something here."

After eating they returned what was left of the food to the pack and zipped it shut. Then they stretched out in the bushes for a much needed nap. About midday they awoke and began to chart their course.

"Good thing this is a weekday," J.J. said as she looked around and saw the park was nearly empty. I'll bet on the weekends this place is crawling with people."

"I'd think so," Angel seconded, "This looks like a nice place. I wonder where the cave is?"

"There are signs everywhere. One of them will probably point the way," J.J. reasoned as she studied the park entrance and headquarters building about fifty yards away.

"Ready to go?" chirped the little one.

"Yup," replied J.J. "Let's move along that row of trees," she suggested as she pointed to a long stand of pine just inside the park and off the highway. "No one can see us there."

Together the Kids dashed into the trees, stopping just long enough to read a sign which pointed the way toward the cave and grab a map of the park's layout.

"This is a neat place," J.J. woofed as she looked at the map.

"Ya," agreed Angel. "They have lakes and stables and even an outdoor theater. That's really something."

"Looks like this road takes us right to the cave," J.J. stated. "Let's get going."

Both dogs were excited by the thought of seeing another historical site. Together they quickly worked their way along the side of the park road and advanced toward the cave. Soon they came to the parking lot at the base of a steep trail which led to the cavern. An informational marker told them that Robbers Cave was once a hideout for some of the region's most notorious bandits. Frank and Jesse James, The Younger brothers, Belle Starr and many others hid out here right after the Civil War. The trail along the nearby Fourche Maline River was called the Robbers Trail and all the outlaws used it.

"I can see why they picked this place," J.J. laughed. "If you didn't know exactly where it was you'd never find it."

"That's the truth," seconded Angel as she looked up at the boulder strewn pathway framed in stubby pine.

"Boy, that's a climb!" J.J. whooped as she studied the jagged trail winding toward the heavens.

"Got to be in shape for this one," Angel grinned. "Ready?"

"Let's go," affirmed J.J. as she flashed a broad smile.

The Kids slowly began to plod the narrow, rocky path that seemed to shoot straight up. As they went they studied the boulders of tan and red all cracked and creased and scarred and worn by the ceaseless assaults of wind, water, and time. Each seemed a rung on a ladder climbing skyward. Huffing and puffing they pushed and pulled themselves higher. Finally but one last jagged cut of sandstone stood between them and their prize; the entrance to Robbers Cave.

"Look at that!" exclaimed J.J. as she peeked over the rocks and into the cavern's broad mouth.

"What a great place to hide," Angel gushed as she studied the cave and the trickling stream that dripped from it."

"Can't beat it," J.J. agreed. "Water and shelter and no one can see you. No wonder the bad guys chose this place." The Kids shimmied down the steep incline and entered the cave. When just inside a light shower appeared from nowhere and began to sprinkle the rocks. In their excitement they hadn't even noticed the bank of clouds and the gust of cool air that had sneaked in between them and the blazing sun above.

"Boy does that feel good," J.J. barked as she held out a paw to catch a few drops dripping down from the cavern's ceiling.

"I didn't even notice the clouds," Angel chirped. "That breeze sure is nice," she added, turning her nose into the wind.

"It could pour and we'd be fine here," J.J. reckoned as she slurped a little water from the trickling little stream on the cavern's floor.

"Just like Jesse James," Angel giggled who followed her sister's lead and drank as well.

"Or the silver thieves," joked J.J. with a loud laugh.

"Ya," agreed the little one. "How about some lunch?" she added. "That climb made me hungry."

"Me, too," J.J. yelped. "Help me with the pack."

"Last of the hot dogs," Angel sighed as she opened the food bag and passed one to J.J.

"We'll give the park a good search before we leave," counseled J.J. as she pawed out a ration of nuggets for each of them.

The Kids finished their light lunch and then relaxed to watch the soft rain turn to light mist. Even through the haze from their high perch they could see far out into the countryside.

"Sure is pretty," J.J. remarked as she gazed out over the lush green of forested hills that painted the horizon.

"I wish we could just stay here," Angel purred. "But I guess we can't."

"I'm afraid not," J.J. responded. "We have a job to do."

Angel gave a loud yawn and then curled up next to her sister. J.J. gave her a gentle pat on the head and then both quickly fell asleep.

An hour later J.J. was awakened by faint voices coming from the trail below. She sharply nudged Angel who quickly snapped to attention. "Someone's coming," J.J. whispered. "Quick. Help me with the pack. We have to get out of here."

Angel did as ordered and then the two scurried from the cave opening to the rocky incline that bordered it. Peeking over the ridge they could see that two men were slowly working their way toward them. Should they run or hide? They had but an instant to decide.

"Back in the cave," J.J. commanded. "They're too close. They'll see us for sure."

In a flash the Kids bolted back into the cave and hid behind a slight bend in the rocky wall deep inside the cavern.

"Get behind me," J.J. snapped, "and lay low."

Both Kids hugged the side and plastered themselves to the cool floor. In a moment the two men entered the cavern and then sat down just a few feet inside. J.J. poked her head just around the bend and watched. She had seen them before.

"Looks like we're in the clear, Rob," one man snickered loudly. "The cops are tearing their hair out trying to crack this case but have
no idea where the stuff is or who took it."

"We did all right," Rob answered with a wide grin. "What now?"

"Nothing's changed," the other man hissed. "Let's not get impatient. Everything's working out just like we planned. Just keep to your normal routine. In a few more weeks I'll get it from you and move it out west. Then we'll just sit tight."

"Okay by me," Rob answered. "When do we meet next?"

"Don't know," the other man answered. "Just remember the phone codes in case something important comes up and I have to get a message to you."

"Got them right here," Rob assured him as he tapped his right temple and grinned.

"Great," the man cooed. "Now let's get going."

Though she could not see, Angel recognized the voices and inched her head forward to get a look. Jaw to jaw the dogs looked on as the men rose and left the cave.

"The thieves," Angel blurted when they were out of earshot.

"I can't believe it," J.J. snorted as she slapped herself on the snout.

"Robbers Cave," Angel laughed as she shook her head in amazement.

"Probably buried treasure all around here," J.J. grinned as she thought about all the outlaws who had called this place home.

"Could be," Angel agreed. "Let's follow them," she added as she thought about the two thieves. "Maybe we can get more clues as to where they're going."

"Good idea," commended J.J. "But keep low and stay way back. We don't want anyone to see us; especially those two."

"Right," nodded Angel as she led the way back to the front of the cave.

The Kids crept out of the cavern and over the trail incline. They could see the men walking down the path far ahead of them. Soon they were in the parking lot. From their perch they could now see the white van parked below.

"I wonder if the silver is still in the van?" Angel mused.

"Could be," J.J. reckoned. "Let's get closer."

Quickly the girls slid down the trail and hid behind one of the large boulders that bordered the parking area.

"Going down is sure a lot easier than coming up," the little one joked as they watched.

"Sure is," confirmed J.J. as the commissioner entered a private car and peeled out of the lot.

"Can you see Silver?" she asked.

"No," answered the little one. "I wonder where he went?"

"He's not in the van," J.J. advised as she looked into the vehicle's cab. "Maybe he's taking a walk."

The Kids looked at each other for a moment. Each knew what the other was thinking.

"Help me get this pack off," J.J. commanded. "We might have to really move."

Instantly Angel pulled as J.J. shed the backpack. After one more quick look around, the two dashed for the van. J.J. stood high on her hind legs and tried the driver's door, pushing the button with her nose. But it was locked. Next they moved to the back where J.J. anchored her legs hard to the ground and reached up toward the handle. With a powerful paw she tugged down hard. Surprisingly the latch popped and the door flew open. Without a word the Kids backed up and then together leaped into the van and began sniffing the floor and poking at boxes, looking for signs of the stolen silver.

"If it's still here it's under the floorboards," J.J. reasoned as she pawed the steel panels that made up the floor. "He'd never leave the stuff out in the open."

In the excitement the Kids had lost their caution. Suddenly Angel yelped loudly as a firm hand roughly grabbed her hind leg and jerked her out of the van. J.J. turned just in time to see the driver tear the pouch from the little one's neck. She wheeled and with all her might lunged for the man, sinking her teeth deep into his wrist. He let out a scream and dropped the bundle while flailing wildly at J.J.'s head with his free hand. But J.J. held fast, letting go only after she saw Angel retrieve the pouch from the ground. Then they scurried away as the man nursed his wrist and swore at them. They retreated deep into the woods before turning to watch as the man shut the van's rear doors. Still holding his bleeding wrist, he entered the cab and drove away.

"That wasn't smart," Angel counseled. "One of us should have been on the lookout."

"You're right," agreed J.J. "If he knew that we knew who he was he would have killed us."

"And we almost lost the pouch," Angel added. "Then we would have been in real trouble."

"We were in trouble enough without that," J.J. huffed, wincing as she rubbed her sore head. "Still, we almost had it. I'll bet the silver was still in the van; a little luck and it would have been ours."

"So close," Angel sighed. "But this is just a little setback. We'll have it in the end," she finished, perking up a little.

"Ya," seconded J.J. "Sometimes you have to try a whole lot before you reach a goal.

You can't quit just because it doesn't work out at first."

"I know," confirmed the little one. "It just seems like everything is always so hard."

"That's kind of a rule in life," J.J. replied. "Just about anything that's worth doing is hard."

"I guess you're right," squeaked Angel as she repaired the tear in the leather string and slid the pouch back around her neck.

"Do you think he'll tell the park people about us?" Angel questioned, worried that the man might report them.

"I doubt it," reckoned J.J. "The last thing he wants is attention. He'll just go on; and we should, too."

"Right," nodded the little one. "Let's go get our things."

Together the Kids returned to the boulder and fetched the pack. Angel helped J.J. load it and then they marched back to the road and turned north. The sun was now fighting hard to burn away the last of the rain clouds. Soon its summer brightness won a full victory.

"I wonder where Poteau is?" Angel queried. "Lucky said to go there."

"I don't know," confessed J.J. "But I guess we'll take Highway 2 north and see where that takes us."

"Might as well," Angel replied.

The Kids soon reached the highway, crossed to the eastern side, and began working their way north. The going was rough. In places the roadway cut through solid rock, leaving only a narrow shoulder for the Kids to travel. Time and again the whirring sound of an approaching car sent them dashing for what little cover the shoulder provided. Soon they came to a break in the hills where a thin strip of gently rolling land replaced the heights all around them.

"This looks like a good place to rest," J.J. stated as she eyed the tiny creek cutting through the valley floor. "Let's wait here until after dark."

"Okay," chirped the little one, eager to get off the roadway.

Together the Kids slid over the grey steel guard rail and followed the creek downstream to a stand of scrub oak along its rocky northern bank.

"This looks good," Angel squeaked as she helped her sister remove the pack.

"Let's get a drink," J.J. advised as the Kids stepped toward the water.

"Boy, this water looks nice and clear," the little one observed. "I wonder if it comes from a spring?"

"Must," reckoned J.J. as she slurped. "It's nice and cool for this time of day."

"I guess the spring waters come from one of the aquifers," Angel reasoned.

"Must," J.J. agreed. "

"Let's check the book and find out more about them," Angel advised as she finished her drink.

The girls returned to the pack and Angel pulled out the book. Together they scanned the contents until they came to a section on water. J.J. found the page and began reading.

"It says here that Oklahoma has a whole lot of them," she spoke as she pointed to a map that identified each by color and name.

"Neat," chirped the little one. "What else?"

"Well in parts of the state where there's little rainfall, the people pump up the water from underground and use it. Otherwise they couldn't live there. They use it for daily living, to irrigate crops and water livestock."

"It's amazing how people can adapt to the land," Angel observed.

"Just like animals learning to live in harsh places," J.J. added.

"How does the water get there?" the little one asked.

"Rainwater seeping through the ground," J.J. answered. "It's called recharge. It says that the water in an aquifer can come from miles away. But sometimes people pump it out faster than it refills and then you can have a real problem."

"No water, no life," Angel stated. "Let's be sure to keep the water bottles full."

J.J. laughed as she closed the book and placed it back in the pack. Then she pulled the food bag out and opened it.

"Getting low," she huffed as she poured out a portion of nuggets for Angel and then one for herself. "But we'll find something soon."

"Hope so," Angel sighed as she watched the last of the day's light began to fade in the west. "Boy, you tagged old Rob Silver," she added with a giggle as she pawed the sacred pouch hanging from her neck. "I'll bet his wrist still hurts." J.J. just grinned as she curled up next to her sister and quickly fell asleep.

The Kids awoke several hours later to a symphony of summer bugs. To the east a crescent moon of silvery white sliced a thin gash in night's starry darkness. Both girls ambled to the little creek for a deep drink, then returned to the pack. Angel helped her sister secure it and then they skipped upstream to the road. Highway 2 was quiet.

"This is better," J.J. commented as she eyed the roadway. "Maybe we can get through these hills before morning."

"Ya," agreed the little one. "Dodging traffic on this narrow road is tough."

Through the night and into early morning the Kids trudged on. Finally they came to the State Highway 31 intersection. In the dimmest of light they could barely make out a sign that pointed the way to Poteau.

"Back to the east," J.J. stated as she read. "I wonder how far?"

"Probably not far if there's a sign here," the little one reasoned.

The Kids ambled on until near dawn when they reached the small town of Kinta on the northern edge of the Sansbois Mountains. Here they called a halt just as the first flickers of a new day trickled over the eastern horizon. Finding refuge in a stand of oak just off the highway, they sprawled out on the shaded ground for a rest. Though tired, dawn's cool dampness refreshed them.

"I think this is my favorite time of day," J.J. remarked as they watched the sun's crown break the plane of darkness. "I never get tired of it."

"I know what you mean," replied the little one. "Every new morning seems like a fresh start in life; kind of like yesterday's failure only means a new day's success; another chance to get it right."

"That's well put," J.J. commended. "You're becoming quite a little philosopher."

Angel grinned at the compliment as she gave her sister a gentle poke in the ribs.

"I wonder if I can philosophize our way into some breakfast?" she quipped.

"We'll find something here," J.J. promised as she gazed east toward Kinta. "There's bound to be something in this town."

"Well, let's get started," Angel ordered as she rose from her perch.

Without a word J.J. sprang to her paws. Squinting her eyes against the new sun, she saw what looked to be several buildings just ahead.

"Looks like a restaurant and a convenience store," J.J. murmured. "Let's scout them out."

Together the Kids flanked the road about twenty yards from its edge, being careful to stay hidden in the trees and brush. Soon they came to the back of the little store and watched cautiously from the trees. Enclosed by a fence, a row of trash cans lined the back of the lot.

"Looks like the gate is open," Angel observed. "We can get in."

"Right," huffed J.J. "Help me with the pack."

Angel did as ordered and together they stashed the pack behind a bush. Each took a food sack; one empty the other nearly so. Then they crept slowly toward the trash cans and scanned the area. No one was near.

"Let's go," J.J. barked.

In a lurch she began her sprint to the cans. Angel matched her stride for stride. When at the gate J.J. ordered the little one to keep watch. Can by can J.J. searched until she hit paydirt; a damaged box nearly full of packaged dog food. She quickly pulled down the can, nosed out the box, and emptied it into a food sack.

"Someone's coming," Angel yelled as she saw a man approach. "Let's go."

J.J. clenched the sack tightly and shot for the gate. Then the Kids made a dash for the bush and their backpack. They looked back to see the man staring at them, but he did nothing; only closed the gate and latched it.

"Pretty close," Angel puffed.

"Good job," J.J. praised, remembering how their carelessness at Robbers Cave had nearly cost them everything. "This looks like a good haul."

"It should hold us for a while," Angel reckoned as she examined the loot. "Not steak but it'll do."

"All that good barbecue spoiled you," J.J. laughed as the little one began to stuff the food sacks back in the pack.

"Let's walk a ways," J.J. advised as she slipped into the pack. "We'll eat after we get out of town."

With that the Kids retreated to the tree line and continued east along Highway 31. Angel noted that in Kinta Highway 2 came in from the north before cutting west and then south again to Robbers Cave. At midmorning the Kids came to a stop along San Bois Creek and took refuge under the bridge. After unloading the pack they pulled out the food bags and enjoyed a well deserved meal. They then shimmied down to the creek for a cool drink. Stomachs full and muzzles wet, they sprawled out in the shade of the bridge for a rest.

"Should we stay here for a bit or push on?" J.J. asked as she flicked a fly away from her face.

"It's a good place," Angel replied, "but it's not that hot yet and it wouldn't hurt to cover a little more ground."

"Ya," agreed J.J. "I guess we should always do as much as we can when we can."

"Right," seconded the little one. "Sometimes that little bit of extra effort can make a big difference."

J.J. nodded in agreement and together the Kids secured the pack to J.J.'s back. Then Angel inched out from under the bridge and checked the road for cars. Seeing none she motioned to J.J. and together they scampered to the tree line and resumed their march east. In a few hours they reached the hamlet of Leguire at the intersection of Highway 82. Here a road sign pointed them south to Poteau.

"South again," spoke J.J. as she peered up at the now blazing sun. "I guess we need to think about stopping for the afternoon.

"Guess so," squeaked the little one. "It's starting to sizzle
. That looks like a good place," she added as she pointed her nose toward a tree lined pasture."

"Ya," said J.J. "Maybe there's a tank there. Let's go see."

The Kids came to the barbed wire fence just off the roadway and Angel stepped hard on the bottom strand to help J.J. slip through. Then she followed. As they had hoped there was a small but full stock tank near a row of pecan and elm. After removing the pack the Kids waded into the clear water to cool down and drink. As they splashed J.J. noticed a large set of eyes peering at them through the brush. She poked the little one and pointed at the figure.

"Just a cow," Angel muttered.

"No, look," J.J. insisted. "That's not just any cow."

"You're right," the little one gasped. "Look at those horns. They must be six feet across."

"The longhorn!" J.J. exclaimed. "It has to be."

"Let's go talk!" Angel squealed as she made a quick leap to the tank's bank and skipped to the brush. J.J. was right behind.

"Are you a longhorn?" the little one quizzed excitedly as the cow advanced toward them.

"Sure am, little lady," the cow confirmed with a twist of her mighty head.

"We're supposed to talk to a longhorn," J.J. informed him. "Lucky the loon told us to find her. Could you be the one?"

"Could be," the longhorn chuckled. "Old Lucky. What's that crazy bird up to now?" she added with a snort.

"You are the one," Angel stated with a knowing grin.

The longhorn just smiled back but the Kids knew that this was the animal Lucky had meant for them to find.

"Oh, I'm J.J. and this is my little sister Angel," J.J. offered. "What's your name?"

"LeFlore," the longhorn answered.

"That's a funny name," Angel quipped as J.J. clipped her on the ear for being impolite.

The cow just laughed and explained to the girls that she had been born in LeFlore County and the name just stuck.

"Is that where we are?" J.J. asked.

"No, you're in Haskell County now," the longhorn replied. "LeFlore is the next county over; back toward Poteau."

"Lucky told us to go to Poteau," J.J. informed her. "Is it far?"

"Nope, not too far," LeFlore informed them. "Just go south to 270 and cut a hard left to Lake Wister. Poteau is just up the road."

"Oklahoma sure has a lot of lakes," Angel remarked.

"Oh, ya," the cow confirmed. "Oklahoma has more man-made lakes than any other state; more than a million acres worth. I hear that you Texans want to buy some of the water. Bad idea," she huffed with a shake of her mighty horns.

"Wait a minute. How did you know we were from Texas?" J.J. stammered, knowing that the Kids hadn't mentioned it before.

"Oh, word gets around," the longhorn responded with a sly grin that confirmed what the Kids already suspected. The old cow already knew everything about them; their whole story.

"You know I'm from Texas, too," LeFlore continued, "although my ancestors came first from Spain and then through Mexico to Texas."

"How did they get to Oklahoma?" Angel chirped.

"Cattle drives," the longhorn answered. "In the old days Texas cowboys would move thousands of longhorns a year through Oklahoma to the Missouri and Kansas markets. The Shawnee Trails in the east, the Chisholm Trail in the center, and the Great Western Trail were all critical roadways cutting through the state. And of course Oklahoma developed her own livestock industry that's still big business."

"Do they still have cattle drives?" J.J. quizzed.

"Oh, no," LeFlore replied. "Railroads cut out the need for them. Besides, the prissy cows they have today aren't tough enough to make a trip like that," she added with a sniff.

"You're the first longhorn we've ever seen," confessed Angel as she studied LeFlore's blotched hide of white and orangy brown. "Are there more of you?"

"More now than there used to be," LeFlore responded. "Years ago they replaced us with other breeds; animals that could put on weight more easily. But then some people began to realize the critical role we'd played in western heritage and didn't want to see that lost so they started breeding us back. We're doing fine now."

"That's good," Angel stated. "Keeping ties to the past is important."

"Sure is," the longhorn affirmed. "Say, it's good you came when you did. They're going to move me to another pasture anytime now. A few more hours and you might have missed me."

The Kids just looked at each other and smiled, knowing that their decision to push on had paid off.

"What should we do now?" J.J. asked as she looked south down Highway 82, "after we get to Poteau."

"If you want to see some real history go north out of Poteau to Spiro Mounds," the longhorn advised. "And look up Artemus."

"Artemus?" Angel questioned.

"Artemus the Armadillo," LeFlore explained. "He hangs out around there."

"What's Spiro Mounds?" J.J. asked.

"Old Indian city up on the Arkansas," the cow answered. "It's an interesting place."

"Sounds neat," Angel chirped. "We'll check it out."

"Well, got to go now," LeFlore stated as she saw a truck and trailer heading toward them. "Why don't you girls wait out the heat here and then press on at dusk. Today's a scorcher."

"That's what we had in mind," J.J. confirmed. "Thanks for helping us."

"My pleasure," the longhorn answered as she turned and slowly ambled for the truck now but a hundred yards away.

The Kids watched the cow disappear into the trailer and then settled down on the tank's bank for a meal and a rest. After eating, Angel pulled out the map and began marking the places they had seen along the way. Then they both sprawled out on the damp earth for a much needed nap.

Near dusk they arose, loaded their gear, and headed south once more along Highway 82. Several hours later they came to the town of Red Oak at the 270 intersection. Here, as instructed, they turned east toward Lake Wister and Poteau. The night was ideal. Stars twinkled brightly through the canopy of black above while the thinnest sliver of moon etched its stark white outline overhead. Onward they marched, finally coming to the town of Caston and the juncture of U.S. Highway 271. Just to the south lie Lake Wister and yet another state park. Poteau was just ahead.

"Almost there," J.J. observed as she read the road sign. "Just a few more miles."

"Should we stop around here?" Angel asked as she noticed a slight brightening to the east. "It's almost dawn."

"Probably should," nodded J.J. "We don't want to get caught in a big town in broad daylight; not if we can help it."

"That looks like a train," Angel remarked as she looked to the south and saw the single light of a speeding locomotive piercing the predawn darkness. "Maybe we should go find a railway bridge. That would be a good place to hide for a while."

"Good idea," praised J.J. "Let's take a look."

The Kids quickly covered the ground to the tracks and then proceeded east. Sure enough they soon came to a tressel spanning the Poteau River just at the northern tip of Lake Wister.

"Looks like a good place," J.J. suggested as she focused on the bank angling gently down to river's edge.

"Not bad," seconded the little one. "There's plenty of cover."

The Kids skittered down the bank to the water and took a good drink. Then they found a tiny but nice clearing in the trees and, after removing the pack, settled in on a sweet smelling bed of summer soft clover. Slumber soon triumphed as the dawn announced a new day.

After several hours they arose to the sound of a turning engine that seemed but a few feet away. Startled, the Kids both jumped to attention as a camper-topped pickup passed by them.

"There's a road there," J.J. huffed. "I didn't even see it."

"Neither did I," Angel chuckled as they watched the truck pull down close to the river and stop.

As they watched an old man and a young tan dog emerged from the cab and slowly plodded back to the camper. He opened the door and pulled out two fishing rods along with a lawn chair and tackle box. Then they headed down to the river bank where he opened his chair, baited his hooks, and sat down to fish. As he did the dog paraded north along the bank sniffing each bush, leaf, and blade of grass. Then she turned back south and, nose high in the air, dashed straight for the Kids.

"She smells us," J.J. noted as the dog approached.

"She looks nice," Angel observed. "I don't think she wants trouble."

In a blink the retriever cut through the brush to the Kids. She stopped for a minute to look and sniff and then patted the ground before them. J.J. and Angel returned the salute.

"Who are you? the new pup asked.

"I'm J.J. and this is my sister, Angel," J.J. replied. "And you?"

"Daisy," the retriever answered. "This is our fishing spot. We come here everyday in nice weather."

"What river is this?" Angel asked.

"The Poteau," Daisy responded.

"We're looking for the city of Poteau," J.J. offered. "We should be close."

"Just upstream," Daisy informed her.

"Are you from around here?" she continued.

"No, we're from Texas," Angel replied.

"Texas!" the new dog yelped. "I've been there many times. What brings you this way?"

The Kids proceeded the tell Daisy their story as the retriever listened with interest. She mentioned that she had heard of the Sooner Silver and that as far as she knew the thieves hadn't yet been caught. She also told them that there was a big reward out for whoever nabbed them.

"We almost had it," Angel sighed, "but the guy caught us in the van."

"Was it just one man?" Daisy questioned.

"No, two," replied J.J. "The other one's a county commissioner.

Daisy slapped her head in amazement and broke out in her best dog laugh as she rolled over and over in the dirt.

"I can't believe it," she chortled as she eyed the pouch Angel was carrying. "What's that?" she asked as she pointed to it.

Angel pulled the pouch from her neck and opened it, showing Daisy the silver arrowhead and relating to her the Indian woman's warning not to lose it.

"The man in the van almost got it but J.J. really chomped him," Angel hooted as she looked toward her sister with admiration.

"It's a good thing," Daisy stated solemnly. "You lose this you lose everything."

"We know," confirmed the little one. "Why do they call you Daisy?"

"That's where I was born," she told them. "It's a little town to the west of here. Maybe you'll see it someday."

"Hope so," J.J. gushed. "We want to see everything we can."

The Kids told Daisy all the places they had been to so far and asked her what she knew about this area. She told them that the river came out of the Arkansas highlands and was the only river in Oklahoma to flow north before emptying into the mighty Arkansas. She added that Poteau was a French word and that many places in the area carried French names.

"We read about the French explorers," J.J. informed her. "They were all over."

"Sure were," confirmed Daisy.

"We read the Vikings might have been here, too," Angel stated. "Do you know anything about them?"

"Sure," the retriever gushed. "They were here way before the French or any other Europeans. They left their writing just to the east of here at Heavener. It's all on a big stone. There's a neat state park there."

"No kidding," J.J. barked.

"Do you know about a place called Spiro Mounds?" Angel interrupted.

"Yup," affirmed Daisy. "His brother lives close to there; just a mile or so away. That's where he'll go when he's through fishing."

"The longhorn told us to go there next," Angel informed her.

"Ohhh," Daisy cooed. "Maybe I can help you."

"Really?" bubbled the little one. "How?"

"In the camper," the retriever explained. "I can hide you there. It might be a little hot, though."

"Not as hot as walking," J.J. quipped with a grin.

Daisy returned the smile and then told the Kids she'd make sure the windows were open and the little fan was on. When they were about to leave she'd signal them and make sure the door was unlatched. After she and her master were in the cab they could quickly sneak aboard. She also told them to snag some food from the cooler.

"There's sandwich meat in there and dog nuggets on the truck bed next to it," she told them. "Help yourself."

"Thanks, Daisy," the Kids gushed in unison.

"Now I've got to get back," the retriever told them. "Why don't you get some rest. We'll probably be here another few hours. I'll get everything ready and when the time comes I'll let you know. Okay?"

"Sure," J.J. replied. "We'll be right here."

With that Daisy returned to the camper and went inside to open the windows and flip on the fan. Then she returned to her master and sat as he fished from his chair. As she had told them, the old man fished for another few hours and then rose to leave. He folded his chair, grabbed his rods, and returned to the truck. After placing his rods in the camper he turned and moved toward the cab. Daisy took the opportunity to quickly move back and unlatch the door. The Kids awoke just in time to see her signal and then follow her master to the cab. After both were inside the Kids dashed to the camper steps, pushed opened the door, and scurried inside. J.J. snapped the door shut just as the man cranked the motor and pulled away.

The Kids watched out the open window as the truck moved north along Highway 271/59, one of those occasions when a single roadway shared two numbers. Soon they were in Poteau and eagerly eyed the town as they moved through it. Running from side to side, window to window, they soaked in the sites of this picturesque place nearly wrapped in a mountain ring. North of town they came to the point where the roadways split: 59 to the west and 271 to the east. The driver veered east, passing through the town of Spiro before coming to a county road that shot to the north. A left turn soon brought him to Fort Coffee, once a military post and site of an early Oklahoma Indian school.

"I think he's stopping," J.J. whispered as the truck slowed and turned up a driveway." Get ready."

"Okay," squeaked the little one. "Wait a minute!" she squealed. "What about the food?"

"Oh, ya!" J.J. muttered as she slapped herself on the head. "I got so interested in the sites that I completely forgot."

Before she had finished her sentence Angel had opened the cooler, dug through the ice, and picked out a pack of bologna. Then she searched the floorboard and soon found the bag of nuggets that Daisy had told them about.

"No time to load it in the pack," J.J. warned. "We'll just have to carry it. Here, give me the sack. You take the meat."

Angel pushed the sack of nuggets toward her sister who quickly grabbed it tightly in her jaws. She then did the same with the meat. The truck came to a stop behind another car. They nestled low as they heard the truck door open and then shut. They could hear footsteps moving toward the house. In a few seconds there was a scratching sound on the camper door. It was Daisy telling them it was safe to come out. Quickly Angel pushed the door open and both dogs scampered down the steps to the ground.

"It's okay," Daisy giggled. "No need to run.He's gone into the house."

The Kids dropped there food bundles and each breathed a deep sigh of relief.

"Did you have a good ride?" the retriever asked.

"Great," exclaimed the little one. "This is pretty country."

"Sure is," Daisy replied. "Spiro Mounds is just up that road; less than a mile. You'll like it. Where will you go after that?"

"Don't know," Angel shrugged. "We never know what comes next."

"We just go from place to place and follow the signs," J.J. added. "The longhorn told us to look for an armadillo named Artemis. Maybe he can tell us what to do."

"All we know for sure is that sooner of later we'll find the silver," Angel boasted, "and then we'll find a new home."

"I bet you will," Daisy barked with a broad smile. "Come back and look me up when it's all over. I want to hear everything. So will all the other dogs in the neighborhood; cats too."

With that Daisy gave the ground a hard good-bye pat and then turned toward the house. The Kids watched as she curled up on the front porch, gave her a last wave of thanks, and then turned up the Spiro Mounds road where they soon melted into the high sweet grass that flanked it. In but a few minutes they were at the eastern edge of Oklahoma's only archeological center.

THE ARMADILLO

"Look at that neat old hut!" J.J. exclaimed as she eyed a nearby ancient structure of packed brown earth and grey-green thatch.

"Let's explore," Angel chirped as she studied the building style of a time long passed.

After a quick look around to make sure no one was watching they swiftly skipped toward the old dwelling and went inside. Once there Angel helped J.J. with the pack and then they began to sniff and scan every nook and cranny.

"Must have been a house," J.J. reckoned.

"Yup," agreed the little one. "It's kind of cozy," she added with a grin.

"Let's take a look outside," suggested J.J. as she turned back toward the entranceway.

Together the Kids exited the hut and began to survey their surroundings. Not far down a trail was a modern looking building which they determined to be the site's headquarters. In the near distance were several grassy hills rising from the nearly flat surface.

"Those look funny," J.J. observed as she pointed her nose towards them. "What do you think they are?"

"Just hills," Angel shrugged as she focused harder, a little blinded by the fiery red of late afternoon that glimmered off their crests.

"I don't know," J.J. countered. "They just don't seem to fit. There's something different about them."

"Let's go back to the hut for a bite and a rest and then have a better look later," Angel counseled.

"Good idea," J.J. commended as she scanned the horizon once more.

The Kids returned to the hut and after a little bologna and a paw full of nuggets stretched out on the cool earthen floor for a little snooze. Shortly after dusk J.J. awoke to a scratching sound coming from just outside the rear of the hut. She quickly poked Angel to attention and then rose.

"What is it?" the little one yawned as she pawed the sleep from her bright brown eyes.

"Something's out there," J.J. whispered as she motioned for Angel to follow.

Quickly the girls went out the passage and began to inch their way along the round-walled little dwelling. Near the rear they saw a faint little animal outline furiously tearing into a large rotting log.

"What are you doing?" J.J. barked as the little creature looked up.

"Getting dinner," the critter squeaked. "What's it look like."

"You eat logs?" Angel sniffed.

"Course not," the creature huffed as he squinted his beady little eyes. "I eat the bugs in the logs."

"Bugs?" winced J.J. with a wrinkled face.

"It's an acquired taste," the critter chuckled. "Would you like a grub?"

"Uh, no thanks," J.J. declined.

"What are you?" Angel asked.

"An armadillo," the funny looking animal answered.

"Oh!" the Kids exclaimed together. "Would you be Artemis?"

"Sure am," he confirmed with a sly grin.

The Kids looked at each other and smiled as they eyed the goofy little critter with the long, pointed nose and thick scales.

"LeFlore the longhorn told us to come here and look for you," J.J. explained.

"Ah, LeFlorë," Artemis beamed. "I've had many a good meal in her pasture. How's that big old cow doing?".

"Fine," Angel replied.

"Good," the armadillo chuckled. "You know we're kind of related."

"How's that?" asked a confused Angel.

"Well her ancestors came from first Mexico and then Texas and on to Oklahoma and so did mine. But I haven't seen her since I moved here."

"Why did you move?" J.J. questioned.

"Better eating; better life," Artemis answered. "Animals are a lot like people. They migrate; always looking for something better. In some ways the history of the world is the history of migration. That's sure true of Oklahoma. And this place is a great example of what happens when things go bad."

"Do you know a lot about this site?" Angel quizzed. "We were going to explore it tonight."

"Great," Artemis gushed. "I'll give you the tour," he finished as polished off one more juicy bug.

Together the three began the trek around the Spiro Mounds site. As they did Artemis explained its history.

"Over a thousand years ago this was one of the biggest cities on the continent, maybe the world," he informed them. "Thousands and thousands of people lived here."

"Why here?" Angel asked.

"Well you know geography is everything," the armadillo explained. "This was a good place; rich soil and plenty of water, and the Arkansas River is just to the north. That made trade with other peoples easy. In fact this was one of the world's great trading centers. The Indian tribes from the American south came here all the time and there was even a trading network that stretched all the way west to California."

"Did the Vikings come here?" J.J. quizzed.

"Don't know for sure," Artemis mused. "But they did get to Heavener and that's close. I'd say it was a good possibility."

They soon came to one of the little hills that had so caught the Kids' interest. J.J. mentioned to the armadillo that they didn't look natural; that there was something about them that didn't seem to fit.

"You have a good eye," complimented Artemis. "You're exactly right. Those are burial mounds. That's where they used to bury the really important people after they died. The archeologist are always studying them trying to figure out just what happened here."

"What are archeologist?" Angel stammered as she tried to pronounce the word.

"They're folks who dig up the past to try to understand it," the little critter explained. "It's a fascinating occupation as long as you don't mind working hard and getting dirty.

"Why did everyone go away?" J.J. questioned.

"Nobody's sure," the critter confessed , "but drought is the most likely answer. They think that maybe five or six hundred years ago the rains failed. And you know the rules; no water, no life, and certainly no civilization. That's why water is so precious."

Just the thought made the girls thirsty and they suggested to Artemis that they all get a drink. They worked their way to the headquarters building where they found an outdoor faucet and turned it on. Each took a deep drink and then J.J. carefully turned the handle, making sure that the faucet was completely shut off.

"That's right," Artemis praised. "Don't waste a drop."

J.J. just grinned, then suggested to her sister that they scout the area around the headquarters building for any kind of useful material. While Artemis looked on they approached the information board and found a few brochures about Spiro Mounds and a good map of the region around it. Then they returned to their little friend and all three lumbered up the trail to the hut. Once inside they plopped down around the pack.

"Where are you two going next?" the armadillo asked.

"Don't know," Angel shrugged.

"The only thing we know for sure is that we have to find the Sooner Silver," J.J. stated. "Have you heard of it?"

"Oh, sure," confirmed Artemis. "There's a poster on one of those telephone poles out on the road offering a big reward for anyone who brings it in."

"That'll be us," Angel boasted as she poked her nose high in the air.

J.J. laughed and gave the little one a swat while the armadillo just smiled and suggested they head north over the river into Cherokee country.

"What's up there?" J.J. asked.

"Green Country," Artemis replied. "Lots of lakes and rivers and forests and all sorts of historical sites. Work your way up to Three Forks and then over to Tahlequah."

"Three Forks?" chirped Angel.

"It's where the Arkansas, Verdigris and the Grand Rivers all come together. It's an important place in Oklahoma history. And see if you can find old Clem along the way."

"Who's Clem?" quizzed J.J.

"Coyote," the armadillo answered. "He knows more about that country up there than just about anyone."

"Should we go back to the highway," Angel asked, "or is there a quicker way?"

"There's a railroad bridge just a few miles upstream," Artemis replied. "I'd try that. But be careful. There's not much room on it if a train comes." With that the armadillo rose to say good-bye.

"Thanks for all the help," J.J. offered.

"My pleasure," Artemis squeaked. "Best of luck to you."

"And to you," the Kids replied together.

The armadillo scurried out of the hut and quickly disappeared into the brush. The Kids pulled out a little food, had a quick snack, and then planned their next moves.

"Do you think we should go back to the highway or just go to the river and follow the bank until we find the railroad bridge?" J.J. queried.

"The river would be quicker," reasoned the little one. "It's just up ahead."

"Ya," agreed J.J. "And he said it was only a few miles upstream. I guess that's our best bet."

"Let's get a few hours sleep and then get going," Angel suggested. "We'll still have a lot of traveling time before dawn."

"Sounds good," nodded J.J. as she curled up near the pack.

Both Kids quickly drifted off and did not awaken until near midnight. Angel arose first and pawed J.J.'s face to let her know it was time to go. An owl's shrill screech broke night's silence as the little one helped her sister secure the pack. Then they headed north through the dew dampened fields. Though the moon was dim the sky was still star bright. In a short time they came to the south bank of the mighty Arkansas and began to work their way upstream. Just as the armadillo had told them, the grey steel trusses of the bridge soon appeared as an outline just ahead. Climbing up the bank they worked their way to the tracks and the structures southern end. Then they stopped to look and think.

"Boy this is a long bridge," J.J. commented as she scanned the far distance to the northern bank.

"Sure is," the little one gulped as she thought about a train coming while they were crossing. "Narrow, too."

Both Kids looked ahead and behind and then at each other.

"What do you think?" J.J. asked.

"I don't know," confessed Angel. "If we go, we'd better move fast."

"Well," shrugged J.J. "We have to get across the river so let's move!"

With that the Kids broke into a fast trot along the bridge's west side rail. With only an occasional quick glance back they stayed focused on their objective; the dim lights framing the tressel's far end. Suddenly a thin beam split the darkness behind them. Without breaking stride J.J. turned to look, then yelled at her sister.

"Train!" she shouted. "Faster!"

Trot turned to sprint as the Kids dug deeply into the splintery wooden track and pulled hard for the far bank. Behind them the light advanced quickly, now just reaching the bridge's south side.

"Almost there," yelled J.J., "just another fifty yards."

In a flash the Kids covered the distance and passed under the last overhead truss that marked the structure's end. Then they rolled into the gully that ran alongside the track and hunkered down. Gasping for breath they watched as the lights came upon them and a pickup truck passed by.

"Some train," Angel giggled as she poked her sister.

"What was I supposed to think?" J.J. barked. "I saw the light."

Angel could only laugh as they watched the red tail lights disappear into the distance. "I guess it's one of those maintenance vehicles," she mused, "one of those trucks that they rig up to ride the rails."

"Must be," agreed an embarrassed J.J. as she smacked herself on the head. "Boy, you were really moving. I've never seen you go so fast."

"I just kicked into overdrive," the little one boasted.

J.J. chuckled as the Kids sank down in a thick tuft of grass to catch their breath and rest their tired muscles.

"Well, at least we're over the river," Angel chirped. "I guess we're in Cherokee Country now.

"Must be," J.J. nodded as she looked back south to the black expanse of water running just below them. "I can't wait until daylight. I want to get a really good look at the river."

"Me, too," affirmed the little one. "It must be important to Oklahoma history."

"Let's move away from the tracks and find a good hiding place," counseled J.J.

"Ya," squeaked the little one. "We can move down by the river."

They soon came to a little clearing at water's edge that looked like someone's fishing spot. A rutted narrow road barely visible under the dim bridge lights ran straight to it along the structure's other side.

"This looks like a good place," stated J.J. as she sniffed around. "There's been a dog here, too."

"What kind?" joked the little one as she too poked around with her nose.

"Look," barked J.J. "A flashlight. I wonder if it works?"

"Hit the button," Angel commanded as her sister poked the switch and a bright light came on. "Great," gushed Angel as she grabbed the barrel and pointed the light at J.J. "Now we can read at night."

"Like right now," J.J. barked. "Help me with the pack."

The Kids removed the pack, pulled out the book, and turned to a chapter about the Arkansas River. Angel read aloud as J.J. listened with interest.

"It says the river's source is way up in the Colorado mountains," the little one started. "It runs across much of Kansas and enters Oklahoma near Ponca City which is just south of the Kansas state line. Then it cuts southeast and meets up with the Cimarron just to the west of Tulsa at Keystone Lake."

"What's Tulsa?" J.J. wondered.

"Big town," Angel answered as she read on, "the second biggest in the state."

"Same old story," laughed J.J. "Big cities always seem to be on rivers."

"Sure seems like it," grinned the little one.

"Anyway," she continued, "southeast of Tulsa is Muskogee in the Creek Nation. Near Muskogee the Arkansas, Verdigris, and Grand Rivers all meet."

"Three Forks!" exclaimed J.J.

"Yup," confirmed Angel. "just like the armadillo said. "And just upstream is the Canadian. It meets the Arkansas to form Robert S. Kerr Lake. The river finally crosses the Arkansas state line at Ft. Smith and runs all the way to the Mississippi. It's all part of a big navigation system that allows people to ship goods by boat all the way to New Orleans and then out into the Gulf of Mexico."

"Neat," gushed J.J. as she remembered their earlier trip through the Crescent City and their travels in the Gulf. "I guess that means that just about anything from anywhere in the world can get to Oklahoma by water."

"Or from Oklahoma to anyplace else," the little one countered.

"Ya," J.J. agreed as she thought back to the huge barges they had seen before on the Mississippi.

Angel shut the book, turned off the flashlight, and placed both back in the pack. Both Kids suddenly realized how tired they were and curled up together to get a few hours sleep in the peaceful pre-dawn quiet.

COYOTES AND COTTONMOUTHS

First light beamed bright as eyelids broke sleep's seal. First J.J., then Angel, stretched, rolled and rose. After a quick skip to the river for a drink, they pulled out a ration of food from the pack and settled in for a light meal. Breakfast done they fetched the atlas, opened it, and pondered their next move.

"We're about here," J.J. reckoned as she pointed to the railroad bridge marked on the map. "I guess we head upstream and try to find Three Forks."

"Sounds right," concurred Angel. "Should we follow the river or go up to the highway?" she continued, noting that a main roadway ran just to the north.

J.J. stroked her chin for a moment as she studied the map.

"Let's just follow the river to the lake," J.J. suggested. "It's right up ahead."

"That sounds like fun," boomed a loud voice behind them.

In an instant the startled Kids whirled around in the direction of the voice and tensed. But just as quickly they relaxed when they saw a large, odd looking dog with a goofy grin chuckling at them.

"You could at least have announced your presence," Angel squeaked with annoyance.

"I just did," the dog laughed. "You two ought to be more observant. Don't let anything sneak up on you like that. It can be dangerous."

"It's a lesson we keep having to learn," J.J. confessed as she studied the newcomer closely. He had huge paws, a thick coat of tan and grey, and a long pointed nose that seemed to flair a little with every word. Right away she knew he was both different and smart.

"Learn your lessons the first time," the dog advised. "You may not have a second chance."

The Kids knew he was right and offered him a bite to eat but he politely declined.

"No offense, but you're a funny looking dog," J.J. spoke as Angel nodded in agreement.

"What breed are you?"

"Coyote," he beamed with pride. "We're not exactly dogs like you know dogs. We're on a little different branch of the canine tree."

"I knew it," Angel chirped. "You're Clem, aren't you."

"Your obedient servant," the coyote boomed with a bow and a grin.

"Artemis the armadillo told us to look for you," J.J. stated.

"Old Artemis, eh," Clem bellowed. "Is he still digging bugs down at Spiro?"

"That's where we met him," Angel replied.

"Good critter," the coyote spoke earnestly. "Tough as a boot and smart as a whip. Why did he send you this way?"

"We don't know for sure," the little one confessed. "All we know is that the Indian woman told us to do whatever the animals said and go wherever they told us to go. We're trying to find the stolen Sooner Silver."

"Ahhh," the coyote purred. "I heard about that. Everyone's tied in knots trying to figure out who took it."

"We know who has it," J.J. informed him. "We just don't know where they are."

"Almost had it once," Angel added with a sad little grin, "at Robbers Cave."

"That's a neat place," Clem snorted. "Been there many times."

"You cover a lot of ground," J.J. complimented.

"Sure do," the coyote acknowledged. "I mostly stay here in Green Country. But I do like to roam some and get the latest news from the other coyotes around the state."

"You must know a whole lot about this country," Angel stated; "history and stuff."

"Oh, ya," Clem answered. "You can hardly take a step around here without running into something of interest. The river alone is worth a whole day's talk."

"We read earlier that the early explorers used this river all the time," J.J. remarked.

"Of course," Clem acknowledged. "The Arkansas was the natural highway into this part of the country. That's why so many settlements sprung up along it. Commerce is what makes places thrive and the river has always been a vital trade link. It was important a thousand years ago and still is today."

"Artemis said we're in Cherokee country now," Angel informed him. "How far does it go."

"Pretty much from here all the way north to the Kansas border," the coyote replied. "There are some smaller tribal areas in the far northeastern corner of the state and of course the Creeks are a big tribe to the west. Just about twenty or so miles straight north from here is the home of Sequoyah, the Cherokee leader who developed their alphabet. They named this county after him."

"We saw a lot of lakes and parks down south," J.J. commented. "Are there a bunch up here."

"Oh," Clem gasped as he smacked himself on the head. "You need a calculator just to counting them. Sometimes I think all Green Country is is one big lake: Tenkiller, Gibson, Hudson, Spavinaw, Lake of the Cherokees, just to name a few. And of course there are dozens of great parks all around the waters. It all makes a dog wish he could just retire at birth and spend his whole life fishing," the old coyote finished with a chuckle.

The Kids both laughed at the idea but reminded their friend that work always had to come first.

"I know," Clem countered with a grin. "But it never hurts to dream a little."

"Where should we go next?" Angel asked, sensing that it was time to start moving.

"Follow the river to Muskogee and Three Forks, then cut back northeast to Tahlequah.

From Tahlequah work your way north all the way to Miami, then back west to Bartlesville and south into Tulsa. See if you can find Kit the fox. He usually hangs out around Claremore and knows a lot of things."

"Why don't you go with us?" Angel squeaked. "We always like good company," she finished, remembering the cat that had traveled with them so far on their last adventure.

"Better not," Clem cautioned. "Dogs are one thing but a lot of folks don't like to see us coyotes running around. We have to be careful about where we go and when."

"Oh," the Kids murmured together. "That's too bad."

"Just the way it is," the coyote sighed. "Now you two better get moving and cover some ground before it gets too hot. Best of luck to you; and find that treasure."

"We will," Angel assured him as the coyote turned and quickly disappeared into the thick woods along the riverbank.

The Kids loaded the pack on J.J. and then set out along the upper bank of the majestic Arkansas. Near noon they came to Highway 59 and the massive dam that held the waters of Robert S. Kerr Lake, named for the former Oklahoma governor and later United States senator.

"Boy that's some dam," Angel quipped.

"Then it must be one big lake," J.J. added.

"Let's check the map and have a bite," the little one suggested as she pointed to a grove of pecans just off the roadway. "We might have to do a little planning here."

"Ya," agreed J.J. as she watched the heavy highway traffic rush by.

"Do you want to take off the pack?" Angel asked as the two settled into the thin grass beneath the trees.

"Better not," reasoned J.J. "We might have to move in a hurry."

Angel opened it and pulled out the last of the bologna, the sack of nugget's, and a water bottle along with the map. "Food's getting low," she commented as she gave her sister a piece of meat and then scraped a few nugget's from the sack.

"There's just enough for a day or so."

"We'll find some more," J.J. promised. "What does the map say?"

"There's a good sized town just to the north; Sallisaw," Angel answered.

"Sounds French again," J.J. laughed. "The French seem to have their name on everything in this state."

"Seems like it," Angel chirped. "And you're right. This lake is a big one," she added as she traced the blue outline with her paw."

"How do we get across the road?" J.J. mused as she studied the land ahead.

"I don't know," the little one confessed. "We might have to wait until dark."

"I hate to waste that time," J.J. scowled. "It's only twelve and we could cover a lot more ground before the heat sets in."

Angel nodded in agreement and then rose to scout the area. "There might be a way," she stated as she studied what looked to be a set of drainage pipes not far up the road. "Maybe those pipes go all the way under the highway to the other side."

"Might," J.J. agreed. "In fact they should. Why else would they be there? Let's go take a look."

Quickly the Kids scampered through the brush until they came to the concrete funnels poking through the steep roadside incline. Just as they had calculated the broad pipes ran under the highway to just above the shoreline on the other side.

"Great!" shouted J.J. "Let's go!" In less than a minute they were looking out over the lake's vast expanse of bluish green.

"What luck," Angel chirped. "Look at all the boats."

"Too many to count," J.J. marveled as she focused on a grain-laden barge working its way through the nearby lock.

"I guess that's how the ships get past the dam," Angel surmised as she followed her sister's gaze.

"Must be," nodded J.J. "Look at all the boats lined up to pass."

The Kids stood for a minute as they watched the produce of Oklahoma work its way downstream, destined for markets around the world. Then they set off once more along the northern shore and walked for two hours until finally surrendering to the midafternoon sun. They staked out a place under a treed cove along a little creek and plopped down for a rest. Angel pulled out the book and began to read.

"It says that one of those big barges can carry more stuff than a whole fleet of trucks," she recited. "It's the cheapest way to move all sorts of things."

"It sure must help cut down on road traffic," J.J. surmised.

"Air pollution, too," reasoned the little one.

"How far is Muskogee?" J.J. asked.

"Looks to be about two inches," Angel grinned.

"In miles," J.J. laughed as she cuffed the little one on the head.

"About forty miles," she answered as she studied the scale at the bottom of the map.

"Long way to walk," sighed J.J. "I sure wish we could pick up a ride."

"That would be nice," the little one agreed. "Do you see any boats heading upstream?"

"Sure," J.J affirmed. "But they're all way out in the water. We can't get to them. Even if we could there's no place to hide."

"What about that one?" Angel noted as she pointed to a large barge anchored close off shore.

"That's still a long swim and our things would get wet," J.J. countered. "The maps, the book, the flashlight; everything would be ruined."

"I guess you're right," sighed Angel.

"Let's hide the pack and scout around a bit," J.J. suggested. "Maybe we can find some food."

"Good idea," commended the little one. "There might be a picnic area around here. Let's find some high ground and take a look." The Kids spied a low bluff about fifty yards inland and climbed to the top. From there they could see a little wooden dock just around a bend from where they had left the pack. On the shore next to it was a tiny canoe placed upside down.

"Are you thinking what I'm thinking," J.J. quizzed.

"Sure am," snapped Angel. "Let's go down and check it out."

After taking a careful look around, the Kids trotted down to the shore and inspected the little craft.

"No holes in it," J.J. observed as she tipped it over with her nose and nudged it into the water.

"It floats," beamed the little one. "But there's no oar. How would we move it?"

"Dog paddle," J.J. giggled. "We'll paddle with our paws. We won't have to go too far. But we'll have to wait until dark. Otherwise they'll see us."

"How do we know the ships going upstream or when it will leave?" Angel questioned.

"We don't," J.J. admitted. "But that's the way it's pointed and it can't just sit there forever. It's just a chance we'll have to take. Let's just hope it doesn't leave before we're ready. Now let's go back to our spot and try to get a little sleep. We've got over three hours until dark."

"Okay," replied the little one.

The Kids returned to their hideout and curled up together next to the pack. They drifted uneasily, each excited by the possibility of taking a good boat ride. They arose just as the sun's last light glistened over the water. A quick look told them that the big barge was still there, but they could hear its engine turning.

"Sounds like she's getting ready," J.J. said with a frown. "We'd better hurry. Help me with the pack."

Angel did as ordered and quickly the Kids scattered along the shoreline to the little canoe, pushed it a few feet out into the water, and jumped in. Then they put paws down and began to paddle, one on each side of the little craft. In the barge's cabin they could see two men looking straight ahead. Soon the grinding of gears announced the ship's departure and it slowly began to inch forward through the calm waters.

"Hurry," shouted J.J. without looking over at her sister.

Both Kids paddled with all their strength and soon came alongside the vessel as it picked up speed. A long rope dangled from the canvas cargo cover and J.J. grabbed it, quickly looping it once around a thin support beam that straddled the inside bough of their little craft. Then she passed the rope's tail to Angel who did the same on the rear beam before threading what was left through a loop on the big boat's side and knotting it tightly. They were off.

"Good work," praised the little one.

"You, too," J.J. countered with a wide grin.

The little canoe was so close to the ship that the men aboard could not see it without leaving the cabin and edging all the way to the side. The Kids were safe in the gentle, cool spray that misted over them. Only the ship's dim yellowy lights broke the darkness of the Arkansas. Fatigue soon triumphed. The Kids slept soundly.

Well before dawn they awoke to a sea of lights that marked the Port of Muskogee. Their barge slowed to a crawl and then gently pulled to a loading dock.

"We'd better go," advised J.J. "Let's unrope our boat."

Together the two unlashed their craft and pushed away from the barge.

"Where do we go?" Angel asked, confused by darkness and their new surroundings.

"Let's drift back downstream to the highway bridge," counseled J.J., noting that they had just passed under Highway 62. "Then we'll check the map and take it from there."

"Makes sense," affirmed the little one.

Slowly the current pushed them back down the Arkansas and in dawn's first light they came to the bridge where they paddled themselves ashore on the river's eastern bank. They found a secluded grove of shrubs and trees and settled in to plan their next move.

"That was a nice ride," Angel chirped as she helped J.J. with the pack.

"Sure was," her sister agreed. "Too bad we can't find taxis like that all the time."

"Clem said to go to Tahlequah," J.J. reminded Angel. "I wonder if this road might lead there?"

"Might," the little one reckoned. "I'll check the map."

Angel opened the pack and pulled out the map and book. Then in the early morning brightness she opened it and found there location just outside Muskogee.

"Yep," she confirmed. "This is the road to Tahlequah. Looks to be about thirty, thirty-five miles."

"Great," barked J.J. "Let's have a little breakfast."

"A little is all we have," moaned the little one as she pulled the food sack out of the pack.

"Ya," sighed J.J. "We'll have to find something in a hurry."

Angel scraped out the last of the nuggets from the bag and pushed them toward her sister.

"Here, you eat it all. "I'm not hungry," she lied.

"No, no!" protested J.J. "I won't eat unless you do."

"But you need it more," Angel insisted. "You have to carry the pack."

"Doesn't bother me a bit," countered J.J. "Now let's eat," she commanded as she pushed half the food in Angel's direction.

Angel could only smile as she scarfed down her share and then opened the book to the chapter about the region.

"What's it say about Three Forks," J.J. asked excitedly.

"Lots," Angel answered.

"It says that a French trader named Choteau and his Osage Indian friends founded the site way back in the early 1800's. They built a big trading post and people from all over came here to do business."

"I guess that makes sense," J.J. mused as she rubbed her lower jaw. "It's a natural location for such a place."

"Ya," Angel seconded. "How many times have we seen that cities have a geographical reason for being where they are."

"Many times," confirmed J.J. "What else does it say?"

"It says that from Three Forks people could easily go down to the Gulf or over to St. Louis. All they had to do was follow the Arkansas to the Mississippi and then go upstream or down. And of course you could push deeper into the interior by going upstream on any of the three rivers. For example, if you go up the Verdigris you'll come to Tulsa's Port of Catoosa which is one of the nation's busiest inland ports."

"I guess that's why they call it all a Navigation System" J.J. reasoned.

"Yep," affirmed the little one as she closed the book and placed it back in the pack.

"I guess we'd better get moving," J.J. suggested.

"Guess so," the little one nodded in agreement. "Let's get the pack and hit the highway."

The Kids came out from under the bridge and staked out a trail just to the north of Highway 10/ 62.

"Another road with two numbers," Angel chuckled. "We see a lot of those."

"Ya, but they don't last long," reckoned J.J. "That usually means the road forks at the next town."

"Let's keep our eyes open for food," Angel counseled. "I sure could use a hot dog."

"Same here," J.J. chuckled. "A chunk of beef wouldn't be bad either."

Soon the Kids came to Fort Gibson, once a critical military post in old Indian Territory. Here they stopped to survey the town.

"See anything that looks like food," Angel squeaked.

"Hard to say," J.J. remarked. "There's the usual; convenience store and what looks to be a restaurant."

"I guess we'd better check them out," reckoned the little one.

"Sure should," confirmed J.J. "Let's try the store first. It's closer."

The Kids worked their way through the trees to the back of the little store and sat in the brush until they were sure no one was watching. Then J.J. stood watch while Angel poked around the cans. Suddenly a truck's whining engine broke the silence and the little one scampered back to the brush and J.J. As they watched, the delivery vehicle straightened out in the lot and then slowly backed up to a sliding overhead door. The driver got out and rang the bell on the frame. Soon the door opened and he went inside, returning in a moment to begin unloading.

"I'll bet he's carrying some food," Angel whispered.

"You can almost bet on it," J.J. retorted as she kept her eyes glued on the truck.

The driver unloaded a stack of boxes outside near the door, and then wheeled another load inside. He repeated the process once more.

"It looks like he's saving that stack for last," J.J. reasoned. "Let's make a dash when he goes back inside."

"What if it's not food?" Angel questioned.

"Then we'll just have to try something else," J.J. replied. "Look he's going back in. Let's go!"

At full sprint the Kids made for the boxes and quickly inspected them. "It's food," Angel squealed. "Grab one!"

Each of the girls quickly latched on to the plastic wrapping around each box and shot back to their hideout, turning just in time to see the man looking quizzically at the stack and then looking back inside the truck. The Kids laughed as with a shrug he wheeled his lightened load into the store.

"He never knew what hit him," J.J. giggled. "What do we have?"

"Some sort of sausage," Angel informed her. "Vienna."

"Never heard of it," J.J. chuckled. "But I bet it'll be good."

"Sure better than what we have now," Angel chirped.

The Kids tore into the first box and pulled out a little can. While J.J. placed a paw on the can to hold it down, Angel grabbed the tab in her teeth and jerked hard, popping the top and releasing the wonderful aroma of juicy fresh meat.

"Boy does that smell good," J.J. gushed as she licked the juice off the top, then pulled out a sausage and gave it to her sister.

"Taste good, too," Angel squeaked as she bit down, chewed, and swallowed.

"I could do with about a hundred of these," J.J. mumbled through a mouthful of food.

The Kids finished off the can and then loaded one box in the pack. Angel put the rest in a food sack, knotted it tightly, and wrapped its strings around her neck.

"You can't carry it all," she informed J.J. "It's too heavy."

"Thanks," beamed J.J., admiring her little sister's selflessness. "Now let's go."

The Kids continued on up the highway past Fort Gibson and then stopped by a little creek for a rest and water and another bite to eat.

"We still need to find more food," Angel advised. "These little cans won't last long."

"You're right," agreed J.J. as she popped open the second can and divided its contents. "But right now I'm just glad to have this."

After finishing their meal the girls resumed their journey, walking until midday. A road sign told them that Tahlequah was just ten miles ahead.

"Almost there," Angel peeped.

"I guess we should stop now," J.J. reckoned, "and wait for nightfall."

"That looks like a good place," Angel remarked as she pointed to a weathered barn just down a dirt lane from the highway. "Plenty of shade," she added as she eyed the tall trees surrounding the structure.

"Looks good to me," J.J. seconded as she turned down the lane with her sister.

As they reached the barn they carefully checked their surroundings. They saw no one. After taking a quick drink from a cattle trough they entered the barn's open doors and went inside.

"Boy that's a load of hay," Angel commented as she studied the bales that filled it from floor to ceiling.

"That will feed a bunch of cows," J.J. laughed as she sucked in the sweet smell of freshly cut fodder. 'But then again Oklahoma has a lot of cows to feed."

"Do you think we should stay here in the barn or outside?" J.J. added.

"Better stay outside," counseled the little one. "Someone might come for some of this hay while we're sleeping."

"Good thinking," praised J.J. "Let's take a look outside."

The Kids left the barn and began to circle it. Near the back they found a well hidden spot in a brush enclosure flanked by two large oaks.

"This looks good," Angel chirped.

"Not bad at all," agreed J.J. as, with Angel's help, she moved to drop the pack.

Angel then pulled out another can of food from the sack and the book and map from the pack. After another light meal, they settled in for a quick read.

"It says that Tahlequah is the capital of the Cherokee Nation," Angel read.

"Does it say where the word comes from?" J.J. asked as she peered over the little one's shoulder.

"It's a Cherokee word, but no one seems quite sure where it came from," Angel answered, "though there are a lot of suggestions."

J.J. unfolded the map and began to study it while Angel continued reading.

"The old coyote was right," J.J. barked. "Look at all the lakes north of here."

"Ya," Angel affirmed as she shifted her gaze away from the book and to the map. "I guess that's the Grand," she reckoned as she studied the chain of lakes.

"Must be," agreed J.J. as she traced the Grand River line to the north.

"And what's that one?" Angel quizzed as she pointed her paw at another blue line.

"The Illinois," J.J. replied. "It looks like another one that comes out of the Ozarks in Arkansas."

"Oh, the Ozarks make it into Oklahoma," the little one whooped as she studied the map.

"That's great," grinned J.J. "We've always had good luck in those mountains," she added as she thought about how she and Angel had found a family there.

"There's Miami," Angel bleated. "That's one of the places Clem told us to go."

"It's way up there, isn't it," J.J. remarked as she studied the map.

Angel was about to make a comment when the sound of a truck broke the peaceful afternoon silence. Quickly the Kids put down their things and turned to look back through the brush. Just as they did a pickup hauling a long, flat trailer pulled up to the barn. Inside were two men. One got out while the driver backed the trailer just a few feet inside the building. Then he got out and together the two began loading the hay bales onto the trailer.

"Where you taking this load?" one man asked.

"Up to my brother's place in Miami," the other answered. "He needs some feed."

"When are you leaving?"

"First light tomorrow," the driver replied.

As they talked, they stacked the bales high along the sides from front to back. Then they filled in the middle halfway back to a height of about four feet and then stopped.

"I guess that will hold him for a while," the driver spoke as he examined his load.

"Should," his helper laughed.

The driver then got into the truck, pulled out of the barn, and went back to unhitch the trailer.

"Looks like you're ready to go," the helper said. "Need anyone tomorrow?"

"Nah," the driver scoffed. Thanks for offering but we can handle it. Let's go home."

The two got back in the truck and slowly rolled down the dirt road to the highway.

The Kids looked at each other and grinned.

"How could we be so lucky?" J.J. chortled.

"Because I kissed the pouch hoping for something good to happen," Angel answered.

"Well do that more often," J.J. commanded as she patted the little one on the head and smiled broadly.

"Let's not get too giddy," Angel cautioned. "We have to time this just right."

"Ya; you're right," J.J. admitted. "He might check his load just before leaving so we'll have to jump on just at the last second."

"And we just have to hope he's not going to stop for anything else," Angel reckoned.

"With those bales piled so high in the front he won't be able to see us," J.J. reckoned.

"But we'll have to make something to cover us from the rear."

"Or at least move a few bales around to block the view," Angel reasoned.

"That's probably our best bet," J.J. agreed. "We can arrange them a little now and hope he doesn't notice in the morning. If he does we can always jump on and move them again."

"Right," replied Angel. "Let's go."

The Kids jumped onto the trailer and begin to arrange the heavy bales. They pulled one from the middle stack and pushed it to within a few feet of the trailer's rear, then did the same with another.

"Let's turn then on their sides," advised the little one. "That will make them a little higher."

"Good thinking. That's really all we need," observed J.J. "Don't you think?"

"Should do it," Angel answered.

The girls stepped back to admire their handiwork, noting that they had a good hiding place but also had plenty of room between the bales to see the road behind and beside them.

"Not bad," beamed the little one. "Let's just hope he doesn't notice the change."

"I don't think he will," J.J. counseled. "But if he does we'll just go to the next plan. The Kids had learned from experience that it was always good to have a backup strategy in case the first didn't work out. They knew that even the best laid plans could be derailed by unforeseen circumstances. But they also knew that the failure of one plan meant only temporary defeat and nothing more. New plans, faithfully executed, would sooner or later bring success in almost any endeavor.

The Kids left the trailer and retreated to their hideout to rest. Near dusk they ate a hearty meal and then pulled out the book and map for a little last-light study. They noted some of the towns; Stillwell to the east, Wagoner to the west, Choteau not far to the northwest. They were captivated by the number of state parks in the region; Sequoyah, Snowdale, and Natural Falls to name just a few. And of course they were always eager to find sites of great historical importance such as Salina, a trading center on the Grand River founded by A.P. Choteau in 1796.

"There are just so many neat things to see here," Angel sighed as she closed the book.

"I know," moaned J.J. as she folded up the map and passed it to the little one. "But if we can't go everywhere at least we can read about it."

"Ya," Angel agreed. "That's the next best thing."

"The very best thing is reading about something first and then going to see it," J.J. commented. "You appreciate it more that way."

"You're right," replied the little one. "We should make a list of all the interesting places we read about and then do our best to go see them."

J.J. said nothing more, just nodded her head in approval of her sister's idea.

After Angel placed the material back in the pack the Kids cozied in to watch the last of a brilliant orange sunset and then sank into a deep, tired sleep.

The throaty trill of a raccoon's wailing snapped them to attention shortly before dawn. After a quick sip of water at the cattle trough, they shared a can of sausage and then prepared to leave. They watched the road closely for their ride's arrival. Just as the morning's first rays spilled over the horizon a pair of headlights pointed their way.

"Here he comes," chirped Angel. "Get ready."

The Kids moved to a row of low bushes just a few feet behind the trailer's rear and crouched down. Soon the truck reached the barn, turned a half circle, and backed the hitch gently under the trailer's tongue. Then the driver emerged, secured the tongue to the hitch, and returned to the cab.

"He didn't even look, whispered J.J. "Let's get on."

Silently the girls hopped on board and quickly slinked behind the two hay bales they had arranged the night before. Then with a jolt the driver was off, slowly bouncing his crimson truck down the rutted trail and out onto Highway 62. The Kids looked at each other and grinned. They were on the move again and one step closer to Sooner Silver.

The sun quickly brightened into a brilliant orange of early morning fullness as the Kids staked out their spots beside the upturned bales; one on each side between the middle and outer rows. There were no cars trailing as they watched the snake of white-striped black cut a stringy path through summer's green. Flurries of grass whipped loose from the bales clouded about them as they strained to read each sign they saw. Soon they reached the intersection of Highway 82 where markers directed them to the Cherokee Heritage Center and the magnificent Murrell Home near Park Hill. A few moments more and they were in Tahlequah and traffic.

J.J. motioned to Angel and the two retreated behind the rearmost middle bales.

"We'd better lie low until we get out of town," J.J. cautioned. "Somebody following will notice us for sure. And be ready to run for it," she added. "He might stop here."

"I'm ready," Angel peeped.

The truck slowed to a crawl as the traffic thickened. Sadly, the Kids could get but a glimpse of the stately old buildings that dotted the town. Soon they emerged on the city's northeast side and the driver cut north on Highway 10 which ran along the pine-green western bank of the sparkling Illinois River. Sparse traffic again allowed the Kids to emerge from their hideout and savor the sites once more. On they went along the scenic highway until meeting Highway 412, the Cherokee Turnpike, at Kansas, Oklahoma. Here State Highway 10 merged with U.S. Highway 59. Just to the east was West Siloam Springs and the Arkansas state line. But they held to their northerly course, passing through Jay and hitting park and lake country once more near Grove.

"There seems to be a different park every mile," Angel remarked as she noted the signs they had seen starting south of Jay.

"There's a bunch," J.J. gushed. "Eucha, Spavina, Honey Creek. They're everywhere."

"I wonder if these are as nice as the ones we've seen already?" the little one amused.

"Probably," J.J. reckoned as she peered west out over the Grand Lake of the Cherokees. "It's hard not to have a nice park in such pretty country."

"You're right there," agreed Angel. "I wonder what's up ahead?"

"Looks like a good sized town," J.J. surmised as she noticed more and more buildings along the roadside. "I sure wish we could see forward better."

"Let's not complain," the little one scolded. "Looking sideways and backward and riding is better than looking forward and walking."

J.J. just grinned, not about to question the logic that her sister had just laid out. She returned her gaze to the roadside and soon saw a sign that told them they were now in Grove. Once more the Kids hid behind the bales as the driver worked his way through the town before veering a little to the west and crossing over the lake. Soon they reached the juncture with Highway 125 which ran straight north. Miami, named for the Indian tribe, was just ahead.

Fifteen minutes later the driver slowed and then gently turned his rig onto a county rock road that led to a tidy white-frame farmhouse. The Kids knew that this was the end of the line.

"Get ready to go," J.J. advised. "As soon as he slows down enough, we'll make a jump."

"Let's head for those trees," Angel suggested as she pointed to a small stand of oaks just about fifty feet away.

"Good idea," praised J.J. "That looks like a little creek running along the tree line."

Soon the driver geared down to a crawl as he came to a cattle guard that marked the entrance to the house's driveway. Without a word the Kids made the short leap to the ground and quickly skipped away to the trees. The driver saw nothing.

"Made it again," J.J. bragged as she and Angel settled in behind a row of scrub bushes that filled the space between the skinny oaks.

"Nothing to it," the little one grinned. "Now what?"

J.J. checked the sun and reckoned it was about ten. She suggested they have a little to eat and then check the map and book to figure out their next move. Angel helped her with the pack and then pulled out another can of food. After sharing it, they opened the map for a quick study.

"Clem said to go to Bartlesville," Angel reminded her sister. "I wonder where that is?"

"Right there," J.J. barked as she traced a line far to the west.

"Oh, ya," chirped the little one as she followed her sister's paw. "That's looks to be a long way off."

"Ya, but look how far we've already come," J.J. remarked as she traced their journey and realized that they had nearly crossed the entire state from south to north.

"Yep," affirmed Angel. "I guess we just keep plugging away."

"That's all we can do," agreed J.J. "Plug away day in and day out and things usually end up okay."

"I guess we should find a road that runs west and take it," Angel reasoned.

"Or go back a little south and follow this one," J.J. countered as she traced the line down the Will Rogers Turnpike to Vinita and saw that a good road led from there to Bartlesville.

"Just as good," Angel confirmed. "I wonder what the book says about Miami," she added as she reached for the text.

"Open it up and see," J.J. commanded.

Angel flipped through the pages until she came to a section on Miami and the surrounding region.

"Good stuff," the little one read. "It says that Miami is a town of about fourteen thousand and the county seat of Ottawa County. It's just a jump north to Kansas or east to Missouri.

"We've been in Missouri," J.J. interrupted. "Remember?"

"Sure," moaned Angel. "That's where the car hit me," she remembered as she thought back to their earlier adventure.

"That wasn't one of our best days," J.J. sighed.

"Sure wasn't," the little one seconded. "Anyway," Angel read on. "There are several little towns around it like Commerce, Cardin, Picher and Quapaw. A lead mine runs underground all the way from under Picher into Kansas and its caused a lot of problems."

"That's too bad," lamented J.J. "What else?"

"Well, Commerce is the home town of Mickey Mantle, one of baseball's greatest players."

"No kidding," gushed J.J.

"And Miami is where Steve Owens comes from. It says he won something called the Heisman Trophy back in 1969. It means he was the best college football player in the country."

"Wow," exclaimed J.J. "He must have been something."

"And it says that just east of here the Neosho and Spring Rivers join to form the Grand," Angel added.

"Ah; that's one of the rivers at Three Forks," J.J. recalled.

"Sure is," Angel confirmed. "That means they could ship goods by water all the way up here."

"What was the other town you named?" J.J. questioned. "Quapaw."

"Un, huh," nodded Angel. "It's another Indian name. It says the tribe holds a big pow-wow every fourth of July," she finished as she closed the book and placed it back in the pack.

"That would be fun," J.J laughed. "Too bad we've already missed it."

"Sure is," Angel sighed. "It's hard to believe we've been traveling for over six weeks."

"Well we've got a lot more ahead so let's pick up our trash and then get moving," J.J. ordered as she folded the map and placed it back in the pack.

Angel picked up the empty sausage can and placed it in the food bag along with several others. The Kids had a hard and fast rule about anyplace they stopped; always leave it a little nicer than they had found it. That meant that they always picked up their own trash and, whenever possible, that of others' as well. They knew that there would always be a trash can somewhere along the way and there was no excuse for spoiling the beautiful land and waters.

Cleanup complete, J.J. strapped on the backpack and, after getting a little water from the shallow little creek, they set off down the narrow county road. Though not marked on the map, they reckoned its due west course would soon connect them with a major artery. In thirty minutes their deduction proved correct as they hit the Will Rogers Turnpike and cut southwest toward Vinita.

For nearly four hours the Kids trudged along the highway. Finally the broiling summer sun won out as always and they stopped to rest on a wooded ridge just above the thorough fare.

"You know, these major highways are all right," J.J. ventured as she plopped to the ground. "But I like the back roads better."

"Me, too," agreed the little one. "You seem to see so much more when you slow down a little."

"There's water," J. J. noted as she looked down the ridge's side slope to a small, algae pond of murky green.

"Doesn't look so great," Angel frowned as she looked down the ridge.

"Does seem awfully dirty," J.J. concurred, "but let's go check it out. It may be better than it looks."

After dropping the pack the two carefully edged their way down the incline into the thick grass and knee high brush that lined the pond. Reaching water's edge, J.J. brushed back a thick tuft of green to examine the water underneath. Angel looked on.

"What do you think?" J.J. asked as she pulled out her dripping paw.

"Better not," Angel cautioned. "It's not a stream; just run-off. There's nothing to keep it clean."

"You've gotten pretty smart," J.J. kidded. "Where did you learn all that?"

Angel just grinned and turned back toward the ridge when she felt a nail-sharp stab hammer her neck just above the shoulder. She yelped in pain and stumbled backwards as J.J. whirled around to see a black, pitted head cocked tight and high to strike again.

"Moccasin!" screamed J.J. "Get back!"

Angel retreated several steps as J.J. circled out of range and came to her side. The coiled mass of scaly, muddy black held fast in the brush, slightly twitching its viper head to follow the vibrations around it. Its jaws parted slightly, revealing the cotton-white mouth for which it was named.

"Where did he get you?" J.J. asked as she

pushed Angel farther away from the snake.

"My neck," Angel whimpered as she shook with anxiety.

J.J. brushed back the little one's blood speckled fur to see two punctures about an inch apart.

"Bad?" Angel asked.

"Not good," J.J. answered honestly. "How do you feel?"

"It hurts," the little one cried.

"I'll bet it does," J.J. replied. "Your neck's starting to swell. Let's get back to our spot. Can you walk?"

"I think so," Angel mumbled.

The Kids trudged back up the slope to their little hideout. J.J. grabbed a water bottle and poured a little on the wound. Then she removed the pouch, fearing that the swelling might cause her to choke on the leather thong which secured it to Angel's neck.

"Water?" J.J. asked as the little one flopped to the ground.

"No," Angel refused with a shake of her head. "I feel a little sick."

"It's the shock," J.J. explained as she took a small sip and replaced the bottle cap.

"And the poison," the little one moaned. "Am I going to die?"

"Don't even think like that," J.J. scoffed. "You'll be all right but it'll take a few days to get over it. We'll just stay here until you're better."

Angel gave just a slight hint of a smile and rolled to her side while J.J. stroked her still trembling head. As she watched the little one's neck continued to swell, soon reaching the size of a melon.

"I can't breathe," Angel cried as her eyes rolled up to meet those of her big sister.

"The swelling's choking your windpipe," J.J. explained. "Suck hard with each breath to get more air in."

Angel did as ordered and, with much difficulty, was able to pull down enough oxygen to keep her lungs nearly filled. But each gasp was painful and she wheezed with every heave.

J.J. watched and worried as her sister slipped in and out of awareness. She hadn't even noticed that the night had chased the sun behind the western slopes. She pulled the flashlight from the pack, popped the lid on a can of meat, and prepared for that long, lonely wait for a new day's coming.

J.J. slept sparingly. Each hour she would awaken and check the little one's breathing, gently placing a paw on Angel's ribs to detect the motion of respiration. She fought hard to drive from her mind any thought that her sister might not survive.

"Not even a possibility," she scolded herself.

Well before dawn she picked up the sacred pouch and held it close, hoping that its power would make all things well. Then she slowly waved it over Angel and whispered words of encouragement. The little one twitched but made no sound other than the gasps of laboring lungs. Exhausted, J.J. fell down in a heap and slept.

"Time to get up," Angel cooed as she gently pawed her sister's face.

J.J. jerked with a start as she shook to chase away sleep's tight grasp. Eyes fluttering, she focused on Angel's outline in the somber shadows of the day's first light.

"Angel!" J.J. blurted. "What?" she continued but could not finish her sentence.

The little one just smiled at her sister's confusion and then grabbed a water bottle and offered it to J.J. The big dog took a deep drink and then returned it to Angel who did the same.

"I can't believe this," J.J. stammered. "How do you feel?"

"Not bad," the little one replied. "The neck's a little sore but the swelling's gone down and I can breathe a whole lot better."

"How long have you been up?" J.J. questioned.

"Just a bit," Angel replied. "You sure conked out after the animal came," she added with a chuckle.

"What animal?" J.J. quizzed.

"What do you mean?" the little one queried. "You were up with me when it came."

"When what came?" J.J. demanded in puzzled voice.

"The big white animal that came out of the woods," Angel explained, thinking that her sister was still hazy from sleep.

"I don't remember anything like that," J.J. huffed. "The last time I saw you you were fast asleep and barely breathing. You didn't budge all night."

"Oh, come on," Angel scoffed. "It came straight out of those trees and walked right up to us. And you talked to it."

"What did it say?" J.J. demanded.

"You did all the talking," the little one replied. "It just listened, looked hard at us both, pawed the ground three times, and then vanished back into the woods. You've got to remember all that."

"Not a bit," confessed J.J.

"After it left I went back to sleep and woke up feeling fine," Angel explained.

J.J. could say nothing more. She scoured the ground around them for some kind of revealing scent but smelled nothing. Then she looked deep into the woods, turned to Angel and shrugged. Baffled, she plopped back to the ground with a shake of her head. Angel could only grin widely as she sat down beside her sister.

"Hungry?" J.J. asked.

"Starved," the little one replied. "I'll get a can of food."

Angel fished another ration of vienna sausage from the pack, returned to J.J. and opened it by herself. Then she divided the contents between them and each had a good breakfast.

"We're getting low on food again," the little one warned. "We're down to just three cans."

"That sure went fast," J.J. remarked.

"Little cans," Angel replied. "What's next? On to Vinita?"

"Yep," J.J. answered. "Get the book and let's see what it says."

Angel grabbed the book and checked the contents page for a reference to Vinita. She found one and flipped to the page.

"Sounds interesting," the little one said as she read. "It says that Vinita is one of Oklahoma's oldest towns and the first one to have electricity."

"No kidding," J.J. remarked. "I wonder why it's there," she added, remembering that there was always a reason for a town being where it was.

"It started as a railroad junction," Angel read, "and now several major highways meet there, too."

"I sure wish we could get another ride on a train," J.J. grinned as she thought back to the train trip they had taken before.

"It was fun, wasn't it," the little one smiled.

The Kids loved trains because their tracks so often ran through the back country. Here they could get a far better feel for the land and a region's history and get away from sameness of so much urban highway clutter.

"I wonder if the map shows any railroad tracks?" J.J. pondered. "I never even thought to look before."

"Me, either," confessed Angel. "I'll get it and see."

Angel quickly pulled the map from the pack, unfolded it, and spread it out on the ground. The fast spreading brightness of a new day made reading for detail easier and the Kids quickly found their location northeast of Vinita.

"Looks like Vinita is still a major junction," J.J. observed as she traced the track lines that converged on the town.

"Ya," seconded the little one. "The tracks come in from every direction," she remarked as she read names like Burlington Northern and Union Pacific.

"But where do they all go?" J.J. quizzed as she scratched her head and studied.

"Look at that one," Angel ordered. "It goes to Claremore and Bartlesville and Tulsa and a bunch of other places," she continued.

"In kind of a roundabout way," J.J. joked as she focused on the lines.

"That makes it more fun," the little one chirped. "You can see more places."

"That's true," J.J. agreed. "Well let's pack up and work our way to town. We'll see what we can do when we get there."

The girls began there early morning walk along the highway towards Vinita. It was surprisingly cool for July. J.J. suggested that there might be a storm brewing to the northwest as the wind kicked up hard from that direction. Along the way they talked about the snake bite and other perils of nature.

"Stings, bites, bad weather," J.J. huffed. "It can all get you."

"It's kind of sad," Angel sighed. "Nature can be so pretty at times yet so unforgiving at others. Especially if you make a mistake like I did."

"We'll sure be more careful next time," J.J. promised.

"We'll beat the bushes with a stick first," the little one laughed.

"And yell," J.J. added with a loud giggle.

"What can really get you is water," Angel remarked. "Those lakes look so pretty and the people you see boating seem to be having so much fun. Yet it's just one small step to disaster."

"That's right," J.J. agreed. "One bit of carelessness is all it takes."

"And those people who try to drive through flooded creeks," Angel continued. "That's just asking for it."

"Yep; yet they do it over and over again," J.J. lamented.

"Speaking of water, it looks like you were right," Angel observed. "That does look like a storm coming in," she finished as she noticed a bank of rolling black quickly moving toward them.

"Let's find a place to hide," J.J. ordered.

"What about there," Angel suggested as she spied a little shed in a tiny pasture not far off the road.

"Looks good," J.J. replied. "Must be a little feed barn."

The Kids cut through a thin row of trees and reached the shed just as the first drops began to fall. Though in bad repair, the aging structure of raw wood and rusted tin sheets offered good shelter. Soon whipping winds sent tree limbs crashing and the eerie skies split from the weight of the water they held. Rain came in buckets as the Kids held fast in a corner, ignoring the steady trickles working through the leaky roof above but covering the precious pack to keep it dry. For fifteen minutes the welcome wash of water nourished and cleansed the land. Then just as quickly blue sky and bright sun chased the leaden clouds far eastward. It was time to move once more.

"Some storm," J.J. cracked as she shifted her body to adjust the pack.

"Sure was," confirmed the little one. "But it's just what the land needed," she added, noting how dry everything had begun to look.

"Yep," agreed J.J. "It'll have everything greened up in no time."

"Sure will," affirmed Angel. "I'm always amazed at how the plants perk up so quickly after a good rain."

The Kids left the shed and skipped back over the field to the highway where they fell into the woods that lined it. Near noon they reached the outskirts of Vinita just where the Burlington Northern tracks crossed to their side of the turnpike.

"Do you really want to look for a train?" Angel questioned as she studied the shining rails heading into town.

"We've done it before," J.J. affirmed. "I know it's not easy getting on but we can cover a lot of ground if we do."

"If we do find a train, how will we know it's going to the right place?" the little one quizzed. "We're supposed to be looking for Bartlesville and Claremore and then Tulsa," she reminded her sister.

"We won't know for sure," confessed J.J. "But those are probably big towns and the trains are bound to go there. If not we can always get off and try something else. You know the rules. If one thing doesn't work just try something else and keep trying until you get it right."

"Guess so," affirmed the little one with a smile. "What now?"

"Let's get a little closer to town and then find a good hiding place," J.J. reasoned. "After dark we'll follow the tracks. There's bound to be a rail yard up ahead."

"Makes sense," peeped Angel as she started to walk.

The Kids trekked down the rail line until they came within sight of a residential area. Here they stopped and scouted the area for a good hiding place. Just off the tracks was a pasture, lush green from the recent rain. A small stock tank brimming with fresh, clean water lay just on the western barbed wire boundary. Framing the tank's northern flank was a thin line of hickory saplings surrounding a giant oak.

"That looks good," Angel commented as she pointed towards the tank.

"Not bad at all," confirmed J.J.

Angel stepped hard on the fence's bottom string as J.J. slid easily, pack and all, through the wire and into the grass. Angel followed. Together they marched toward the tank under the eyes of two white faced momma cows and a pair of wobbly legged calves. They soon reached the oak's shelter where J.J. dropped the pack. After a much needed slurp of rain freshened water they sprawled out on the cool dirt to rest.

"I wonder what those cows are thinking?" Angel laughed as she watched them watch her.

"Probably thinking about the Sooner Silver," J.J. retorted with a wide grin.

"More likely they're just looking out for their calves," the little one replied, her smile withering as she thought about their difficult mission ahead. "Do you think we'll find it; the silver I mean. We haven't seen a sign of it since Robbers Cave."

"Sure we will," J.J. comforted. "We just have to stick with it. It'll all work out."

"Yup. You're right," the little one replied as she nodded her head in agreement. "We go so far and work so hard. It just kind of gets discouraging sometimes; not knowing if all the work's going to pay off."

"That's just life," J.J. counseled, "working your way through discouragement and disappointment."

"Same for just about everyone," Angel reasoned.

"Just about," confirmed J.J. as she set her chin down in the dirt and closed her eyes.

Angel watched as her sister quickly fell asleep, then rolled to her side and did the same. Near dusk both arose to the rattling clack of steel wheel on track.

"Maybe that's our train," J.J. joked as she pawed away the sleep from her still droopy eyes.

"Could be," Angel grinned as she stretched hard to chase away slumber's stiffness. "That's a long one," she added as she stared at the endless string of cars snaking through twilight's shadows toward town.

The girls ambled slowly to the tank and drank deeply, then splashed themselves with cool water until fully alert. Returning to the pack they pulled out the last two cans of sausage and had a good meal.

"Last of the food," sighed Angel as she checked the water bottles. "We'd better fill these, too. They're almost empty."

J.J. took one bottle and Angel the other, then together they moved back to the tank and filled them to overflowing before capping them tightly. Skipping back to their spot, Angel placed first her bottle and then her sister's back in the pack and then pulled out the map. In the fading light they began to study, hoping to find some clue as to the path they should take.

"We'll have to go through town," J.J. huffed. "There's no getting around it. All the tracks lead straight in."

"That may not be so bad," the little one reasoned. "We need to find some food."

"We'll have to wait awhile longer," J.J. counseled. "There's too much traffic this early."

"Let's give it one more hour and then just creep along the tracks," suggested Angel. "We'll take our time and see how things shape up."

"Sounds good," affirmed J.J. as she settled down once more to wait for full darkness.

Angel sank down beside her and for an hour they just watched and talked.

"Too bad they don't have many passenger trains anymore," J.J. quipped. "That would be a neat way to see the country."

"Sure would," agreed the little one, remembering how she had heard the family talk about the time when trains carried people everywhere. "I wonder why they quit running?"

"I'm sure it had something to do with money," J.J. surmised.

"And convenience," Angel added.

"That, too," agreed J.J. "I guess our modern road system makes driving just about as quick and cheap."

"And of course planes are so much faster," Angel noted as she spied the lights of a jet high overhead in the star sparkled darkness.

"But freight trains must still make sense," J.J. reasoned. "Think about how much stuff that long train can carry."

"Kind of like those river barges," Angel remarked as she thought back to the cargo ships they had seen on the Arkansas.

"Both are probably cheaper than trucks," J.J. reckoned.

"Especially for big, bulky loads like grain, coal and oil," Angel concluded as

J.J. stood.

"It's good and dark," she observed. "Ready to get moving?"

"Might as well," the little one replied.

With that Angel rose and, after securing the pack on J.J., cut back through the pasture and fence and then on to the tracks. They could see the lights of Vinita shining brightly just ahead. Traffic was still heavy so they moved cautiously as they approached the first street crossing.

"Too many cars," J.J. huffed. "We'll have to wait."

"Let's hide behind that," the little one suggested as she pointed to a silver painted utility building just off the tracks.

"Good place," affirmed J.J. "We'll just sit awhile until things calm down."

The girls quickly scampered behind the structure and waited for over an hour. Finally, as the traffic lightened, they emerged to once more try a crossing. Now in the open, they had to move quickly. J.J. checked each way and saw one car coming far down the road.

"Now!" she ordered. "Step on it!"

Silently the Kids dashed through the crossing, coming to rest in a clump of bushes far on its western side. Here they once more took time to survey the surroundings.

"Looks like more of the same up ahead," J.J. pouted, "only worse."

"More streets, more buildings, more people, more cars," Angel moaned. "Maybe we should get off these railroad tracks and find a back way through town."

"You're right," commended J.J. "Let's find someplace where the traffic's not so thick. It's either that or sit here for another hour or two."

"Let's go that way," Angel suggested as she pointed to a quiet looking spot just to the south. "Maybe we can find some food."

"Now's a good time to look for it," J.J. agreed. "But let's keep our bearings and remember where the tracks are. Staying on them is our best bet to find a rail yard and catch a ride."

"It won't be hard," the little one chirped. "There are supposed to be a lot of lines meeting in this town. We're bound to run into one even if we go in a different direction."

"Good thinking," praised J.J., having forgotten for a moment that Vinita was a major railroad junction.

The Kids crossed over the tracks and slowly, cautiously began working their way through town. They soon came to another thoroughfare which a road sign labeled as Historic Route 66.

"I wonder what 66 is?" J.J. pondered as she read the sign again.

"Must be pretty special to have a sign like that," the little one ventured. "Let's remember the number. Maybe the book will say something about it."

"Might," agreed J.J. who was now holding her nose high in the air. "I smell food."

"Me, too," confirmed Angel who had also turned her nose into the warm southern breeze blowing the aroma their way. "Good food."

"That way," J.J. ordered as she struck a path in a line of shadows just off the highway.

Soon the girls came to the source of the wonderful smells; Clanton's Cafe. The Kids hunkered down in the distance and watched.

"Looks like their closing down for the night," Angel remarked as she watched what appeared to be the last car leave the lot.

"I think so," concurred J.J., noting that the lights inside were dimming. "Let's get closer."

Without a word the girls inched their way toward the restaurant until they came to its side. After taking a quick but thorough look around J.J. motioned Angel to follow and the two scattered around to the back where they took refuge behind a large dumpster. The door to the kitchen was open and through the screen they could see but one man busily engaged in his after hours duties.

"Stay here," J.J. ordered. "I'm going to look inside."

"No," countered Angel. "I'll go. The pack slows you down too much."

J.J. gave a nod of approval and Angel slinked along the back wall to the screen door. Inside the man was busy moving back and forth through the swinging door that led from the kitchen to the dining area. On a stainless steel bench just inside the door Angel could see and smell several trays of meat; beef and ham and sausage. Mouth watering she returned to her sister who was watching intently.

"Tons of food!" she whispered excitedly. "It's just inside the door!"

"Pull out a food sack!" J.J. commanded. "We'll fill it up."

Angel quickly reached into the pack and grabbed a sack in her teeth. Then together the Kids pranced toward the door with the little one in the lead. Angel poked her head around just in time to see the man return to the dining room once more.

"Now!" she squealed softly after dropping the food sack.

Instantly Angel latched onto the the screen's wooden frame and tugged hard to open it. J.J. shot past her and quickly placed her front paws on the steel bench just next to the food. Angel grabbed the sack, fell in behind, and opened the bag wide while J.J. began sweeping the food off the first tray. Then she moved to another and did the same. In a short time the bag was nearly full. Too heavy for one, both girls clamped down hard on each side of the bag and then flew back out the door and to their hiding place behind the dumpster. They looked back just in time to see the man standing over the counter and scratching his head in confusion. Then the main door shut and the Kids heard the lock.

"Pretty close," J.J. wheezed as she leaned hard against the container. "But boy does that smell good."

"Mmmm," agreed Angel as she poked her nose into the sack and sucked in the smoky scent. "There's enough food here for a week."

"Let's have a bite and then divide the loot," J.J. suggested. "We can put some in the pack and you can carry the rest in the sack."

"Sounds good," chirped the little one as she pawed out several portions of ham scraps and pushed them to her sister.

"Haven't had any ham for quite a while," J.J. gushed as she wolfed down several mouthfuls.

Angel said nothing, just continued to eat, stopping every so often to lick the sweet, fatty juice from her lips. When full they emptied part of the sack's contents into the other bag and placed it in the pack. Angel then looped the other sack's drawstring around her neck and they were off once more. When back on the street they noticed the restaurant sign: 'Since 1927' it read.

"That's eighty years," remarked the little one.

"Hard to believe," added J.J. "They must do something right to stay in business that long."

"Must," seconded Angel. "They've certainly earned my stamp of approval," she added with a wide grin.

As the night darkened the traffic lightened until but few cars posed a threat. The Kids struck out on 66, staying as much in the shadows as possible. They knew that a major intersection must be ahead as Route 66 was also labeled Highways 69 and 60. A sign told them that Highway 2 was just ahead.

"Next time we get a chance I want to study the book and see if it says anything about Route 66," Angel spoke as they walked. "I have a feeling it's really historic."

"Me, too," confirmed J.J. as she noticed a railroad crossing just ahead.

"Union Pacific," Angel noted as they reached the tracks. "I'll bet this crosses the line we were on."

"Ya," agreed J.J. "Let's follow it north. They have to meet up close by."

The girls struck north and soon came to the switching yard where several trains stood, each pointing in a different direction. The Kids drew closer and examined the box cars, looking for an open door. They soon found one about midway down an incredibly long string of some eighty carriers.

"What do you think?" J.J. asked as Angel looked at the nearly six foot jump into the car.

"Way too high," the little one moaned. "Besides, we don't even know where this train's going or even if it's leaving anytime soon."

"Well it can't sit here forever. It has to go somewhere," J.J. countered. "We'll just have to take our chances."

"I guess you're right," Angel conceded. "But how do we get on, especially with all our stuff."

"Let's think," J.J. advised. "There's almost always a way to do something if you use your imagination."

"Yup," the little one confirmed as she brightened. "Let's look around. Maybe we can find something to help us; a tool maybe."

"Good idea," praised J.J. "There must be something around here."

The Kids began to poke their way up and down the tracks and soon found several empty wooden crates in a shallow gully. J.J. quickly nuzzled one to determine its weight. Surprised by its lightness, she turned to Angel.

"These could help," she remarked. "I think I could make the jump from the two stacked one on the other if I didn't have to carry the pack. What about you?"

"I don't know," the little one sighed. "It would be awfully close. But we can't leave the pack no matter what. And we can't leave the crates next to the door. Someone would see them for sure. I can't think of anything that would look more suspicious."

"You're right," J.J. affirmed with a sad shake of her head. "But if I could get on you could push the crates away and then I could pull you up; our gear, too."

"With what?" Angel asked. "We'd need a rope of something."

"Let's look around some more," J.J. commanded, determined to find what they needed now that she had a plan.

The Kids continued their search until they came to a pile of scrap metal sitting just off the tracks next to an open top boxcar. They poked around until through the faint yard lights Angel spotted what looked to be a long, rusty steel cable sitting loose about halfway up the pile.

"What about that?" she squeaked as she pointed to it.

"That might do," J.J. reckoned. "I'll see if I can pull it down."

She carefully worked her way up the pile and grabbed the cable with her teeth, then pulled hard as she backed her way down. The cable came loose and the Kids found that on its end was a thick metal hook.

"Perfect," she gushed as she spit the rust from her mouth. "But it's not too tasty," she added with a laugh.

Angel grinned and helped her sister fold the cable into two-foot lengths. Then they carried it back to the car, placed it on the ground, and returned to get the crates. With great effort they carried first one, and then the other, back to the siding just below the open door. They then placed one on top of the other. Angel helped her sister remove the pack and then J.J. began to measure her jump.

"What about the cable?" Angel quizzed.

"You get on the crates and push it to me once I'm in," J.J. ordered. "It's stout enough to go up several feet before it starts to bend."

"Okay," peeped Angel.

J.J. took a position about twenty feet from the stacked crates and then began to run. In a few steps she was at a full sprint. When but three feet from the rough wooden boxes she leapt to the top, bounced, and in full extension easily cleared the distance and height to the boxcar's floor. Turning to Angel she smiled and motioned for her to send up the cable. The little one quickly grabbed an end, climbed onto the crates, and poked it through the air to her sister. Grabbing it tightly, J.J. pulled backwards deep into the car until the hooked end was dangling near the ground. Angel opened the pack and pushed her food bag inside before zipping it shut. She then grabbed a strap and secured it to the hook. At her signal J.J. pulled on the cable until she cleared the doorway and had the pack in the car. As she worked to unhook it, Angel began to push away the crates, slowly nosing them away from the tracks. Far up ahead they heard the rumble of an engine as the train came to life.

"Hurry!" screamed J.J. "The train's leaving!"

In a panic Angel scampered back to the boxcar as J.J. dangled the hook end of the cable back to the ground. As the train began to slowly lurch forward she placed a back paw in the curve of the hook and wound her front around the cable, clutching it tightly to her chest. J.J. clamped her powerful jaws on the steel and began to back into the car, pulling with all her might as Angel slowly inched her way upward. As the train picked up speed J.J. began to falter, fighting both Angel's weight and the train's momentum. She spent the last of her strength in one gigantic tug that brought her sister to the lip of the door frame. Angel bit hard on the cable to secure herself, then released her grip and placed her front paws firmly on the floor. J.J. held fast as the little one raised her free rear paw to the deck and pushed hard, propelling most of her bulk into the car. J.J. released the cable and scrambled to Angel, grabbing her by the shoulder and dragging her the last few inches to safety. Both dogs collapsed in exhaustion, their hanging tongues nearly touching the splintery wooden floor.

After several minutes Angel rose and shook, then went to the pack and retrieved a water bottle. She returned to her sister, popped the cap, and offered her a drink. J.J. stumbled to her feet, tipped the bottle, and drank deeply. Angel followed. "Boy, that was close," she wheezed as she popped the cap back on the bottle.

"I didn't think I could hold on another second," J.J. confessed.

"Ya, you could have," the little one teased. "You wouldn't have dropped me."

J.J. just grinned and gave her sister a quick pat on the head. Then they turned to the door just as the morning sun was breaking out to the east. They watched in silence as the beauty of a new day spilled brightly over the land.

"We must be heading south," J.J. reckoned, noting the position of the sun.

"Must be," agreed the little one. "I kind of got turned around in the yard. I wasn't sure which way we were going. I wonder what's ahead?"

"Pull the book and the map," J.J. suggested. "Let's see what we can find out."

"Good idea," chirped Angel as she turned toward the pack.

Angel returned and handed the map to J.J. while she pawed through the book. Soon a page on Route 66 caught her attention. "Here it is," she squeaked excitedly. "Route 66."

"What's it say?" J.J. demanded.

"It's maybe the most famous highway in the country. It runs from Chicago to Los Angeles and cuts all the way across Oklahoma. Listen to some of the towns: Vinita, Claremore, Tulsa, Bristow, Oklahoma City, Weatherford and on into Texas. There's probably more interesting things to see on Route 66 than any other road in the nation. It was also the route so many Oklahomans took to California back during the 'Dust Bowl' days."

"What was that?" J.J. questioned.

"It was back in the 1930's," the little one explained. "There was a terrible drought and the soil just blew away in the strong winds. It ruined the farms and ranches and people had to go someplace else to make a living."

"Those must have been tough times," J.J. remarked.

"Sure were," Angel confirmed. "It was called the Great Depression. Even those people who did manage to keep their places had a tough time because prices for their produce collapsed to nothing."

"I guess farming's always a risky business," J.J. reflected, "even in the best of times."

"Yep; ranching, too," added Angel. "You have to admire those people who stick with it. It would be tough to work so hard everyday and run the risk of getting nothing for it."

"Sure would," agreed J.J. with a nod. "But I guess when you think about it, there's not much of a guarantee for anyone. That's why you always have to work hard, plan ahead and try to be ready for anything that might go wrong."

"Yup, you know what they say," the little one trumpeted. "Expect the best but prepare for the worst."

Angel closed the book while J.J. opened the map and tried to determine where they were. She found Vinita and then began tracing the rail lines with her paw.

"Hey, I think that's 66 right there," she nearly shouted as she pointed out the door to the highway running just parallel to the rail line. "Look at the map."

Angel edged over and took a hard look while J.J. pointed to the thin, black crossed line that represented the railroad. Then she shook her head in agreement as J.J. folded the map and placed it back in the pack. Moving to the open door the Kids watched the new day's sun climb higher above the horizon, sprinkling the land in a brilliant yellow. From their perch they could see deer by the dozens out for an early morning browse. His night's work done, a fat, tired looking raccoon dragged his way down a rutted trail of dirt. Above a hawk of splotched brown and white gracefully floated the currents. The calendar flipped to August.

THE KIT FOX

"This is great," the little one peeped as they watched the countryside roll by. "I'm glad we're not going too fast," she added, thankful that the train was barely crawling.

"Me, too," J.J. agreed. "Now we can see more."

"I wonder what's ahead?" Angel quizzed.

"Some little towns," J.J. answered, remembering what she had seen on the map. "And then we get to Claremore."

"Isn't Claremore where the fox hangs out?" Angel questioned.

"That's what the coyote said," J.J. confirmed.

"What about Bartlesville?" the little one queried. "I thought we were supposed to go there first."

"I don't know," J.J. shrugged. "We just have to take things as they come. We'll get to Bartlesville sooner or later."

"Guess so," affirmed Angel as she continued her watch.

Through the morning the train slowly followed Route 66 to the south. The Kids passed by Chelsea and then Foyil. They were disappointed at not being able to see Totem Poll Park just to the east of the little town on Highway 28A. The book told them that it was a really interesting place and contained several examples of beautifully crafted icons. By mid morning they were pulling into Claremore. Here the train came to a stop just north of town.

"We'd better load the pack," Angel suggested. "We might have to get off here. You never know what might happen."

"Yup," agreed J.J. as she moved to the backpack and positioned herself to sling it up on her shoulders. "Help me with this thing."

Angel lifted and pulled as her sister passed her front legs through the straps and secured the pack on her back. Then the Kids went to the door and peeked out. Far up ahead a few men were working near the engine but they showed no interest in the rest of the train. The Kids waited and watched. Two hours passed.

"Looks like we're stuck here for a while," J.J. huffed. "I wish we could get out and see the town."

"Me, too," moaned the little one. "It looks like a neat place. But we can't do it in broad daylight. Besides, we'd lose our ride. It was tough enough getting on this train the first time."

"That's the truth, J.J. laughed as she continued her watch.

"Might as well have some lunch," the little one suggested as she opened her food sack and passed a huge, juicy piece of brisket to her sister and then took one for herself.

"Beef today," Angel chirped.

"What about that sausage?" J.J. chuckled.

"That will be next," Angel. "Ham, then beef, then sausage. Not bad."

"Not bad at all," laughed J.J. as she swallowed the last bite.

"Hey, what's for dinner?" A shrill voice came from the ground beneath them. The Kids looked at each other in surprise and then poked their heads out the door. Just below was a small tan-colored creature with huge ears, a black-tipped tail, and a sack around his neck. They immediately suspected that this was the critter they were supposed to find although it was unlike any fox they had seen before.

"Brisket," J.J. replied as she looked down. "Want some?"

"Sure," the newcomer answered. "Just a second."

The Kids watched in amazement as the little creature backed up, broke into a sprint, and then effortlessly leaped through the boxcar door. After shaking himself off he turned to the girls and grinned broadly.

"Wow, that was some jump," complimented Angel. "I wish I could do that."

"Nothing too it," bragged the little fox. "Kit's the name," he added with a smile.

"I'm J.J. and this is my little sister Angel," J.J. announced.

"I heard about you two," the fox offered. "Heard you're looking for that stolen silver."

"That's right," peeped Angel. "Do you know anything about it?"

"Not much," the fox confessed. "But I do know that nobody's found it yet. The cops are stumped."

"Wait a minute," J.J. stammered. "How do you know all this about us?"

"Oh," the kit answered coyly, "the grapevine is an amazing thing."

"The grapevine?" Angel questioned with a cock of her head. "What's that?"

"Just an expression," the fox replied. "Always remember that people love to talk; and so do the animals. Nothing's a secret for too long."

"You must have talked to Clem the coyote," J.J. surmised.

"Baby, I'm a fox. We don't get close enough to coyotes to talk. To one of them I just look like another meal," the kit explained.

"No offense," Angel quipped, "but you're kind of a funny looking fox. The ones I've seen were red and a lot bigger."

"Different breed," the kit answered. "I'm a kit fox, part of the swift fox family. We're about the smallest breed of fox there is. And we're fast; so fast not even the wind can catch us."

"Are there a lot of you around here?" J.J. questioned.

"Not a whole lot. Most of us live farther west. But we've learned to adapt to different kinds of country and I've come to like it here," the fox responded.

"Oh, I almost forgot," Angel chirped. "How does some beef sound?" she finished as she handed the fox a chunk.

"Oh, boy," the fox chortled as he took the morsel from Angel and bit into it. "Oh, have some of this," he added as he dropped the sack from his neck.

"What's that?" J.J. quizzed as she smelled the sack and then opened it.

"Cheese," the fox answered between chews. "Local stuff from Swan's Dairy. Really good."

"Great," squeaked Angel as she tore off a chunk. "What do you know about Claremore?"

"Interesting place," the kit replied as he swallowed his lunch. "It was named for an Osage Indian chief named Glahmo who later became known as Chief Clermont; that's French for 'Clear Mountain'. The Osage set up a settlement on the Verdigris called Clermont Mounds. and did a pretty big business with the French traders who came up the river."

"We've been down to Three Forks," J.J. informed their visitor. "That's where the Verdigris empties into the Arkansas."

"Hey, you're pretty smart," the fox praised.

"We like to study," Angel explained. "The only problem is there's just so much to know."

"That can complicate things," the kit sympathized. "But you just have to take in as much as you can whenever you can. You'll be amazed how much you can learn over time."

"Anyway," the kit continued, "after the Louisiana Purchase the government assigned this region to the Cherokees. They came and built a prosperous settlement. Later, when the railroad came, the town was moved to meet it."

"It's funny that they'd move a whole town just to be on a rail line," J.J. laughed.

"It wasn't the first time and it wouldn't be the last," the kit informed them. "In those days a railroad could mean life or death to a town. Many a thriving settlement perished when the railroad took another route. They're all over the country."

"How come they call it Claremore instead of Clermont?" Angel asked.

"Oh," chuckled the fox. "Somebody at the Post Office wrote the name down wrong and nobody ever bothered to fix it."

The Kids giggled at this quirk of history and then asked about Will Rogers. They had seen the name on several signs and wondered who he was.

"He was probably the most famous man from around here and one of the best known men in the world," the kit informed them. "He was part Cherokee and born just up the road around Oologah, but he called Claremore home. You're in Rogers County right now."

"What did he do?" the Kids asked together.

"He was a bit of everything," the fox recounted. "a first rate cowboy, an outstanding writer, and a big movie and stage star. But above all he was a humorist. He had some great lines and told funny stories. He worked his last years during the Depression of the 1930's and that was a time when the whole country needed cheering up. He probably helped a bunch of folks get through those tough times. The Will Rogers Museum and Memorial is just up the road."

"Wish we could see that," Angel squeaked.

"What are some of the other towns around here?" J.J. asked.

"Well, Pryor about twenty miles east on Highway 20 and Collinsville about the same distance in the other direction. Pryor got its name from Nathaniel Pryor. He was on the Lewis and Clark Expedition.

"No kidding!" piped the Kids together.

"Collinsville sits on a lot of coal and one of the country's biggest gas fields," Kit continued. "Then of course you have Tulsa and all the suburbs around it."

"What about Bartlesville?" Angel questioned. "We're supposed to go there."

"North and west," the fox answered. "There's a good chance this train will go by it. It usually runs north out of Claremore, through Nowata and almost to Kansas before looping back south.

"Oh, I forgot to ask," the kit continued. "Where did you get that good food?"

"Up in Vinita," Angel replied. "We found a good restaurant."

"Good price, too," joked J.J.

"Too bad you didn't get to go through Choteau. There's an Amish community there and those people sure know how to cook," the fox drooled as he licked his chops.

"Amish?" J.J. quizzed as she cocked her head.

"Religious community," Kit explained. "They live life like it used to be lived. No electricity; no modern conveniences; no nothing. Pretty interesting folks."

"Sounds like it," Angel responded. "Where do you think we should go next?

"Hmmm," the fox mumbled as he stroked his chin. "That's a good question. I know you need to get to Bartlesville and you sure need to see Tulsa. After that I'd just stay on the train and go where it goes. Be sure to see the Tallgrass Prairie. After that work your way back to the Red. Somewhere along the way you need to find the mule. He'll set you straight."

"The mule?" mused Angel. "I've never seen one of those. What does he look like?"

"Dumb," the fox chortled. "But don't let his looks fool you. He's smart as a whip. He just doesn't like to show it too often. Oh, don't worry. You'll know him when you see him."

In the distance came the rumbling sound of the train's engine sparking to life. A lurch of the car told them that it was time to move again.

"Well, I'd better get going," the fox announced. "Best of luck to you two."

"And to you," J.J. countered. "Thanks for you help."

"Do you want some food?" the little one offered.

"No, I'm fine," the kit responded. "You'd better keep all you have. You might need it. As a matter of fact you might need the cheese, too. You keep it," the fox finished as he pushed his little sack toward the girls.

"Double thanks," the Kids purred in unison.

In a shaved second the fox flew to the ground and disappeared into the weeds. As the Kids, watched the train began its slow roll forward. At a switching station it veered to the north and began to pick up speed. Soon the entire train had cleared Claremore and was now out into open, rugged country. The Kids settled in to study the land as it passed.

Near Oologah the tracks bumped Highway 169 and turned to parallel the road on its eastern flank. Far in the distance they could just make out the massive expanse of blue that was Lake Oologah.

"Looks like a big one," Angel remarked as she looked to the east. "I wonder what feeds it?"

"Maybe the Verdigris," J.J. reasoned.

"Good guess," affirmed the little one. "It takes a pretty big river to cover such a large area."

"Ya," remarked J.J., "and probably some smaller feeder streams, too."

The Kids had observed that most lakes were usually constructed in low areas where several bodies of water met. They had seen that in Texas and now here in Oklahoma. They were always amazed at the size of the dams that held the water back. And at times they pondered the wisdom of altering stream flows and flooding so much good land.

The train chugged on. Just to the west of the northern tip of Lake Oologah they passed Nowata, a town famous for substantial oil production that dated back over one hundred years. The Kids marveled at the number of rocking pumps that even now kept the black gold flowing. The thick forests and high hills of the east had now given way to a rolling prairie of sweet grass that nourished the livestock and made Nowata an important ranching center. Here the train switched to the western side of 169 and rolled ahead to South Coffeyville, just a few miles south of the Kansas border where it sidetracked and in a crawl turned back to the southwest.

"We're running low on water," Angel advised as she drained the last from one of the bottles and then opened the other for her sister.

"You're right," J.J. agreed. "We really need more than two bottles."

"It'll be dark soon," the little one noted as she watched the sun's bottom touch the western horizon. "Maybe the train will stop."

"Might," reckoned J.J. "If it does, there's no problem getting off. We can jump. But getting back on is something else."

"We need a better system," Angel counseled.

"We need a ladder," J.J. countered with a laugh.

"Then let's make one," Angel replied.

"With what? J.J. questioned.

"I don't know," Angel confessed. "But let's think on it."

"You're right," answered J.J. "There's bound to be something we can do."

Soon the train passed through Dewey, a town named for a famous United States Navy admiral. Then, in the day's last light, it pulled into Bartlesville and slowly geared down to a full stop. The Kids peeked around the edge of the open door. In the twilight shadows way up ahead they could see several men busily working on a cargo platform. But there was no one near their car.

"It'll be safe to get off," J.J. stated. "There's no one close enough to see us. Do you want to do a little exploring?"

"Why not," shrugged the little one. "But let's wait a few hours. It's still early. The traffic looks pretty heavy."

"Yup," concurred J.J. "Let's have some dinner and catch a little nap. Then we'll see what things look like."

"Sausage night," Angel beamed as she pulled two chunks of pork and a little cheese from the pack and passed it to her sister.

"Good stuff," J.J. gushed as she tore off a portion of pig and chased it with a small dab of cheese.

After eating the Kids quickly curled up and fell fast asleep. Several hours later they stirred to alertness and surveyed the town.

"Looks better now," Angel observed. "Not so many cars."

"Ya," confirmed J.J. "Do you think we should leave the pack or take it with us?

"Leaving it's a gamble," Angel reasoned. "The train could leave at anytime."

"Ya, I guess you're right," agreed J.J. "Let's drop it down and hide it behind those cans," she added as she pointed to a row of black painted barrels lined against a wall on a nearby platform.

"Good idea," praised the little one as she grabbed a strap and began to pull the pack to the doorway.

The Kids dropped the pack to the ground and then followed. First J.J., then Angel made the jump down.

"Easy jump," smiled J.J. "I wish jumping up was as easy as jumping down," she added as she latched on to the other strap.

"Don't you though," coughed Angel as they tugged the backpack to the barrels and placed it behind them.

After concealing the pack and pulling the empty water bottle the Kids set out to study the town. They moved slowly through alleys and side streets, carefully scouting their surroundings as they went.

"Pretty good-sized city," J.J. commented.

"Seems to be," affirmed the little one. "I wonder what they do here?"

"Oil, mostly," came a shrill voice from a tree behind them.

The Kids turned to see what was talking. Sitting on a tree limb about ten feet off the ground was a huge feline of splotched orange and gold. From his perch he looked down on the girls through bright blue eyes that seemed to flash with his every movement. His long, fluffy tail curled around his front paws, its tip rising up then dipping down each few seconds.

"Who are you? J.J. demanded as she looked up to the limb.

"Phillip," the cat purred.

"And you?" the feline countered.

"I'm J.J. and this is my sister Angel," came the reply.

"You must be those crazy dogs from Texas that everybody's talking about," the cat chuckled.

J.J. and Angel just looked at each other quizzically. It seemed the deeper they got into their journey the more critters knew about it.

"Oklahoma animals seem to have quite an intelligence network," J.J. deadpanned.

"Have to keep on top of things," Phillip informed them. "Oh, I was just kidding. I really don't think you're crazy. In fact I admire what you're doing."

Swiftly the feline clawed his way down the tree trunk to the ground. He perched himself in front of Angel, then pawed the pouch around the little one's neck. Twinkling eyes twitched sharply as he gave a slight nod of approval.

"Seen a lot so far, have you?" the cat asked in a tone that was more statement than question.

"Whole lot," confirmed Angel brightly.

"By the time we're through we'll know more about Oklahoma than most Oklahomans," J.J. assured him.

"I'll bet you will," agreed the cat.

"Tell us about Bartlesville," Angel squeaked. "It looks like a neat town."

"It is," Phillip offered. "Lot of history here. The town's well over a hundred years old. It took its name from an early settler named Bartle. But way before the town, the area was home to the Osage, Cherokee, and Delaware tribes. Today Bartlesville is best know for Phillips Petroleum. It's one of the world's biggest oil companies and old Frank Phillips started it right here. That's why they named me Phillip."

"There sure are a lot of big buildings here," J.J. remarked as she looked around.

"Quite a few," the cat confirmed. "And some of them are real gems. Bartlesville has some of the most interesting architecture around. Some of the biggest names in the business came here to build; guys like Frank Lloyd Wright."

"What else is here?" Angel asked with interest.

"Well there are museums, a theater, and a ballet. And of course just southwest of town is Woolaroc. That's the old Frank Phillips ranch out in the Osage Hills. It has a first rate museum and an incredible nature preserve. You can drive around it and see all sorts of things; loads of animals, old cabins, beautiful scenery; the works."

"Sounds great," J.J. said with a grin. "Maybe we'll get to see it."

"I hope you do," the old cat offered. "What are you supposed to do now?"

"Go to Tulsa," Angel told him. "We want to stay on the train if we can. Do you have any idea when it might leave?" she continued, worried that it might leave without them.

"That train usually stays here until just before dawn," Phillip informed her, "and then it cuts through Tulsa before looping way out to the west."

"That's just what we need," J.J. barked. "Do you know where we might find something to build a ladder with?"

"A ladder?" the cat coughed, a little surprised by the request.

"Yup," replied J.J. "Getting in that open car is tough. It's so high up."

"We thought we'd build something to help us get in and out," Angel added. "A ladder seemed logical."

"I guess it does at that," agreed the feline. "Why can't you dogs learn to jump better," he added with a laugh.

The Kids could only grin and explain to the cat that they made up for their physical limitations with heavy doses of imagination, planning, and will power. To the dogs, handicaps were only spurs to greater effort.

"That's admirable," the cat commended. "Attitude is everything, isn't it."

"Sure is," seconded the little one. "I was thinking about the ladder," she continued. "All we need is some wood and some twine or wire."

"Oh, and we need another couple of water bottles," J.J. added.

"That's easy enough," Phillip informed them. "They're everywhere. The people next door keep a whole case of bottled water on the back porch. They won't mind if we snitch a few."

"They won't mind or they won't know?" Angel cracked.

"Same thing," the old cat grinned. "How can they mind if they don't know?"

The Kids just laughed at the feline's convenient logic and then thought once more about the ladder. Phillip put a paw to his jaw and then brightened.

"I just thought of something," he exclaimed. "Survey stakes."

"Survey stakes? J.J. questioned.

"Just what you need," the cat spat. "They're wooden stakes survey crews use to mark property lines. The short ones are only about a foot long. They're thin and light but strong enough to hold your weight. Slap some of those crosswise about a foot apart on a 2X4 and you've got a ladder. All you need then is something to tie 'em down with."

"That'd be the twine or wire," Angel reasoned.

"Yup," agreed the feline. "There's a construction site close to the rail line. I'll bet we could find everything you need right there. We'll swing by my place and grab a few bottles of water and then head for the tracks."

"Sounds great," the Kids gushed together.

The three cut through a residential area and soon came to Phillip's house, a solid white two-story of prairie style construction with a large, inviting front porch. The Kids studied the old dwelling from top to bottom before ascending the steps to the porch.

"This is some old house," Angel commented.

"It's nearly as old as the town," Phillip informed them. "They don't build them like this anymore," he added with a twinge of sadness in his voice.

"It gives you a taste of an older Oklahoma," J.J. remarked as she nosed the smooth, painted, tongue and groove slats that comprised the landing. "Too bad so many places have lost that sense of history."

"A real shame," the cat concurred.

"I like this porch," the little one chirped. "I can imagine a time when the horses and wagons came down the street."

"Great place to sit when the weather's nice," the old cat noted. "My buddies hang out here all the time."

The three sat for a minute, soaking up the still night air. Then Phillip suggested they go next door and get a little water. Quietly they slipped through the next door gate and sided up to the back porch. An opened carton of bottled water sat at its edge just as the cat had told them. Each girl quietly grabbed one and then they returned to Phillip's porch. J.J. filled the empty bottle they carried at an outdoor spigot and then the three marched off toward the railroad tracks, each carrying one bottle. Just after midnight they came to the construction site the cat had noted. It was but a hundred yards from their rail car. Phillip quickly located a bundle of stakes while J.J. looked for a bigger piece of lumber. She soon found an eight foot grey-splotched board that had been used as a concrete form.

"Perfect," she said to Angel who had tailed close behind her. "Help me carry this."

Each dog grabbed an end and moved back to Phillip who was sitting near the stakes. They then laid down the lumber and sat.

"Just what you need," the old cat purred. "Now if we can find something to lash it all together with, you'll be in business."

"There's bound to be something around here," Angel chirped.

"Well, let's take a look," Phillip recommended.

The three began poking around the site until they came to a big wooden box with a heavy lid. J.J. wedged her nose under the lid's corner and pushed hard, flipping it up and open. The cat jumped to the box's edge and looked inside.

"Tools," he informed them. "Hammers, shovels, a handsaw, a few screwdrivers and a utility knife," he stated as he jumped in the box and began to root around. "Ah, what's this?"

In a second the feline sprung up from the bottom of the box and landed cleanly on a sidelip before gliding to the ground. In his mouth was a spool of thick yellow, nylon twine often used in construction projects. Then he returned to the box and retrieved the knife he had seen.

"This might come in handy," he counseled as he dropped it to the ground.

"Good thinking," commended J.J. as she picked it up.

Angel grabbed the twine and the three returned to the wood they had gathered. They first laid out the 2x4, placing it on top of two bricks to raise it off the ground. Then they picked up a stake and placed it across the board's front near the top. Phillip latched onto the twine's end while Angel grabbed the spool and moved backwards until they had unraveled about four feet of string. J.J. popped the blade on the utility knife and with a quick slash cut the first section of twine. Loop by loop the Kids threaded the twine, tugging hard with each wrap to keep the slat tightly secured to the big board. Then with a mighty yank they knotted together the last few inches of string.

"Good job," praised the cat as he looked on. "Do that about seven or eight more times and you've got a good ladder."

Stake by stake the Kids repeated the process. Finally, after more than an hours hard work, they stepped back to examine their creation.

"Should hold us," J.J. remarked as she pawed hard at a slat. "Seems nice and snug."

"And it's not too heavy," the little one observed as she raised the bottom end of the 2x4.

"Not bad at all. Let's get it to the car," J.J. ordered.

Each dog grabbed an end, raised the ladder, and began a slow walk to the tracks. The cat led the way. When at the boxcar door they tipped the ladder skyward until its top end came to rest about two feet above the threshold.

"Couldn't be better," the feline stated as he quickly skipped up the rungs to the boxcar entrance and hopped inside. "You try it," he suggested.

J.J. placed a back paw on the lower rung and pushed upward while balancing with her front paws on the slats above. In no time she had scaled the ladder and joined Phillip in the car. Angel followed.

"Oh, boy," she shouted. "This is great."

"Beats tugging that old cable," J.J. laughed as she pointed it out to the cat.

"We can still use it to haul up stuff," the little one remarked. "Let's not forget the pack."

"Oh, ya," J.J. barked as she slapped herself on the head. "For a minute there I did forget. Let's go get it and the water."

Phillip made his jump to the ground and the Kids followed. They retrieved the water bottles and then moved to the pack, opening it and placing the water inside. After zipping it shut they lugged it to the ground beneath the boxcar door. J.J. scaled the ladder, grabbed the cable, and lowered it to Angel who attached the hook to a strap. With a few sharp tugs J.J. soon had the pack in the car.

"Good system you have," commended the cat. "What's in the bag besides the water?"

"Food, maps, a book, and a flashlight," answered the little one.

"You come prepared, don't you," the feline chuckled.

"We've learned," J.J. explained. "You never know what you might need."

"How about dinner?" Angel piped. "I'm starving. Got ham, sausage, and beef."

"No, you go ahead," the old cat declined. "I ate earlier."

Angel pulled out two thick slabs of ham from the bag and nudged one to J.J. The two ate heartily and then the little one reached into the bag once more for a few bites of sausage.

"I don't know what's better," J.J. quipped. "Ham or sausage. I never can make up my mind," she finished with a grin.

"Don't forget the beef," giggled Angel.

"What about fish?" argued the cat as he looked on. "That's the best eating around."

"Like that, too," Angel squeaked. "We just haven't found any in a long time."

"Now you've done it," J.J. joked. "making us think of what we don't have instead of what we do have."

"That's the nature of man," Phillip remarked with a long chuckle. "Advertisers figured that out a long time ago."

"Ya but animals should know better," Angel countered as she slapped a paw on the wooden floor.

J.J. rose solemnly to her feet and proclaimed: "I hereby swear to always be happy with what's in the bag." Then she paused and added: "except when there's no fish in it."

Phillip and Angel rolled on the floor in tearful laughter. J.J. could only stand and grin. "I guess we always want more," Angel mused. "But you know, it's not just having more but doing more as well."

"Sure," agree the cat. "You reach one goal and then shoot for the next. You do the work and the stuff will usually come."

"Yup," concurred J.J. "The real satisfaction usually comes more from the doing than the having."

"Then it's all agreed," concluded the feline with a wave and a thump of his padded paw. "Doing beats having; doing makes for having."

"We should be writing this down," squeaked a smiling little one.

"Ya," seconded J.J. as she put on a solemn face. "We'll put it in a book and then send our findings to The Oklahoma Society of Learned Animals."

"Socrates would be proud," Phillip finished with a low bow.

"So would Will Rogers," Angel added as she flashed a broad grin.

"Him, too," J.J. agreed.

"Him would be proud," Phillip scolded. "What kind of English is that?"

J.J. sunk her head in embarrassment as Angel broke into laughter once more.

"He would be proud," the big dog corrected.

"She's better at geography and history than English," the little one chided as she moved to open a bottle of water. "She'll learn. I'm teaching her."

"We may joke about it but it's little things like that that can make a big difference in someone's life," the cat offered in a more serious tone. "How well you speak can say a lot about you. It might make a difference in getting that good job."

"Writing, too," added the little one as she took a sip and then passed the bottle first to Phillip and then to her sister.

"That, too," confirmed the cat.

"Well, Kids, I guess it's time I got moving," the feline purred. "I sure have enjoyed this."

"So have we," the girls said together. "You say the train will leave just before dawn?"

"Yup," the cat affirmed. "Goes straight into Tulsa." With that the cat jumped to the ground and quickly disappeared into the shadows. The Kids hauled their ladder into the car and then curled up together to get some sleep.

"I sure will miss that cat," Angel confided with a loud yawn.

"So will I," J.J. agreed as her eyelids snapped shut.

THE MULE

The jarring jolt of slamming steel shook the Kids to attention. Ever so slowly their car began to move in a clacking creep through the quiet stillness of early dawn. The air hung heavy with a night's dew that coated all with the thinnest sheet of dampness. First J.J., then Angel, rose, shook and looked. To the east a pencil line of light fought hard to climb earth's curve. To the west blackness still held firm. Though still August, just the slightest scent of crispness hinted of a coming new season. Sleep's thirst sent Angel to the bag for a bottle.

"Look at this," she shouted as she turned back to her sister.

"What is it?" J.J. spoke as she moved toward Angel and the bag.

Next to their pack was a small sack, its top carefully twisted and tied shut. Angel worked at the tie until it came loose and then peered inside.

"Get the flashlight," she commanded. "I can't see."

J.J. obeyed, pointing the light into the sack while Angel pawed through its contents. A still smaller sack filled with fried fish and dog nuggets sat at the top. Beneath were two small, paper-bound books along with yet another bottle of water and a compass.

"We can sure use this stuff," J.J. remarked as she studied the compass that the little one had handed to her.

"Shine the light," Angel commanded. "Look," she squealed as she read the books' titles: "History of Tulsa and Geographic Regions of Oklahoma."

"Great," barked J.J. "They look like school workbooks."

As the little one opened the first book a piece of paper fell to the floor. It was a note to them from Phillip.

"What's it say?" demanded J.J. as she flashed it with her light.

"Best of luck to the Blacktail Kids from the Bartlesville Regiment of the Oklahoma Cat Command," Angel laughed.

"Signed: Phillip Feline-Presiding Officer."

"I didn't know he was so important," J.J. chuckled.

"Oh, wait, it says something else," Angel read. "P.S. Look to Highway 60."

"That's all?" J.J. quizzed.

"That's it," Angel answered.

"When did he come back?" A befuddled J.J. asked with a hard shake of her head.

"I don't know," the little one shrugged. "I sure didn't hear anything."

"We must have been conked out," J.J. stammered, a little concerned that anything, even a quiet cat, could sneak up on them like that.

"Must have been," Angel affirmed. "How did he get up here without the ladder and carrying that sack?"

"Cats can really jump," J.J. replied, without admitting that she was just as puzzled as her little sister.

"Boy does that fish smell good," Angel gushed as she took a deep sniff.

"Let's have some," J.J. suggested as she pulled two thick pieces from the sack.

"I guess now we don't have to worry about wanting something we don't have," Angel laughed.

"I sure would like some ice cream," J.J. countered with a huge grin and a low howl.

"Never satisfied," the little one chided as she shook her head and munched down on her breakfast.

For nearly an hour the train barely budged, advancing but a few feet at a time as cars were hitched or unhitched and the train assembled. Finally, as dawn's light chased away the night's last shadows, the engine groaned loudly and the cars began a slow but steady forward movement. The girls watched out the western door as the train picked up speed. Ahead they could see a highway crossing which a sign identified as Highway 60, a main thoroughfare through the city and one of northern Oklahoma's major roadways. As they approached the crossing a white van waited behind the barricades for the train to pass.

"There he is!" shouted J.J. "Rob Silver!" she nearly screamed as she read the sign on the van's side.

Angel crowded in and focused hard on the cab, trying to get a glimpse of the man they had traveled so far and worked so hard to find; the man who could punch their ticket to a new home.

"Just missed him," J.J. barked as she pounded a paw three times into the splintery wooden floor. "I wish we could stop the train."

"Then what?" the little one asked as the train sped on. "Knowing where he is, where the silver is, isn't the same as getting it. We found that out at Robbers Cave."

"I guess you're right," a more sober J.J. agreed with a deep sigh.

The Kids watched as the train's last car cleared the crossing. Behind them the van sped over the tracks and headed east on Highway 60 and deeper into Bartlesville.

"I guess the old cat knew from the beginning," Angel surmised with a tight grin.

"Must have," agreed J.J. "I wonder why he didn't just tell us. Maybe we could have gotten it last night."

"Maybe," concurred the little one. "But it could be that the Indian woman meant for us to do other work first; ever think of that? Maybe finding the silver's not the real prize, just a reward for a job well done."

"I suppose you're right," huffed J.J. as she plopped to the floor. "I suppose it's kind of like last night when we were talking about the importance of doing and not just having."

"There you go," complimented the little one. "I'm going to see what's in the books Phillip left us."

"Good idea," praised J.J., brightening at the idea of seeing new material.

Angel first picked up the book on the geographic regions of Oklahoma and returned to seat herself next to her sister. She pawed through the first few pages and came to a map that had been taken from the Oklahoma Almanac.

"Here we go," Angel beamed as she placed the book on the floor for both girls to study.

"Hmmm," J.J. pondered. "Ten distinct regions."

"Yup," Angel confirmed. "We've already been through some of these: the Red River Valley, the Ouachitas, and the Ozark Plateau."

"Looks like we're in the Prairie Plains now and getting close to the Sandstone Hills," J.J. observed. "They should be just a little to the west."

"Could already be there," reasoned the little one.

"That's possible," confirmed J.J. "We're right on the line. What's that word down there?" she continued as she read from the map.

"Almanac," Angel read aloud. "I wonder what that is?"

"Don't know," confessed J.J. "Maybe it's kind of a book that tells all the facts about a place; like a country or a state."

"Ya," peeped Angel. "Maybe it has more stuff like this map."

"That'd be a great tool," gushed J.J. "I wish we had one."

"Sure would," agreed the little one. "You could learn a lot from it. Let's keep our eyes open for one."

"Right," affirmed the big dog.

The Kids soon saw a sign that told them Tulsa was just ahead. At Ramona the tracks crossed to the east side of Highway 75, the main route from Bartlesville to Tulsa.

"I'm going to get the book on Tulsa," J.J. barked as she skipped toward the boxcar's corner. Returning to Angel she set the book down and opened it.

"What's it say?" the little one demanded eagerly.

"Whole bunch," J.J. informed her. "We're back on the Arkansas. The river cuts right through town."

"That figures," popped the little one.

"This area has been home to many tribes," J.J. continued. "First the Osage and later the Creek and Cherokee. The name Tulsa probably came from a Creek word from way back. In fact, in 1836 the Creeks had their first big council under a huge oak tree called the Council Oak. It says it's still there in Council Oak Park just south of downtown."

"I sure would like to see that," Angel mused.

"So would I," J.J. seconded as she read on. "It seems that a lot of what is now Tulsa was Creek tribal land and a few families like the Perrymans owned most of it."

"What did they do?" Angel quizzed.

"Ranching and commerce," J.J. answered. "And It says the first post office in the area was located on the Perryman ranch."

"It'd be neat to have your own post office," Angel giggled. "I wonder if they got free mail?"

"Don't know," J.J. chuckled. "Anyway, the railroad came in the 1880's and in 1898 Tulsa incorporated and officially became a city."

"What about oil?" Angel questioned, noting all the pump jacks they had seen in the area.

"That's what I was just coming to," J.J. offered. "That's what made Tulsa boom; oil and lots of it. The first strikes came in the early 1900's and people flocked here to get a piece of the action. Some of the biggest oil companies in the world had their start in Tulsa. The city's history reads like a Who's Who in the oil business: names like Getty, Sinclair, Cosden, and Skelly to name just a few."

"Kind of like Frank Phillips in Bartlesville," the little one observed.

"Same thing," J.J. confirmed. "And just like in Bartlesville the oil men put their money into some fantastic buildings. Look at some of these," J.J. ordered as she and Angel flipped through the pages and looked at some of the architectural gems.

"Especially the insides," Angel gushed as she studied the pictures and noted the fine detail of the interior finish outs. "They don't make them like that anymore."

"Sure don't," agreed J.J. "There ought to be a law against ever tearing them down."

"Sure should," affirmed the little one as she turned the pages.

"And there are some great museums here, too," J.J. continued. "It says that the Gilcrease Museum has one of the world's finest collections of western art."

"Was he another oil man?" Angel asked.

"Uh, huh," J.J. replied as she turned the page to read some more.

"Tulsa rose from a sleepy little village to now be the second biggest city in the state at nearly 400,000 people. And it's ringed by big suburbs: Owasso, Broken Arrow, Jenks, Bixby, Sand Springs, Sapulpa, Glenpool, and more. It looks to me like it's all pretty much just one big town. You don't really know where one ends and another starts."

"We've seen a lot of that," Angel squeaked. "You really can't judge the true size of a region by just its one big city."

"No you can't," J.J. agreed as she flipped to yet another page.

"I wonder what else they do here?" Angel quizzed.

"Lots of things," J.J. read. "The book says that oil is still important, both production and refining. But the history of oil is a history of booms and busts. Things are great during booms but they never last. And the busts can be really bad."

"I guess that's true for all types of businesses," Angel reasoned.

"Yup," affirmed J.J., "and everyone figured that out. People not just around Tulsa but all over Oklahoma learned a long time ago not to tie their fortunes to just one or two industries. Now they use the term 'diversify'. That means having a broad mix of businesses."

"Makes sense," peeped the little one. "That way if one of two go bad there are still plenty of others to keep things going."

"Exactly," woofed J.J. "That's why around Tulsa they do a lot of work in things like aircraft and aerospace, chemicals, and telecommunications, just to name a few."

"But oil money never hurts," giggled Angel.

"Nope," laughed J.J. "But you have to look at it as just a bonus, not your base pay."

"Well put," congratulated the little one.

J.J. closed the book and took it back to the bag, then rejoined her sister just as they came to Collinsville. A short while later the train chugged into Owasso and the Tulsa skyline soared to the south.

"There it is," beamed Angel as she strained to focus on the city ahead.

"Pretty, isn't it," J.J. remarked as she looked at the surrounding green hills.

"Sure is," replied Angel. "I wonder if the train will stop?"

"Who knows," shrugged J.J. "We'll just have to wait and see. But we'd better load up just in case."

"Better," agreed Angel as she moved to the pack.

The Kids had a drink of water and then stuffed all their things into the bag. Angel zipped it shut and then helped her sister strap it on. They could see a rail yard not far up ahead. The train slowed to a crawl. The Kids watched anxiously, hiding their bodies behind the boxcar wall and peeping out the door. Though still just midmorning, the sun sizzled; that teasing hint of autumn burned away.

"Not just yet," summer seemed to say.

Once in the yard the train slowed still more. Ahead the Kids could see the engine veering slightly to the southwest. The cars followed in a long curl of black and grey and rusty brown. For an hour the creep continued.

"It's not stopping," J.J. reckoned as she watched the engine exit the yard.

"I wonder where it's going?" Angel puzzled.

"We'll just have to see," J.J. replied with a shake and a shrug.

As they watched the train slipped along Tulsa's west side, first crossing Highway 75 and then 64 before cutting straight south to Interstate 44, the Turner Turnpike. It was the main route to Oklahoma City. At 44 the train cut sharply west, following the tracks that ran parallel to the main highway. J.J. read a road sign aloud: "Oklahoma City-105 miles."

"They're not too far apart," Angel quipped, noting the distance between the state capital and Tulsa. "And look. We're back on Route 66."

"Oh, ya," J.J. responded. "I didn't notice that. I guess the old road runs right next to the turnpike."

"Must," peeped the little one. "I'm glad it's still here. Nothing like an old road to get a sense of history."

"Agreed," her sister barked. "Just close your eyes and imagine times past. You can bet Route 66 has a real story to tell."

"It would make a good book,'" Angel added with a laugh.

"Maybe we can write it," J.J. chuckled as she tapped her sister on the head.

The Kids resumed their watch as the train cleared Sapulpa and headed for

Bristow. Near noon they had a good meal of fried fish and the last of the meat from Vinita.

"How much food is left," J.J. asked.

"Two or three days worth," Angel answered. "I'm really glad the old cat brought us this bundle."

"Ya, it helps," confirmed J.J. "But we'd better keep our eyes open for more."

"It does disappear in a hurry," the little one noted.

After lunch the Kids took a short nap, then rose once more to see the sights as the train moved slowly westward along Route 66. As they went they noted the towns: Stroud and Chandler and Warwick, where they crossed the Deep Fork of the Canadian River. By late afternoon they could just make out a city skyline punching through the flat horizon.

"Must be Oklahoma City," J.J. barked.

"Has to be," chirped Angel. "Boy does it look big," she added as she poked her head a little farther out the door to get a better look.

"Have you noticed how different the land looks?" J.J. asked, as she thought about the high hills and thick forests farther east.

"Ya," answered the little one. "It's really changed. I'll bet you we've crossed into another region."

"What was the last one?" J.J. questioned.

"Sandstone Hills," replied Angel. "Judging by the color of the dirt I'd say we're in the Red Bed Plains now."

"Sure looks like it," J.J. coughed as a gust of wind blew a haze of dust into the car.

"I guess we better load up again," suggested Angel. "We don't know what the train's going to do."

"Good idea," praised J.J. "We have to be ready for anything."

The Kids went through their now well rehearsed procedure of preparing for a get away if they ran into trouble. Except for one bottle of water, they were packed and loaded. Standing in their car they watched the train enter the city. The late afternoon sun was at its worst. The ground was a skillet; their car an oven.

"What happened to that little cool snap this morning?" Angel moaned.

"Just a teaser," J.J. sighed. "Happens every year about this time."

"Looks like another rail yard," Angel remarked as she studied the tracks merging just ahead.

"Must be," seconded J.J. as the train slowed to a crawl. "We'll just sit tight and see what happens."

"We'd better hide," the little one suggested. "There are bound to be people working here."

Quickly the Kids pulled back from the door. J.J. stayed in front, occasionally peeping around the sidewall. In a few minutes the train came to a dead stop. From her perch J.J. could see a few men far up ahead.

"No one back here," she whispered. "I'm going to take a better look."

Poking her head farther out she studied the layout. She could see three other trains in the yard, each pointing in a different direction. Some were chugging;

others silent.

"This is a huge yard," J.J. exclaimed. "Oklahoma City must be a really big railroad junction."

"Sure looks like it," Angel replied. "This place is mighty busy."

"I sure wish we had some way to get out and see the city," J.J. woofed. "I always hate missing something, especially when we're so close."

"I know," agree the little one. "But we can't risk getting caught on foot in such a big place."

"Or losing our ride," J.J. added.

"Or that," concurred Angel.

"At least we have the books," J.J. brightened.

"That's the next best thing," Angel replied.

"That's right," smiled J.J. "Let's get the Oklahoma history book and have a look."

Angel skipped to the bag and pulled out the book and map and returned to her sister. She quickly flipped the pages until she came to the chapter on Oklahoma City.

"What's it say?" J.J. asked.

"Well, it's the state capital. We already knew that. But it hasn't always been. There's a town just north of here named Guthrie. It was the first capital, but they moved it to Oklahoma City just a few years after statehood."

"I wonder why they changed it?" J.J. quizzed.

"It doesn't say much, Angel answered. "But it sounds like a lot of politics."

"Oh," sniffed J.J. "Why is it always politics?"

"It does say that Guthrie's a neat place today, Angel laughed as she read on. "About the whole town's been restored and looks like it did a hundred years ago. And on the site where they were supposed to build the state capital building is one of the world's biggest and prettiest Masonic Temples. It says it's quite a site. Here, look at the picture."

"Wish we could see that for real," J.J. barked as she studied the photo. "That's amazing."

"Cheer up," Angel squeaked. "Maybe we will."

"Anyway," the little one continued. "Oklahoma City is the largest city in the state with around 600,000 people. And like Tulsa it's ringed by big suburbs: Edmond, El Reno, Midwest City, Moore, and Norman to name just a few. The University of Oklahoma's in Norman. And guess what?"

"What?" quipped J.J.

"It's on a river," Angel informed her with a wide grin. "Two of them really."

"I never would have guessed," J.J. smirked sarcastically. "What are they?"

"The North Canadian cuts through town," the little one answered. "It says they've fixed it up nice with a river walk downtown. It has shops and entertainment; the whole works. And the main branch of the Canadian runs just to the south."

"Where's the capitol building?" J.J. asked.

"Downtown," Angel replied. "And right across the street is the new State Museum of History. It says if you don't see anything else you should see that."

"Must be pretty neat," J.J. whooped. "Say, I just thought of something," she added as she looked at the book. Look at the different spellings. Oklahoma City is the C A P I T A L of the state but the building itself is spelled T O L. I never noticed that before."

"You're right," complimented Angel. "I didn't notice it either." Angel continued to read aloud, noting to her sister other interesting facts about the city. It was home to numerous other museums and historic sites, including the Cowboy Hall of Fame and Western Heritage Museum. Like Tulsa it was an important oil center. There was even a well on the capitol grounds. It was both a major rail and highway junction. Interstate Highways 35, 40, and 44 all met here. And it was the site of the annual Oklahoma State Fair. Oh, and we're right smack dab in the middle of the state. The geographic center is just a few miles north of town."

"No kidding," gushed J.J. "There's sure a lot to do here," she continued as Angel closed the book.

"Ya," chirped the little one. "You could stay here for weeks and not see it all."

"Maybe someday we can," J.J. sighed.

"After we get the silver and find a new family," Angel smiled as she patted J.J. on the shoulder. J.J. beamed at the thought.

The last traces of orange melted away in the west as the Kids settled in for the night. After a meal of nuggets and fish they loaded and zipped the pack, then stretched out to sleep. It had been a long but rewarding day.

Well before dawn the now familiar lurch of their car told them the train would soon be on the move. Inch by inch it began to crawl. Just as first light's first tease began to brighten the eastern sky they cleared the yard and headed slowly west.

"I'm sure glad this is a slow train," Angel quipped. "This must be a lazy crew. They sure don't want to work too hard."

"Can you blame them? " chuckled J.J.

"Not really," giggled the little one. "They're probably just like us. They want to take their time and see more."

"This is a good way to do it," commented J.J.

"About the best," Angel said with a grin. "When you think about it it's even better than a car."

"Ya," concurred her sister. "You go whatever speed you want and don't have to fight the traffic."

"Right," affirmed the little one.

In a short while the train came to U.S. Highway 81 and veered straight north. In another hour they reached the town of Kingfisher at the Highway 33 intersection. Here they saw a sign advertising the Chisholm Trail Museum.

"Hey, this must be the Chisholm Trail," Angel peeped as she remembered the story about the great cattle drives that came up from Texas.

"Must be," confirmed J.J.

"Funny how they built these highways along the old trails," Angel remarked.

114

"Ya, but when you think about it, it just makes sense," reasoned J.J. "I'll bet a whole bunch of today's roads started out as trading routes years ago. And a lot of the trading routes probably started out as game trails."

"Good thinking," praised the little one as the train cleared Kingfisher and continued north.

"If this is the Chisholm Trail, then this road must go up to Kansas," J.J. added.

"Must," seconded Angel. "It's going north and we know that Kansas is north."

"I'm going to check the compass," J.J. barked as she moved to the pack. "I'd forgotten all about it."

J.J. retrieved the compass and took a reading. It confirmed their direction.

"These things sure are handy," chirped Angel as she took the compass from her sister.

"Especially when you're in open country and away from the roads," J.J. added.

The train chugged north as the Kids studied the endless expanse of prairie rolling by. In a short while they crossed the Cimarron River and then passed through the little town of Dover.

"I wonder what's up ahead?" J.J. pondered.

"Let's look at the good map," Angel advised as she moved to the pack.

"Get the book, too," J.J. suggested. "I want to look up something."

"Coming up," Angel squeaked as she pulled both from the bag. Returning to her sister she placed the map on the floor and opened it up. J.J. took the book and began flipping through the pages.

"What are you trying to find?" Angel questioned as she drew alongside her sister.

"Couple of things," J.J. answered. "Rainfall and population."

"It sure looks dry here compared to the east," Angel offered as she looked out over the land. "And the Cimarron didn't look like much compared to the eastern rivers."

"Nope," agreed J.J. "A lot less depth and flow."

"Ah, here it is," she continued as she came to the rainfall map.

"Boy look at the difference!" Angel exclaimed as she pushed next to her sister and looked at the map. "No wonder this place looks so parched."

The Kids studied the map closely, noting that extreme eastern parts of Oklahoma often received more than fifty inches of rainfall annually while the far west and Panhandle areas normally got less than twenty.

"This area must get around thirty or so inches a year," J.J. reckoned as she pointed to their location on the map.

"Looks about right," Angel affirmed. "What else did you want to look up?"

"Population," J.J. answered as she sifted through the book. "We know there are about 400,000 in Tulsa and about 600,000 in Oklahoma City, but I was wondering how many people live in the whole state."

"There it is," Angel chirped as J.J. turned to the table. "About 3.8 million."

"Hmm. 3.8," J.J. pondered. "I guess they've got it just about right."

"Ya," agreed the little one. "That's plenty for a land this size. I sure hope they don't make the same mistake they made back home," she added, noting how so much of Texas had been ruined in so many ways by rampant population growth.

"What do you want to bet that Oklahoma's a lot like Texas; most of the people live in the eastern half," J.J. surmised, remembering how nearly 80% of Texans lived along and east of I-35.

"That would make sense," Angel reasoned. "That's where the water is."

"Yup," stated J.J. "Seems to be far fewer towns out here."

"I know," affirmed the little one. Farther east there's a town every few miles."

"There does seem to be a pretty big one not too far up ahead," J.J. offered as she turned to the map laid out on the floor; Enid."

"Ya," squeaked Angel. "It looks like another highway and rail junction. Highways 81, 412, and 60 all meet there."

The train continued on through the cattle and wheat country of north central Oklahoma. Shortly before noon it pulled into Enid and stopped.

"Enid looks like an interesting place," Angel commented as she and J.J. passed a sign advertising the Railroad Museum of Oklahoma. "I wonder what the book says about the town?"

"Let's see," J.J. offered as she looked through the book and found the place. "Lots of history here," she began with a smile. "Back in the old days they called this region the Cherokee Outlet because it belonged to the tribe. It was a pretty big chunk of dirt; around seven million acres. After the Civil War the U.S. government forced the Cherokees to sell it."

"How come?" Angel quizzed.

"They were mad because so many of the Cherokees had sided with the Confederacy during the war," J.J. explained.

"That's what Boomer said," Angel frowned.

"Yup," confirmed J.J. "Anyway, the Cherokees had been leasing the land to cattlemen for grazing. But a lot of folks wanted land to farm, so in 1893 the government opened the region to homesteaders and they came by the thousands. They called them Boomers."

"Ah," grinned Angel. "That's where the word came from. "How did they decide who got what?" she continued.

"Land run," J.J. laughed as she read.

"What's a land run?" the little one puzzled.

"Everyone lines up and at the signal they all dash into the territory and stake claims to whatever land they can," J.J. explained.

"That must have been quite a sight," chuckled Angel. "Was there just one?"

"Nope," replied J.J. "There were others, but this one was the biggest."

"Oh. One more thing," she added. "It seems some folks jumped the gun and sneaked in a little early. That's where the word 'Sooner' came from and that's why they call Oklahoma "The Sooner State."

"You mean they cheated?" Angel gasped.

"That might be a little harsh," J.J. answered. "Let's just say some people couldn't tell time so great."

"Watches might have been running a little fast," Angel countered with a wide grin.

"That's as good an excuse as any," J.J. laughed as she turned to the next page. "Oh," she continued. "Enid's another example of moving a town to meet the railroad."

"Not again," Angel sighed humorously.

"Yup," confirmed J.J. "And of course they found oil and gas around here, too."

"I figured that," Angel replied. "We've seen all the pump jacks."

"I wonder if the dust bowl hit up here?" Angel wondered.

"Oh, ya," J.J. answered as she continued to read. "They plowed up all this land for farms and there was nothing left to hold the soil in place once the native grasses were gone."

"Then the drought and winds came," offered Angel.

"Exactly," confirmed J.J.

"I tell you it's not wise to press nature too hard," Angel sighed. "That's a lesson some people never seem to learn."

"She always wins in the end," J.J. responded with a hard shake of her head.

J.J. closed the book and returned it to the pack. After a drink and a light meal the Kids resumed their watch. In a short while the train cranked up once more and began a slow crawl through Enid. Soon it came to a crosstrack and turned to the east.

"We're changing directions," Angel noted.

"Heading back east," J.J. advised as she checked the compass that now hung from her neck. "I'm going to check the map and see what's ahead."

"Good idea," chirped Angel.

"Looks like we'll run into another set of tracks just ahead," she stated as she rubbed her jaw. "We could keep going east or cut south again. It all depends."

"South takes us right back to Oklahoma City," Angel observed. "I hope we keep going east."

"Ya," agreed J.J. "We want to see something new."

Near the little town of Fairmont the tracks crossed. Their train held due east. Delighted, the Kids once again looked at the map.

"Looks like we'll hit I-35 again," Angel stated as she raked her paw across the map. "And there's a good sized town not far up ahead; Perry."

"And then the tracks fork again," noted J.J. "North and east."

"Oh, and look!" the little one exclaimed. "Way out here," she continued as she pointed with her paw. "The Tallgrass Prairie!"

"Oh, ya," howled J.J. "We're supposed to go there. I forgot all about it."

"Boy, it's a long way off," moaned Angel. "And it doesn't look like the tracks go anywhere near there."

"Well, if we have to walk we'll just walk," J.J. counseled. "We'll get there one way or another."

"I guess you're right," peeped the little one. "I've just gotten a little too used to first class travel."

"You do like luxury," J.J. teased as she gave her sister a tap on the head.

At midday the train reached I-35 and Perry. A sign told them that it was another landrush town and the site of a major manufacturer of heavy machinery. Once through town they continued north until coming to the junction.

"Which way will we go?" J.J. pondered as she looked first north and then east.

"We're not slowing," Angel observed. "I'll bet we're going straight ahead."

"Must be," J.J. concurred.

As they suspected their train held to the northern course. The Kids studied the map to see what came next.

"Looks like Ponca City's our next stop," J.J. barked.

"What are those towns off to the west?" Angel asked.

"Tonkawa and then Blackwell," J.J. informed her. "They're just off I-35. Ponca City's on 77/ 177," she finished, a little surprised that two major highways ran so close together.

"77 must have been the main highway before they built the Interstate system," Angel reckoned. "Remember that's really pretty new."

"You're right," commended J.J. "Just like Route 66 and I-44 and I-40."

"I like Route 66 better," chimed the little one. "More stuff to see."

"Me, too," confirmed J.J. "I wonder if the kids today even know about the old roads?

"If they don't someone should tell 'em," Angel sniffed.

Late in the afternoon the train slowed as it neared Ponca City. The Kids knew that this was the end of the line if they wanted to go east to the Tallgrass Prairie.

"I wonder if the train will stop here?" J.J. mused.

"If it doesn't we're on our way to Kansas," Angel advised, noting that the border was but twenty miles north.

As if on demand the train slowed to a crawl. Up ahead the Kids could see the rail yard. As the orange of day began to fade their car shook then stopped.

"Bingo!" barked J.J. "We'll lay up here until after dark and then head east."

"I'm going to miss this train," sighed the little one.

"I know," sympathized J.J. "But we'll find something even better."

Angel brightened at the thought and then suggested they have some dinner. J.J. agreed and the little one went to the food bag and retrieved the last of the fish and a pawful of nuggets.

"Really getting low on food," she remarked as she gave J.J. her share.

"We'll look around after we get off," J.J. counseled. "We're bound to find something here."

"Let's look at the book and see what it says about this area," the little one suggested.

"Why not," agreed J.J. "There's still enough light to read."

Angel went back to the pack, pulled out the book, and returned to J.J. who was looking once more at the map. A quick flip of the pages brought her to the section on Ponca City and the surrounding area.

"What's does it say?" J.J. demanded.

Well Ponca City is named for the Ponca tribe. It's also another land rush town," she read. "Tonkawa and Blackwell, too. And guess what?"

"What?" woofed J.J.

"They're all on rivers," the little one laughed. "Ponca City's on the Arkansas. Tonkawa's on the Salt Fork of the Arkansas. And Blackwell's on the Chikaskia."

"The what?" J.J. puzzled with a cock of her head. "That's a real tongue twister."

"Sure is," agreed Angel as she spelled it out. "Anyway," she continued. "One of the reasons they chose the site for Ponca City was because of a good spring nearby."

"Figures," J.J. remarked with a shake of her head. "Water; water; always water."

"Tonkawa was named for the Tonkawa tribe," Angel read on. "And of course this region's a major oil and gas producer. Ranching and grain farming are also big."

"I wonder how far we are from Oklahoma City?" J.J. pondered as she studied the map.

"Looks to be not quite a hundred miles," Angel replied. "Make it ninety."

"Seems about right," J.J. confirmed. "That makes it about 110 miles from the capital to the Kansas line.

"Yup," agreed Angel. "Oh, this looks interesting. The Pioneer Woman Museum. It says there's a big statue out front dedicated to the women who helped settle this area."

"I'll bet they were tough," J.J. offered.

"They had to be plenty plucky," Angel grinned. "Life in those days wasn't easy."

"For anyone," J.J. added.

Angel flipped the page and began to read again when the Kids heard voices just outside their car. In a flash they moved back to the dark corner and huddled together behind the pack. Their hearts thumped as the talking grew closer.

"Close'er up on this side," a gruff voice ordered. "I'll get the other."

In seconds the girls heard the clinking sound of rolling metal as first one door slammed shut and then the other. A snapping click of each told them the doors were latched. In a panic the Kids scurried forward and pushed hard on a sliding steel wall. But it wouldn't budge. They were trapped.

"Oh, no," cried Angel as she hung her head. "Now what do we do?"

"I don't know," J.J. confessed as she sank to the rough wooden floor and sighed.

For several minutes the girls said nothing as they tried to focus in the near total darkness. Only the light from a few vents pierced the blackness. Finally J.J. rose and began a slow pace around their wheeled prison. Then she moved to the pack and fumbled through it until she pawed the flashlight. Turning it on she began to study every inch of their tomb.

"That vent," she barked as she pointed to a narrow opening in the wall near the top of the car.

"We can't get through that," Angel protested. "It's way too small."

"That's not what I meant," J.J. explained. "We can get up there with the ladder and then maybe we can fish the cable hook down and spring the latch."

"Might work," Angel shrugged.

"Has to," J.J. countered. "Help me with the ladder."

Angel helped her sister maneuver the rickety ladder in place and then held it firm while J.J. climbed to the top. With no room to spare she squeezed her head through the vent. Looking down she could just make out the latch's outline just a few feet to the left of the opening.

"I think I can get to it," she informed Angel who was looking up at her. "Bring me the cable."

Angel quickly turned the light on the corner and grabbed the hooked end of the steel string. Returning to the ladder she met J.J. halfway. Securing the hook in her mouth J.J. ascended once more.

At the top she pushed the hook through the vent and began to work it down the side of the car to the height of the latch. Then she began to slowly swing the cable back and forth as she tried to snag it. Time after time she tried. Time after time she failed.

"Can you get it?" Angel whined.

"I don't know," huffed J.J. "I keep missing by just a bit."

She drew a deep breath and then pushed her head the last inch she could through the vent. Cable in mouth she swung once more. Her jaws ached from the strain. Finally the hook found its prey.

"Got it!" she shouted after securing the cable in place with her paw. "Grab the end and pull hard."

The little one eagerly clamped down on the cable end and jerked. J.J. did the same from her perch. The lock popped.

"Good work," praised J.J. as she grinned down at her sister. "It's open. Now let's get this door open."

Descending to the floor, J.J. moved to the door. Angel followed. After pulling the cable back inside they studied the door for the best place to push. Halfway up was a U-shaped round iron bar welded to a steel strip that ran the length of the door.

"That's our spot," J.J. boomed.

"Looks good," agreed the little one.

The Kids positioned the ladder next to the door and J.J. climbed to the bar. Bracing her hind legs against a ladder slat she pushed against it with all her strength but the door wouldn't budge.

"We need some leverage," she reasoned. "I can't move it this way."

"What about the cable?" Angel suggested. "That way we can both pull."

"Good thinking," J.J. commended. "We can loop the hook through the bar."

Angel grabbed the cable while J.J. climbed the ladder yet again. Handing her the hooked end, J.J. attached it to the bar and then dropped to the floor. Then she and Angel clamped down on the cable's tail and pulled once, then twice, then three times. Finally the massive door moved, sliding back but a few inches.

"Whew," gasped J.J. "That's some kind of heavy."

"Sure is," puffed the little one as she tried to fill her lungs. "I just had an idea," she continued. "That looks like a big enough crack for the 2x4. Let's wedge it in there and then push on the board. That'll be easier than tugging on this cable."

J.J. brightened then pushed the ladder down and lined up its 2x4 spine with the crack in the door. Then she and Angel maneuvered it forward until its end slipped through. Changing positions, they pushed hard on the board's opposite end. The 2x4 bent with the strain but held and the door slid open another foot.

"That's all we need," hooted Angel.

"Should do it," confirmed J.J. with a broad smile. "It's really amazing what you can do with such simple tools."

"And imagination," the little one added with a grin. "They're no good without that."

"Agreed," woofed J.J.

At that moment the sudden lurch of the car told them that the train was preparing to leave. Their victory celebration ended quickly.

"Hurry. We have to move," J.J. barked as the car rocked once more. "Help me with the pack." They quickly loaded the pack and strapped it to J.J.'s back. They then pushed the ladder out the door and gently lowered one end to the ground. Angel skipped front paws first down to the ground and then turned to watch J.J. do the same.

"We forgot the cable," the little one cried.

"Got to leave it," J.J. snapped. "It's too heavy to carry anyway. The ladder, too."

The Kids quickly backed away from the tracks as the train began to move. Both watched in silent sadness as it inched its way northward. They felt as if they had lost a good friend.

Slowly and carefully they worked their way out of the yard and into the town. It was near midnight and the streets were quiet.

"How did it get so late?" J.J. mused.

"It took us awhile to break out of that car," Angel reminded her. "Some things take time," she added with a chuckle.

"Funny how time passes when you're busy," J.J. joked.

The girls soon came to the impressive statue of the Pioneer Woman and stopped to rest. After a drink from an outdoor faucet they moved under a light on the side of the museum and studied the map. The Tallgrass Prairie was due east and a shade to the north.

"Looks like we take Highway 60 east for a bit," J.J. advised. "Either that or go north to and then cut east from there."

"Well let's not worry about that just now," Angel warned. "Let's see about finding some food. We're down to our last meal; and a small one at that."

"Well let's eat what we have and then get moving," J.J. commanded as she dropped the pack.

The Kids ate the last of the nuggets, filled their water bottles full, and then looked at the map once more. A nearby site caught their attention.

"The Marland Mansion," Angel read aloud as she pointed to a spot on the map. "That's just ahead. Want to check it out?"

"Why not," replied J.J. "Might be interesting."

"And there's no better place to look for food than a mansion," the little one grinned.

"That's right," laughed J.J. "Help me with the pack."

Angel did as ordered and the two then set off into the night. In a short while they reached the grounds of the sprawling Marland estate. A plaque told them that the site was a National Historical Landmark.

"This must be some place!" gushed the little one as she focused on the palace outline just ahead.

"It is," came a scruffy voice from a bush just behind them.

The Kids jerked around in the direction of the voice and assumed a fighting stance. Just as quickly they relaxed as an old mutt of solid white waved a paw in friendly greeting.

"I'm Scooter," he beamed as he eyed the Kids. "I live here."

"I'm J.J. and this is my sister Angel," J.J. spoke for both of them.

"Ahhh," grinned the old dog. "I thought so."

"You've heard of us?" Angel quizzed, a little surprised.

"Oh, ya," Scooter answered. "You're the Texas dogs looking for the silver."

"That's right," J.J. confirmed. "How'd you know?"

"A little bird told me," the old dog joked. "Actually it was a big bird."

"Lucky the Loon," Angel nearly shouted.

"Yup," Scooter affirmed. "I met him over on Ponca Lake not too long ago. He said he was heading back to Canada and stopped in for a snooze. He gave me your whole story. I wasn't sure he was setting me straight. You know loons," he finished with a smirk.

"Tell us about this place," pleaded J.J. "It sure looks interesting."

"Well," Scooter began as the Kids crowded in closely, "this was the home of E.W. Marland. He was one of Oklahoma's first oilmen. He leased land around here from the Ponca tribe and hit it big; really big. His company became one of the world's largest."

"Sounds a lot like Frank Phillips," J.J. commented, remembering the similar story in Bartlesville.

"Yup," Scooter affirmed. "In fact it's all one big company now. Marland Oil became Conoco and not long ago it merged with Phillips."

"What about the mansion?" Angel chirped.

"It's something," the old dog began. "It's modeled after a palace in Italy and took years to build. You should see the inside."

"Wish we could," J.J. sighed.

"Well, maybe we could arrange a tour," Scooter responded with a twinkle in his eye.

"Really," the Kids squealed together.

"Why not," the old dog answered. "No charge," he added with a grin.

"Oh, thanks," Angel laughed.

The Kids followed Scooter to the mansion and through a doggy door that led into one of the kitchens. Though the lights were dim and few the girls could easily make out the elaborate detail of delicately carved wood and trimmed gold and marble that seemed to adorn every room.

"This is some place," they marveled together. "I'll bet you they had a lot of parties," J.J. added with a laugh.

"Still do," Scooter responded. "People use it all the time for parties and weddings and stuff. But I guess this place's grandest days were when Mr. Marland was governor."

"He was a governor?" Angel quizzed.

"And a Congressman, too," Scooter informed them. "Back in the thirties," he finished as he led them back to the kitchen.

"We're out of food," J.J. informed their new friend as they entered the kitchen. "Do you think you could help us?"

"Sure, the old dog answered. "One of the advantages of being a mansion dog is that you get really good eats," he finished as he moved to the icebox door and opened it. "Now let's see."

Scooter eyed the bottom shelf and then quickly scooped out four, large tinfoil packets and dropped them to the floor. Then he moved to a large box sitting next to the refrigerator and pulled out a dozen packages of regular dog food. As he worked Angel helped J.J. remove the pack and together the Kids unzipped it and pulled out an empty food sack. Scooter read off the labels as he helped them fill it.

"Well, looks like we have quail, pheasant, veal, and smoked salmon," he informed them. "That should hold you for a while."

The Kids stood in a state of shock, their eyes wide and their mouths watering. They simply could not believe their good fortune.

"We've never eaten like this before," Angel gurgled.

"I could grow to like mansion life," J.J. added as she did a little tap dance on the kitchen floor.

"Don't kid yourselves," the big old mutt chortled. "I have to beg for the good stuff same as every other dog."

"I'll bet you've got your sad-eyed look down pat," Angel giggled.

"Down to a science," Scooter grinned. "I'm absolutely impossible to say no to."

The Kids laughed loudly, knowing that they had met a true professional. Then they looked as Scooter's grin melted away, his eyes narrowed, and his face turned somber.

"Always remember that the biggest and best mansions are built in the mind. The other stuff's just stuff; nothing more," he admonished. "You've a hard road ahead and to make it you'll have to build that mental mansion of imagination, grit and persistence. Do you know what that word means?"

"Never give up," the Kids answered in unison.

"Exactly," complimented the old dog. "Now if my information is right you're supposed to be heading for the Tallgrass and looking for Matthew."

"Matthew?" Angel puzzled.

"The mule," Scooter replied.

"Ya," confirmed J.J. "We didn't know his name. Where will we find him?"

"Somewhere along the way," the old dog answered. "I can't tell you exactly where. But when you do find him, pay attention to what he has to say. He's a smart one."

"Any idea when he might turn up?" the little one quizzed.

"Probably when you least expect it," Scooter advised. "That's kind of his way."

"Which way should we go?" asked J.J. "The map shows two different roads; 11 or 60."

"I'd go north to 11," the old dog counseled. "The traffic's a little lighter. But you'll have to cross Kaw Lake and it's a long bridge so you'll have to be careful."

"Then what?" questioned the little one.

"Keep heading east. One way or another you'll get there," their friend told them.

With Angel's help J.J. strapped on the pack and then Scooter led them out the doggy door and back onto the mansion grounds. Then he pointed down a narrow road which would take them to Highway 11. The Kids gave their friend a sad look and then gazed once more at the Marland Mansion. Scooter turned to look as well.

"Just stuff," he muttered with a grin. "Just stuff. I'd give it all up to go with you. What an adventure."

"Why don't you?" Angel asked.

"Too old," he sighed. "Besides, this ones for you. It's written all over."

Confused by his last statement, the Kids started to speak but the old dog shushed them with a wave of his heavy paw. Then he turned and quickly vanished into the bushes. The girls went north.

In a short time the Kids reached the Highway 11 intersection and cut to the east. Marching all night, they reached Kaw Lake just before dawn. Near the bridge they settled under a giant cottonwood in a shallow gully just off the road. It was a good place to hide.

"Breakfast?" J.J. asked as she motioned for the little one to help her with the pack.

"Sounds good," chimed Angel as she unzipped the bag and pulled out a packet. "What will my lady have this morning, quail or pheasant?" she laughed.

"I believe today's a quail day," J.J. sniffed as she stuck her nose proudly in the air.

Angel quickly pulled open the foil and served her sister a generous portion, then took one for herself. As they ate they watched the morning's first brightness peek over the eastern horizon and then spill over the lake's blue waters.

"I guess the Arkansas feeds the lake," Angel reasoned as she licked the tasty juice from her mouth.

"Must," agreed J.J. as she did the same. "That river seems to be everywhere we go."

"It's a big one," replied the little one with a shake of her head. "I'll bet you could

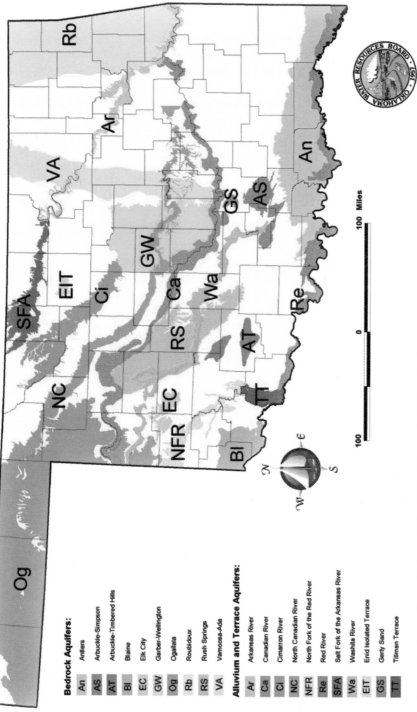

Bedrock Aquifers:

An	Antlers
AS	Arbuckle-Simpson
AT	Arbuckle-Timbered Hills
Bl	Blaine
EC	Elk City
GW	Garber-Wellington
Og	Ogallala
Rb	Roubidoux
RS	Rush Springs
VA	Vamoosa-Ada

Alluvium and Terrace Aquifers:

Ar	Arkansas River
Ca	Canadian River
Ci	Cimarron River
NC	North Canadian River
NFR	North Fork of the Red River
Re	Red River
SFA	Salt Fork of the Arkansas River
Wa	Washita River
EIT	Enid Isolated Terrace
GS	Gerty Sand
TT	Tillman Terrace

Map showing major aquifers in Oklahoma (Oklahoma Water Resources Board, March 2003).

write a big. thick book on it and still have plenty left to say."

"A lot of history," J.J. concurred. "Let's get some water?"

"I'm right behind you," the little one squeaked as J.J. moved toward the lake.

For an hour the Kids lounged lakeside and watched the early morning traffic traverse the bridge. Most went west.

"I guess a lot of people from the countryside work in Ponca City," Angel reasoned. "For every car heading east there are three moving west."

"That'd make sense," agreed J.J. "The towns are where the jobs are."

"It's hard to believe how quickly things can change," Angel spoke. "For most of history most people lived on the land. The cities were just little islands. Now it's the other way around."

"Yup," responded J.J. "I don't think it's been like that for too long; maybe 60 years or so."

"At least in this part of the world," Angel stated, recalling something she had seen in a book not long ago concerning the American transition from a rural to an urban society. Historically speaking that's almost overnight," she added.

"Just the blink of an eye," agreed J.J. whose own eyes were not blinking but drooping.

Fatigue and full stomachs soon conquered both as they sprawled out in the warmth of a new morning sun. A cooling breeze sprang up in the north and filtered smoothly over lake and land. Autumn was near.

For four hours they slept and dreamt. Near noon J.J. awoke with a tremor then rose. She smiled as she turned to Angel whose head and body quivered with the little squeaks of a dreaming dog.

"Visions of silver," J.J. laughed to herself as she gently poked the little one to alertness. "If only dreams alone could make it all so."

"Time to get up sleeping beauty," she purred.

Angel twitched then jolted as her shuttered eyes fluttered. With a quick cough she wobbled upright, then shook her head hard left then right then left again. The cobwebs cleared, she grinned at her sister and stretched.

"Sorry to interrupt," J.J. chuckled. "You looked like you were having a quite vivid dream."

"The silver," Angel smiled, "And that big white animal. She came again."

"How do you know it's a she?" J.J. teased.

"I don't know how," Angel admitted with a cock of her head. "I just know now," she finished with a shrug.

"Well, let's get back to reality," chided J.J. as she cuffed the little one's shiny black nose. "Let's figure out what we're going to do next."

"Let's get a drink first," Angel suggested.

The Kids skipped down to the water, drank deeply, and filled a near empty bottle. Then they returned to their spot and grabbed the map from the pack.

"That bridge is our only real option," J.J. remarked. "Going around the lake would take hours and we'd still have to cross the river somewhere."

"Do we dare risk it in daylight?" the little one questioned as she looked out over the long, thin ribbon of concrete and steel.

"Nope," J.J. huffed. "Way too risky. We'll just have to wait for dark."

"Makes sense," puffed Angel. "We'll get some good rest and chow down really well. It might be a long night."

"We might as well have stayed asleep," joked J.J.

"Why didn't you let me finish my dream," twitted Angel in mock irritation.

"You were drifting too far away," chortled J.J. "I had to reel you back in before you got lost forever."

"I knew exactly where I was the whole time," Angel sniffed with a giggly grin.

J.J. just laughed as she plopped to the ground. Angel joined her. For an hour they chatted about their old home and how far they had come on this journey. But as usual they had no way of answering the big question: How far did they have to go?

"One foot in front of the other," J.J. counseled. "That's all we can do."

"Guess so," agreed the little one. "But sometimes my feet get tired," she chuckled.

"So do mine," seconded J.J. with a shake of her head. "But have you ever noticed how that tiredness kind of melts away once you've really accomplished something?"

"Ya," replied Angel. "Like when you've met a tough challenge or achieved a big goal."

"Exactly," praised J.J. "That'll energize you like nothing else. It's hard to describe that awesome feeling; that incredible satisfaction that comes from it."

Angel said nothing more but nodded her head in understanding. Then she suggested they take a look at the book and see what else they could learn about this region.

"This looks kind of neat," chirped the little one as she came to a section on Oklahoma geography. "It says Oklahoma is nearly 70,000 square miles and has seventy-seven counties."

"Does it say exactly what a county is?" J.J. asked.

"Ya," responded Angel. "It's pretty simple really. A county is just an administrative region of the state. That means you can do state business close to home; like get your car tags or go to court. Otherwise you'd have to go to Oklahoma City for everything."

"Oh," J.J. beamed."That makes sense. What's the biggest county?"

She continued. "Oklahoma County, that's Oklahoma City, has the most people; about 700,000. And the smallest is Cimarron with only about 3000," the little one read.

"What about land area?" J.J. quizzed.

"Hmm," Angel murmured. "Ah, here it is. The smallest is Marshall down on the Texas border. It's only 370 square miles. And the largest is Osage at nearly 2300. From the looks of this map it's just a little to the east of us," she noted as she pointed to the spot. "Oh, this is neat, too," she continued. "Oklahoma is bordered by six other states: Texas, Arkansas, Missouri, Kansas, New Mexico, and Colorado."

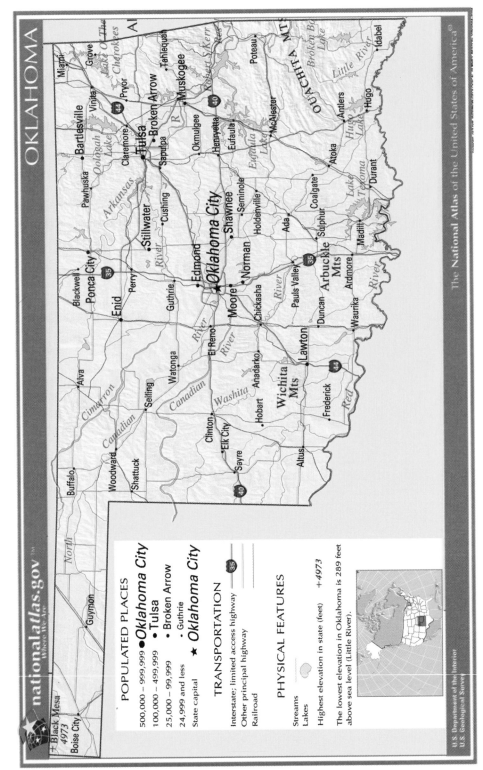

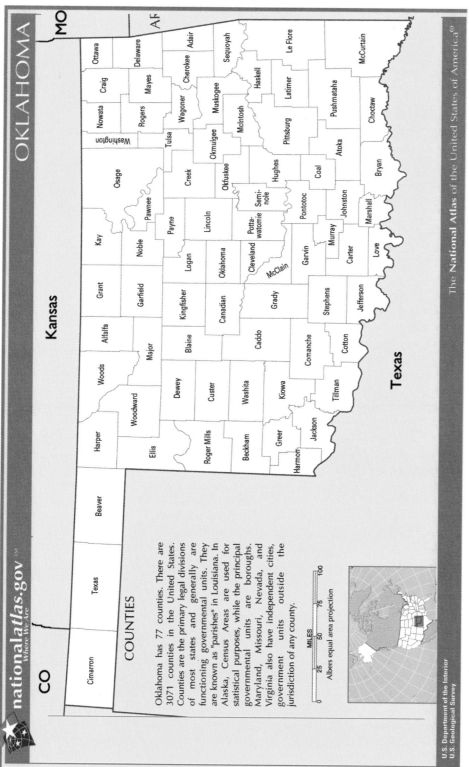

"I wonder how big Oklahoma is compared to other states?" J.J. questioned.

"It's right here," Angel answered. "It's larger than any state east of the Mississippi except Minnesota but one of the smallest to the west of the river. Believe it or not," she laughed. "Oklahoma was once part of Carolina, or so the English said."

"What!" blurted J.J., remembering from their earlier adventure just how far away the Carolinas were. "That's crazy."

"Yup," giggled the little one. "The English claimed everything from the east coast to the west and a straight line across would put this state in Carolina."

"Greedy, weren't they," J.J. chuckled. "Why can't we claim some land that way?"

"Why not," Angel squealed. "Everybody else did. We'll call it the Republic of Dogestan or something like that and it'll be a place just for critters. Oh, and I'll be president."

"Whoa! Aren't we ambitious," J.J. scoffed, exploding in laughter as she poked the little one in the ribs. "Why should you be president?"

"Because," Angel sniffed. "Everybody knows that Border Collies were meant to rule."

"Well Madam President," retorted J.J. "You might as well claim the moon as long as you're at it."

"Believe I will," chimed the little one as she shut the book and returned it to the pack.

The Kids enjoyed their lighthearted attempt to remake the universe and then treated themselves to a hearty lunch. After stuffing themselves with scrumptious smoked salmon and a bit of tasty veal they settled in for a long snooze.

"I want to be president," J.J. yawned as gravity grabbed her eyelids.

"After me," Angel joshed as she curled up next to her sister.

The Kids slept soundly until dusk, arising together just in time to see the sun start its nightly tumble to the west. They quickly focused on the bridge where the traffic was thick. Unlike that morning, it moved mostly east.

"Everybody's going home," Angel commented. "We're going to have to wait awhile."

"Looks like it," agreed J.J. "Might as well have some dinner," she suggested. "But let's keep it light. We might have to move in a hurry later on."

"Okay," the little one squeaked as she moved to the pack. "What'll it be?"

"How about some pheasant," J.J. replied. "And a little regular dog food," she added with a tight smile.

"Oh," Angel groaned with a grin, knowing that her sister was warning her about eating up all the good stuff too quickly. "Discipline again," she huffed.

"Yup," confirmed J.J. "And balance."

Angel retrieved a packet of dog food and a foil of pheasant and returned to J.J.. She passed the tin to J.J. then ripped open the plastic bag of dog food and divided the contents between them. J.J. did the same with the meat. Together they plopped down to the ground and ate. When finished they put their trash back in the pack and then skipped down to the lake for a drink. Their thirsts quenched, they returned to load the pack.

"Traffic's thinning," Angel observed as she looked out over the bridge. "We can go soon."

"I think you're right," affirmed J.J. "Another half hour and we should be okay."

Angel helped her sister secure the pack and then they cautiously moved toward the bridge. In the east a splendorous moon of yellowy orange climbed skyward in all its fullness.

"Good moonlight tonight," noted J.J. "That'll help us."

"Should," piped the little one as the last set of headlights passed and then disappeared into the prairie darkness.

"Nothing's coming," J.J. barked. "Let's move!"

Swiftly the Kids darted onto the Kaw Lake bridge. J.J. took the lead as they anchored themselves to its southern railing and bolted full throttle for its eastern end. Halfway across a truck appeared, its lights blinding the girls.

"Keep moving!" J.J. yelled back as she turned her eyes away from the brightness.

Angel obeyed as she lowered her head and pulled still harder. The truck slowed to a crawl as it reached the Kids. In the moonlight they could see the driver's head poke out the window, his face locked in a puzzled gaze. With a shake of his head the truck sped up while the Kids sped on. In another minute they reached their goal. Gasping for breath, they skittered down a low rise that flanked the road and rolled onto the prairie grass that covered it. Tongues hanging out, they lay wheezing, sucking hard for each measure of air. Finally J.J. arose with a hack and a shake.

"You okay?" she coughed as she placed a paw on Angel's thumping side.

"Ya," sputtered the little one as she rolled to her chest and stretched her back legs. "That was some sprint."

"Sure was," laughed J.J. "We might have set a record."

"I feel like it," grinned Angel as she rose to all fours. "That old man sure looked shocked."

"Probably wondering what on earth a dog was doing carrying a pack," cracked J.J.

"I'll bet he's still wondering what we were doing," giggled the little one as she took another deep breath. "Now what?"

"We just stay on 11," J.J. counseled. "The map says it goes nearly straight toward the Tallgrass and that's what we need to see."

"Sounds good," panted Angel. "Let's get some water."

"I'm for that," J.J. huffed.

The Kids inched their way through the moonlight and down to the lake for another well-earned drink. Even through night's dark the moon's brilliance allowed them to see their own reflections in the glistening water. When quenched they returned to the highway and began their march to the east through Osage County. Well past midnight they came to the tiny hamlet of Shidler and the intersection of Highway 18. Here the eastern route ended. The Kids stopped to

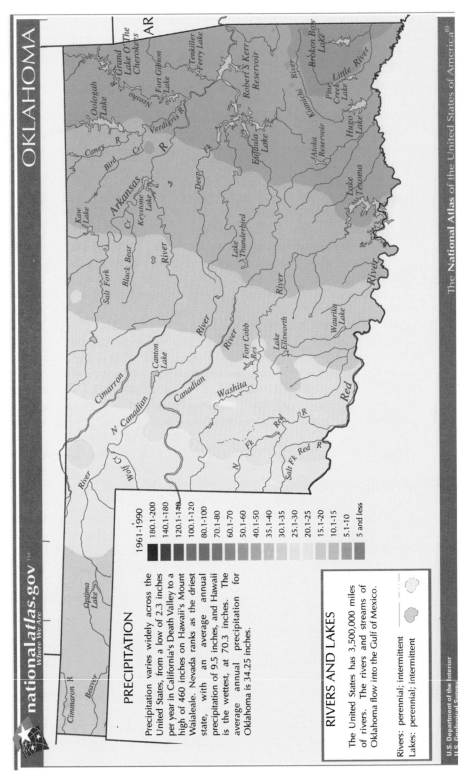

OKLAHOMA

nationalatlas.gov™
Where We Are

PRECIPITATION

Precipitation varies widely across the United States, from a low of 2.3 inches per year in California's Death Valley to a high of 460 inches on Hawaii's Mount Waialeale. Nevada ranks as the driest state, with an average annual precipitation of 9.5 inches, and Hawaii is the wettest, at 70.3 inches. The average annual precipitation for Oklahoma is 34.25 inches.

1961-1990

180.1-200
140.1-180
120.1-140
100.1-120
80.1-100
70.1-80
60.1-70
50.1-60
40.1-50
35.1-40
30.1-35
25.1-30
20.1-25
15.1-20
10.1-15
5.1-10
5 and less

RIVERS AND LAKES

The United States has 3,500,000 miles of rivers. The rivers and streams of Oklahoma flow into the Gulf of Mexico.

Rivers: perennial; intermittent
Lakes: perennial; intermittent

The **National Atlas of the United States of America**®

U.S. Department of the Interior
U.S. Geological Survey

BLACKTAIL KIDS VISIT SAPULPA JUNIOR HIGH

plot their next move. Angel unzipped the pack and pulled out the map and flashlight.

"No straight shot to the Tallgrass," commented J.J. as they studied the map. "We'll either have to go cross country or take 18 north and then cut over. What do you think?"

"Overland's shorter," remarked the little one as she ran her paw over the map. "And the terrain doesn't seem too rough. Look's like this stream is the only thing in our way," she finished as she pawed at the blue line representing Salt Creek, an Arkansas River tributary that met the great river near Ralston."

"It doesn't look too bad," J.J. reckoned. "Not much more than a wade."

"We have good light, too," Angel added. "I think that's our best bet. I'll get the compass just in case."

"Good idea," praised J.J. "We might need it."

"We just need to set a course due east and just a shade to the north and we can't miss it," Angel stated as she turned off the light, folded the map, and placed them both back in the pack.

"Don't forget the compass," J.J. reminded her.

"Got it," affirmed the little one as she zipped up the pack. "Ready?"

"Ready," J.J. answered with a broad grin.

Through the night the Kids trudged over the gently rolling land of Osage County, stopping each hour to take a compass reading and have a drink. Near dawn they reached a back country road and the little town of Personia. A moonlit sign told them that they had reached the edge of The Tallgrass Prairie Preserve.

"We made it!" Angel squealed in delight.

"Not a bad night's march," beamed J.J. "I wish the sun would hurry up. I want to see this place."

"We really don't know exactly what it is," Angel popped. "Ever think of that," she added with a laugh.

"Nope," agreed J.J. "But it must be important or they wouldn't have told us to come here."

"Maybe we can find some information somewhere," the little one reckoned.

"What about the book?" J.J. quizzed. "It's bound to say something about it."

"Ya," gushed Angel as she tapped herself on the head. "Let's find a place to camp and we'll have a look."

The girls found a tiny, open-sided shed about one hundred yards off the road and settled in for a much needed rest. After removing the pack and nearly draining a water bottle they stretched out on the cool earth to await a new day's coming. They had walked nearly twenty miles. Sleep soon seized them.

"I thought we were going to study," Angel chuckled as she nudged her sister's nose.

"Huh. What's going on?" J.J. mumbled as her eyes fluttered and slowly opened. "What time is it?"

"Looks like about eight," Angel answered as she studied the sun's full orange orb now with each minute rising higher in the eastern sky.

"Boy, I really conked out," J.J. laughed as she rose to her feet.

"We both did," the little one grinned. "We had a long walk."

J.J. went to the pack and pulled out a water bottle, then offered it to Angel who drank deeply before passing it back. Between gulps J.J. studied the area now glowing a golden bright in the morning light. After fastening the lid she returned the bottle to the pack and pulled out the book.

"Let me see," she murmured as she flipped through the pages. "Ah, here it is; Tallgrass Prairie."

"What's it say?" Angel demanded impatiently, her deep brown eyes beaming and her ears perked up in excitement.

"Whole bunch," J.J. whoofed. "The Tallgrass Prairie Preserve is a big conservation area; about 36,000 acres. It's one of the few places left that's pretty much the same as it was hundreds of years ago; before the land was plowed up for farming. It's teeming with plant and animal life. Some of the grasses like the bluestem can grow taller than a man. There's deer, rabbits, and all kinds of birds; just about every type of critter you can think of. Oh, and there's a bison herd here, too," she added.

"What's that?" Angel quizzed.

"Another word for buffalo," J.J. informed her. "Don't you remember?"

"Oh, ya," cooed the little one as she slapped herself on the side of the head.

"Look," pointed out J.J. "Look at that fence line. You can tell by the land that that's where the Preserve ends."

Angel followed J.J.'s lead and focused on the spot not far away. On one side of the fence was the lush thickness of native prairie grasses while on the other just the dried brown and tan stubble of the last wheat crop.

"I like the park side better," the little one stated dryly. "I wish there was more of it."

"Ya, but people have to have wheat to eat," countered J.J. "We need both; just maybe in better balance."

"I guess you're right," squeaked Angel. "Say, I wonder if land that's been plowed up can be restored to its old state; you know, replanted in native grasses?"

"Maybe," shrugged J.J. "I really don't know. That would be a good project for someone."

"Sure would," agreed the little one. "I'll tell you, every kid in Oklahoma should see this place."

"Sure should," seconded J.J. "They'd really get a feel for what the first European explorers saw. It's places like this that give you a real sense of history."

"A lot more than you can get out of a book alone," Angel added.

"Speaking of which," J.J. chuckled as she began to read again. "It says that this whole region used to be covered with buffalo. And not just in Oklahoma but as far south as Texas and all the way north up to Canada. Might have been as many

PAUL AT HOME WITH J.J. AND ANGEL

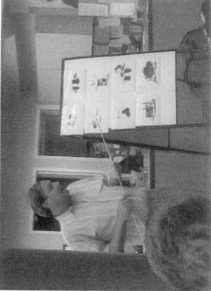

ABOVE: PAUL TALKING WITH STUDENTS AND TEACHERS AT JENKS EAST INTERMEDIATE

LEFT: LESSONS GIVEN AT LEE ELEMENTARY SCHOOL, LEE STUDENTS PETTING J.J.

as sixty million of them."

"Where'd they go?" questioned Angel.

J.J. was about to look for an answer when the rattling sound of a truck shook them to attention. They both turned to see an old pickup loaded with cattle feed bearing down on their shed.

"Quick," boomed J.J. "We have to get out of here. Help me with the pack."

The girls quickly filled the pack with their things, zipped it shut, and hoisted it onto J.J.'s back, a move they had now practiced to near perfection. A quick glance showed the truck to be but yards away and slowing to a stop.

"Where do we go?" whispered the little one.

"Through that fence and into the grass," ordered J.J. "It'll make good cover."

Silently the Kids shot from the shed and sprinted the short distance to the fence. Angel held down the bottom strand of wire as J.J. slipped through, then followed. In seconds they were safely hidden behind the reverse slope of a thickly matted grassy rise. A quick peek back showed they had escaped unseen.

"Mighty close," huffed J.J. as she wiped her brow.

"Too close," seconded the little one. "Now what?"

"Let's explore," J.J. suggested.

"Just what I was thinking," replied Angel. "I want to see buffalo."

"Well, let's get to it," J.J. barked with a broad smile.

Throughout the day the Kids slowly worked their way along the game trails of the Tallgrass. Near noon a cooling northern breeze rushed in the take the edge off the late summer sun. An hour later they stopped by a tiny spring to eat and rest.

"Water must come from another aquifer?" J.J. reasoned as she dipped her muzzle into the shallow pool. "There's no stream here."

"Must have," Angel agreed. "I wonder what this one's called?"

"Check the book," J.J. suggested.

"Ya," Angel chirped. "Let's find its name."

Angel quickly pulled the book from the pack and studied the Table of Contents. She soon came to a chapter on water and flipped to the page.

"Here we go," she said. "A good map."

Together the Kids studied the map which told them that Oklahoma had over twenty designated underground water deposits. They pinpointed their location in the Tallgrass and determined that they were above the Vamoosa-Ada aquifer, a narrow but long formation that ran for over one hundred miles from north to south.

"I'll bet these things are important," Angel mused as she shut the book and returned it to the pack. "I wonder how much water they hold?"

"Don't know," confessed J.J. "Each one's probably different. But you're surely right about one thing. You can bet people depend on them for water."

"I guess those windmills we've seen tap into them," Angel reasoned as she pulled out a packet of meat and one of dog food.

"Must," agreed J.J. as she tore open the packet. "What else is on the menu?"

"Smells like quail," the little one answered as she sniffed the partially opened foil. "Here."

The Kids finished their lunch and then sprawled out in the bed of grass for a snooze. An hour later they arose and continued their trip through the rolling hills, spotting a small herd of deer and at least a dozen types of birds. Late in the afternoon they came within site of the Preserve's headquarters and stopped behind a clump of bushes to survey the scene. No one was near.

"Want to check it out?" Angel quizzed. "Might find some information."

"Why not," J.J. answered.

The Kids skipped up to the old ranch house building and quickly found the information rack. Pulling a few flyers from the display they made a circle of the site and then retreated back to their hiding place.

"Hey, they even make movies here," J.J. woofed as she read a pamphlet.

"Maybe we can be in one," the little one hooted. "We'll be big stars and eat pheasant everyday."

"No barbecue?" questioned J.J.

"Okay, both," grinned the little one.

"Hey, what's that?" J.J. barked as she looked down the road about one hundred yards.

"Cattle?" Angel shrugged.

"Uh, uh. Too big," J.J. shot back. "Look again."

The Kids focused down the road on a gentle rise just off it. Here three hulking forms of furry brown stood motionless, their backs turned to the sinking sun.

"Bison!" the little one shouted. "Has to be."

"Let's go look!" J.J. yelled.

The Kids eagerly trotted down the park road and approached the three mammoth beasts, for the first time coming face to face with that magnificent symbol of the west. Moving to within ten feet, they carefully studied the giant horned heads and hill-like humps that made them creatures like no others. Angel spoke but they made no response, only staring back through piercing brown eyes. J.J. took another step forward but they retreated in kind.

"I guess they don't talk," sighed the little one.

"Doesn't look like it," J.J. agreed. "Too bad; the stories they could tell."

That remark seemed to bring just the slightest of smiles to the animal closest. With a snort he looked to the others and with a flick of his tail all turned and ran. The ground shook. Two soon disappeared behind a near low rise while the leader held the summit. He turned to the Kids and pawed the golden ground twice, then rejoined his tiny herd. The girls were terribly disappointed that their first encounter with real buffalo had proved so fruitless.

"They don't talk but maybe they hear all right," Angel reckoned. "I could swear that the one smiled a little when you said that. Maybe we're just not supposed to talk to them yet."

"Could be," J.J. replied. "If we've learned anything it's that things aren't always as they seem."

"And everything has its time," added the little one.

PHOTO BY PAUL MARTIN

PAWNEE BILL'S RANCH

"Yup," concurred J.J. with a nod of her head.

"Something else," Angel continued. "The big white animal we've seen sure looks a lot like a buffalo."

"Naw, it has to be something else," J.J. sniffed. "Those critters were all brown."

"I guess you're right," affirmed her sister. "But."

"But what?" J.J. queried.

"Ah, nothing," Angel answered. "Just my imagination I guess."

J.J. chuckled and gave her little sister a gentle cuff on the head, then suggested they cover a little more ground before stopping for the night. Remembering their instructions to cut back to the Red, they set their course south. Just at dusk they once again came to the road that marked the preserve's boundary. Crossing it they found a tiny but nice grove of hickory that lined a shallow gully and bedded down for the night.

"Still no mule," sighed J.J. as she removed the pack. "I wonder if we'll ever find him?"

"Of course we will," assured the little one as she helped her sister. "Although I have to admit this has been one of the longer chapters in our lives."

"Yup; long time between animals," J.J. laughed. "How about a little dinner?"

"I'm ready," affirmed Angel as she zipped open the pack.

"Which way do we go in the morning?" Angel quizzed.

"I don't know," J.J. muttered. "Let's check the map."

Angel pulled the map from the pack and returned to her sister, unfolding it in front of her. Together they studied the routes to the south.

"Looks like this road takes us by a lake and into a good-sized town," Angel as she pointed to Bluestem Lake and the city of Pawhuska. "And then Highway 99 is pretty much a straight shot south, at least for a while."

"I guess that's our best bet then," reasoned J.J.

"Seems to be," agreed the little one. "We'll have a good night's sleep and get an early start."

J.J. said nothing, just gave a nod and then sprawled out on the cool bank of the dampened gully. Angel did the same. Another slight hint of a coming autumn's crispness soothed them. They slept well.

An hour before sunrise they arose. After a quick, light breakfast they loaded up and left, charting a course southeast through the prairie just off the narrow road to Pawhuska. Soon dawn's first teasing light broke through in the east, coloring the land the dimmest of yellowy gold.

"I just love this time of day," Angel remarked as she watched the sun's crown climb.

"It's my favorite, too," affirmed J.J. "There's something so calm and peaceful and pretty about it. No other time is its equal."

"That's for sure," confirmed the little one. "Looks like a little road up ahead," she added as she focused south.

"Doesn't look like much," huffed J.J. "Just a private ranch road."

"It has a name," Angel puffed as they drew closer. "Pleasant Valley Road," she stated when drawing near enough to read the sign.

"Name seems to fit," J.J. offered, noting the pretty countryside.

"Do you hear a whining sound?" asked Angel, "or is it just my imagination?"

"Just the wind," replied J.J. as they reached the rutted little trail.

"No, listen," insisted the little one.

J.J. stopped, cocked her ears high, and strained to hear. Sure enough she faintly caught what seemed to be the cry of an animal in distress.

"You're right," confessed J.J. "It's coming from behind that hill," she added, pointing to the low, round rise not fifty feet away. "Let's have a look."

J.J. took the lead as the Kids trotted down the road and over the rise. At its crest they peered down into a tiny valley and a sight they had never before seen.

"What is this?" Angel spat in disgust.

"You got me," J.J. gasped with a shake of her head.

On the floor below were dozens of animal cages lining several deep pits dug out from the ground. From the cages came the whines and whimpers and cries of thirsty, hungry dogs. At full speed the girls dashed down to the valley floor and approached the first cage. Inside was a famished dog of tan and white, breathing heavily and panting for water.

"Would you help us," he cried.

"What is this place?" Angel snapped as she popped the latch on the cage and yanked open its steel mesh portal.

"You don't want to be here," the canine warned. "This is where they make us fight."

"Who?" J.J. growled.

"Some really bad people," the dog answered. "And today is Saturday. That's when they come."

Angel quickly unzipped the pack and pulled out a water bottle which she uncapped and passed to the dog. Then without a word she and J.J. moved from cage to cage, unlatching each as they went. From each stumbled an animal in the same condition. Halfway through the first dog squealed a warning.

"They're coming!" he cried.

The Kids whirled to see a truck poking just over the crest of the hill and heading toward them. Another truck and a white van followed. Quickly they popped two more locks and then screamed for the other dogs to run. Some were too weak from hunger and thirst. All were confused by neglect and abuse. The lead truck's door flew open and the driver emerged. Cupping his hands on his forehead to better focus, he looked down on the scene then jumped back in his seat. A cloud of brown dust plumed from his spinning back wheels as he accelerated down the hill. Nearing the first cage he slammed his brakes hard and slid to a stop. The others pulled alongside. From each truck filed three men; from the van but one. He was Rob Silver.

"Look!" shouted J.J., her face knotted in both fury and fear. "It's Silver."

Angel stared hard at the man they had for so long been trying to corner. He quickly joined the others as they approached the dogs. Some carried long whipping sticks while the lead driver raised a rifle and took aim at J.J. The rifle cracked as his first shot missed. The second grazed her left loin and sent her sprawling into the pit. All around the other men were whipping the dogs, trying to force them back into their cages. They fought valiantly, one locking onto the wrist of his tormentor and breaking it. Angel flew into the pit to help her sister. As they looked up the man with the rifle was taking aim again. Suddenly, from just over the rise came the drumming sound of pounding hooves striking the hard prairie ground. Men and dogs all turned toward the hill. In seconds the figure of a strange looking horse broke the plane and came into view. Behind him were three mighty bison. Lining up and running abreast, they charged at full gallop. The horse singled out the man with the rifle. Too stunned to fire, he froze in fear as the horse bowled him over, trampled him into the ground, and then savagely bit his upper arm to bleeding. Near the second truck, two tried to flee, each fighting the other for the cab's safety. The man left out turned just in time to have his chest crushed against the door by a bison's bouldered head. He crumpled to the dirt below. The lance-like thrust of another bison's horn ripped the truck's left rear tire, flattening it in an instant. Scattering in panic, the others fled on foot, only to be run down and mauled by the angry animals with their superior speed. But one escaped; Rob Silver. Flying through the open window, he cranked his van and threw it in gear, first speeding backwards, then nearly tipping over as he cut the wheel hard to turn around. The Kids watched in silence as the van's rear end bounced out of sight over the rise. The one man left cowered in the truck. He had no keys. Rolling up the windows and locking the doors, he sat in the middle, shaking as the animals surrounded him and peered through the glass. One buffalo arched his mighty hump and then shattered the glass with his mighty head. Another did the same on the other side. Covered in shards, the man sunk to the seat and cried. Disgusted, the animals all turned away. He wasn't worth the effort.

"Not so tough now, is he," the horse snorted as he turned to the Kids still stuck in the pit. "Let me help you out of there."

The Kids looked hard at the horse as he shuffled to the incline and came down beside them. They hadn't had time to look at him closely but now that they did they could see that he wasn't a horse at all. Though they had never seen one, they knew he was a mule.

"Are you Matthew?" the little one gurgled as she pawed at her sister.

"Sure am, sweetheart," the mule chuckled with a wink and a smile. "And let me guess who you two are," he added with a pearly grin.

The mule quickly looked to the bloody wound on J.J.'s leg. As he did Angel helped her sister to her feet. Wobbly at first, she soon regained her balance and tested the leg with a few limping steps.

"Looks like he just nicked you," the mule observed. "You're lucky he was such a bad shot."

"We'd better clean that up," Angel suggested as she pulled a bottle from the pack.

J.J. stood as the little one poured a slow stream of water on the wound. As she did the mule climbed out of the pit to look at the other dogs. When Angel was finished, the Kids joined him. They counted a total of fourteen dogs who had been held in the cages. One by one they told their stories. Some had been bred to fight while others were captured strays trained to do so. They were seldom fed or watered. Those who came to watch and bet represented every level of society; from the uneducated laborer to the prominent professional. Dogs who wouldn't fight were savagely beaten and often shot. They could not count the number they had seen killed or severely injured in just the short time they'd been here.

"Hard to believe humans can do such things," Angel blubbered, the tears rolling down her cheeks.

"Human!" spat the mule. "It's quite a stretch to call trash like that human. They're something less; a lower order."

"We'd heard rumors that this happens in Texas," J.J. choked with a sob. "But we didn't believe it."

"Happens just about everywhere; every state and every nation," Matthew hissed. "Evil knows no borders."

"And it's timeless," Angel added with a frown.

"And that," agreed the mule.

"Well at least we got some of them," J.J. angrily laughed as she looked at the five men still down on the ground around them.

"Maybe that one will get the word out," Angel sneered as she peered at the man with a two-day stubble and filthy hands still cowering low inside the truck.

"Ya, but the one we wanted got away," lamented J.J., explaining to Matthew their mission.

"Maybe it's not time yet," he neighed with a twinkle in his eye "Might be more work for you, first."

The Kids just laughed and shook their heads in bafflement. Then the three turned to the other dogs as the buffalo kept watch on the man in the truck, bumping the doors with their heads whenever he got too close to a side window.

"Okay, guys," Matthew addressed the dogs. "I'm sorry you've been through such a tough time. But we've got to get going. There'll be help here for you in just a few minutes and things will be a lot better. You'll all get good homes. No one deserves it more than you do."

"Really!" whimpered the lead dog. "How do you know?"

"Mules know everything," Matthew winked. "Just trust me on this one," he added as he broke a broad smile. "Oh, and keep an eye on this scum until the cops come."

"We will," several of the dogs answered as they paired off to guard the men, some of whom were now starting to stir.

"One more thing to do," the mule spoke as he turned to the buffalo.

"Good job, fellas," Matthew praised the bison as he bowed his head to them. "Not a bad day's work."

"Thanks, guys," the Kids seconded together, hoping that the buffalo would finally talk to them.

Sadly for the girls the mighty bison merely snorted, pawed the ground hard, and turned to leave. Before doing so the leader rammed the truck's door once more, forcing the man to sink in the seat yet again. Then with a smirk he led the others at full gallop up the hill, quickly reaching the summit then disappearing behind the slope.

"How can something so big be so fast," marveled the little one.

"They can fly," Matthew chuckled.

"Why won't they talk?" J.J. quizzed, disappointed that their second encounter with the magnificent beasts had yielded the same result.

"They don't say much," the mule informed them. "They use their ears a lot more than their mouths."

"Probably wise for all of us," Angel chirped.

"Hey, you're learning," Matthew lauded.

"Have you ever seen a white one of those?" J.J. asked.

"Why do you ask?" the mule shot back.

"In our dreams we've seen this big white animal that kind of looks like a buffalo," J.J. replied. "It's always kind of hazy so we can't be sure."

"Naw, that was probably an elephant," Matthew countered with a smile.

"Elephants aren't white," protested the little one.

"Oh, ya," insisted the mule with a twinkle in his eye. "The world is full of white elephants."

The Kids knew that Matthew was teasing but the conversation came to a quick end with the sound of roaring motors. All turned to see a fleet of trucks and cars heading toward them along the road.

"Quick; we have to move," the mule ordered. "Can you walk all right?" he asked as he looked to J.J.

"I think so," J.J. answered.

"We just need to get to the top of that little bump," Matthew advised as he pointed his nose toward a grassy knoll not far to the west. "Then we can hide on the other side and watch."

The three bade a final farewell to the other dogs and then shuffled toward the slope. At its base one of the men was struggling to rise. As they passed Matthew gave him one last swift kick in the side and he fell once more with a painful groan. Then Angel helped a limping J.J. climb to the summit where the three turned and plopped down to hide in the high grass. Below police cars and Humane Society vans fanned out over the area. Starting with the man in the truck, the police took all six men into custody while the animal people began to care for the dogs.

"I wonder how they knew to come?" a baffled Angel asked as she turned to the mule.

"I called in," the mule deadpanned with a loud laugh.

"Ahhhh," J.J. scoffed as she waved a paw at him.

"Do you think they'll get good homes?" the little one questioned.

"Guaranteed," Matthew promised. "There are a lot of good folks around here."

"What about those rotten men?" J.J. spat.

"Well the law's on animal abuse aren't nearly tough enough," the mule snorted in disgust. "So I don't know."

"Now what do we do?" Angel pondered.

"What were you told to do?" Matthew queried.

"Cut south all the way to the Red," J.J. answered.

"Then there's your answer," the mule chuckled with a shrug of his powerful shoulders. "I'll tag along for a while."

"Great!" gushed the Kids together. You're the first one to want to go with us."

"By the way," J.J. inquired. "Just where do you live?"

"Oklahoma," the mule replied.

"No, I mean where's your home?" she continued.

"Oklahoma," he said again. "From the Panhandle to the prairies to the pines; I'm right at home anywhere in this state."

"You sound like some Texans," Angel peeped. "At least the real ones."

"We have a lot more in common than some might think," Matthew quipped. "Love and respect for the land is what counts. And not just in Oklahoma or Texas but throughout the southwest. It's a wonderful region, almost magical, and we have to work together to guard it. A whole slew of problems don't start or stop at a state line."

"Maybe we should work together in everything," J.J. offered. "Even football," she added with a smirk.

"Let's don't crowd things," Matthew cringed. "Even a first rate mule and two brilliant dogs can't accomplish one of life's few impossibilities."

Matthew and the girls enjoyed a merry laugh, then he suggested they walk to a nearby tank for water. As they went, the mule cited some of the places they should see in this region. It was also obvious to both him and Angel that J.J.'s leg was hurting her although she said nothing. Reaching the tank they drank deeply and then refilled their water bottles. Thirsts quenched, Matthew turned to graze on a patch of sweet grass while the Kids ate a hearty meal of pheasant and dog food. When finished the mule suggested that he carry J.J. for a few days while her leg healed.

"I'm okay," protested J.J. "I don't want to burden you."

"No bother at all," Matthew scoffed. "I've carried big cowboys before. In fact I can carry you both without any trouble. Bet neither one of you has ever ridden a mule."

"Never have," they confessed together.

"Well now's your chance," he chuckled. "You'll be surprised by my mulepower."

"Is that like horsepower?" Angel giggled.

"Better," the mule whooped. "Now let me get down and you climb on."

Matthew folded his knees and dropped to the ground. Angel gave J.J. a boost aboard and then followed, taking a seat just behind her sister. Then with a huff and a groan he rose.

"How's it feel back there?" he quizzed. "Nice and snug?"

"A little wobbly," Angel squeaked as she tried to balance herself.

"You'll both get the hang of it pretty soon," Matthew promised. "You'll be first rate cowdogs in no time."

"Where'll we go?" J.J. asked.

"Lots of places," the mule answered. "You get the big tour."

"We have a map," the little one informed him. "Do you want to look at it?"

"Don't need it," Matthew declined with a snort. "Ready?"

"Ready," the Kids replied together.

With a slight lurch the mule began to walk through the rolling prairie. By midafternoon they reached the shores of Bluestem Lake just outside of Pawhuska. Here they stopped for a rest.

"What do you know about Pawhuska?" Angel quizzed between laps of lake water.

"It's the county seat," Matthew informed them. "The name means "white hair" in English. It's the headquarters for the Osage people and has some great museums. And there was a Civil War battle near here."

"Sounds neat," J.J. smiled as she wiped the water from her muzzle. "What's next?"

"We'll kind of follow 99 south and then turn toward Pawnee," the mule answered. "You need to see Pawnee Bill's."

"Pawnee Bill's?" Angel questioned.

"Old West place," Matthew replied. "You'll like it."

The three rested for about fifteen minutes. Then the mule fell to his knees and gave the order to mount up. The Kids eagerly complied, each splaying her back legs over his massive back and balancing with her fronts.

"You two are catching on in a hurry," Matthew praised as he began a slow lope.

"We're getting better," J.J. whooped. "We want to be trick riders one day."

"Let's don't rush things," Matthew chortled with a shake of his high-eared head.

The mule carried the Kids east along the lake's northern shore until coming once more to the road leading back to the Tall Grass. Here he turned south and soon crossed Highway 11 which was also Highway 60. Then he passed just outside of Pawhuska before picking up Highway 99 and skirting the town just to the west. By late afternoon they had reached the intersection of Highway 20 and the town

of Hominy, site of the historic Drummond Home. The last few hours of light brought them once more to the mighty Arkansas where they stopped for the night.

"We seem to run into this river no matter where we go," Angel piped as she looked out over the waters now reflecting the day's last orange.

"It's a big one," mewed the mule as he dropped to the ground to let the Kids slide off.

"Good place to camp," J.J. quipped as she looked up at the giant cottonwood that now sheltered them.

"Can't beat it," agreed the mule.

Angel helped her sister remove the pack and then the three moved to the river for a drink. After slurping their fill they returned, carved out a nice spot on the sandy bank, and sank to the ground. In the near distance they could see the headlights passing to and fro over the river's bridge. The little town of Cleveland lie just across it.

"I know you don't need it," J.J. joked as she looked to Matthew, "but I want to look at the map."

"Be my guest," the mule encouraged her.

J.J. skipped to the pack and pulled out the map, the flashlight, and that night's dinner. Then she returned to Angel and Matthew, unfolded it, and flipped on the light.

"We're nearly back to Tulsa," she exclaimed as she dragged a paw eastward across the map.

"Covered a lot of ground, haven't you," the mule observed.

"Sure have," Angel chirped. "Still a long way to go, I think," she added with a sigh.

"Most likely," Matthew huffed softly as his twinkling eyes focused on the Kids.

The girls had a feeling that the mule knew exactly what was in store for them but knew he would never tell. To do so would spoil their journey of discovery.

"Tell us about mules," piped J.J. as she grinned at Matthew. "Aren't you part horse?"

"Just the good part," Matthew nearly hollered.

The girls fell out in laughter as the mule lifted his head and pointed his nose proudly toward the sky. Then with a loud sniff he lowered his head and broke into a broad smile.

"You have to admit," Angel giggled, "horses are pretty."

"Pretty doesn't always get the job done," Matthew shot back. "If you want to show off, get a horse. If you want to get some work done, find a good honest mule. Ever heard the expression, 'Work like a mule'. Life takes more than prissy prancing."

"What about herding cattle?" J.J. countered. "Horses aren't bad at that."

"Okay, I'll grant you that," Matthew admitted with a little pout. "That's where our good part comes from; the working side of horses."

Matthew tossed his head back and shot the Kids a wide smile. The Kids knew he was teasing them.

"The fact is," he continued, "mules probably did as much to make this land as anything. Plowing up these prairie grasses to create farmland was hard work and there were no tractors in those days; just a man, a mule, and a plow; all muscle and a little steel."

"Why did they plow up so much?" Angel queried. "We read that that was a big reason for the dust bowl."

"They overdid it for sure," the mule answered. "But you have to remember that man is a learning animal and much of what he learns comes from mistakes; quite often painful mistakes. The dust bowl was a perfect example of what can happen when nature's pushed over the edge."

"I guess everybody knows better now," reasoned the little one.

"Some do; some don't," Matthew sighed. "For some it's a lesson that never seems to sink in. And those are the folks who can make it rough on everyone else."

"What about the buffalo?" J.J. questioned. "The book said there used to be millions of them."

"Another good example of something that seemed wise at the time turning out to be pure idiocy," Matthew commented. "The buffalo was the animal best suited to the land as it was. But the cattlemen wanted grazing land and the farmers wanted farm land and to them the buffalo were just in the way. I still say killing them off was one of the saddest events in this nation's history. Nothing made less sense," he finished with a deep frown.

"At least there are some left," J.J. offered.

"Ya," agreed the mule. "Thanks to a few wise folks here and down in Texas. They managed to save just barely enough to keep the species going. But now the herds are growing again and that's good news."

"Were they just bad people?" the little one queried.

"Oh, no. No. No. No," Matthew countered. "It's always dangerous, and frankly dumb, to judge people and events from one era by the standards of another.They were just people of their times; didn't know any better. Remember what I told you. People have to learn as they go along. Folly and genius; genius and folly. That's always been the human condition, and they're still nowhere near done. There's lots of work left to do."

"Ya," teased J.J. "As a puppy you did not know anything. I remember. And you sure weren't a born cowgirl," she added as she playfully swatted Angel's nose.

"Was too," Angel sniffed. "It's in my blood."

"She is getting to be pretty good," praised the mule. "Let's eat. You have your dinner and I'll find a good patch of grass."

Matthew rose to find a grazing spot while Angel opened a foil, took a portion, and passed it to her sister. J.J. did the same with the packet of dog food. After eating they cleaned up their trash and took the map back to the pack. Then they sprawled out on the sand to rest and talk. Matthew soon returned, informing them that he had found a carpet of fresh fodder and had eaten his fill.

"Now we're all fat and happy," Angel cooed.

"Mules don't get fat," Matthew cracked as if insulted. "We work too hard. Happy, yes. Fat, no, " he added as he flashed his huge, pearly teeth, hawed loudly, and twitched his long, pointed ears of greyish black.

The Kids laughed as the mule's good natured teasing. They knew that Scooter the mansion dog was right when he told them to listen to him.

"What's up for tomorrow?" J.J. quizzed as she looked toward Matthew.

"We'll get up early and cross the river before dawn," he answered. "Then we'll catch 64 and swing by Pawnee and Pawnee Bill's. After that we'll cut over to Stillwater."

"What's there?" Angel chirped.

"Nice town; pretty good sized. It's home to Oklahoma State University," the mule offered. "They're the Cowboys."

"Sounds like my kind of place," squeaked the little one as she smiled proudly, "as long as they allow cowgirls, too."

"They do," laughed Matthew. "Got a whole bunch of them."

"I want a cap," Angel demanded, remembering the people she had seen wearing them.

"Me, too," countered J.J. "Only I'll stay a Sooner."

"I guess there's just no peace in this state," the mule sighed as he tossed his massive head from side to side and chuckled loudly. "Now Sooners and Cowgirls, we'd better get some sleep. We'll need an early start tomorrow."

Matthew slid his massive body to the ground and rolled to his side. The Kids curled up together and laid their heads on his warm stomach.

"Great pillow," yawned the little one as her eyelids drooped.

"Can't beat it," agreed J.J. in a tired whisper.

"No charge," chuckled the mule.

A loud snort jolted the Kids to alertness as Matthew began to stir. Quickly they rose and stretched as the mule did the same. The predawn air carried the first true chill of their adventure.

"First real cold front," Matthew observed. "The others have just been teasers."

"Feels kind of nice," Angel piped. "Fall must really be here."

"Funny how things can change so quickly," J.J. mused.

"Fast as a fox," the mule offered with a twinkle in his eye.

The Kids said nothing but knew that Matthew was referring to their friend the Kit. They also knew that he would never admit it. To do so would be to acknowledge that he knew everything about them; the past, the present, and of greatest importance, the future.

"Let's get a drink and then why don't you two get everything ready while I scout the highway," the mule suggested.

"Right," Angel chirped as J.J. nodded in agreement.

Quickly the three sidled down to the river and drank deeply. Then Matthew ambled toward the road while the Kids loaded the pack. He soon returned and told them all was quiet.

"Not a car in sight," he stated with a smile. "Let's load up."

Matthew sank to his knees while the Kids climbed aboard. When secure he rose and began a quick walk through the brush toward the bridge. After one last look he stepped from dirt to concrete.

"Hang on tight," he yelled as he stepped up his gait to a fast trot. "We gotta move."

The still morning air broke with the clackety-clack of rock-hard hooves on asphalt as the mule shot for the opposite end. The Kids bounced on his back, straining mightily to keep their legs locked tightly around his upper ribcage. Far up ahead the faint lights of an early traveler pierced the dark curtain that shrouded the land. With one last lashing thrust Matthew cleared the bridge and quickly veered into the brush that lined the Arkansas's south side. Pulling to a rapid stop he looked back to see the truck dash by.

"You two okay?" he wheezed as he sucked hard to fill his lungs.

"Okay back here," J.J. huffed.

"That was quite a ride," the little one added. "J.J. might make a cowgirl yet."

"What do you mean 'might'," J.J. protested. "I did as well as you did."

"Naw, you had to hold on harder," Angel countered with a giggle. "I just glided along; no trouble at all."

"You both did great," Matthew laughed. "Now why don't you just slide off and give this old mule a break."

Matthew bent his knees and allowed the Kids to dismount, then the three headed down to the bank for some water. After drinking their fill they returned to a large clump of bushes near the highway and sat for a rest. In the east the first hint of light now announced a new day's coming.

"That's 64," Matthew informed them as he pointed to the U.S. highway running to the west. "That'll take us to Pawnee."

"Is it far?" Angel questioned.

"Not really," the mule answered. "Just a few hours unless the storm slows us down."

"What storm?" J.J. quizzed as she looked at the clear sky above. "There's not a cloud in sight."

"Take my word," Matthew assured her as he cocked his head to the west and took a deep sniff.

The Kids gave each other a puzzled look and just shrugged as the mule looked on in amusement. Finally he suggested that it was time to get moving. The Kids agreed.

"We'll walk awhile," J.J. stated as Angel nodded her approval. "We don't want to wear you out."

"I doubt you'll do that, Matthew chuckled. "Leg must be feeling better."

"Much," affirmed J.J. "I want to test it out."

"Besides," Angel squeaked. "We need the exercise after all this pampering."

"Ya," chortled J.J. "We don't want to get out of shape."

Matthew gave a loud guffaw and then started west down the flank of Highway 64 with the Kids walking alongside him. Behind them shone a new dawn's brightness. But in moments a bank of black began forming just ahead. Steadily it moved toward them as it chased away the sun's early rays.

"Looks like you were right, Matthew," confirmed the little one as she watched the leaden clouds creep closer.

"How did you know?" J.J. demanded.

"Just instinct," he explained. "Animals sense a lot of things that people don't. You've been in the house too long. A wild dog would know it, too."

"We should get out more," Angel deadpanned as she began to search for shelter. "Anyone see a good place to ride this out?"

As they looked, the first jagged jolts of lightning lanced downward, their bright spits daubing the land in eerie shades of yellowy-white. Matthew gave warning.

"No time for anything," he shot calmly but firmly. "Let's head for the little gully just below that rise," he finished as he pointed to a barren spot about fifty feet off the road.

Like the mule, the Kids knew that in a lightning storm lower meant better and trees could mean death. Quickly they scampered to the place Matthew had spotted. The first drops of rain began to splat as they curled up together; J.J. first, and then Angel who covered the pack with her body. Matthew then wrapped around them, his broad back facing the storm's biting gusts.

"Hang on Kids. This won't be long," the mule assured them, knowing that such forceful winds meant a fast moving system.

The rain quickened and thickened as the three huddled fast. But in minutes it slackened then stopped. The wind went with it, marching on east. Matthew on top looked up and then turned his head west. Sunlight splashed the prairie in brilliant orange. A rainbow rose in a gentle arc to the north.

"Not so bad," the mule chuckled as he struggled to his feet. "Pack get wet?"

"Just a little," Angel peeped as she uncovered her sister. "No damage though."

"We should look for some kind of tarp," J.J. remarked, "or at least a good piece of plastic."

"Wouldn't hurt," the little one agreed, "just in case we get caught out in the open again."

"That's good thinking," Matthew praised. "It never hurts to be prepared."

The three ambled back to near the highway and resumed their trek west. Soon the mule spied something stuck on a barbed-wire fence and went to take a look.

"Here's your cap," he laughed as he returned and dropped it on Angel's head. "Might have blown in all the way from Stillwater."

The Kids grinned as they looked it over; OSU in orange pressed on grey flannel. Angel put it on backwards to keep the bill from covering her eyes. J.J. pulled it down tightly and then nosed the little one's ribs.

"Boy do you look dumb," she teased.

"At least I have a cap," Angel boasted as she pointed her nose high with pride.

"Ya, I want one, too," pouted J.J. jealously.

"We'll find one for you, " promised the mule. "Then you can both look goofy."

J.J. brightened at the prospect and shared a laugh with the others. Then all were on the move once more. Through the morning they skirted Highway 64 toward Pawnee, reaching the edge of town just after noon. Here they stopped in a grove of oaks along Black Bear Creek for rest and a meal.

"Where does the word 'Pawnee' come from?" J.J. asked as Angel pulled a lunch from the pack.

"The Pawnee people," Matthew explained. "We're in their territory. It's an interesting place," he continued. "A lot of famous people come from here. I guess the best known is a man named Chester Gould. He created the Dick Tracy comic strip that was read worldwide.

"Who was Pawnee Bill," the little one quizzed, remembering Matthew's earlier reference to him.

"His real name was Gordon Lillie," the mule explained. "Years ago he had a Wild West Show that toured all over the U.S. and Europe. His home place is now a big museum. There's a lot of neat stuff there; even some buffalo."

"Close by?" mumbled a full-mouthed J.J.

"Yup; just to the south," the mule responded. "We'll swing by there on the way to Stillwater. You'll enjoy it."

"Sounds great," gushed the Kids together as they finished their meals.

"Why don't you two clean up and rest a bit while I find grub. Then we'll get going," Matthew suggested as he began to scout around for forage.

The Kids did as ordered while the mule ventured out to find a little lunch. Thirty minutes later he returned to find them dozing in the afternoon warmth. With a haw and a stomp of his hoof he woke them. After loading the pack they set off, swinging south to bypass the town, then picking up the highway once more. In a short time they came within sight of the massive stone gate that marked the entrance to the Pawnee Bill Ranch.

"Look at that gate!" Angel stammered as she studied the structure. "Let's go inside."

"Hold up there," warned Matthew. "There are people here this time of day. We'd better stay in the trees so no one will see us."

"Oh, ya," moaned the little one. "I just got a little excited."

"Easy to understand," the mule replied. "This is an exciting place."

"We can get a little closer," J.J. remarked, noting the good cover all around.

"Sure can," agreed Matthew. "Let's work our way over there," he added, pointing to a row of trees behind an old building.

The three circled from east to west and came to a stop behind Pawnee Bill's original ranchhouse, an old log and mud structure typical of its day. From there they could see the mansion now serving as the site's museum. Nearby was a beautifully restored red stage coach that had been a part of the show. "Pawnee Bill's Wild West" was stenciled in yellow on its side, just above the door. Near the gate was an observation tower made of stone which the Kids desperately wanted to climb but knew they couldn't at this time of day.

Matthew noted their disappointment and told them that one day they would be able to come back and see all the sites closeup. Then he suggested they follow the ranch road and look for buffalo. The Kids perked up at the idea and together they picked up the trail and followed it. Soon they came to several head of bison grazing on a little rise. Matthew took the lead and approached the mighty beasts. Looking up they tilted their heads and twitched their tails in greeting. The mule tapped the ground with a hoof to do likewise. Then all focused past the mule to the Kids standing just behind him. Matthew motioned the dogs forward. Walking abreast they moved to the front. The old bull stepped ahead of the others and studied the girls carefully. His eyes twinkled as a faint smile seemed to cross his face. With a slight nod he twice pawed the ground hard, turned, and with the others in tow trotted off.

"He knows about you two," the mule remarked. "That was a good luck sign."

"Why won't they talk?" Angel blubbered in exasperation.

"I told you they don't say much," chuckled the mule. "They'll have something to say when they figure there's something worth saying."

The Kids shook their heads in bewilderment as Matthew turned back toward the trees. The girls followed. After stopping at a little spring for a drink the mule advised that it was time to move on.

"Stillwater?" the little one asked.

"Yep," the mule replied. "Then we'll cut south and back to the east."

"East-west-west-east-south-north-north-south," complained J.J. "It seems like we're just going in circles."

"You want to see everything, don't you?" Matthew teased.

"Sure," confessed J.J., a little ashamed of her outburst.

"Well things don't always run in a straight line, whether it be this trip or life itself. Think of it all as kind of a road through the mountains. It has to follow the contours of the land and wind its way around. You can't always just cut right through."

"That sounds like school," Angel peeped.

"Exactly," complimented Matthew. "You might want to be a doctor but you have to study a whole lot of other things before you can get there; things that really have nothing to do with medicine."

"Like learning to read," J.J. popped.

"Yup, that's the start of everything," the mule smiled. "And on this trip you might have to go all sorts of places before you end up where you need to be."

"Ya," Angel scolded as she bopped her sister lightly on the nose. "We have no idea where we're supposed to go. Don't forget the rules. We do what the animals tell us. Do that and we'll be all right; at least I hope so."

"There you go," hawed Matthew. "You ready to get going?"

"Ready," the Kids answered.

"Then let's hit it," the mule cackled.

The three worked their way back to the south side of Highway 64 and followed it until late afternoon when they came to Highway 412, the Cimarron Turnpike. Here they trailed south to the Stillwater cutoff where they stopped. Settling in amongst the trees along a tiny creek they plopped to the ground for some much needed rest.

"Boy we've covered a lot of ground today," Matthew gurgled. "How's the leg holding up?"

"A little tight," J.J. admitted. "But not too bad."

"Well, tomorrow you'd better ride," the mule ordered. "You, too," he added as he nodded toward the little one.

"We don't want to wear you out," insisted Angel.

"Who, me!" he laughed. "I told you I walk better with riders. They keep me from bouncing so much; takes the strain off my knees."

The Kids knew that their friend was teasing but they were delighted by the idea of riding once again. Sitting up higher they could see more, although riding seemed about as tiring as walking.

"Different set of muscles," the mule informed them when they made the comment. Muscles you don't normally use as much. That's why you get tired; like some people get tired when they try to think," he finished with a flashy grin.

"Dogs, too," giggled the little one as she and her sister choked with laughter.

"Don't forget the mules," J.J. added.

"Mules, too," Matthew confessed, "as much as I hate to admit it."

"I guess we stay here tonight?" J.J. reasoned.

"Yup," the mule replied. "This is a good place; nice and quiet and covered. We'll have a good rest and then start out fresh in the morning."

"I guess we can't go through town," Angel sighed, disappointed that they would have to skirt it.

"Nope," Matthew agreed. "We can't let all those people see us. Now you two had better have a little dinner."

"Good idea," J.J. barked. "Veal sounds good."

Angel helped J.J. with the pack while the mule ventured out to graze. After pulling out the last of the meat and a pack of dog food, she sat down next to her sister and together they shared a good meal.

A hard day's work and a hearty meal soon sank the Kids. When their four-legged friend returned he found them curled up together, sleeping soundly. With a grin he rolled down beside them and did the same.

Well before dawn he arose to the sound of traffic on 412. With a gentle nudge he awakened the dogs.

"Let's get going my adventuresome pups," he whispered as he rolled to his hooves and wobbled to his feet.

The girls uncurled and stumbled upward, shaking and stretching to break sleep's grasp. Then all three ambled to the little creek for a morning drink. The air was chilled.

"Fall is really here," Angel quipped.

"Sure is," confirmed J.J. "Where do we go now?" she continued as she turned to Matthew.

"Well, we're going to have to cross the Cimarron sometime. We could just shoot south on 177 but that's a major highway. I think it'd be better and safer to work our way east on 51 and then cross the river on a quieter road. There are a couple not too far away. Why don't you load up your gear and climb aboard."

The Kids returned to their camping spot and did as Matthew ordered. Then he fell to his knees to let them mount. When secure on his back they gave the signal and off he went. With a quick skip he was across the highway and heading east. The sky's slight brightening told them a new day was near.

Soon they picked up Highway 51 and set a course straight into the first orange rays now spilling over the horizon. By midmorning they crossed Highway 108 where they stopped for a brief rest. Lunchtime brought them to Highway 18 where empty stomachs commanded they halt. Matthew found a clump of high brush where he sunk to the ground and the Kids slid off.

"This is good cover," he noted as he peered back toward the road.

"Not bad at all," agreed the girls together as J.J. slipped off the pack and opened it.

"What's around here, Matthew?" Angel asked as she took a little food from her sister.

"Well, Jim Thorpe's home is just down the road at Yale," the mule answered as he pointed east down Highway 51.

"Jim Thorpe?" quizzed J.J. "Who's he?"

"Oh, nobody special," Matthew deadpanned, "just the greatest athlete of his time."

"Really!" the Kids exclaimed.

"Yup. A Sac and Fox Indian who could scoot like a deer. He ran track and played football for the Carlisle Indian School in Pennsylvania. Then he went to the Olympics in Stockholm in 1912 and stole the show; won a slew of gold medals. The King of Sweden called him the world's greatest athlete. But he wasn't through there. After that he played pro baseball and then switched to football. He really did make professional football go when a whole bunch of folks thought it wouldn't. I really don't think the world has ever seen another quite like him. And he came from just down there," Matthew finished as he pointed towards Yale.

"This state seems to put out a lot of fine athletes," J.J. remarked, remembering some of the others they had read about.

"Whole bunch," confirmed the mule. "But there are plenty of brains here as well."

"Is the river close?" Angel asked.

"Just a few miles," Matthew answered. "Sometimes the water's low. Maybe we can wade across and not have to risk the bridge in daylight."

"That'd be great," J.J. barked.

The Kids shared a pack of dog food while Matthew chomped away at a patch of grass. Then he returned to pick up the Kids who were packed and waiting.

"Finished already?" he snorted as he dropped to his knees.

"Ready to go," the little one chirped.

"All right then, all aboard."

The Kids crawled onto Matthew's back and gave him a tap to let him know they were ready. Then, after a quick check for traffic, he crossed over Highway 51 and began to move south along the western side of 18. In an hour they reached the Cimarron and, much to their delight, found it low and easily fordable. Reaching the southern bank he shimmied up the slope and walked straight into someone's old camping spot. There they found a cooler that someone had left behind. Sitting on the cooler was a crimson cap with the letters 'OU' stamped in white on the front.

"There you go," the mule chortled. "Looks like this is your day."

Matthew dropped to his knees and the Kids hit the ground. J.J. quickly grabbed the cap in her mouth and flipped it back over her head. Angel turned it around and pulled it down tightly.

"Okay, now, no fighting," the mule warned as he tried to keep a straight face.

The Kids just giggled as J.J. suggested they check the cooler. Inside they found two packs of bologna still cool from the water of the melted ice.

"Oh, boy," J.J. whooped. "Food and my cap."

"Shaping up to be a pretty good day," Angel squealed.

"So far," Matthew agreed.

Angel placed the meat in the pack and then the Kids climbed once more onto the mule's broad back. They set out south again. Not far ahead lie Cushing.

"What's in Cushing?" J.J. asked as she read the road sign.

"Major oil and gas distribution center," Matthew replied. "One of the most important in the country."

"Is that what those pipelines are for?" the little one questioned, noting how many she and J.J. had seen along the way.

"Yep," affirmed the mule. "Those lines crisscross the country and a whole bunch of them connect right around here."

"Must be a lot of work to lay those pipes," surmised J.J.

"Lot of work and a whole lot of money," laughed Matthew. "But the country couldn't survive a week without them. Everything would come to a halt if those pipelines shut down."

The trio soon reached the northern edge of Cushing and turned east to bypass the town. They then came to Highway 33 and cut toward Drumright. Just before dark they hit the Highway 99 intersection just a few miles east of the town. Here they found a nice, quiet pasture and stopped for the night.

"We sure hoofed it today," Matthew wheezed as he dropped to the ground.

"Sure did," confirmed the little one as she slid off his back and hit the dirt.

"Or at least Matthew did," corrected J.J., a little embarrassed that the mule had done most of the work.

"There's water close by," Matthew informed them as he tilted his head upward and sniffed. "Put down the stuff and we'll go find it."

The Kids did as ordered and the three cut off through the field. Just as the mule had said they found a small tank just over a rise and drank deeply.

"I can't remember the last time we drank from the bottles," quipped J.J., noting how lucky they had been to find water at every stop.

"Well you hang on to them," the mule lectured. "You'll need them sooner or later. And always keep them full."

"Oh, we will," assured the little one. "You can count on that."

The three returned to their campsite where Angel pulled out the last of the dog food from Marland Mansion and a little bologna. Matthew spotted a cattle barn nearby and decided to look for a meal there.

"I sure miss that quail," sighed the little one as she swallowed a bite and then licked her lips.

"Ya, bologna's really a step down," J.J. laughed.

"It's still a step up from regular dog food," Angel quipped as she swatted at her sister's new cap.

"It's a good thing Matthew doesn't eat meat," woofed J.J. "He'd clean us out in a few bites."

"It's a wonder there's any grass left in Oklahoma," joshed the little one. "As much as he eats."

The mule returned just as the Kids were cleaning up and sank to his knees beside them. With a wide grin he informed them that he had found a whole sack of fine horse feed and had helped himself.

"Beats plain old grass, doesn't it," barked J.J.

"Every time," hawed the mule.

"What do we do tomorrow?" Angel asked.

"We'll trail south toward Interstate 40 and the North Canadian," Matthew answered. "Then we'll see from there."

"We really do appreciate how much you've helped us," J.J. cooed. "You're a great friend."

"Hey, I'm having the time of my life," Matthew blurted. "Seeing good country with good company. You can't beat it. I'm the happiest mule north of the Red."

The Kids beamed at the thought of Matthew being so pleased. They could not believe their good fortune in finding him. Still, deep down inside, they knew that the day would come when he would have to leave them. Then they would be on their own once more. Success in their mission would mean staying sharp and tough.

"We haven't looked at the map and the book in a long time," chirped the little one.

"Who needs to with Matthew around," joked J.J. in return.

"Oh, no," countered the mule with a hard shake of his head."I don't know everything. Why don't you pull them out and let me have a look."

Angel skipped to the pack and retrieved both, then returned. After unfolding the atlas, the three pinpointed their location.

"We're nearly back to Route 66," chirped the little one, as she traced the line just to the south that paralleled I-44.

"Heard you saw part of that road by rail," the mule hooted.

"How did you know that?" J.J. barked. "We never told you about the train trip."

"Now where did I hear that?" Matthew chuckled as he scratched his head.

Matthew gave each a nuzzle from his massive nose, laughed, and then turned his attention back to the map.

"Well let's see here," he spoke as the Kids crowded in. "Just about forty miles nearly due east is Okmulgee."

"That's the capital of the Creek Nation," Angel interrupted as she read from the book she had just opened. "Okmulgee" means 'boiling water' in the Creek language."

"Really," exclaimed the mule. "I didn't know that."

"See there's a little he doesn't know," giggled J.J. as she patted Matthew on the back."

There's a lot I don't know," confessed the mule once more. "Anyway, just a short skip south from Okmulgee is Henryetta, an important crossroads where I-40 and U.S. 75 meet and the starting point of the Indian Nation Turnpike. It runs south to Hugo near the Texas border."

"Henryetta," the little one read. "That's where Jim Shoulders is from."

"Jim Shoulders?" J.J. quizzed.

"One of the all time great rodeo cowboys," the little one explained.

"Didn't know that either," the mule acknowledged as he continued to study the map. "East of Henryetta is Checotah along Lake Eufaula. It's the biggest lake in the state; over 100,000 acres."

"That's huge!" barked J.J. "What feeds it?"

"The two Canadians; north and south," answered Matthew. "Eufaula is where they meet."

"Makes sense," reasoned J.J. "I'll bet there are a bunch of nice parks around it."

"Quite a few," the mule confirmed as he studied the map. "Arrowhead is the one that stands out. It must be a big one."

"The book says that just north of Checotah on U.S. 69 is Rentiesville," Angel read. "It was founded right after the Civil War and was one of the first black settlements in Oklahoma. There are others, too; Taft, and Boley, and Langston, to name just a few."

"U.S 69 is pretty much the old Texas Trail," Matthew informed them.

"Where does it cross the Red?" J.J. questioned.

"Just below Durant at Colbert's," the mule answered. "You'll need to go there before you're through."

"And after that?" Angel asked.

"We'll see," he hawed. "We'll see."

"Oh, come on, tell us," begged the two together.

"All in good time," he hedged. "All in good time."

The Kids pouted at his refusal to tell them what lie ahead but knew by now that he had a reason for everything. Information would only come in dribbles from this wise mule. Turning back to the map the three began to explore the routes and territory to the south and west. Matthew suggested they stay on 99 and work their way south to Seminole. With that Angel returned the map and book to the pack and all settled in for a well earned rest.

Before dawn they arose and resumed their march down Highway 99, staying about a hundred yards off the road to avoid being seen. Today the Kids walked, giving the mule a break. Darkness still cloaked the land when they crossed I-44, the Turner Turnpike. As the sun spewed out its first yellow flashes they pushed past the town of Stroud. Soon they came to the same railroad tracks they had traveled earlier in their journey.

"Sure would be nice to hop a ride again," J.J. laughed as they stepped over the rails.

"I'll bet that was fun," Matthew chuckled.

"Sure was," confirmed the little one. "We had a great time, at least until the end when we got locked in a car."

"How'd you get out?" the mule inquired.

"Canine ingenuity," J.J. woofed.

As they walked J.J. explained the whole affair. After hearing the story Matthew shook his head in disbelief and expressed his deep admiration for their creative powers.

"It's amazing what you can do when you have to," he bubbled.

"And how you can turn just about anything into a tool," Angel added.

"That, too," acknowledged their friend. "In fact, when you think about it, some of the greatest work has been done with the simplest tools. It's really the mind that matters most. Everything springs from that."

"Right now my mind says breakfast," the little one peeped.

"Mine, too," affirmed J.J.

"The Deep Fork's not far ahead," advised Matthew. "That'll be a good place to stop. I could do with a chew myself."

In less than an hour they reached the Deep Fork of the Canadian and stopped for a break. The road sign told them that here State Highway 99 was also U.S. 377.

"Funny how so many roads have two numbers," Angel quipped as she helped her sister with the pack. "We've seen it so often before."

"Sometimes federal and state roads overlap," Matthew offered. "It's not uncommon."

"Why do they call some 'turnpikes'? J.J. questioned.

"They're toll roads," Matthew began. "You have to pay to use them."

"Why?" the little on queried.

"It's a quick way to get them built. Sometimes there's no money in the budget for a needed road so they borrow the money to do it by selling what are called 'bonds'. The toll charges are then used to pay off the bonds," he explained.

"Then the road is free once the bonds are paid off," reasoned J.J.

"Supposedly," Matthew smiled. "But not always. Will Durant, one of the world's great historians, once said that one of life's few impossibilities was giving government more money than it could spend."

"Like trying to give a dog more food than he can eat," laughed the Kids together.

"Something like that," hawed the mule.

Matthew excused himself to look for some good grazing while the girls pulled out some bologna and the last few bits of dog food. After a light breakfast they sprawled out on the ground to await Matthew's return.

"Find anything good?" J.J. asked as he plodded back into camp.

"Yup. Hit a good little patch," he answered as he folded down beside them. "Sure do miss that good horse feed though."

"We miss the smoked salmon and quail, too," giggled Angel.

"Endure we must," pronounced J.J. solemnly as she rose and arched her head toward the sky.

All had a hearty laugh and then prepared to set off once more. After loading up and drinking from a cool pool of the Deep Fork they resumed their journey south. Midafternoon brought them to the the little town of Prague at the Highway 62 junction, a turn-of-the-century community founded by Czech immigrants. Near dark they reached the bank of the North Canadian just above Interstate 40.

"Call it a day, Kids?" Matthew puffed as he surveyed the ground looking for a good place to camp.

"I'm ready," J.J. coughed as she sidled up to the mule.

"That looks like a good spot," the little one huffed as she pointed her nose toward a soft spot of sand beneath a large cottonwood.

"Looks great," agreed J.J. and Matthew together.

The three tired travelers shuffled the short distance to the site and, after dropping the pack, fell to the ground. The last of an early autumn sun cast a sparkling yellow tinge over the river's low, muddy waters. A crisp wind whipped in from the north to cool and soothe them. Just upstream a weathered old barn graced the crest of the bank. Down river there was no sign of man, just the sand ,the shrubs, the weeds and the trees, their leaves now fast-turning to obey the commands of a changing season.

"It's almost nippy," J.J. woofed as the three slid down the low bank towards water.

"Well, I think we've turned to October," Matthew remarked as he waded into the shallows along the shore.

"River sure seems dry," Angel noted as she looked out over the sand toward the opposite bank. "Just a few ripples here and there."

"Dry summer," advised the mule. "Fall rains should fill it some. If we get them," he added. "Don't always."

"Seems to be feast or famine with rain," observed J.J. "And you never know which."

"Totally unpredictable ," concurred Matthew as he shimmied back up the bank with the Kids following. "Why don't you two break out your dinner while I'll check out that old barn."

The Kids returned to their spot and pulled out the bologna while the mule worked his way upstream and uphill to the barn While they ate they watched for his return. The day's last shimmers shadowed his march back to them about ten minutes later. In his jaws he carried a large sack which he dropped at their feet.

"This will hold you for a while," he quipped as the girls eyed the bag. "A little plain old crunchy dog food. Nothing fancy but good for you."

"Was that in the barn?" J.J. asked as she looked inside the half full sack.

"Yep," he answered. "In a can. Must be for the cow dog."

"Great," gushed the two. "What about you?"

"Nothing for me," he admitted. "Did find a few bites of feed in a trough but the horses must have pretty much cleaned it out."

"We're sorry for you," sighed the little one.

"No problem," Matthew sniffed with a wave of a hoof. "I'll be fine."

The Kids scooped out a few pawfuls and crunched down on the tasty nuggets. After eating their fill they closed up the sack and placed it next to the pack. Nearby Matthew found a good clump of grass and filled himself.

"Good grass. Just doesn't stick to you like feed," he chuckled as he returned to the Kids.

"We'll look hard for something for you tomorrow," promised Angel as she laid her chin on the now chilly ground.

"No need," protested the mule. "I do fine on grass; would like a nice fresh apple though. Call it dessert," he finished with a broad smile.

The Kids shared a laugh with the mule and then the three tucked in for the night. The early autumn chill drew them close together with both snuggling up against Matthew's soft, warm stomach.

As was their custom they arose well before first light. There was another bridge to cross and just beyond that a major highway.

"No reason to muddy ourselves up crossing the bottom," Matthew reckoned as he and the girls drank at the nearby pool of river water. "We'll just take the bridge. I'll carry today. I'm feeling frisky."

"Are you sure?" questioned the little one.

"Sure I'm sure," he grinned. "I told you I walk better with baggage."

The Kids were glad to have a ride. J.J.'s leg had tightened up some and both were a little tired and stiff from so much walking. Returning to their spot they loaded their gear as the mule kneeled to receive them. When securely aboard he rose and moved toward the bridge. A quick check in both directions showed no traffic. Quickly he hit the structure and broke into a swift trot that in less than a minute took them across. Safely on the opposite side he moved back into the brush along the road and struck south. In minutes they reached Interstate 40 where he scampered through the underpass to clear it. Safely passed he moved off the road and resumed the trek south.

"You're in the Seminole Nation now," Matthew informed the Kids. "The whole of Seminole County; everything from here to the South Canadian."

"Is Seminole the county seat?" Angel quizzed.

"Nope That's Wewoka, the county seat and tribal headquarters," the mule informed them. "It's not far to the southeast. We'll swing by there."

"Didn't I see a couple of other big towns on the map not too far from here?" asked J.J., thinking back to their studies the previous night.

"Yup, to the west," affirmed Matthew. "Shawnee and Tecumseh."

"Tecumseh rings a bell," squeaked the little one as she recollected some of their reading.

"Great Shawnee leader," the mule replied.

"Must have been if they named a town for him," J.J. surmised.

"Maybe someday you'll have one named after you," Matthew teased. "J.J. ville."

"How about Angel's Heights," the little one added.

"Good name, too," approved the mule.

"She does want to be president of something," snickered J.J.

"Well everybody should be some sort of president at least once in life," the mule cackled. "Or at least have a town named after them. I do in Texas."

"What?" inquired the Kids together. "Matthewtown?"

"Naw. Muleshoe," he hawed as he gave them his toothiest grin.

"Oh, look," squeaked the little one as she stifled a giggle. "Town up ahead; another highway, too."

The three stopped to check their surroundings. Just ahead lay the hamlet of Little at the intersection of 99A.

"I wonder what the A stands for?" asked J.J.

"Alternate," replied the mule. "Usually just means another route to the same place."

"Oh," quipped J.J. "Thanks."

Quickly skirting the town the three moved on south. By midmorning they came to the northern reaches of Seminole, a city of about 7000. Here they swung to the east once more and after a short while crossed Highway 9, a major east/ west route through Oklahoma's southern half. Another hour brought them to U.S. 270, the main route into Wewoka. Here they stopped, taking cover behind a low rise just off the roadway.

"Relay station," Matthew joked as he dropped down to let them off.

"Relay station?" the Kids asked as they slid to the ground.

"Don't you remember your western movies?" the mule teased them. "A relay station was where the stagecoach stopped to change tired horses and allow the passengers to rest a bit."

"Oh," laughed the little one. "I don't remember ever seeing that?"

"You would if they still made good movies like they used to," Matthew lamented. "Good westerns are hard to come by nowadays. Too bad."

"They need to get cracking at Pawnee Bill's or the Tallgrass again," J.J. barked.

"Sure do," Matthew agreed as Angel nodded likewise.

Not far away the mule spotted what looked to be a little tank and all three skipped over for a drink. Then he found a bale of hay near a little shed and munched away while the Kids returned to their spot to await the mule's return.

"Sure is awesome country," the little one observed as she looked around at the surrounding hills spotted with oak and hickory and even the occasional pine.

"Ranches look pretty," added J.J., thinking about the years of hard work that went into making them so.

"Yep," concurred the little one. "It almost looks like each blade of grass is tended by hand. It's all so neat and tidy."

"Here comes Matthew," J.J. barked.

"Did you get your fill?" the little one queried as he drew near.

"Sure did," he puffed. "Good, wet, fresh-cut hay. Now if I could just find that apple."

"We're bound to find one sooner or later," J.J. promised with a giggle. "Just hang on."

"What's next?" the little one asked as the mule fell down beside them.

"Wewoka then on to Holdenville," he answered.

"Wewoka's only eight miles," J.J. stated, noting the sign they had seen just before stopping. "We'll be there in no time."

"Ready to push on?" Matthew asked.

"Ready," the girls affirmed together.

The Kids loaded the pack and then Matthew buckled his knees to let them mount. Once snug and tight he jolted forward and then ambled slowly alongside 270. In a few hours they reached Wewoka and swung to the north to miss the town, passing by the Seminole Nation Museum on the way.

"I can't count the number of museums we've already passed," J.J. remarked. "You could spend a lifetime just trying to cover them all."

"Oklahoma's full of them," replied Matthew as he turned his head back toward the girls. "If they just had a Mule Museum. That'd round it all out."

"What about dogs?" protested Angel with a loud sniff.

"Well, okay; one of those, too," conceded the mule with a chuckle.

"That's better," hooted J.J. as she patted Matthew on the side.

By late afternoon the trio came to Holdenville, the county seat of Hughes County. Swinging south they picked up Highway 48 and, in the fading light, followed it to the northern bank of the South Canadian just downstream from its juncture with Oklahoma's other Little River. Here, exhausted, they stopped for the night, making camp under the bridge.

"What a day," huffed J.J. as she slid off Matthew's back.

"All the way from the North Canadian to the South," wheezed the little one as she did the same.

"More than thirty miles," Matthew coughed. "Pretty fair walk."

The last flickers of daylight beamed in from the west as the trio stumbled down to the river for water. As they drank they could hear a car bouncing on the bridge above. Just as it neared the northern end they heard a loud clunking sound, followed by the thud of a large box hitting the ground below the bridge.

"Huh," laughed the mule. "Must have fallen off the luggage rack."

The three walked to the box and J.J. nosed it upright. Bound shut by one long strand of stout rope, she worked to open it.

"Give me a paw," J.J. ordered as the little one grabbed one side of the knot firmly in her mouth.

"There we go," J.J. grinned as she pulled the other and untied it. "What do we have here?"

Opening the flaps she began to pull out the box's contents; clothing on top, including two thick, burgundy colored sweaters, a tin of ham, some cookies, and at the very bottom, a small paper bag. Inside it she found three large, shiny bright red apples.

"Hey, buddy. You're in luck," J.J. hooted as she placed the apples on the ground in front of Matthew.

"Mmmmm, boy!" the mule glowed as he crunched down on one. "Absolutely delicious," he added as the sweet apple juice dripped down his lower lip.

As Matthew devoured the other two apples the Kids looked at the clothing. The sweaters seemed extremely fine and Angel fished out the flashlight to have a better look. Pointing the light at the labels she read the words: "Miss Jackson's-Tulsa."

"Must be an elegant clothing store," J.J. reckoned as she ran her nose over the soft cashmere.

"Must be," agreed the little one.

"You better hold on to those," Matthew cautioned. "It might get really cold before you're through."

"Ya," nodded the little one, noting how in this part of the country the weather could turn savage in a matter of minutes. "We'd better save the rope, too. It might come in handy."

"Good thinking," praised J.J. and Matthew together.

The Kids carefully folded the sweaters and placed them in the bag. Then they turned to the tin of ham. Angel held it firmly while J.J. pulled the tab and peeled back the top. The sweet smell sent them drooling. J.J. pulled the meat from the can, tore off a large chunk, and passed it to her sister. Then she jerked one for herself. After each had had two more helpings J.J. returned the ham to its tin and pulled out some nuggets which she shared with Angel. While they finished supper the mule topped off his apples with some grass from the river bluff. Then he returned and in no time all three collapsed from fatigue and full stomachs. After a few brief words all eyes snapped shut. Angel dreamt deeply.

Dawn's first rays slithered under the bridge and awakened the Kids, now huddled together against the morning chill. Rising stiffly but quickly they yawned then stretched then looked around. Matthew was gone.

"Must be out grazing," J.J. reasoned.

"No," cried the little one. "He's gone for good. I saw it in my dream last night. That strange white animal came and Matthew went with her. I could see them almost gliding together over the hills."

"That was just your imagination," scoffed J.J. "He wouldn't leave without saying good-bye," she argued.

"He did say good-bye," countered Angel, wiping tears from her eyes as she pointed to the box. "Look."

The girls stumbled to the box and focused on the paper attached to its top. It was a letter from Matthew.

Dear Kids,

Words can never express how much I've enjoyed our travels but it's time for an old mule to rest. I have to say that you two are the pluckiest pair of dogs I've ever known. I have no doubt that your intelligence and spirit will guide you to success in this quest and in all others that might follow. Always remember the words: 'By Endurance We Conquer'. That means to never give up no matter how tough things get.

Now take the river downstream to the next highway and cross the old bridge. Then trail south to the Blue and find the eagle. He'll tell you where to go from there. Good luck.

Your best friend always,
Matthew

The Kids finished the letter and then Angel, fighting back tears, carefully folded it and placed it in the pack. Then she gently pawed the pouch around her neck, thinking back to her dream, if it was a dream.

"Well," J.J. mumbled glumly, "at least we had him for a good long while."

"Yup," seconded the little one. "But I sure am going to miss him."

"We learned so much," sighed J.J.

"He taught us a lot," Angel agreed. "But maybe the eagle will be just as smart."

"Well, let's go look for him," J.J. barked.

Silently the girls loaded the pack and strapped it to J.J.'s back. Then they walked. Not far downstream they turned to take one last look at the bridge where they had lost their friend, wheeled once more and marched. The rusty dirt of the South Canadian dusted up behind them.

THE EAGLE

"Looks like we'll have to go up," J.J. remarked as she eyed the sheer wall of the riverbank stretching for nearly a hundred yards ahead.

"Or down," countered the little one. "The bed's nearly dry here. We can walk through it. It's not far."

"Would be easier," admitted J.J. as she stared up at the high climb. "Let's do that."

The Kids skittered down the bank to the bed and proceeded through the squishy red sand that topped it. Each step left a deep print.

"Looks like we're not alone," Angel joked as she studied the string of animal tracks that dotted their roadway.

"Yup," confirmed J.J. "Lots of critters come through here."

"I'm going to get a quick drink," Angel chirped.

J.J. watched as her sister hopped toward a shallow pool of water about thirty feet away. In a flash she sensed danger. The mud around the water looked different; more spongy; more like a thick red soup than ground. "No, Angel!" she yelled. "Get back!"

But it was too late. The little one began to sink. In a panic she quickly turned and furiously pawed the muck to gain a firm foothold. But each lunge forced her down more deeply. In seconds she had sunk to her chest. J.J. shed the pack and first ran as close as she could toward her sister, carefully pawing the ground for firmness at each step. More than five feet away she had to stop as the earth quaked beneath her heavy paws.

"The rope!" shrieked the little one. "Get the rope!"

In an instant J.J. rushed back to the pack and pulled out the rope that had wrapped the box. It was long enough if she could just find a way for Angel to secure it around her. Frantically she looped one end to form a large lasso, knotting it down with her powerful jaws.Then she turned to see her sister now nearly up to her neck in muck. With a hard thrust she tossed the loop toward Angel's head and missed, the lasso falling a foot off the mark. Once more she tried and once more she failed. The third try was a ringer, the looped end falling perfectly around her sister's head. Quickly inching away, she tugged the loop tight. Angel gasped as her windpipe constricted. With a mighty jerk J.J. lurched backwards, digging her powerful legs deep into the sand. Angel rose slightly, her pink tongue shooting out from her mouth as she gagged on the loop, her deep brown eyes rolling into near unconsciousness. Step by painful step J.J. strained. Inch by choking inch Angel slid toward her. Finally, in one last supreme effort of will, J.J. dug in and tugged with all her strength. Wheezing for air and muscles burning with stress she saw Angel's front legs pull free from the sinkhole and reach dry ground. One more slight jerk and her back legs followed. Dropping the rope she ran to her sister and dragged her several more feet from danger. Then she collapsed beside her.

For more than ten minutes the Kids did not move. Caked in slimy red mud, Angel lie still, working hard to draw fresh breath into her empty lungs. Aching all over, J.J. wheezed and coughed as she did the same. Finally they stirred and stumbled to their feet.

"Boy, that was close," J.J. hacked. "How do you feel?"

"Awful," confessed the little one as she too sucked hard to breathe. "You?"

"Same," replied her sister with a gasping laugh. "Even worse than you look, and that's bad. You're a mess."

"Ya," the little one sighed. "I'm a red dog now," she finished as she looked herself over.

"Maybe you should change your name to Rusty," J.J. cracked. "Now let's get you cleaned up."

"I'm ready," she admitted. "but I think I'll find another pool."

"That'd be wise," hooted J.J. "This time be a little more observant."

The Kids moved back closer to the bank and walked downstream about twenty yards. Here the river channel cut closer. After checking the ground and removing the pouch, Angel inched her way into the cool water and washed away the red. J.J. watched and couldn't help think about how her sister had always tried so hard to avoid taking baths at home.

"First bath you ever liked," joshed J.J. as Angel emerged from the water.

"First one I ever really needed," countered the little one with a grin.

Angel retrieved the pouch and gently washed away the mud from its lower half. Then she returned it to her neck. That done the two walked back to the pack. J.J. wound up the rope and placed it back inside.

After cleaning up the Kids set out, following the riverbed for a short distance until the bank flattened out once more. In less than an hour they came to the Highway 75/270 bridge. A closer look revealed a second bridge just beyond the first.

"Two bridges," J.J. remarked. "Matthew said to cross the old one."

"Must be the second one," observed Angel as she studied the structures. "It looks ancient."

"Must be," agreed J.J.

The Kids hugged the red dirt road which ran under the first bridge until they came to the second. Called the Calvin Bridge, it was named for the small town just across the river to the south.

"Wow, look at this!" Angel exclaimed as she studied the massive steel structure that spanned the South Canadian.

"Ancient is right," barked J.J. as she read the sign. "Built in 1919. That's nearly ninety years ago."

"They sure did this one right," cooed the little one as she carefully eyed the solid construction. "I'll bet it'll be here ninety years from now."

"Good bet," J.J. concurred. "Too bad they don't make the new ones as pretty. This bridge has class."

"Well, let's get going," Angel advised.

After checking for traffic the Kids swiftly skipped across the bridge and into a thicket on the south bank. Here they stopped briefly to take a look at the map and take a sip of water. Their tracking told them they were on Old Highway 75. They would later find it to be one of Oklahoma's best kept secrets; lightly traveled but delightfully scenic. To the north lie small towns like Horntown, Wetumka, and Weleetka; to the south Coalgate and then Atoka on Muddy Boggy Creek at the U.S. 69 intersection. Due east on U.S. 270 was McAlester, an important city at the junction of 69 and the Indian Nation Turnpike. Nearby at Savannah was the U.S. Army Ammunition Plant. Some thirty miles to the southwest down State Highway 1 was Ada, another large university town at the northern tip of the Chickasaw Turnpike. Finally they located the Blue River far to the south.

"Long way to the river," J.J. commented, remembering Matthew's instructions to go there.

"Yup, but it looks like we'll see a lot of neat places along the way," noted Angel as she folded the map.

"Sure should," agreed her sister. "Ready?"

"Let's go," chirped the little one.

Just as they began to exit the thicket a white van appeared on the highway. Slowing to a crawl it left the main road and steered onto the dirt track which flanked the Kids' hiding place. Scampering back into the brush the girls huddled down and watched.

"It's Silver!" J.J. whispered excitedly as she read the sign on the van's side.

"Look over there!" Angel ordered as she pointed back to the bridge's north side.

Lumbering slowly toward them over the old structure was another car; the county commisioner's. Soon it cleared the span and pulled alongside Rob Silver's van. Then each man got out. After taking a quick look around they began to talk. The Kids strained to hear them.

"Looks like we're still in the clear," the commissioner cackled as he spit into the wind and grinned broadly. "It's time I take it out west."

"Just what I was thinking," confirmed Silver. "We'll just lie low for a little bit longer and then unload it. Show me where you're taking it," he finished as he cracked open his map and spread it on the hood of his car.

The Kids squirmed to catch a glimpse as the commissioner pointed to the spot but could see nothing from so far away. J.J. softly huffed in disgust, knowing that it they could only see they could solve the puzzle right then and there. But it was not to be.

"Great spot," praised Silver as he folded the map. "An eagle couldn't find it way out there."

"An eagle," mumbled Angel as she looked toward her sister, knowing that their next task was to find one.

"Yep," J.J. whispered softly, still mad about not being able to get even a glance at the map.

The Kids hovered low as the two men talked for a few more minutes and then quickly transferred the loot from the van to the car. Then both quickly sped away in different directions.

"Well, at least we know that it's not in the van anymore," J.J. spoke as she watched Silver disappear over the nearby hill.

"Ya, but where exactly is he taking it?" sighed the little one. "He could be going just about anywhere and by the way they were talking we don't have much time."

"I know," answered J.J. "And if they sell it before we can find it......" she added, failing to finish the sentence.

"Then we're out of luck," Angel pouted as she finished it for her sister.

"That's right," J.J. concurred. "But we haven't come so far and worked so hard to lose now. We'll beat them to it yet," she spat through tightly clenched jaws.

"Right," barked the little one in a low, forceful tone rare for her. "Let's get moving!"

Silently the girls struck south on Old 75, scurrying off the road only at the sight of the occasional car. Near nightfall they crossed Highway 3 just outside the town of Coalgate. Pressing on in near darkness they reached the town and found a good spot to hide in an empty garage near the Mining Museum.

"We must be in coal mining country," J.J. surmised.

"Very astute," Angel teased. "Coalgate in Coal County."

"That is a dead giveaway, isn't it," J.J. laughed.

Angel helped her sister remove the pack and then the two went to a nearby little draw for a drink. Thirsts quenched, they returned to their spot. After eating Angel retrieved the book, map, and flashlight and sprawled out next to J.J.

"Let me see here," Angel mused as she flipped the pages. "Coalgate. Ah, here we go."

"This used to be a major coal producing area but the mines played out a long time ago. Now it is more ranching and agriculture. There's still a lot of coal farther north and east, over around Stringtown and on into Pittsburg County."

"That's McAlester; right?" J.J. asked.

"Right," confirmed the little one.

"What's south?" J.J. asked as she pointed the light at the map.

"A few little towns, Phillips and Lehigh," Angel answered as she studied. "Then we hit 69 again at Atoka. Looks like a pretty good sized town."

"The Texas Trail again," J.J. commented. "What a story that road could tell if it could talk."

"Yup," agreed the little one. "Probably enough history to fill ten volumes."

"Ten big, thick volumes," chuckled J.J.

"Atoka was named for a Choctaw leader," Angel read on. "And there was a Civil War battle fought nearby; the Battle of Middle Boggy. It's also just about exactly halfway between Tulsa and Dallas."

"Bet there's a lot of traffic through there," reasoned J.J.

"After Atoka comes Durant," Angel went on. "Just below the Blue."

"That's where we're headed," J.J. woofed. "Doesn't look too far."

"Nope; maybe thirty-five from Atoka," Angel affirmed as she checked the mileage scale. "We should get there tomorrow without any trouble."

"Sure wish we knew exactly where to find the eagle," sighed J.J., remembering their instructions.

"Don't worry," Angel soothed as she patted her sister's nose. "He'll show up."

J.J. nodded in agreement as Angel returned the things to the pack. Then they curled up together on the cool dirt floor and quickly fell asleep. In her dreams Angel saw a mighty bird of prey soaring majestically high above. She knew the eagle was near.

Dawn broke grey and damp and cold. Each red ray fought hard to pierce the gloom. The Kids awoke together, each taking a quick peek to see the other stirring. Rising as one, they shook off the chill and ambled to the draw for a morning sip. Refreshed, they returned to their spot, closed the pack and strapped it to J.J.'s back. A quick check of their surroundings sent them on a slight circle east to avoid the town. They zipped across Highways 131 and then 43 before picking up 75 once more. By midmorning they reached its juncture with U.S. 69 just north of Atoka.

"End of the road," Angel chirped. "No more Old 75."

"A nice road," J.J. added. "Too bad."

"Yup," affirmed the little one. "I guess we should swing a little west around the city."

"Makes sense," agreed J.J. "It looks like the land is starting to flatten out some that way. It'll make for easier walking."

"Right," peeped Angel.

The Kids swung south and west and soon crossed Highway 7, a major road that ran from Atoka to Lawton in the far west. This was cattle country; a wide open expanse of well tended, thick grass pastures and red-banked tanks. Boggy Depot State Park lies just to the west.

Midafternoon brought them to Clear Boggy Creek where they took a break. Settling in to a thick stand of trees along the creek's northern bank, J.J. shed the pack while Angel scouted around.

"Watch out for the mud," J.J. teased as the little one moved toward the green water.

"Got ya," shouted Angel as she turned and flashed a wide grin.

J.J. followed and together they drank deeply of the cool water. To their relief the skies had cleared and a warm sun now bathed them.

"Leaves are turning fast," Angel chirped as she looked up at the giant cottonwood that stood nearby.

"Pretty, isn't it," J.J. remarked as she noted the brilliant yellows that painted the sky's blue canvas.

"Beautiful," the little one purred as she splashed a pawful of water at her sister.

"I don't know which I like best, the soft, fresh green of spring or the snapping crispness of the yellow and orange and red of autumn."

"Tough call," agreed J.J. "I guess I like them about the same. It's best to appreciate each season for what it gives us. We wouldn't like any of it near so much if it stayed the same all year round."

"Good point," praised Angel. "It's like always having something to look forward to."

"Every living thing needs that," J.J. mused. "People, dogs, you name it."

"Especially dogs," the little one puffed as she grinned and pulled back from the water.

"Well now I'm looking forward to some ham," J.J. chuckled as she and her sister turned back towards the pack.

Angel pulled out the map and found the Blue River where it crossed the highway just north of Durant.

"Might not quite make it before dark," she sighed as she pointed it out to J.J. and then looked to the sky. "It's still about fifteen miles."

"Ya," agreed her sister. "It'll be close. But let's try. It's our goal for the day and we don't want to miss it."

"You're right," concurred the little one. "If you don't meet the little goals sometimes the big ones slip away forever. Let's get going."

Quickly the Kids loaded the pack and set off south once more, wading the shallow Clear Boggy and then striking a steady but rapid pace as they glided through the rolling countryside. Just as the sun began its final dive they reached the glimmering waters of the Blue.

"I think we made it," gushed J.J. "This must be the river."

"Has to be," Angel hooted as she looked to the opposite bank.

"Now aren't you glad we stepped things up?" J.J. grinned.

"Sure am," confessed the little one. "It's funny how reaching a goal gives you a shot of energy. I feel fresh as a daisy."

"Want to make another ten miles tonight," J.J. joshed.

"Pleeeaaassse. I'm not that fresh," the little one giggled as she helped her sister with the pack. "But I am ready for dinner."

"I second that," J.J. whooped as she opened the pack and pulled out the food.

"I guess the Blue ties into the Red," Angel reasoned as she peered out over the water."

"Must," agreed J.J. as she studied the river's flow. "It runs in that direction."

"Hard to believe we're not far from the Red," the little one mused. "It's just below Durant. But I wonder where we go from here?"

"Good question," J.J. huffed with a shake of her head. "Maybe we'll just follow the river."

"And look for the eagle," Angel reminded her.

"And that," nodded J.J. "Well; we'll worry about that in the morning."

"Ya," Angel squeaked as she returned the food bag and ham tin to the pack.

"Get the book," J.J. shouted. "Let's see what else we can find out about this region."

Angel did as ordered, returning to J.J. with the book, map, and flashlight. First she looked up Durant and then turned to the page.

"Pretty good sized town," Angel read. "About 13,000. There's a university and a lot of industry. They even have a sausage factory; J.C. Potter."

"I wonder if they give out free samples," J.J. laughed.

"That would be nice," Angel hooted as she licked her lips. "Anyway, the town was named for a part Choctaw family that settled here after the Trail of Tears. It used to be a major stop on the stagecoach mail route to California. And of course the railroad comes through it. Oh, and listen to this," Angel continued. "There's another big river just to the west; the Washita."

"That sure sounds familiar," J.J. barked remembering the Ouachita region to the east.

"Same sound," Angel explained. "Different spelling. Washita must be the English version of the French word."

"Must be," concurred J.J.

"Durant is Choctaw but the Chickasaw country starts just to the west," the little one stated. "And there's a huge lake near here; Lake Texoma; a wildlife refuge, the Tishomingo, and an old fort; Fort Washita."

"Boy there's sure lots to see around here," J.J. remarked.

"Sure is," affirmed the little one as she shut the book and folded up the map. "The next few days should prove interesting."

"Every day seems so," laughed J.J. as she watched Angel stash their things in the pack and return with the sweaters.

"Might get a little nippy tonight," she stated as she looked up at the darting lights of a clear night sky. "Look at all the stars."

"Which one's the good luck star?" J.J. joked.

"Anyone you choose," Angel retorted as she curled up on one of the sweaters. "Luck's in the mind, not in the skies."

"Well put," praised J.J. as she settled in next to her sister. "Still, I like that one," she added as she pointed to the brightest of stars near the Little Dipper."

"Does look like a good one," responded Angel with a broad smile. "Now go to sleep."

"Hey lazy bones," drilled a commanding voice from the lowest branch of a high, soaring cottonwood. "You two ever gonna get up?"

Canine eyes flared open as the Kids rose and shook and looked above. Sitting stoutly on a thick swaying limb sat the largest flying critter they had ever seen; its cap of white crowning a trunk of darkest brown; its beak of curving gold blending with the turning leaves of a shimmering autumn dawn. Four foot wings flashed a new day's greeting in a spread that might have spanned the Blue. Spike-sharp talons anchored him vise-like to his bark-rough perch.

"Come on folks," he chortled. "Day's a wastin'."

"I knew you'd come," chirped Angel with a grin as wide as the eagle's wings.

"See, I told you," she purred as she looked to J.J.

"You are the eagle, aren't you?" J.J. asked as she looked up. "The one Matthew told us to find."

"Yep," the bird affirmed. "How is that crazy mule?" he added with a laugh.

"Fine," the Kids answered together. "He traveled with us a long way."

"Bet you learned a lot," the eagle ventured.

"Whole bunch," confirmed the girls. "Will you teach us, too?"

"Might," the bird chuckled. "Looks like you're learning an awful lot on your own. That was pretty smart the way you got the little one out of that quicksand; good thinking under a lot of pressure. That's admirable."

"You saw that?" Angel quizzed.

"That and a whole lot more," the bird cackled as he fluttered his wings and gently floated to the ground. "Oh, they call me Edmond," he offered as he sunk his claws into the cool earth. "After the town. That's where my folks are from."

"We've seen it," gushed the Kids together. "Right outside of Oklahoma City."

"That's right," praised the bird. "You're getting to know this state pretty well."

"We're trying," woofed J.J.

"And we're having a lot of fun doing it," added Angel as she moved closer to the eagle and sat down beside him.

"Well why don't you have a little breakfast and then see some more," Edmond suggested.

"Sounds good," grinned J.J. as she turned to the pack. Hey what's this," she blurted as she nosed a large bag sitting next to their own.

"Thought you could use a little extra," the eagle chuckled.

J.J. quickly pulled open the new sack and found it full of dog food and meat scraps. Angel skipped to join her.

"Thanks," she gushed. "We were just about out."

"I know," stated Edmond with a sly smile.

"You seem to know everything," chided the Kids as they shared out a big meal.

"The only thing I know is that I know nothing," he hooted.

"What!!!" giggled the Kids together as they munched their breakfast.

"Never heard that, huh?" the eagle snorted. "That's from Socrates; the ancient Greek philosopher."

"We met a dog named Dogenes in Arkansas," the little one chirped. "They related?"

"Distantly," chortled the bird as he shook his massive wings.

"The Greeks had a lot of smart guys, didn't they," J.J. barked as she crunched on a nugget. "We used to hear our family talk about them."

"Some of the best," Edmond answered. "Any time studying the Greeks is time well spent; the Romans, too."

Breakfast finished, the Kids trotted down to the river for a wash and a drink. Then they returned to the eagle and packed their bag while he watched. A brilliant sun was quickly chasing away the autumn night's chill. Angel helped J.J. strap on the pack and then they turned to the eagle.

"Where to now?" the little one asked excitedly.

"Upstream to the highway and then west to the fort," Edmond answered.

"Fort Washita?" J.J. beamed.

"Yep," the eagle affirmed. "That's one place you need to see."

"Are you going to walk with us?" Angel mused with a twist of her head.

"Of course not," the bird cackled with a hard shake of his snow white crown. "What kind of an eagle do you take me for? I'll be right overhead. You two just watch."

With that Edmond cranked his massive wings into motion and quickly soared high into the blue morning sky. The Kids turned and began their march up the Blue. In less than an hour they came to the intersections of highways 78 and 48. Here the eagle motioned for them to cut due west on 78. After flanking the little towns of Cobb and Brown they hit Highway 199. In a short time they were standing at the gates of Fort Washita. Up above their friend the eagle glided to a landing atop a mighty oak.

"Boy this looks like a neat place!" gushed J.J. as she gazed at the wonderfully preserved icon of early Oklahoma history.

"Look at all the old buildings!" squeaked the little one as she eyed the wood and stone structures that graced the grounds in every direction.

"They built them to last," laughed J.J. as she glued her eyes to the rock frame of one of the largest. "Look there's an information board," she added. "Let's take a look."

The Kids ambled to the plaque that told the fort's story and began to read. They found that the fort was established in 1842 by General Zachary Taylor, a man who would later be a United States President. Its purpose was to protect the Choctaw and Chickasaw peoples from raiding tribes living farther west. It was named for the nearby Washita River. Many officers stationed here would become famous Civil War figures; men such as George McClellan and Braxton Bragg. Early in the war Confederate forces occupied the fort, making it an important supply depot. After the conflict it was abandoned as a fort with the land being given to a Chickasaw family, the Colbert's. Finally, in 1962, the Oklahoma Historical Society purchased the site and began restoration work, a task that continues to this day.

"That's some history," J.J. nearly shouted as she finished reading.

"It must be a chore to fix up these old buildings," Angel chirped. "They've done a good job so far."

"Sure have," agreed J.J. "It all looks so real. You can almost see the soldiers going through their daily routines."

"Let's walk," Angel insisted. "I want a closer look."

"Good idea," beamed J.J. as she looked up at Edmond who was watching them closely from his high perch.

The eagle rose and spread his wings in a sign of approval as the Kids began their tour. Cautiously they walked the grounds, inspecting each building from the massive barracks to the tiny little cabins that served as the officers' quarters. The lone cannon standing in the yard, the Confederate cemetery, the cook shed and the post water well all received the Kids' careful attention. Rounding their way back to the entrance they peered up at a smiling Edmond who then floated down to the ground just behind a thick hedge. Moving to meet him, the Kids were all smiles as they approached. Exploring the fort had been a fascinating experience.

"Great place, isn't it," hooted the bird. "I thought you'd like it."

"Thanks for bringing us here," gushed the Kids together.

"Everyone should see this place," Angel chirped.

"What's next?" J.J. quizzed excitedly.

"We'll go by Tishomingo then work our way west to the Arbuckles," the eagle advised.

"The Arbuckles?" Angel questioned.

"Mountain range," the bird explained. "One of Oklahoma's geographic regions. It's really nice."

"What about Tishomingo?" J.J. barked. "We saw a reference to it in the book."

" Well, it's a town just up ahead; named for a famous Chickasaw. Nearby is a big wildlife refuge; over 16,000 acres," Edmond answered. "It's has all sorts of trees and it's full of critters. Some of my cousins live there."

"Sounds great," Angel chirped. "We've seen other refuges," she added. "How do they get started?

"Different ways," the eagle explained. "Sometimes people will donate land for one or the government finds a good site and buys it. They're usually run by U.S. Fish and Wildlife Service. The primary objective is to keep large blocks of land from being chopped up and paved over. That way the animals will have plenty of space and the land won't be ruined."

"It's a great idea," purred J.J. "Too bad there aren't more of them."

"Yup. Should be," agreed the eagle as he arched his back and straightened his wings. "Ready to move?"

"Which way?" squeaked the little one.

"Well, Madill's just down 199 to the west, but we'll go north to Tishomingo like we said," the bird advised. "Watch my feathers."

With that the mighty bird went airborne, soaring into the blue with but a few pounding thrusts of his powerful wings. The Kids watched as he set a course north and then began to follow his trail. Floating aloft, he was never out of their sight. In a short while they reached Highway 22 which bordered the reserve on the east. To the west was the 4600 acre Cumberland Pool which formed the northern extreme of Lake Texoma. Beyond the pool was the Washita flowing gently to the southeast. Ahead the Kids looked up to see their friend gracefully land at the top of a giant elm.

"I think he's marked a spot for us," J.J. surmised.

"Looks like it," affirmed the little one as the two set a course for the tree.

"Look at all the tracks," J.J. yowled as she studied the animal prints pressed into the mud of the Cumberland's bank.

"Deer, raccoon, bobcat, you name it," Angel chirped as she studied the ground.

"Ducks, too," J.J. purred as she looked out over the water.

"Hundreds of them," the little one squealed as she followed her sister's gaze. "And all types."

Breaking through the brush they came to a picnic site which Edmond had marked for them. As they approached a table the giant bird floated down to meet them.

"Looked like a good place for lunch," he informed them.

"What are you going to eat?" J.J. quizzed, remembering that all they carried was dog food and a little bit of ham.

"Don't worry about me," Edmond laughed as he shot back into the air and out over the lake.

The girls watched as he glided for a moment over the water and then shot straight down, his razored talons fully extended. With a gentle splash his feet hit the water and then in an instant he rose once more turning toward the Kids and then gliding to a landing beside them.

"Boy that was easy," laughed the little one as she eyed the bird's lunch; a nice fat bass.

"Wish we could find food like that," hooted her sister as Edmond chuckled.

"Got to have the equipment," he grinned as he took his first bite.

"Good claws?" ventured J.J.

"They help," counseled the bird. "But it's the eyes that make the difference."

"Eagle eyes," giggled the Kids together as they remembered hearing that expression.

"That's right," coughed Edmond between bites. "I see more at a hundred yards than a man can see at ten."

"That must make the fishermen mad," howled J.J.

"Not my problem," the bird cackled with a grin from his red-stained beak.

"Can't you fry that thing up for us," joked Angel, remembering how long it had been since they'd had fish.

"Are you part cat or something?" hooted the eagle. "I thought you liked meat."

"Meat, fish, whatever," J.J. joshed. "We're not too particular."

"We've learned to make do with what's there," Angel added proudly.

"That's a good way to be," praised the bird. "Adaptability's won many a battle. It can get you through some tough spots."

"It has for us before," J.J. admitted.

"No doubt it will again," Edmond cooed. "You two are pretty smart," he continued. "I couldn't help overhear when you were talking about goals; how missing on little goals can cost you the big ones later. You were right on target."

"You heard that!" exclaimed the Kids together.

"I just happened to be in the tree above," he smiled as he spat out a bone. "You'd be amazed by how much you can learn by just keeping your mouth shut and your ears open. That little bit of wisdom reminds me of a story about Stupid Sam."

"Stupid Sam?" giggled the little one.

"Tell us," demanded J.J. as she and Angel drew closer to the eagle.

"Well," Edmond began. "Sam was a squirrel who talked a lot more than he worked. One year he totalled up the number of nuts he thought he'd need to store to get him through the next winter. Then he tallied how many he'd need to gather each day to have enough. Each morning he'd start collecting but he'd always stop to tell any other squirrel that came along just what his plan was. And he spent so much time talking that he always fell short of his daily goal, either that or he'd get a little tired and knock off way too early. Anyway, like I said, each day he came up short but said he wasn't worried because there was still plenty of time before winter came. As you might imagine, when winter did come he didn't have nearly enough. By late January he was forced to go out each day to see what he could find to eat. One day my cousin Reno was out hunting and saw that little brown ball of fur standing out like a sore thumb on a carpet of fresh white snow. And to his day old Reno said that Sam was one of the best lunches he'd ever had.

"Poor Sam," sighed the little one.

"Lazy Sam," countered J.J. "If he'd got done each day what he'd set out to do he'd still be with us."

"That's right," cooed the eagle. "He didn't get the day's work done. And when you don't get the day's work done you don't get the week's work done and so on. And then in some ways you end up like Sam, although I doubt anyone would have you two for lunch," he finished with a hard laugh."

"I guess, in a lot of ways, life's just a series of small steps," reckoned Angel as she rubbed her jaw.

"Exactly," praised the bird. "And a big goal. Don't forget that. Without a big goal the small steps take you nowhere."

"And every once in awhile those small steps turn into big leaps," added J.J. with a broad smile.

"That's right," nodded the eagle. "Those big leaps that come along every so often really let you know you're getting somewhere. And that gives you the energy and the confidence to see the job through. You wake up one morning and just know you're going to succeed. And that's a great feeling."

The eagle's words soothed the Kids as they thought about how far they had come. Though they knew not where their journey would take them, they were determined to reach their goal and find the silver.

"Hey," blustered J.J. as she looked at the bird. "You knew about the quicksand and you heard us talking. Just how far have you been tracking us?"

"I picked you up way back at the Tallgrass," the eagle admitted. "I go up there a lot. But of course I heard about you before that. These critters out here are nosy."

"And I suppose you know about what happened at the dog fighting place?" Angel quizzed, already knowing the answer.

"How do you think Matthew knew where to find you?" he confessed. "The police, too."

"I wonder what happened to those guys?" J.J. mused as she wondered aloud what kind of people could be involved in something like animal fighting.

"Too early to say yet," Edmond offered. "But I'm afraid not a whole lot. Oklahoma laws aren't nearly tough enough. It's a little better in Texas but not much. The penalties should be a lot harsher."

"Do you know where the silver is?" J.J. asked bluntly. "You do know about it?"

"Oh, sure I know about it," confirmed the bird. "Everyone out here does. But where it is exactly I can't say. Besides, it's your job to find it, not mine. All I can do is put you on the right trail. The rest is up to you. Now get packed. We've got ground to cover."

The girls shrugged and began to load their things. When ready Edmond told them to follow the shoreline and skirt Tishomingo to the south. Then they would pick up the Washita and follow the river upstream and into the Arbuckle country.

"I'll be close," he promised the Kids as he cranked his wings and began his effortless ascent into the pale blue autumn sky.

"Wish we could do that," Angel laughed as she watched the eagle float high above. "Look how easily he glides," she finished.

"He just locks those big wings in place and the currents carry him right along," marveled J.J. "I'll bet he could stay up there about as long as he wants to."

"Long time, anyway," agreed the little one as she looked back down to the sun-drenched land that lie ahead.

Soon the girls came to Highway 99, the main route between Tishomingo and Madill to the south. A short while later they reached the railroad bridge that marked the last reaches of Lake Texoma.

"That was some lake," piped J.J. "I didn't think it would ever end."

"I wonder how far it stretches," pondered the little one. "Let's measure it on the map tonight."

"Good idea," replied J.J. as the girls took a quick look up at Edmond and then turned to follow the Washita upstream.

"I guess this river's a tributary of the Red, too," reasoned the little one as they walked. "Or at least it was before they built Texoma."

"Must be," agreed J.J. as she skipped over the rotting trunk of a long-fallen elm. "I wonder how far it runs; where's its source?"

"I suspect we'll find out sooner or later," chirped Angel as she followed her sister over the log.

The Kids walked until near dark, finally coming to a halt near the Johnston/Carter county line just north of Mannsville. Edmond gently glided down to meet them.

"Tired," he laughed as the girls unhitched the pack and fell to the soft earth along the bank.

"Beat," confessed the little one with a huff. "Wish we could fly."

"It's not as easy as it looks," coughed the bird with a wide grin. "My wings can get as rundown as your legs."

The Kids laughed as they rose and skidded down the bank for water. Mouths wet, they returned to the eagle and the three watched as the coming night tugged hard on the sun's orange skirt.

"I always did love to watch the sunset," sighed Edmond. "Dawn and dusk; my favorite times of day."

"Ours, too," confirmed J.J. as she patted the little one on the head. "We never get tired of either one, do we."

Angel only smiled, then rose and went to the pack. Pulling out some food she returned to J.J. and Edmond.

"Want some meat?" she asked the big bird.

"Naw, I had a little meal earlier," he informed her. "Another fish. You two go ahead."

After eating she returned the food sack to the pack and came back with the map, book, and flashlight.

"I wonder what's around here?" she pondered as she unfolded the map and flipped on the light.

"Just ask Edmond," J.J. chuckled. "He can probably tell you more than the map can."

"Well study it anyway," countered the bird with a loud hoot. "That's always good practice if nothing else. I won't always be here."

"Well, okay," woofed J.J. "Let's see what we have."

The girls found their location on the map and began to study this new region. Directly to the west was Highway 177 near the juncture of Caddo Creek. From there it was just a short hop to the important city of Ardmore on Interstate 35. To the south of Ardmore was Lake Murray State Park. To the north lie the Chickasaw National Recreational Area and the city of Sulpher, and due west from there the Lake of the Arbuckles and the Arbuckle Mountains.

"The Arbuckles!" barked J.J. "Found 'em."

"Now wasn't that more fun than having me tell you," chided the eagle as he gave J.J. a gentle poke with his beak.

"Sure was," confessed J.J. as Angel looked on.

"What are those towns farther north?" the little one quizzed as she turned back to the map.

"Paul's Valley and Purcell," J.J. read as she traced I-35 north. "From there on it's pretty much Oklahoma City and its suburbs."

"Looks like the river takes us right to the Arbuckles," Angel mused as she pondered the map once more. "And it doesn't look too far."

"Should get there by this time tomorrow," Edmond advised. "Maybe quicker."

"Great," hooted the little one.

"How big is Ardmore?" J.J. asked as she looked back south on the map. "Doesn't look like we get to go through there."

"Pretty good sized town," answered the eagle. "Close to fifty thousand in the town and surrounding area. Like most big towns it's at a highway intersection; I-35 and U.S. 70."

"We've crossed 70 before," chimed the little one. "Only it was way to the east."

"It's a long one," the bird advised. "Runs nearly to Texas in the west."

"What's 77?" J.J. pondered as she studied the map and saw that that highway ran right through the center of town.

"It was the main highway before they built the Interstate," Edmond answered.

"Like Route 66," J.J. reasoned.

"Exactly," commended the eagle. "Near just about every Interstate you'll find an old U.S. highway."

"What made Ardmore so big?" questioned Angel.

"Cotton first," Edmond replied. "And then they struck oil; lots of it."

"We've seen that before," J.J. quipped as she thought about all the oil producing regions they'd seen so far.

"No doubt you'll see more before you're done," the big bird laughed. "But let me give you a warning about commodities," he added with a sober gaze.

"What's that word?" Angel fumbled as she tried to pronounce it.

"Commodities," Edmond stated again. "Oil, cotton, wheat, lumber, you name it; the things that come from the ground. If history teaches us anything it's that commodities are always a boom or bust proposition. Let me give you an example. Back in the late 20's or early 30's, I don't remember exactly when, cotton went to nearly 60 cents a pound and everybody thought they could get rich quick. So they bought or rented as much land as they could get their hands on and grew as much cotton as they could. But by the time the harvest came in cotton had slumped to only about 6 cents and a lot of folks went flat broke; ruined; some of them forever. Mind this warning. When everyone thinks something's a "can't miss," get out if you're in and steer clear if you're not. And always remember there's more gold in your head than you'll ever find in the ground. So mine your mind, not the earth. Over the long haul it will always be worth more."

The Kids looked hard into the eagle's shining eyes. Then knew that it was an important lesson he was trying to teach them.

"But don't some people make a good living off those kind of things?" questioned Angel.

"Oh, sure," Edmond responded. "Always have and always will. But they're the ones who know their business and have the smarts to ride out tough times. Once I heard a great line from an old oilman. He said, 'Any fool can make a million dollars in the oil business but it takes someone who knows what he's doing to make a living at it'."

Edmond hunched his massive shoulders and focused hard on the Kids, trying to see if they clearly understood his message. He could sense their confusion.

"But," stammered Angel, "do you mean that we should always expect things to go badly?"

"No, no," countered the eagle with a hard shake of his white-feathered head. "All I'm saying is that life's seldom a smooth ride. It's full of bumps; sometimes big ones. And how hard those bumps bounce you often depend on how well prepared you are for them. Always expect the best but also prepare for the worst; just in case. That's what I always say."

"Ya," sighed J.J. "Sometimes things happen that you just can't control; like the weather."

"Exactly," praised the bird. "You can't control the weather but you can build a good, strong shelter before a storm hits. That makes it a lot easier to ride out. Or take the case of a cotton farmer. He might be just days away from harvesting a bumper crop and then up comes a hail storm wiping out a whole season's work in a matter of minutes. So to protect himself he buys crop insurance. All of us should have a little insurance built in on whatever it is we're doing."

"I see what you mean," cooed the little one. "I guess reaching a daily goal is a kind of insurance."

"Almost," countered Edmond with a snort. "I know we've talked about this before but let's touch on it just once more. It's important," he huffed as he drew a deep breath. "Meeting daily goals only means that you get the job done on time if nothing goes wrong. The problem is, something usually does go wrong and when it does you slip behind. It's best to add a little cushion; do a little more. That way if you lose a little time you can still make it up."

"That makes sense," the girls barked out together.

"And of course if you do that, you might finish early and have time for a little fun," J.J. added with a laugh.

"Yep," agreed the bird. "And everyone else will still be working; worrying themselves to death and scrambling to meet the deadline. And believe me, that's a rotten feeling," he spat in disgust.

"Ya," chortled the little one. "We don't want to end up like Stupid Sam."

Edmond paused for a moment and looked at the Kids. He could tell from the gleam in their eyes that his message was getting through.

"Oh, and one more thing," the bird continued. "Do your own work. Get your own facts. Don't listen to the crowd when making decisions. Contrary to popular belief 'they' is not always a reliable source," he finished with a wide grin of his golden beak.

The Kids broke into laughter as they thought about the number of times they had heard the expression "they say". They promised to ignore it from now on.

"Good mutts," the eagle praised. "Now let's all get some sleep. We've a lot to do tomorrow."

Angel returned the book, map, and flashlight to the pack and then skipped back to J.J. and Edmond. The eagle said good night and then zipped to the top of a short sycamore. A brilliant full yellow moon framed his outline as he curled his head under a wing and quickly fell silent. The Kids curled up together and soon did the same.

The next morning broke chilly but calm as Edmond floated down to wake them. After pecking them to alertness he turned to face the orange rim now rising lazily in the east.

"Looks like a great day," he cawed as he watched the Kids paw at their faces and stumble to their feet. "Grab a drink and a quick bite and then let's get moving."

The girls did as ordered and then loaded the pack. After securing it on J.J.'s back they looked to the bird for directions.

"We still follow the river?" Angel asked as she studied the land ahead.

"Yep," confirmed Edmond. "It'll take you right to the mountains. I'll be up above."

With that the eagle flashed his wings and their awesome power quickly propelled him skyward. Once more the Kids began to walk the Washita. In a few hours they crossed Highway 53 just to the east of Gene Autry, a town named for the legendary singing cowboy. Ahead they could see the land rising, the hills covered by the flaming orange and yellows and reds of autumn. Two more hours brought them to Highway 77D where up above Edmond motioned for them to stop. Settling in on the riverbank they sank to the ground as he glided in for a landing.

"You're making great time," he commended them. "Welcome to the Arbuckles," he grinned, noting that they were now on the range's eastern fringe. "Ever seen such color?" he added. "I always like to hang out here in the fall."

"Fantastic," gushed the girls together as they studied the flashing yellows of a bank side cottonwood.

"Well, you have some lunch and then we'll figure out how to cross the freeway," Edmond advised, noting that I-35 was just to the west. "Then we'll be in the heart of the range."

"How much ground do the Arbuckles cover?" J.J. quizzed as Angel pulled a little food from the pack.

"About 300 square miles," answered Edmond. "And it's an old formation; been here for millions of years."

"Seems kind of out of place in this flat country," Angel mused as she wolfed down a piece of meat.

"Well, you know mother nature," chuckled the bird. "She's always playing tricks. That's what keeps things interesting."

"And nice," added J.J. as she finished her lunch.

"That, too," agreed the eagle as he watched Angel return the food sack to the pack. "Now here's what we'll do," he continued as the girls looked on. "I want you to leave the river now and cut straight west. I'm going to scout ahead and look for a good place to get past 35. You'll run right into Price Falls and I'll meet you there."

"Okay," squeaked the little one. "Is it far?"

"Naw. Just a few miles," Edmond advised as he spread his wings. "See you in a bit."

The eagle bolted skyward as the Kids looked across the Washita to the west. A railroad bridge nearby offered them a dry crossing to the opposite bank. Once over they charted a course and began to walk. In a short while they were deep into the woods. A back road sign pointed them toward Price Falls which they reached in less than an hour. Here they settled in to wait for their friend.

"Pretty place," Angel chirped as she placed her front paws in a cool pool of water just below the falls.

"Mighty nice," confirmed J.J. as she took a drink and then did the same.

"Look!" shouted the little one as she looked skyward through the trees. "Edmond."

"Right on time," grinned J.J. as the eagle zeroed in on the girls and began his descent.

"How was your flight?" the little one giggled as the bird landed next to them.

"Not bad," he laughed. "Good thermals today; could have floated for hours."

"Did you find a good place?" J.J. asked excitedly.

"Yup," confirmed the bird. "A big drainage pipe that goes right under the road. You can slip right through and no one will see you."

"Great," yapped J.J. "How far?"

"Just up ahead," he chattered. "You'll be there in no time."

"Then let's get moving," squealed Angel, itching to get into the heart of the mountain range.

"I'll scout up top," Edmond stated. "You just keep your eyes on me and I'll lead you straight to it."

With that the eagle took off once more and the Kids began to walk. In a short while they came to a low, wooded hill. Cresting the rise they could see I-35 just ahead. Edmond hovered above just a few hundred yards to the north.

"Boy, it's a good thing the old bird knew how to get us across," J.J. mused. "We'd never make it in daylight; not with all that traffic."

"No way," agreed Angel as she watched countless cars and trucks barreling up and down one of the nation's busiest roadways.

"There!" barked J.J. as they came to a small clearing near a deep culvert. "The pipe!"

Hurriedly the Kids scurried down the bank to the bottom of the shallow ravine. After taking a quick look around to make sure no one was watching they entered the drain pipe and soon found themselves in the open on the west side of the freeway. Leaving the pipe's shadows they looked up to see the eagle hovering low right above them. With a flick of his wings he shot straight for a short, sturdy oak poking through a rocky outcrop just up the ravine. The Kids skipped to meet him.

"Now wasn't that easy," he laughed as the girls approached his perch.

"No problem," Angel squeaked. "Thanks."

"What's next?' J.J. hooted, still giddy over the ease with which they dodged a dangerous obstacle.

"Turner Falls," Edmond squawked. "If you see nothing else around here you have to see that."

"Is it like Price Falls?" Angel chirped. "That was sure nice."

"Better," counseled the eagle. "You'll see. Just follow that road."

Edmond pointed his beak at the two-lane blacktop that ran to Turner Falls Park, a stunning 1500 acre wonderland run by the nearby City of Davis. Just ahead was one of the scenic overlooks that lined the roadway.

"I'll meet you over there," the eagle cawed as he motioned toward the parking area.

A single flap of his wings sent Edmond airborne while the Kids cautiously made their way north along the road. There was no traffic. In a few minutes they reached the viewing area and settled in behind a thick clump of bushes. The bird was waiting.

"The park entrance is just up ahead," he informed them. "You can sneak in just behind that bluff," he added as he pointed to a rise just a little to the west. "I'll see you at the falls."

"Great," chirped Angel.

Edmond shot skyward as the Kids readied to leave. Turning back toward the road they poked their heads through the bushes and then froze. A white van was pulling into the parking lot. "Quick! Duck!" J.J. ordered. "A car."

The two quickly retreated back into the shrubbery and then turned to look. The van pulled to within ten feet of their hiding place and parked. The driver got out. It was Rob Silver.

"Well what do you know," Angel whispered. "Our old buddy."

"Shhh," J.J. murmured as she put a paw to her lips. "Listen."

Silver walked around to the van's rear and pulled out his cell phone. After quickly dialing he began to talk and loudly enough for the Kids to hear clearly.

"We're still in the clear," he chortled. "Three or four more weeks and we can go get it. We're close to being rich."

The Kids looked at each other and then back at Silver who was slowly pacing around the van. They could barely here the voice on the other phone.

"Bury it deep?" he laughed.

He grinned at the answer and then went on.

"I'll call you from Antelope Hills in a few weeks. Just sit tight. Our buyer's all lined up. This baby's in the bag," he snickered as he turned off his phone.

Angel started to speak but J.J. motioned for her silence. As they watched, Silver got into his van and sat for about ten minutes. Then he fired the engine and streaked south out of the lot.

"Antelope Hills," J.J. huffed. "Where is that?"

"I don't know," confessed the little one. "But it must be to the west. Let's look at the map."

"Ya," coughed J.J. as she buckled her knees and eased to the ground.

Angel quickly unzipped the pack and pulled out the atlas. After unfolding it and setting it on the ground the girls began to study the lands to the west. They soon found their spot far to the northwest in a great bend of the South Canadian.

"There it is!" chimed the little one, her voice shaking with excitement. "If we can get there before he does, we get the treasure."

"Hold on there," cautioned her sister. "He didn't say the silver was there, just that that's where he would call from next. Keep your head on straight."

"I know," pouted Angel. "But it puts us on the right trail if nothing else. Doesn't that make sense?"

"Sure," agreed J.J. "No doubt that's the right direction. Why else would he go way out there?"

"That's a lot of ground to cover in two weeks," Angel added with a frown.

"We're going to have to speed things up," counseled J.J. Let's get to Edmond and tell him what happened. He'll know what to do."

"Ya," concurred the little one. "Let's go."

Quickly the Kids skittered out of the lot and over the road to the rise that bordered the park. After cresting it they came to the boundary fence and shimmied through the wire. A sign on the park road pointed to Turner Falls.

"Just ahead," barked J.J. as she and Angel reached the near bank of Honey Creek. In a matter of minutes the girls stood at the base of the waterfall, a 77 foot drop from the rocks above. Edmond was waiting.

"Wow, this is some place," the little one gushed as they looked up at the eagle perched on a low elm branch.

"It"s Oklahoma's oldest park," their friend informed them as he noted the trails and pools and rock formations that made this area so unique. "I didn't think you would ever get here. What took you?"

"You'll never guess," shouted J.J. with a wide grin.

"I'm all ears," Edmond puffed as he glided to the ground.

The Kids told him the story about seeing Silver and hearing the conversation with his accomplice. They asked him what he knew about Antelope Hills.

"Great place," he told them. "But it's a long way off."

"It sure looked like it on the map," J.J. agreed. "Do you know the quickest way there?"

"Throttle down," cautioned the bird. "The quickest way's not always the best. If you go straight to it you'll miss seeing an awful lot of good country."

"But we only have two weeks," stammered the little one. "If we don't make it we might not find the silver."

"Remember the rules," the eagle scolded. "You have to follow orders and do your job just like the Indian woman told you. Yes, I know about her," the eagle smirked, reminding the Kids that he knew their whole story even though they had never mentioned the woman. "But it just might be that we can speed things up."

"How?" quizzed the Kids together, their frowns fading away to smiles.

"Railroads," answered the eagle with a twinkle in his eye.

"Hop a train again?" J.J. questioned.

"Not exactly," Edmond replied as he reached under his wing and pulled out a faded old map.

The Kids looked on as he dropped it to the ground and told them to unfold it. After doing so they realized that it was an old track map, one that showed not only active rail lines but also many of those abandoned years ago.

"That's your express ticket to the Antelope Hills," he advised them. "That and a handy piece of equipment."

"What kind of equipment?" J.J. puzzled.

"I'll show you in the morning," Edmond answered, noting that the night was fast approaching.

"Can't we do it now?" pleaded Angel as she pawed the ground in anticipation.

"Nope. It's a few hours walk from here," countered the eagle. "Best to stay put until dawn."

The girls reluctantly agreed that the old bird was right and once more turned their attention to the water. A nearby information plaque told them about all the neat places to visit and things to do while in the park.

"Caves!" blurted the little one as she told Edmond about their visit to Robbers Cave.

"I'll bet this place is full on summer weekends," J.J. hooted.

"Busy as can be," confirmed the eagle. "That's why I like it during the week. It's usually nice and quiet, especially in the fall."

"Lot of critters here?" asked the little one.

"Every kind," chirped the bird. "But if you want to see some real critters you need to check out the Arbuckle Wilderness Area close by. Giraffes, lions, my buddies Ollie the ostrich and Pete the peacock; every kind of animal imaginable. And you can drive right through it. It's really something."

"Sounds like fun," cooed Angel as she thought about how much little Amy would have enjoyed such an adventure.

J.J. seemed to sense her little sister's thoughts and reached over to give her a soft pat on the head. Then all three settled in to watch the dusk drape gently over the rugged but majestic country. Their late lunch still filled them. The soft, steady roar of falling waters and the sweet whisper of cool running currents soothed both minds and bodies. As was his custom, Edmond returned to his perch to pass the night. The Kids drank deeply from the pool and then sank to its bank and quickly collapsed into an exhausted slumber.

All awoke to a dismal dawn as autumn's bad side coated the land in a drizzly grey of wind and cold. Shivering, first J.J. and then Angel wobbled to attention and then shook hard to loosen the seasons frosty grip. Edmond looked down from his tree.

"Nippy, isn't it," he cackled as he plunged to the ground, his outstretched wings breaking his fall. "Autumn in Oklahoma," he added as he sidled up to the girls. "Beautiful one day, miserable the next; you never know."

"I'll take yesterday," huffed J.J. as she looked up to the leaden sky.

"Got to take it as it comes," counseled the old bird with a wide grin. "Today is what makes you really appreciate yesterday."

"Yup," agreed the little one as she dropped her head to drink from the now frigid pool. "It'd be awfully boring if every day were the same," she reasoned as she licked the water from her lips."

"That's a great attitude," complimented the eagle as he poked his beak into the water and took a short sip. "Why don't you two have a little breakfast and then we'll get going."

"I'm for that," woofed J.J. whose stomach was reminding her that they had missed dinner the night before.

"How you doing on grub?" Edmond asked as Angel moved to the pack.

"Getting low; almost out," she looked back and answered.

"Well why don't you check out that camping area," the eagle suggested as he pointed to a spot not far down the park road. "Yesterday some people were having a picnic there. Maybe they left something."

"We'll do it," promised J.J.

"I'd do it right now," advised Edmond, "before the cleaning guys come by."

"Good idea," agreed Angel. "Let's go."

The eagle stayed behind while the Kids jogged down the road to the camp site. In the distance they could see a man cleaning another spot not far away. Hurriedly the girls sniffed and poked before finding a nearly full pack of hot dogs and some lunch meat in the trash can as well as a quarter-filled small sack of crunchy dog food on the ground next to it.

"We're in luck," hooted J.J. as she began loading their haul into the food sack.

"Must have had a dog with them," reasoned Angel.

"I'm sure glad," grinned J.J. as she once more looked down the road to check on the cleaning man.

"He's coming," she barked. "Let's move."

Twisting the top of the food sack closed, the girls scampered back to their spot. Edmond was waiting.

"Looks like fortune smiled," he cawed as he eyed the sack. "Now see, if you would have waited just a few more minutes you would have missed out," he finished with a loud chuckle.

"Fortune favors the bold," J.J. laughed as she bit into a hot dog.

"And the prompt," Angel added with a giggle as she did the same.

"All right, you two philosophers; chow down and then get ready," the eagle sniffed.

"No time for dawdling if you want to get to Antelope Hills in two weeks."

Quickly the Kids finished breakfast and loaded the pack. Then they looked to Edmond for instructions.

"Where to now?" J.J. asked.

"West," snapped the eagle. "I want you to follow the southern rim of the range until you're out of the mountains. You'll run right into an old rail site sitting next to an abandoned barn. I'll meet you there."

"How far?" quizzed the little one.

"About two hours hard walking," Edmond informed her. "I'll keep watch from up high just in case you get off course."

"Okay," the Kids replied as one.

"See you soon," the eagle chirped as he put his powerful wings in motion and shot skyward.

Silently the Kids traced their path back to the park boundary and slipped through the fence. Then, as ordered, they set their sights to the west just as a cold rain began to pepper them.

"Nasty day," coughed J.J. as she took the lead.

Sure is," hacked Angel as she followed. "But maybe that strong north wind will chase the clouds away before long."

"Should," reckoned J.J. "The faster the front the quicker it's gone."

"You should be on television," Angel hooted. "You'd make a good weather dog."

J.J. turned, smiled, then looked back ahead. Before them the land was changing as the sharply rising hills smoothed to rolling prairie. J.J. quickened her pace as the rain let up. Angel did likewise. Two hours passed and just as Edmond had told them they soon spotted an old barn sitting all alone on the prairie about a mile ahead. No roads reached it.

"Must be it," Angel offered.

"Must be," J.J. nodded as she scouted the land around it.

The girls' walk turned to a trot as they rapidly splashed through the pools toward the structure and approached its open door. From the barn and out through the pasture ran a set of rusted rails, in places barely visible through the grass and the dirt. Poking their heads inside they found Edmond sitting on an old pump-handled flat car.

"I believe you beat that two hours," he cackled, "at least by a few minutes anyway."

"Nothing to it," bragged J.J. as she stared at the contraption. "What's that thing?"

"Your taxi," he chortled.

"Whaaaat?" hollered the little one as she stared at the funny looking platform on wheels.

"It's an old fashioned hand cart," the eagle explained. "An old barn owl told me about it."

"How does it work?" quizzed J.J. as she examined the cart which ran about six feet in length and four across.

"Just pump that handle," the bird explained as he pointed to the shaft of weathered wood that ran lengthwise about four feet and connected to a gear on the bottom side of the platform. "It turns the gear and the gear turns the wheels."

"Wow!" popped J.J. as she jumped to the platform and placed a paw on the handle. "Come on little sister," she shouted to Angel who was already climbing aboard.

"It might be a little stiff," warned the bird. "It's probably not been used in a long time."

"How did it get here?" Angel peeped as she placed her paws on the shaft's rear cross-bar and pushed downward.

"I think this might have been an old maintenance station a long time ago," reasoned the eagle as he looked around the barn and saw several old tools scattered about. "And those old rails must have been a spur."

"A spur?" questioned J.J.

"Ya. Spur or trunkline. That's what they call short stretches of track that connect to the main lines," Edmond explained. "Looks like this one's been idle for years."

"Do you know where it goes?" asked Angel as she looked back through the door to the tracks outside.

"Not for sure," confessed the eagle. "I don't get over this way too much. But I'd guess it runs west and ties into the UP line somewhere along the old Chisholm Trail; Highway 81."

"Well come on J.J., let's see if it works," insisted the little one as she grabbed her end of the handle.

J.J. latched on to the opposite end and together the Kids began to push and pull up and down. The frozen gear creaked with decades of idleness then finally broke free to do its job as the cart inched forward.

"Wish we could grease that gear," laughed J.J. with a loud huff.

"Let's search the barn," offered Edmond. "Maybe there's some around."

All three jumped to the floor and were quickly drawn to an old wooden box in the barn's far corner. Popping the top they found an old can of greenish grease and a tin of Marland oil.

"This is old!" Angel blurted as she read the label. "Remember Marland?"

"Sure do," confirmed J.J. as she told Edmond about their visit to the Marland Mansion.

Returning to the car J.J. dipped out a large glob of grease and spread it over the gear. Then after wiping off her paw on a mound of old straw she and Angel pumped the handle once more. This time the handle rocked with ease and the car pulled forward and out of the barn.

"It works!" the little one hollered loud enough to be heard in the next county.

"Sure does," grinned J.J. as Edmond smiled approvingly.

"I wonder how fast we can go?" Angel puzzled.

"A lot faster than you can walk," the eagle assured her with a hearty laugh. "Oh, you'd best oil those wheels while you're at it," he counseled.

Without a word J.J. grabbed the oil can and went wheel to wheel, pouring generous amounts on each bearing. When finished she capped the can and placed it back on the platform.

"Now it will run smoothly," cawed the bird. "Always take care of your equipment," he added. "You'll never know just how long it might have to last."

"Sounds like good advice," agreed the little one as she grabbed the handle once more.

"And are your water bottles full?" Edmond inquired. "You'll be heading west where water's sometimes hard to come by."

"I'd better check," chirped the little one as she opened the pack on J.J.'s back and looked. "It's been a long time since we've had to use them."

"Got enough?" asked J.J.

"Full to the brims," Angel reported.

"Good," beamed the big bird. "Now ladies, let's get this crate moving."

"Are you going to ride with us?" asked a happy J.J.

"For a bit," Edmond replied. "I'll give my wings a rest. Besides, I've never done this and I want to try everything at least once."

The handcar glided easily over the old rails, running first due west and then taking a hard curve toward the south. Gleefully the Kids pumped the handle as they glided over the open country.

"This is great!" hollered J.J. "I'll bet we're going ten, maybe fifteen miles an hour."

"I told you it'd beat walking," chuckled the old eagle as he perched on the handle's center shaft, turning his white-capped head every so often to study the surrounding land.

Through the morning the Kids pumped away on their wheeled ferry. Dawn's rainy rawness became but a dismal memory as a flashing autumn sun drenched the land in light and warmth. They soon crossed Highway 53 near its intersection with 76, then came to a stop just outside Healdton, a town named for the massive oil and gas formation deep beneath it.

"Lunch time," beamed the little one as the wheels clicked their last.

"Want something?" J.J. asked Edmond still lashed fast to his perch.

"Naw, you go ahead," mumbled the old bird. "I had a mouse this morning. That'll hold me for awhile."

"A mouse," sniffed J.J. as she puckered her lips and scowled.

Edmond just laughed as the girls dug into the bag and pulled out the food sack. After eating they hopped off the car to drink from a little ditch still brimming with water from the morning's rain.

"Good and cold," piped the little one between slurps.

"Mighty good," added J.J. as she pulled her dripping snout from the pool. "I wonder what's ahead. Do you know, Edmond?"

"Not sure," he confessed. "I haven't been out this way in a long time. But I think there's a pretty good sized town not far to the southwest," he finished as he patted his head as if to jar loose a few distant memories.

"Well," joked the little one with a broad smile, "at the rate we're going we'll find out soon enough."

"If that's where the tracks lead," cautioned J.J.

"It's a good bet they do," reasoned the bird. "They don't lay tracks to nowhere."

"Good point," praised J.J. in return. "Let's get going!"

Quickly the girls climbed back aboard and began to pump the handle once more. In no time they reached full speed. Soon they came within site of Ringling, a small town at the intersection of Highways 89 and 70. Here the tracks cut hard to the west.

"U.S. 70 again," chirped Angel as she eyed the major road just to the south. "You can bet that that'll bring us to a big town sooner or later."

"Yup," agreed J.J. "Always does."

"I'm going to scout ahead," advised the eagle as he spread his giant wings. "I'll be back soon."

"Okay," chirped the Kids together.

Edmond soared into the sky as the Kids continued to pump. He soon returned to tell them that U.S. 81 and the city of Waurika were just ahead. Here they could tie into the U.P. line and follow the old Chisholm Trail north.

"What's in Waurika?" Angel peeped.

"Chisholm Trail Museum," he answered.

"Wish we could see that," sighed J.J.

"What I wish we could have seen was a real cattle drive," countered Angel with a huff. "That must have been something."

"Should of been born earlier," laughed the bird. "My ancestors saw them. It's a story that's been passed down through the years. They said that the cattle would be stretched out for miles; one herd after another on their way to Kansas."

"I guess it meant big money," pondered J.J.

"For a few," cracked the eagle. "Just a bare living for the rest."

In less than an hour the three crossed under U.S. 81 and reached the Union Pacific junction just outside of Waurika. Here Edmond ordered them north.

"Antelope Hills?" woofed J.J.

"Not yet," counseled the eagle. "But soon enough; I promise."

"Now we'll really have to watch for trains," the little one sighed. "What do we do if one comes?" she added as she looked to the eagle.

"Won't be any," he answered sharply, "at least not for awhile."

"Why not?" quizzed J.J.

"Strike," replied the bird.

"A what?" mused the little one.

"Strike," repeated the eagle. "Folks want more pay and refuse to work until they get it. Won't be a train on the tracks until it gets settled; nothing except your little craft. This is a big break for you."

"How did you know about it?" demanded J.J. as she cocked her head.

"The air has ears," Edmond quipped as he clicked his beak and chuckled.

The Kids just shook their heads and began to pump once more. Late in the afternoon they passed a sign that told them Duncan was just ahead. Here the eagle suggested they halt and rest until after dark.

"The tracks run straight through town and we don't want to try that in daylight," he warned. "Let's just wait until things get nice and quiet."

"Makes sense," commended J.J. "It must be a pretty big town."

"Let's look it up in the book," Angel suggested as she reached for the pack and fished out the book and map.

"Good idea," praised J.J. and Edmond together.

"Here it is," Angel squeaked as she flipped to the right page. "Duncan's another railroad town. Back in1892 a Scotsman named William Duncan found out the line was coming through and opened a store here. He thought this would be a good place to do business."

"What's a Scotsman?" J.J. questioned.

"Somebody from Scotland," Angel sniffed, disappointed that her sister didn't know something so simple. "Don't you remember your geography. Scotland's just north of England."

"Oh, ya. I forgot," huffed an embarrassed J.J. as she pounded a paw into the wooden deck.

Angel gave her a light pop on the nose and then continued reading. Edmond laughed and looked on.

"It says that before the railroad nearly ten million cattle came this way on the drives," she exclaimed.

"See," the eagle interrupted. "I told you."

"Anyway," the little one went on, "Duncan's had some rough times; tornados and fires, but the people toughed it out. Of course they found oil and that really helped. A man named Halliburton came here and started an oil field service company. Now it's one of the world's biggest and a branch is still in Duncan."

"How many people live here?" questioned J.J.

"Over 20,000," answered the little one. "Oh, and it's the Stephens County seat," she added as she turned the page.

"What about farming?" asked the eagle as he looked out over the endless expanse of prairie.

"Lot of wheat," Angel replied. "And of course cattle. This is big ranching country. "Oh, and we haven't been paying attention," she scolded herself and J.J. "We've passed into another region; two more really. The Arbuckles are considered to be a separate geographic area and now we've crossed into the Red Bed Plains, the largest region in the state. It runs all the way from Kansas south to the Red River and into Texas," she finished as she closed the book.

"Red Bed Plains," joked J.J. as she looked down at the rusty red soil. "Never would have guessed it," she laughed.

Angel and Edmond chuckled together as the little one opened the map where she pinpointed their spot. Then she ran her paw north along the U.S. 81 line which exactly paralleled the tracks.

"What's ahead?" her sister quizzed.

"Next big town's Chickasha," she chirped. "Looks to be, oh, about forty miles."

"Then what?" J.J. continued as she looked to Edmond.

"We'll see," he replied. "One step at a time. It's always more fun if you don't know what's coming next."

Angel just shook her head at their baffling companion and folded the map. Then she returned it and the book to the pack. In the west the sun was making its final stand against the creeping darkness, its last energy sending short streamers of orange across the Red Bed Plains.

"Beautiful sight," gushed Edmond as he watched the sun's crown slip slowly below the horizon.

"Sure is," affirmed Angel as she pulled a meal from the sack. "Are you ready for a bite now?" she chirped, reminding the eagle that he hadn't eaten since morning.

"No, no," he declined. "I'm fine. It was a fat mouse."

The girls were grateful that the old eagle was so unselfish. Deep down they knew that he was hungry but didn't want to take their food. Perhaps he knew that they might soon need it all; and more. Finishing a frank each and a few nuggets, the Kids closed the sack and placed it back in the pack. Then they jumped from the car to sniff for water, finding but one inch-deep pool in a shallow gully by the tracks.

"Not much," sighed J.J. as she plunged her tongue into the water and took a few laps.

"Nope," agreed the little one as she did the same. "Must not have rained as much here."

"Or it all sank in already," reckoned J.J. "That happens in a dry land."

Thirsts quenched they trudged back to the handcar where they found Edmond still stuck on his perch but fast asleep. Quietly they hopped to the bed and curled up.

"I guess even eagles get tired," whispered J.J. as she looked up at the bird.

"Everything gets tired," the little one quipped. "Even the land."

"Wish I could sleep standing up," giggled J.J. softly as she laid her chin on Angel's back.

"Let's hit it Kids," cranked a loud voice from just above. "We want to get through town before first light."

Quickly the girls snapped to their feet and shook hard to loosen sleep's tight grasp. Angel scooted to the pack and pulled out a water bottle, popped the cap, and offered it to Edmond who took a tiny sip. Then she passed it to J.J. before helping herself. Mouths wet once more, they looked to the north and the lights of Duncan.

"Good time to go," the eagle advised. "Whole town's asleep."

"Nice and peaceful," seconded J.J. "Let's move."

Quickly and quietly the girls took up their positions at the pump handle while Edmond maintained his perch on the shaft. A few pushes and pulls brought them to speed. Only the clicks and clacks of wheels on tracks broke the early morning silence. In twenty minutes they had cleared the city and were once again in the open country to the north. Only the rare farmhouse light pierced the darkness. By first light they were halfway to Chickasha.

"Let's shut'er down here," ordered the eagle. "You need a rest and I want to scout ahead."

Two sets of tired shoulders gratefully obeyed. Releasing the pumphandle, the

Kids looked to Edmond as the handcar slowly coasted to a stop.

"With all that exercise you two are going to look like superdogs before you're through," teased the eagle as he watched the girls stretch their tired muscles.

J.J. responded by tensing her torso in the manner of a bodybuilder. The little one watched and laughed. Then Angel shot a front leg straight out and twisted the paw back to her face to show off a dog's version of a bicep. J.J. mockingly moved to feel it.

"What a rock!" she shouted with a feigned swoon.

"Frightening," quipped the bird. "Now if I could just get her to work her brain as hard as her body she could really be something," he kidded.

Angel gave a fake pout and then all three broke into uncontrolled laughter. Still, the eagle's teasing did have a serious side and the girls knew it. They recognized long ago that mind and body both grew strong through use; that it was necessary to challenge both to their absolute limits.

"Okay folks," the old bird hooted. "I'm going airborne for a little while so why don't you catch a dognap. I'll be back soon."

With that Edmond quickly flapped his way high into the fast brightening sky and soon caught a thermal to push him north. In minutes he was but a tiny dark speck in a sea of sky blue. Angel pulled out the food sack and returned to J.J. Breakfast done, the Kids hopped to the ground to look for water. They soon found a nearly dry tank in a nearby pasture and crossed the curling, crackling, caked mud to drink from its last shallow pool.

"Hardly enough here for one cow," observed J.J. as she brushed the scummy film from the top and took a sip.

"Or any other critter," frowned Angel as she did the same. "Boy is this land different from the east."

"Yup, water everywhere back there," agreed J.J. as she took another slurp. "Maybe we'd better fill that bottle."

"Good idea," praised Angel. "We didn't drink much from it but every drop might be important. I'll go get it."

The little one skipped back to the cart and retrieved the bottle from the pack. Then she returned to J.J. and filled it. Putting the cap back in place, they scurried back to the tracks to rest and wait for Edmond. He returned in twenty minutes to find them both snoozing.

"Up and at 'em, girls," the eagle squawked as he gently landed on the bed. "I brought you something," he added as he dropped a small sack of crunchy dog food onto the floor.

"Great," gushed Angel who stirred first. "We were all out."

"I know," grinned the eagle. "I found this just outside someone's back door. The old dog there wasn't too happy," he chuckled. "He really got after me when he saw what I was doing."

"What's ahead?" asked Angel as she placed the sack in the food bag.

"There's a spur just south of Chickasha that cuts west to Anadarko and another main line," he told them. "That's where we'll go."

"Did you fly all the way up there?" J.J. quizzed, wondering how even an eagle could cover that much ground that quickly.

"Oh, no," he laughed. "I ran into an old friend, a cousin, not far up the line and he filled me in. Told me where to find that dog food, too," he added.

"Thank him for us if you see him again," chirped the little one as she moved toward the handle.

"I'll do it," promised the eagle. "Now let's get pumpin'."

Edmond returned to his perch while each Kid grabbed her end of the handle and began to pump. Soon they were gliding smoothly through the vast emptiness. In two hours they neared the intersection of U.S. 81 and I-44, the Bailey Turnpike. Here they found the spur that the eagle had noted and took a hard left west. Another hour brought them to a rickety old bridge where they stopped for lunch and a rest.

"Hope this old thing will hold us," joked J.J. as they looked out over the ancient structure lying just ahead.

"Sure wouldn't hold a real train," laughed Angel.

"What do you know about Chickasha?" J.J. asked as she looked to Edmond.

"And Anadarko?" added Angel.

"Not much," admitted the old bird. "Why don't you get the book."

"Good idea," squeaked the little one as she placed the food sack back in the pack and grabbed the book and map. "Let's see here. Ah, here we go," she stated as she turned to the right section. "Both cities are on the Washita," she began.

"What a surprise," joshed J.J. "Cities on rivers."

"Ya," grinned the little one as she began to read once more. "Chickasha's the same age as Duncan and also started as a railroad town. It's home to about 17,000 people and a liberal arts college, The University of Science and Arts of Oklahoma. There's a lot of industry there like the Delta Faucet Company. And every Christmas they have a big party; the Festival of Light."

"That sounds like fun," chimed J.J. who had always loved a good Christmas celebration.

"And of course there's tons of good stuff about the native peoples and western heritage. Same with Anadarko," she continued. "It's smaller at about 7000 but it's full of great museums and exhibits. Anadarko's was named after an early plains people and is now home to a whole bunch of different tribes. In fact it's sometimes called 'The Indian Capital of the Nation'.

"Does it name some of the tribes?" quizzed J.J. as she looked over Angel's shoulder.

"Yep," affirmed the little one. "Delawares, Kiowas, Comanches, Arapahos, Cheyenne, and several more."

"Ya," barked J.J. as she began to read as well. "Wichitas, Caddos, and Apaches. A lot of peoples represented there."

"Sure a bunch for just one town," chirped Angel as she read on. "Looks like Anadarko has some fantastic sites and events," she continued. "The Southern Plains Indian Museum and replicas of some Indian villages."

"I'll bet those would be interesting," hooted J.J. with excitement. "And what's that?"

"The American Indian Exposition,' answered the little one. "It's held every August."

"Wouldn't you like to see that, Edmond?" J.J. asked as she looked up at the old bird.

"You bet," confirmed the eagle, happy to see the Kids so excited about Oklahoma's cultural heritage. "I'd stake me out a shady spot way up high and watch the whole thing. It'd be a great way to spend a weekend; maybe a whole week," he added with a wide grin.

"Sure would," agreed Angel as she closed the book.

"I wonder how far we are from Anadarko?" J.J. asked as she reached for the map.

"Doesn't look far," Angel replied.

"Only about fifteen miles from here," J.J. reasoned as she used the map's scale to measure. "Shouldn't take us long at all to get there."

"Sounds like you're ready to roll," hooted the eagle as he looked out over the old bridge just ahead.

"Ready," puffed Angel as she reached for her side of the handle.

With a few quick rocks of the pump the cart began to roll. When it hit the bridge the ancient structure began to creak and moan.

"Hurry!" shouted J.J. "I don't trust this old thing."

Edmond quickly flapped his wings and jetted into the air to reduce the weight on the bridge while the Kids pumped furiously to pick up speed. Just as they reached the middle the rickety frame began to sway like a skinny branch in a strong wind. Finally they reached the other side just as the center planks and a section of rail gave way and crashed to the ground below.

"Whew," huffed J.J. as she wiped her brow with a paw. "That was close."

"Bridge needs work," deadpanned Edmond as he fluttered down to his perch.

"Could stand it," agreed Angel dryly. "We'll write a letter to the governor."

"Or the County Commissioner," hooted J.J.

All three had a good laugh at J.J.'s quip and then they were off once more. In just over an hour they came to the southern edge of Anadarko and met the tracks Edmond had mentioned.

"Going south again folks," he advised as he pointed his beak to the left.

"Back south?" questioned Angel as she looked up at the bird. "But Antelope Hills is to the west.

"I told you to be patient," the eagle reminded her. "We'll get there."

With a shrug the Kids eased onto the main line and began rolling south into the teeth of a stiff but pleasant, warming breeze. They soon reached U.S. 281 near the town of Apache and the blue of Lake Ellsworth. A road sign told them that just ahead lie the large city of Lawton and the massive Fort Sill Military Reservation. Another pointed to the west and the Wichita Mountains Wildlife Refuge.

"That's what I want to see again," Edmond informed them. "It's been an awfully long time."

"Is it really nice?" questioned J.J.

"Some of the prettiest country in the state," he replied. "I wasn't more than a chick when I saw it for the first time."

"Lots of animals?" quizzed Angel.

"All kinds," the old bird answered. "Buffalo, deer, longhorns, you name it. And great water; pretty pools for such a dry land."

"How do we get there?" asked a puzzled J.J. "Do the tracks run to it?"

"I doubt it," the eagle reasoned. "But it's worth the walk, or in my case the fly."

"Well, let's go then," Angel chirped. "I don't want to miss anything.

"What about Antelope Hills?" protested J.J. "I'm afraid we won't make it."

"Yes you will," assured the eagle. "Trust me on this one. Have I ever steered you wrong?"

"Nope," admitted J.J., feeling a little guilty about doubting their friend.

"Then let's roll down to the cut-off and find a place to park this crate," Edmond ordered.

The Kids gave a few hard pumps to pick up speed while the eagle studied the land closely from his perch. Soon he looked down and told the Kids that the road to the Wichitas was just ahead. To the west they could now clearly see the chain of hills rising sharply from the flat prairie.

"They look so close," squeaked the little one.

"They're not," cautioned the bird with a loud hoot. "Mountains will fool you like that," he added with a grin. "You'd be wise to remember it."

The Kids quit pumping and coasted to a stop near an abandoned building just opposite the cut-off. Its sign read 'Richards Spur'. In a stroke of luck they found that an old spur did in fact run west toward the Wichitas.

"Doesn't look like this line's been used in a hundred years," quipped J.J. as she studied the rusted tracks and the weed filled bed. "I wonder how far it goes?"

"We'll find out," puffed the little one.

"Wait a minute," spat J.J. "How do we get our cart on that track?"

"Oh," hissed the little one. "Didn't think of that," she finished as she turned toward Edmond.

"There!" he hooted as he pointed to a tall, flat steel bar sticking out of a metal box just outside one track. "That's a switch. Pull it and the tracks will move."

J.J. quickly sprinted to the bar and gave it a tug. It wouldn't budge. Angel moved to help. Both Kids latched onto the bar and gave it a mighty pull. Still no luck.

"Wait a minute," Edmond pondered. "Maybe I meant push, not pull."

The Kids laughed and pushed the bar in the other direction. It gave slightly. Then a second try cracked its crust of idleness and freed it, moving a section of track to align with the western spur.

"Got it," gushed J.J.

"Good work," praised the bird. "Let's go. We still have an hour of daylight."

Quickly the girls jumped back on the cart and began to pump the handle.

Slowly they approached the junction where their craft veered to follow the new alignment. Through day's last light they wheeled westward, finally coming to a stop just past Highway 58 on the northern tip of Lake Lawtonka. A sign told them they had reached the refuge's eastern boundary.

"Great spot," Edmond stated as they parked under a giant pecan. "Good water; good cover."

"Can't beat it," agreed Angel as she hopped to the ground.

"Let's get a drink," J.J. suggested as she followed.

The three moved down to the water and quickly quenched their thirsts. Then they returned to their cart to eat and rest.

"I can't wait for the dawn," Edmond gushed. "I think you're going to like this place."

"Sure looks good so far," J.J. spoke as Angel nodded in agreement.

The last waves of light washed away in the west as all three settled in for the night. Angel suggested they read up on Lawton and Fort Sill and pulled the book and map from the pack.

"Better pull that flashlight," barked J.J. "It's getting dark."

Angel followed the advice and returned to the two. She quickly found the section on this new region and began to read.

"Lawton's a pretty good sized town," she read, "biggest in this part of the state; way over 90,000 folks. It dates back to 1901 when this area was opened to white settlement. The Kiowas, Comanches, and Apaches are the main tribes here. There's a big university, Cameron, and Lawton's also a major highway junction. I-44 and U.S. 62 meet here."

"Doesn't 44 go down to Texas?" Edmond queried.

"Yup," confirmed the little one. "It crosses the river and runs to Wichita Falls where it stops. Oh, and in case you didn't guess, this is big oil and gas country."

"Never would have figured that out," joshed J.J. with a grin. "What about Fort Sill?" she continued.

"It's awfully important to Lawton's economy," Angel answered. "And it's been around a long time; goes all the way back to 1869."

"Pretty big?" J.J. questioned.

"Huge," replied the little one, "about 95,000 acres."

"Wow!" woofed J.J.

"It's a national historic landmark," Angel added.

"That'd make for a great tour," cawed the eagle as he looked down from his perch.

"Sure would," affirmed J.J.

"I wonder what forms this lake?" Angel quizzed herself as she opened the map. "Medicine Creek," she read. "And there are other creeks going through the reserve."

"We'll see them tomorrow," J.J. beamed. "Now let's get some sleep."

Angel closed the book, folded the map, turned off the flashlight, and put all away. Then the dogs curled up together near the center shaft while Edmond stuck his head under a wing. In minutes all were dreaming deeply.

Shortly after dawn the Kids awoke to find Edmond gone. A chilling breeze blew in softly from the north. In the east a brilliant orange marked the new day.

"I wonder where he went," a concerned Angel coughed as she studied the sky.

"Don't know," replied J.J. as she did the same. "I know he wanted us to explore the reserve together. Let's just wait. Maybe he'll be back shortly."

"Let's hope so," the little one moaned as she jumped to the ground and headed for the lake.

The girls ambled down to the water and soaked in now cold waters. Then they skipped back to their cart and began to watch the sky once more. Soon a dark speck appeared just below a bank of wispy-thin clouds. It was heading toward them and moving fast.

"Edmond?" mused the little one.

"Could be," reckoned J.J. "Sure looks like him."

The Kids watched as the figure neared, then smiled when they could clearly see that it was their friend. Wings stretched wide, he shot down like a rocket before coming in for the softest of landings on the center shaft summit. He carried another sack which he dropped to the cart.

"Where have you been?" Angel demanded. "We were worried."

"Shouldn't have been," he laughed. "Brought you some more grub. Got me a little breakfast, too," he hooted as he looked down on the dogs.

The Kids quickly smelled the sack and caught the sweet, strong aroma of freshly fried fish. Opening the sack they found six large pieces still nearly warm.

"Where'd you get this?" J.J. whooped in excitement.

"Guy on the lake was having an early morning fish fry," he laughed. "He wasn't paying much attention so I helped myself," he finished with a sly grin.

"Hope he doesn't starve," quipped the little one.

"I doubt he will," the eagle chuckled. "He had about a dozen more going. He must have had some real luck yesterday. Lake Lawtonka's my kind of place."

"Ours, too," chirped Angel as she passed pieces to Edmond and J.J. before pulling one for herself. "Each one of these looks to be good for about two meals," she added as she tore into her crispy portion.

"Big fish are always my favorite kind, no matter what the flavor," the old bird hooted.

All three finished breakfast and then turned to the day's business. Angel helped J.J. secure the pack and then the three looked to the west and the line of mountains they so eagerly wanted to explore. They found a little used trail that cut straight into the refuge and the Kids began their march. Edmond took to the sky. Circling low he soon spotted the main park road and pointed the girls to it. Here they found an information board and pulled out a brochure which they studied as they went along. Edmond would join them on the ground when they stopped.

"This place has everything," J.J. gushed as she studied the material. "Look at all the lakes and creeks," she marveled. "Quanah Parker Lake, French Lake, Deer Creek, Panther Creek," she read, naming a few of the places.

"Quanah Parker sure rings a bell," Angel chirped as the bird swooped down and landed.

"Comanche chief," Edmond informed her. "Mother was a captive white Texan; a really amazing man. You should read up on him."

"How big is it?" Angel asked as she moved closer.

"About 59,000 acres," J.J. answered.

"Isn't it great that they set this aside," Angel purred.

"Well let's go see some more," J.J. barked.

Edmond took to the air once more and guided the girls through the refuge. Along the way they saw deer, bison, longhorns, elk, and an animal they'd never even heard of before; the prairie dog. When they approached a town, the name given to a colony, the little critters would rise from their holes and chatter loudly as a warning to all their friends, an act which amused the Kids to no end.

"Noisy little brats, aren't they," Angel giggled as she walked past a mound and gave a loud bark.

"They'd better worry more about Edmond than us," J.J. joked. "To him they look like lunch."

"They look too tough to be tasty," the little one countered.

Later the Kids would learn that once prairie dogs covered the plains in their billions. Now the Wichitas were one of their few safe havens. Above Edmond came in low and when he did the dogs quickly dipped down in their holes.

"Nature at work," chuckled J.J. "Eagles must be a natural predator."

"Must be," affirmed Angel. "Dogs too, probably; or at least coyotes."

"Eveything's got to eat," reasoned J.J.

By noon the Kids had neared the western edge of the refuge and stopped at a picnic spot below Elk Mountain for lunch and a rest. Edmond drifted down to join them.

"How do you like it," he grinned as he anchored himself to the table.

"Love it," they woofed together. "Everyone should see it."

"Hungry?" Angel asked.

"No," Edmond declined. "That big fish I had for breakfast was almost enough to keep me grounded," he chuckled as he rubbed his bulging stomach.

The girls laughed as Angel poked her nose into the old bird's midsection, an act which caused his wings to shoot straight out. Folding them back in, he broke into a huge smile and told the girls how pleased he was to see them enjoy this trip so much. "I've heard of another great place farther to the west," he told them. "We'll shoot for that next."

"What's it called?" the little one queried.

"Not sure," he confessed. "But it's another mountain chain or so I've been told."

"Worth checking out," reasoned J.J. "I sure hope a rail line runs close to it."

"So do I," seconded the eagle. "Now, you two set a spell and then we'll start back."

After a half hour of lounging the Kids rose to begin the long walk back to their cart. Edmond shot skyward once more. Several hours later they came to the Holy City, an important site to the Wichita people for whom the mountains were named. From there they picked up the trail back to the lake, reaching it just before dark.

"That was some hike," J.J. huffed as she flopped down to the ground next to their handcar.

"Tired, girls," Edmond teased as he made his landing next to them.

"Naw," Angel retorted. "That was just a little stroll, " she finished as she licked a sore paw.

All three laughed as Edmond informed them that his wings were on their last legs; bone tired. Then all skittered down to the water for a well earned drink.

"We'd better chow down and then get to sleep," the eagle advised. "We need to leave nice and early if we're going to get through Lawton before daybreak."

"Going west?" asked J.J.

"Yup," answered the old bird.

"Do you know where the tracks are?" J.J. questioned.

"Nope; but we're bound to run into an east/ west line someplace," he reasoned.

"Makes sense," chirped Angel. "Too bad these tracks don't keep going," she sighed, noting that this spot was the end of the line.

"Sure is," agreed the eagle. "But we were lucky to get even this."

"Sure were," concurred the little one. "Saved us a lot of walking."

"Say, I just thought of something," moaned J.J. "How do we go back the other way? This thing's only geared to go in one direction."

"Hmm," Edmond frowned as he placed a wingtip to his chin. "Good point."

"Maybe there's a switch or something," Angel reasoned. "It wouldn't make sense to build one of these things only to go one direction."

"You're right," affirmed J.J. "Let's take a look."

The girls quickly began to examine their craft and soon spotted a steel lever near the edge on its bottom side. J.J. gave it a hard tug and the gear moved, clanking as it did so. Then she hopped to the top and gave the handle a hard rock which sent the cart rolling the other direction.

"Got it," she puffed. "We're ready to roll."

"Good work," praised the eagle. "You're pretty smart dogs."

The Kids just grinned as Angel helped J.J. remove the pack. Then she grabbed their dinner and the girls plopped down on the ground to eat. Edmond took a small piece of fish as well.

Dinner done, the three went down to the lake to drink and clean up. Then they returned to the cart, the dogs to the floor and Edmond to his perch. Sleep came soon.

Well before dawn they arose, drank, and ate. Then the Kids took their positions on the pump while Edmond maintained his watch on the shaft. Soon the cart began to roll forward, shortly taking them back to the main line. Without a hitch they switched tracks and began gliding south, first through the lands of Fort Sill and then the city. An hour before dawn they reached a junction where, just as the eagle had reasoned, another line shot to the west. The tracks were aligned to receive them.

"What luck," J.J. gushed as she looked at the lights all around them.

"This is going to be a good day," Edmond cracked.

Soon they had cleared the town and broken through to open country, running parallel to Highway 62 on its south side. Behind them the first blush of light pushed hard at the night, breaking its grip and bathing the land in a soft, gentle white. Near the town of Indiahoma they crossed under the road and continued on its northern flank. Midmorning brought them to Snyder, where, luckily for them, the tracks took a northward swing, missing the town and protecting them from view. In another hour they reached the North Fork of the Red River where the tracks switched sides once more. Here they stopped for a break.

"Didn't know there was a North Fork," Angel peeped as she pulled out the map. "There's an Elm Fork and a Salt Fork, too," she added.

"And look," barked J.J. as she moved close to her sister. "Big park just to the north; Great Plains State Park. "Ever seen that one, Edmond?" she asked as she looked up to the bird.

"Never have," he answered as he rustled his feathers and moved his wings.

"Looks like a big town not too far up the line; Altus" Angel observed as she stared at the map. "Might give us some trouble."

"Hmmm," the eagle murmured as he looked down from his perch. "I'd better scout it out," he cautioned.

"Oh, and look Edmond," the little one nearly shouted. "Mountains; just like you said; the Quartz Mountains; just north of town."

"Quartz Mountains," repeated the eagle. "That's what I want to see."

"Not far now," gushed J.J. as she looked at their friend and smiled.

"I tell you what," the old bird reckoned as he flopped down on the platform to study the map himself, "you two rest here for a bit. I'm going to take a little jaunt and see what I can see. Give me an hour or so."

"Okay," chirped the little one. "Are you going to check out the city?"

"Yep," he replied. "It looks like those tracks go right through town and you can't take 'em in daylight. Maybe I can find a way around."

"Good idea," praised J.J. "Maybe another old spur."

"That's what I'm counting on," he cawed. "Save a little fish for me," he chuckled as he made his jump and shot skyward.

The Kids watched with awe at the eagle's effortless climb to the heavens. In but minutes he had vanished from sight. Only the striking blue of a Great Plains sky remained. They settled in for a good lunch and, after eating, Angel pulled out the book.

"Altus," she stated as she flipped to the page. "About 21,000 people and a big Air Force base. It was called Frazer back in 1886 but a big flood washed it out. So they moved the town a little to the east and renamed it Altus. That means 'high ground'," Angel read.

"Must have been the Salt Fork," J.J. reasoned as she looked at the map. "Hard to believe such a small stream could wash away a whole town, especially in this dry land."

"History's full of things like that," Angel remarked, remembering the stories she had heard about natural disasters wiping out entire cities, even civilizations. "Anyway," she continued. "This is farming and ranching country; grain, cotton and cattle. Oh," she added. "Texas used to claim this area."

"Really," hooted J.J.

"Yep," Angel read. "Texas claimed the North Fork was the boundary between it and Indian Territory. They called all of this land around here Greer County. The Oklahoma folks thought otherwise and it all created quite a mess for quite awhile. Finally, in 1896, the U.S. Supreme Court settled it by ruling in favor of Oklahoma," she finished as she closed the book.

"I guess that made a whole bunch of Texans Oklahomans," laughed J.J.

"Must have," chuckled the little one as she looked to the sky. "Ah, that must be Edmond," she added as she pointed to the bird zeroing in on them.

"Good news," he shouted as he plopped to a stop. "Found an old trunk line running just a few miles east of town. We can shoot straight back to the main line just to the north and it'll take us right into the mountains."

"Great," woofed the Kids together. "Why don't you have a bite and then we'll get going."

"No need to dawdle," he cawed. "Besides, I found a little something to eat along the way."

"What'd you have?" Angel chirped. "Oh, never mind," she retracted as her mouth puckered with the thought of what he might have eaten.

The eagle just cracked a wide smile as he took his position on the shaft. The Kids manned the pump and in seconds they were once more gliding over the plains.

In an hour they reached the spur on the eastern edge of Altus. Here again they had to throw the switch that moved the track. After doing so they rolled onto the spur and headed north. In a short time they hit the main line. This time the tracks were aligned to receive them. Ahead they could see the mountain outlines.

"There they are," shouted Angel as she peered to the north with building excitement.

J.J., whose position on the cart had her facing south, turned to look. Edmond said nothing, but the glow in his eyes and twitching of his wings suggested eagerness.

"Really never been here, Edmond?" Angel asked as she began to pump harder.

"Nope; first time," he answered. "I just heard about it like I said. Should have come a long time ago. It looks well worth the effort."

For another thirty minutes the trio rocked through this flat land of grass, mesquite and stubby oaks. Then they began to climb through the steep, rocky heights that marked the mountains' beginning. Soon they reached a secluded little canyon where the eagle motioned for them to stop.

"This looks like a good place to hide," Edmond advised. "You stay here for a bit and I'm going to do a little scouting."

"Are you going to check out the park?" J.J. queried.

"Yep," he answered. "I'll be back in just a bit."

The old bird took off while the Kids drank and rested. In fifteen minutes he returned.

"Park entrance is just ahead," he informed them. "And things look pretty quiet inside. Load that pack and we'll go in and do a little exploring. This is not a place you want to miss."

"Great!" hooted the Kids together.

Angel helped her sister secure the pack and then the three moved toward the park, Edmond taking to the air to guide them. They found a good place to slip in not far from the main entrance and soon found themselves on the main park roadway. Along the trail was a small but beautiful lake and along the water numerous camping and picnic spots.

"This is nice," Angel gushed as she grabbed an informational brochure from a stand near one of the open air events buildings.

A loud caw from above jolted them as they looked to see a car heading for them. Quickly they dashed behind an old rock structure until it passed.

"We have to pay more attention," J.J. lectured, certain that the old eagle would remind them of it soon enough.

"I just get lost in thought when we find these neat places," confessed the little one.

"I know what you mean," laughed J.J. "But let's be a little more careful."

"Okay," promised Angel with a soft grin.

For another hour they explored the area while Edmond kept watch from above. Finally, with but little daylight left, the eagle signaled them to return to their cart. Retracing their steps they soon reached the tracks as the bird swooped in for a landing.

"How'd you like it?" he quizzed with a broad smile.

"Fantastic," woofed J.J. as her sister nodded in agreement. "We found a brochure."

"Good work," praised the eagle.

Anxious to read, J.J dropped the pack and then opened the pamphlet.

"Quartz Mountain is part of the Wichita chain," she began. "and the rock's mostly granite."

"Then why do they call it 'Quartz'?" the little one joked.

"Because there's quartz all through the granite," J.J. explained.

"Oh," cooed Angel, still a little confused.

"Anyway," continued J.J., "the whole range dates back millions and millions of years.

"How big is it?" Edmond asked.

"Pretty big," J.J. answered. "Over 4000 acres and one of Oklahoma's seven original state parks; goes back to 1937. And listen to this Edmond, every January they have an Eagle Watch. It seems some of your relatives nest here during the winter and everybody comes to watch them."

"Good place for it," the old bird hooted. "Wouldn't mind staying here myself."

"And not just eagles," J.J. went on. "Hundreds of different kinds of birds live around here. People come from all over to see them. There are nature trails all through the park, a lot more than what we saw. And there's a big lake nearby; Lake Altus-Lugert. They dammed up the North Fork of the Red to make it. Oh, and one more thing. Just west of here is the old Western Cattle Trail, one of the routes they used to drive Texas stock north."

"How many does that make?" Angel chirped, "about four?"

"Sounds right," nodded J.J. as she thought about the others they had seen and read about."

"I wonder how long people have been using this area?" the little one pondered as she looked around.

"Long time," J.J. replied. "Native peoples for centuries; Wichitas, Comanches, and Kiowas mostly. Some of the first whites came as early as 1834. They were U.S. soldiers who were sent here to make treaties with the Indians. And of course more came later," she finished as she folded the brochure and set it aside.

"I'll bet a lot of explorers came through here before that," Angel speculated. "This would have made a great place for a camp."

"You're probably right," agreed J.J. and Edmond together.

J.J. put the brochure back in the pack and pulled out the food sack. Dinner done, they each took a big swig from a water bottle.

"Better fill that in the morning," cautioned the old bird, noting that it was nearly empty.

"As soon as we get to the lake," promised J.J. "That should be pretty quick."

"Just up ahead," confirmed the bird. "Getting chilly," he added.

Autumn meant cold when the sun went down, no matter how nice the day had been. Angel went to the pack and pulled out the sweaters, passing one to J.J. and offering to share hers with Edmond. He was touched by her generosity but assured her that he would be fine. His feathers were the best blanket one could have. The three chatted for a while longer but then one by one dropped off to sleep, the dogs wrapping themselves in the warmth of Miss Jackson's cashmere. The day had been productive and rewarding. They had covered more than sixty miles, seen some wonderful country, and learned still more about Oklahoma.

Around 4:00 a.m. a howling wind ripped in from the north; a gale so strong that it blew the pack off the cart and the caps off their heads. Tiny pellets of ice began to pepper the girls as they struggled to rise and run down their headgear. Above, Edmond had quivered to attention.

"Welcome to your first blue norther," the old bird hacked as he turned his head away from the stinging wind. "This is how things can be on the plains."

Angel struggled to get into her sweater as J.J. helped. Then the little one returned the favor. Darkness draped the land, the dense black bank of clouds above blotting out completely the light of moon and stars. Only the gleam of Edmond's eyes pierced the gloom.

"Bet you're glad to have those sweaters now," the old bird joked as Angel shivered and shook hard against the cold and pulled her cap down tightly.

"Sure are," J.J. coughed as she focused on the eagle's glinting squint above. "I guess the best way to get warm is to get moving," she reasoned.

"Might as well," the eagle agreed. "No sense just sitting here freezing."

Quickly the three shared sips from a water bottle and then the Kids took their positions at the pumphandle. Edmond stayed on his perch. A few rocking motions and they were moving once more. In minutes they reached the southern end of Lake Altus-Lugert. A slight break in the clouds gave them just enough moonlight to see the water and bridge. Here they coasted to a stop. Quickly Angel skipped down to fill the near-empty water bottle. Then she returned to the cart and they were moving once more. The air had warmed just enough to turn stinging sleet to light but frigid rain. The crew pushed on.

Dawn finally brought dryness as the rain ceased. In first light they slowed to a rest just north of Lone Wolf along Highway 44. J.J. showed concern. Her sense of direction told her that they were off course, moving away from rather than towards Antelope Hills. Reaching for the map in the pack, she looked to Edmond.

"These tracks are veering off to the east," she huffed as she studied the map, "away from the hills."

"You're not going to the hills just yet," the eagle spoke as he looked at the Kids. "There are other places you to have to see before that."

"But!" the little one protested. "What about Silver?"

"Ya," barked J.J. excitedly. "What if we miss him?"

"Now settle down a minute," Edmond ordered. "You still have, what, eight or nine days? That's plenty of time to do what I want you to do. Remember the rules. You have to stay disciplined and do things right."

Both Kids heaved heavy sighs and then looked once more to the bird whose quick, wide smile calmed them. They understood that he knew things they didn't; that his sole purpose was to help them in their quest. Yet they sensed their time with him was short.

"You're going to leave us soon, aren't you?" J.J. asked sadly.

"This is our last day," the old bird confessed, his voice cracking in sorrow as he looked down at the girls. "This afternoon I'm turning you over to Soddy."

"Soddy?" the Kids questioned together.

"Yup; Soddy the Skunk," he answered.

"Skunk!" sniffed J.J. as she wrinkled her nose and winced.

"Oh, boy," seconded Angel with a worried shake of her head.

"Old Soddy's all right as long as you stay on his good side," the eagle chuckled. "Just don't say anything that might make him mad."

"We promise," the Kids gushed together, this time unusually quick to recognize what was in their best interests.

"All right now," cawed the bird. "Let's get this raft rolling."

The Kids hit the handle and were soon gliding north. Just after noon they stopped to eat and rest. Ahead they could see the outline of a large town and the major highway that served it.

"I'll bet that's I-40 again," Angel reasoned as she studied the heavy traffic moving east and west.

"Must be," agreed J.J. "I wonder what the town's called?" she added as she pulled out the map.

"I think that's Clinton," Edmond advised. "Clinton or Weatherford."

"Clinton," confirmed J.J. as she whipped out the map and found their location. "Weatherford's just to the east; both on I-40."

"What are those two towns way to the west?" Angel asked as she looked on with J.J..

"Elk City and Sayre," J.J. read. "And then you're almost to Texas."

"Yup," confirmed the little one as she ran her paw along the line that marked the interstate. "We'll have to read about them when we get the chance."

"Maybe tonight," J.J. mused as the wind picked up the map and nearly blew it away.

"Whoa," Angel howled as she snapped a paw down to save it. "We can't afford to lose this."

"Sure can't," seconded J.J. "Then we'd have to go back to using your old outline."

"I need to get back to work on that thing," Angel squeaked as she thought about how long it had been since she done any marking.

The Kids looked up at Edmond who was busy studying the land ahead. He told them to stay put while he looked for a way around the city. In ten minutes he reappeared in the sky to the north.

SKUNKS AND SCISSORTAILS

"Looks like he's carrying something," J.J. mused as she strained to focus.

"Maybe more food," Angel purred.

"Could be," J.J. barked. "Hope so."

As the eagle closed in for a landing the girls could see that he was carrying not a sack but an animal; a small black one. Grinning widely, Edmond swooped in and hovered just off the ground as he turned his passenger loose. Then he touched down himself.

"Blacktail Kids," he squawked, "meet Soddy the Skunk."

The skunk shook himself and then turned to the girls, outstretching his paw and twitching his tail in greeting. The girls returned the gesture.

"I can't believe this," Angel giggled as she gave the newcomer a thorough inspection.

"How much did he charge you for that ride?" J.J. chortled.

"On the house," the skunk replied with a laugh. "Edmond runs a great air taxi service. Say,I've been wanting to meet you two for a long time," he added.

"You knew about us?" the little one quizzed.

"Oh, sure," Soddy snapped. "You're big news all around the state. Word has it that you've covered a lot of ground in the last few months."

"Close to five," J.J. remarked.

"Five months!" the skunk exclaimed. "You're some real spunky canines."

"Got some good news," Edmond interrupted. "There's an old spur just off to the west. You can go around Clinton and link up with the main line going north along U.S. 183."

"Where will that take us?" the little one asked.

"Close to a place I want you to see," the skunk explained. "The Great Salt Plains."

"What about Antelope Hills?" a worried J.J. stammered.

"Be patient," Soddy countered. "I'll get you there and I'll get you there on time."

"I told him the whole story," the eagle chirped. "He knows what you have to do."

"Okay," the Kids replied in unison. "We just can't be late."

As was always the case during times of anxiety, Angel began to paw the pouch around her neck. The skunk reached out and gave it a light touch.

"Might as well spread some of that power," he squeaked. "Dogs aren't the only ones who need it."

"Hope there's plenty to go around," the little one quipped.

The Kids now looked once more to Edmond. They knew his job was done.

"I guess this is it," Angel slobbered as she turned to the old bird.

"Yup," he answered. "Time for me to head back to the Blue."

"We can't thank you enough for all you've done," J.J. purred as she gently ran a paw down the eagle's feathery back.

"I'm the one to do the thanking," he countered as he broke into his trademark grin. "If you two hadn't come along I'd have missed a real high time; seeing all this great country again after all these years. You pups made me feel young again; in mind and body."

"Got to keep them both healthy and strong," Angel puffed, "just like you said."

"Well, no use drawing this out," Edmond sighed. "I want you to think about me when you find that silver. Oh, and give one of those guys a hard bite for me."

The Kids laughed and promised to do their best when the time came. Then the eagle spread his wings, gave the Kids one last smile, and took off to the east. In moments he was but a speck on the horizon.

"I'm sure gonna miss him," J.J. moaned as she looked first to Angel and then to the skunk.

Angel wiped a tear from her cheek but said nothing. Soddy felt their distress and knew that the best way to overcome sadness was to get busy with something important.

"Well folks," he peeped as he looked to the handcar. "Show me how this contraption works."

The girls hopped to the floor and took their positions on the pump. The skunk followed, settling in near the main shaft that Edwin had used for his perch. A few pumps and they were gliding north along the shiny tracks.

"How neat," the skunk popped as he walked from one side of the cart to the other. "Sure beats walking."

"We figured that out, too," yelled J.J. over the loud clicking of the wheels.

"How far have you taken this thing?" Soddy asked.

"All the way from the Arbuckles west to Quartz Mountain and north to here," Angel answered proudly.

"That's a lot of ground," squealed the skunk as he watched the country roll by.

"Why do they call you Soddy?" J.J. quizzed. "That's kind of a strange name."

"Named me after an old house," the skunk began.

"A house?" laughed Angel.

"Yup," Soddy continued. "Look around out here. Do you see any trees?"

"Just a few," J.J. confessed.

"That's right," the skunk affirmed. "And no trees, no wood. Now back in the old days, the Indian peoples in this part of the country made their shelters from buffalo skins. But by the time the white settlers got here the buffalo were pretty much gone."

"Ya, we studied that," shot Angel as she gave the handle a hard pump.

"Anyway," continued the skunk, "the settlers had to have places to live. But with no wood for lumber and no hides for tepees what do you do? You use what nature gives you," he explained without waiting for an answer. "And if there's one thing that nature provides in abundance out here it's dirt and grass; sod. They cut it from the prairie in big squares and that's what they used to build their homes. 'Soddies', they called them; not exactly pretty but quite functional. Soddies were a classic example of how living things adapt to their environment."

"Geography dictates all," remarked J.J. as she looked at the skunk. "We've seen that so many times."

"It sure does," agreed the skunk. "Now I was born in an old soddy long ago abandoned," Soddy went on. "So that's the name my momma gave me," he finished with a chuckle and a broad grin.

"Do you have any brothers or sisters?" Angel asked.

"Brother named Stinky," Soddy replied. "Human called him that once and the name just stuck. I never have understood why people seem to dislike us so," he finished with a deep frown of confusion.

The Kids covered their faces and tried not to laugh as they rolled on. In a few minutes they reached the cutoff that Edmond had found and stopped to check the tracks. They were aligned just right and the trio turned west, soon reaching another line that ran back to the north. Here J.J. had to pull the switch and move the track, an act which greatly impressed Soddy.

"You look like an old hand at that," he praised as she jumped back on the cart.

"Pretty simple, really," she explained as she grabbed her end of the pump and went back to work.

In a short time they reached I-40. A tunnel passed beneath it. Here the three stopped for a rest, a drink and a bite of food.

"Do you like fish?" Angel asked Soddy as she pulled out the food sack. "That's all we have. That and a little plain old dog food."

"I'll eat just about anything," the skunk advised as the little one handed him a chunk.

"Down to the last," moaned the little one as she passed a ration to J.J. "One more fish and a day's worth of nuggets."

"We'll have to start looking around," concluded J.J. as she took a bite.

"Any ideas, Soddy," the little one asked their new friend.

"Pretty good trash dump up ahead," the skunk advised. "Lot of people food."

"Trash dump?" sniffed J.J. as she curled her nose.

"Yep," the skunk confirmed. "You'd be surprised at all the perfectly good eats people throw away."

"I guess we'll have to try it," Angel squeaked, figuring that they could eat whatever a skunk could.

"We'll pass by it soon," Soddy counseled as he looked to the north.

Soon a horde of circling birds caught their attention.

"Trash dump," offered the skunk. "Those birds are permanent residents."

The Kids laughed as they pumped on. In a few minutes they cleared a slight rise and below to the east was the landfill. One man worked a bulldozer at its far southern end. They could see no one else.

"We can hide behind that mound," Soddy informed them as he pointed to a small mountain of trash and dirt. "That's where the birds are feeding. It must be pretty new stuff."

Angel pulled the food sack from the pack and quickly the three hopped from the cart and scurried to the mound. Just as the skunk had reckoned there were several fresh loads lying on the ground behind it. The birds scattered at their approach.

"We'll just be a minute," Soddy yelled as if talking to the birds.

The dogs laughed as they put their sniffers to work. In no time they found enough to fill the sack; fresh meat in two unopened packages, a sack of dog food still sealed, and to Angel's delight, three fresh doughnuts in a closed baggie.

"What a haul," J.J. gushed as the three turned back toward the tracks. "What's that you're carrying?" she added as she looked over at Soddy.

"Farm fresh eggs," he joked as he set down his package to speak. "Nothing like a good raw egg for breakfast."

"Fried's better," Angel deadpanned as she grinned at their comical friend.

"Never had one of those," chuckled the skunk. "Why would you ruin a good egg that way?"

The dogs could only shake their heads in disbelief, forgetting that it was a rare skunk that ever saw the inside of a kitchen. Still laughing as they reached the cart, they quickly climbed aboard with their loot. Soddy fell in right behind them.

"Still a few hours before dark," he observed as he looked west towards the sun. "We can cover a good bit of ground before then."

"Where are we going again?" Angel asked.

"Great Salt Plains," he answered.

"How far?" J.J. quizzed.

"Long way," the skunk replied. "Nearly a hundred miles."

"You've been there?" Angel questioned.

"Several times," he affirmed.

"Why do they call it the Great Salt?" J.J. barked.

"You'll know when we get there," Soddy counseled.

Through the afternoon the Kids pumped away, making good time on the flat land and energized by the cool air. In this part of Oklahoma people were few and towns were fewer. They passed first Arapaho and then the tiny hamlet of Putnam before reaching the South Canadian once more at Taloga. Here they stopped for the night.

"Hard to believe we're at the Canadian again," huffed Angel as she plopped to the ground.

"Seen it before, huh?" the skunk queried.

"Yep; third crossing," J.J. answered. "It's not Angel's favorite place," she added with a laugh.

The dogs told Soddy the story of Angel's near miss farther downstream. He was impressed with their resourcefulness in getting out of a bad scrape. He sensed that they were good companions to have if trouble arose.

"Dinnertime," Angel chirped as she skipped to the cart and retrieved the food sack. "Good eating tonight."

"Don't forget an egg for me," Soddy quipped.

"Thought that was breakfast?" Angel quizzed.

"Breakfast anytime," the skunk retorted.

Angel hooted as she returned to the pack and removed one large white egg for the white-striped critter. As she and J.J. watched he carefully cracked the egg and sucked out its contents without spilling a drop.

"Pretty good!" the dogs gushed as they each gave him a soft thump.

"Good for you, too," he insisted. "And it keeps your coat nice and shiny."

"We'll keep that in mind," J.J. woofed as she tore off another piece of meat.

"Now for dessert," the little one whooped as she tore one doughnut into threes. "This is what I've been waiting for," she finished as she passed pieces to Soddy and J.J.

The three each savored the sweet and then moved down to the river for a drink. Thirsts quenched, J.J. skipped to the pack and pulled out the book, map, and flashlight. Then she returned to the others and unfolded the map.

"We must be here," she reasoned as she poked at a spot. "And the Salt Plains?"

"Up here," Soddy remarked as he placed a paw to the north.

"Yup; here we go," barked J.J. as she found the park. "It is a long way."

"Tomorrow?" quizzed the little one, wondering how quickly they could get there.

"Fast as this thing moves we just might make it," the skunk offered. "Day after for sure."

"What about those other towns along I-40?" Angel piped as she grabbed the book. "What were their names?"

"Weatherford first," J.J. reminded her. "Just east of Clinton. Oh, Elk City and Sayre," she added as she looked at the map.

"Let's see here," Angel mumbled. "Hold the light for me."

J.J. did as ordered and Angel began to read.

"Weatherford," she chirped. "About 10, 000 people. A famous astronaut comes from there; Thomas P. Stafford. Back in the '60s he worked on the Apollo project that took us to the moon. And there's a big university in town along with a space museum. Clinton; about 9000 and home to the Cheyenne Cultural Center; Elk City, about 10, 000 and the National Route 66 Museum; and Sayre; smaller at 4000. It says they used the courthouse to shoot part of a famous movie; The Grapes of Wrath."

"I wonder what that was about?" quizzed Soddy.

"It was about life in the Dust Bowl," the little one answered as she read the passage aloud. "We've read about it before. The bad weather destroyed people's farms and they had to leave. A whole bunch went to California to find work."

"I've heard those stories myself," the skunk remarked. "Must have been really tough times."

"Terrible," sighed Angel as she remembered their earlier studies. "But somehow or other the people endured. They always do."

"Almost always," corrected J.J. "Some just can't adjust."

"Yup," agreed the little one and the skunk together.

Angel closed the book while J.J. folded the map and then returned all to the pack. A soft full moon was rising steadily in the east, bathing the country in a stunning brightness.

"Almost light enough to read," Angel quipped as she looked skyward. "Mr. Stafford must have been excited about being nearly close enough to touch it."

"Would have been a thrill," J.J. barked as she gazed at the circle of white drilling that wide hole through night's darkness.

"Better get some sleep," Soddy advised. "Long day tomorrow."

The Kids had shed their sweaters by midmorning as the cold front had blown through and the air had warmed. Now J.J. laid them out on the ground and invited the skunk to share. He readily obliged, curling up between the Kids and resting his chin on J.J.'s warm chest. Eyes drooped. Sleep followed.

A chilly but crystal clear dawn greeted them. Angel yawned loudly as she fluttered her eyes and stood. Soddy uncurled and rolled to a stand while J.J. snapped to attention and stretched.

"Looks like a nice day," she purred as she turned to the buckets of light now spilling brightly over the eastern horizon.

"Perfect," seconded the little one, her breath clouding thickly in the cold morning air.

A drink and a bite and we're off," the skunk shouted as if to announce their intentions to the land's far corners.

The three sauntered down the bank to water's edge and sipped from a frigid, shallow pool. Angel filled an empty water bottle to overflowing and then capped it tightly.

"How many bottles do you have?" Soddy asked as he splashed his face.

"Four," the little one answered. "But we try to keep them all full. You never know what might happen."

"Smart," squeaked the skunk as he gave an approving nod and turned to crawl back up the bank with the girls in tow.

"I guess you want another egg?" Angel joked as she hopped to the cart and the food sack.

"You read my mind," Soddy squeaked as he licked his lips.

Angel carried the sack to the others and then pulled out an egg for the skunk. Once again they were amazed at the ease with which their new friend cracked the shell and drank it dry.

"Spilled a drop," J.J. teased as one small drip ran down the skunk's lower lip.

"Got it," he popped as his tongue shot down to retrieve it.

Breakfast done the three loaded the pack and then took their places; Soddy by the shaft and the Kids at the handle. With a few hard pumps they were rolling over the railroad river bridge and heading north. They would see the South Canadian yet again. The North was just an hour away.

After crossing U.S. 270 near Seeling the crew quickly reached the broad expanse of the North Canadian. Nearly dry but wide, they clicked their way over the long bridge that spanned it.

"Better rain hard soon," Soddy remarked as he looked down at the inch deep stagnant pools that dotted the bed. "No flow at all," he finished with a sigh.

"Dry country," Angel commented. "What about ground water?"

"Hit or miss around here," the skunk explained. "Good water some places and none in others."

"Hmm," Angel murmured as she looked to J.J. who was working the rear handle.

"Turn up ahead," her sister barked.

Angel and Soddy quickly focused to the north and the great bend in the tracks. Here they curved to almost due east along Highway 60. A few miles more and another turn sent them veering a little to the north once more.

"Good," the skunk hooted. "Right on course. I was a little worried there for a minute; thought we might end up going the wrong way."

For another hour the Kids pumped their way through the broad expanse of flat rolling prairie. Then a high rise to the north caught J.J.'s attention.

"Look!" she shouted. "Hills!"

"Those are the Glass Mountains," Soddy informed them as Angel turned to look. "Sometimes called the Gloss."

"Why do they call them that?" the little one queried.

"Got some sort of mineral in 'em; selentite I believe they call it. Makes 'em shine like glass."

As they drew closer the girls could see exactly what the skunk was talking about as the chain of hills glistened in the bright autumn sun.

"How high are they?" J.J. quizzed.

"Not real high; less than 2000 feet. But that's pretty steep for out here," he added with a laugh. "There's a nice park here, too."

"I'll bet you places like this were important landmarks a long time ago," J.J. reckoned.

"You bet," confirmed the skunk. "Back in the old days getting lost out here didn't take much doing. I imagine many a lost soul used those hills to guide himself home."

"Now we use the tracks," chuckled Angel as she began to pump again.

"Yup; tracks and roads," the skunk affirmed.

Near noon the trio pulled to a stop along a little draw just east of the mountains. Here Soddy jumped to the ground. The Kids followed.

"More water here than in the whole Canadian," the skunk joked as he moved toward the draw and took a look at the deep pool under the bridge. "You two go ahead and eat," he told them. "I'm going to see what I can find here."

The girls skipped back to the cart where Angel grabbed some lunch. As they ate they watched their friend digging along the bank and poking his nose in the water. Finally he marched back to the Kids sporting a wide grin.

"Good pond," he smiled. "Three big fat worms and some minnows that should have taken nature's cold cue and hibernated last week."

"Worms and minnows," J.J. spat as she puckered her lips.

"You're not hard to please," the little one sighed. "How about a little doughnut," she added as she passed a small piece to the skunk.

"Great way to top off a grand meal," he laughed as he gobbled the sweet. "Everyone ready to roll?"

"Ready," advised J.J. as the Kids took their positions on the cart.

"This draw must run into the Cimarron," Soddy piped. "Looks to be running that way."

"We've seen that river before," Angel squeaked as she gave the handle a hard pump.

"It's just up ahead," the skunk remarked. "Haven't seen it in awhile though. Might have water; might not."

Just as Soddy had told them, they soon came to the river bridge just north of the Highway 412/ 60 intersection. A few quick pumps shot them over the nearly dry bed. Fifteen minutes later the skunk motioned them to quit.

"Something I want you to see," he said with a wide smile.

"What?" quizzed the little one as they coasted to a stop.

"A real soddy," he quipped.

Quickly the skunk led the Kids over Highway 8 to the Sod House Museum. The site, maintained by the Oklahoma Historical Society, is home to the last true soddy on the Oklahoma prairie.

"Is this where you were born?" whooped J.J. as she studied the structure.

"Oh, no," laughed the skunk. "I was born in an old ruin. But this is the real thing. A man named McCully built it way back in 1894 and it's the only original house left standing."

"Looks kind of cozy," Angel chirped as she ran her paw along the rough dirt exterior and then peeked through the door to the inside.

"Probably was," Soddy reckoned. "Sure beat living outdoors anyway."

"What happened to all the others?" J.J. asked.

"Weather got them," the skunk explained. "They weren't meant to last forever, just long enough to build something better."

The three finished their examination of the McCully soddy and then returned to the cart and continued north. They first passed Aline and then came to Highway 45 near Carmen. Here the tracks stopped, tying in to the main Burlington Northern line running west.

"Looks like we'll have to hoof it from here," Soddy informed them. "We should get there by dark, he added as he checked the sun.

"Haven't walked in quite a bit," J.J. joked as she reached for the pack.

"Might do us some good," the little one counseled, not quite sure she believed herself.

"Hope no one finds our cart," J.J. worried as Angel tightened the pack straps for her sister.

"Let's roll it behind that old shed," the skunk suggested, pointing to the structure along the tracks just about fifty yards ahead. "That'll hide it."

"Good idea," barked J.J. as she and Angel pumped the cart to the spot.

"This should do it," Angel squeaked. "Can't see it from the road."

"Well, let's make tracks," Soddy hooted. "Follow me."

The skunk set a course over open country, knowing the route was much shorter than taking the roads. Just as he had reckoned the three hit the southern end of the park just at dusk. In the day's last light they reached the shores of the Great Salt Plains Lake, a nearly 9000 acre reservoir fed by the waters of the Salt Fork of the Arkansas. Here they found a deserted campground and stopped for the night.

"Plenty of water," Angel mused as she looked out over the wide lake, now just barely visible in the rushing darkness.

"Don't drink that," Soddy cautioned. "Too salty."

"I think there's a faucet over there," J.J. stated as she squinted through the gloom and pointed to a nearby campsite.

"That'll do," the skunk affirmed as the three moved toward it.

After drinking the three returned to their campsite and sprawled out on the ground beneath a high bench.

"Legs a little tired?" Soddy teased as he grabbed at the little one's paw with his mouth and gave it a gentle tug.

"Little bit," confessed Angel as she swatted the skunk lightly on the nose and giggled.

"Too bad you're so short," J.J. chuckled. "You could work the pump if you were taller."

"I'm the engineer," Soddy sniffed as he stuck his black nose high in the air and then broke into a wide, white grin. "We don't do the hard stuff."

"Well what would the brains of this outfit like for dinner?" Angel chided as she began to help J.J. remove the pack.

"About ten of those doughnuts would be nice," he cracked as he licked his lips.

"How about some meat instead?" the little one scoffed. "Didn't your momma warn you about eating dessert first."

"Nope. She was strict. Never had dessert, period," he quipped in return. "But she was still a good momma."

The Kids buckled over in laughter as Angel passed out dinner. Stomachs full, the three talked for an hour before drifting off to sleep atop the sweaters.

The next morning broke clear but windy and cold as a new front had pushed in during the night. The Kids awoke to find Soddy at lake's edge, quickly dipping his nose in and out of the water as he tried to catch his breakfast.

"Any luck?" yelled Angel as she marched toward him.

"A few little ones," the skunk replied between thrusts. "Enough for a meal anyway. Well, you ready to see the park?" he asked as he swallowed the last little bit.

"Yep," confirmed the Kids together as J.J. loaded the pack and, with Angel's help, strapped it to her back. "Which way do we go?"

"I'll lead," counseled the skunk. We'll work our way around the water."

Soddy took off as the Kids followed. At a campsite they found an information board where J.J. pulled the brochures and read as they went along. They also found a map of Oklahoma's Great Plains Trail, one that detailed the many interesting places in this part of the state and the driving routes to take to see them.

"Bunch of great stuff out here," gushed J.J. as she studied the map.

"Oh, and look!" Angel nearly shouted as she read a brochure. "There's another wildlife refuge right here."

"Never can have enough of those," J.J. offered as Soddy looked on.

Through the morning the three worked their way around the park. They found it got its name from the huge salt deposits that covered much of the area.

"Hard to believe that people have fought wars over this stuff," Soddy spoke as he and the Kids crunched through a thick layer of salt that covered a broad plain.

"Really?" Angel asked, truly surprised.

"Yep," the skunk affirmed. "I heard they had a big fight down in Texas; out around El Paso, I believe they said."

"Does seem hard to believe," J.J. spat as she looked out over a vast expanse of white.

"Salt's valuable," the skunk informed them. "That was especially true in the old days when they used it to preserve meat; meat that might have to last through a long winter."

"Oh; never thought of that," coughed J.J. as she inhaled some salty dust.

"Where does it come from?" the little one asked.

"Underground," Soddy answered. "Percolates up with the water through the soil. When the water evaporates it leaves all these layers."

"The brochure says there's about twenty-five square miles of it," Angel read aloud.

"That's a bunch," remarked a surprised J.J. as the three reached the park's southern boundary.

"Well, back to the railroad and my cushy job," gloated the skunk as they set course back for their cart.

Through out the afternoon the trio retraced their steps and reached their taxi in late afternoon. Tired from the long hike, they decided to stay put for the night and leave early the next morning. Soddy informed them that now they would work their way back to the southwest.

"Antelope Hills?" J.J. queried as she tried to calculate how much time they had left.

"Antelope Hills," confirmed the skunk. "But there'll be a few stops along the way."

"We can't be late," J.J. cautioned. "I think we have about six days left; five or six."

"We'll make it," Soddy promised. "As long as this old crate holds up."

"She's been pretty good so far," chimed Angel as she patted the splintered wooden platform.

"Sure has," seconded J.J.

"How'd that old bird know about this thing anyway?" Soddy pondered aloud as he looked at the handcar and shook his head.

"Who knows?" whooped J.J. "I'm just glad he did."

"We should give it a name," the little one peeped.

"Good idea," concurred J.J.

"Sooner Schooner," suggested the skunk.

"Schooner?" quizzed the Kids together.

"A ship," explained Soddy. "Except back in the pioneer days they called the wagons that carried them 'prairie schooners' because they went by land instead of sea.

"Pretty good," hooted J.J.

"Maybe they put sails on them like a boat," reasoned Angel, wondering if the wind could push a big wagon.

"They tried," chuckled the skunk. "Didn't work too well. Those old crates were heavy."

All three had a good laugh at the idea and then settled in for the night. As the sun began its dive the winds died but left a blanket of bitter cold to drape the ground around them. Tonight the dogs would wear their sweaters while Soddy kept warm between the two.

Morning brought a wondrous scene, the frost covered prairie grass reflecting the sun's first light like a million little mirrors. Squinting against the blinding brightness the Kids awoke, jostling the skunk to awareness as they rose.

"Look at that!" Angel gushed as she stared out over the shining plain.

"Absolutely magnificent," hooted J.J. as she moved to a tuft of frosty grass and gave it a whack, laughing as the thinnest of ice shattered and sprinkled to the ground.

"This is fun," exploded the little one as she joined her sister.

"Enjoy it while you can," chuckled Soddy, knowing that the sun would soon turn ice to dew.

"Where to today?" asked J.J. as she crunched one last piece of ice.

"Down the tracks," Soddy replied as he pointed to the west. "Then we'll see. If I remember right these tracks cut another line that will take us right by the Little Sahara."

"Little Sahara?" the little one quizzed.

"Interesting place," the skunk explained. "Like nothing you've ever seen, I bet. Just wait."

"Okay," Angel agreed, knowing the Soddy wanted to surprise them with something new.

After loading up, the three were off, the Kids pumping hard against the morning chill. Just as the skunk had recollected, they soon came to another rail line near the tiny town of Avard. Here the tracks cut to the southwest.

"Yup; just like I remembered," Soddy squeaked as their line curved to meet the new one.

"What's around here?" J.J. barked as she studied the tracks ahead.

"Wide open country," the skunk replied. "Alva's just to the north though. Pretty good sized town of about 5000; has a big university and the Cherokee Strip Museum."

"Cherokee Strip?" questioned J.J. "Same as the Cherokee Outlet?"

"Same thing," affirmed the skunk.

"We read about that," Angel informed him. "It's still hard to believe so many people wanted land."

"And what they'd do to get it," J.J. interjected.

"Yup," Soddy agreed. "Always seems to be more people than land. That's the history of the world in a nutshell.

"Hard to believe a country this big could ever run out of land," Angel mused as she thought back to their earlier adventure and the vast expanse of ground they had covered.

"It can," advised the skunk. "And pretty much did. That's why we have to protect what little bit is left."

"I guess that's true with just about everything," J.J. stated. "There always seems to be plenty until it's gone; land, oil, food, water, you name it."

"Don't forget money," chuckled the skunk. "It can drain off in a big hurry. Ask any government."

The three said nothing more as the girls pumped the handcar down the tracks. They soon crossed the Highway 281/ 14 intersection near the town of Wynoka. In a few minutes Soddy motioned the Kids to halt.

"What now?" J.J. asked as the cart slowed to a stop.

"Little Sahara," the skunk yelled as he pointed to the east.

"Great," shouted Angel, excited even if she didn't know what it was."

"Bring a water bottle and let's go," Soddy ordered as the three hopped to the ground.

"Now are you going to tell us what it is?" J.J. joked as they walked up a rise.

"Wont' have to in just a second," the skunk chimed as the three reached the crest.

"Wow!" shouted J.J. as she looked out huge expanse of rolling sand before them. "Where did all this come from?"

"Flooding from the Cimarron River years ago," offered the skunk. Some of those peaks are seventy-five feet high," she added as the Kids carefully studied the dunes.

"Why do they call it Little Sahara?" Angel quizzed.

"Because it looks kind of like the big one," Soddy explained.

"Oh ya, the one in North Africa," the little one countered.

"Very good," complimented the skunk.

"Is this one as big?" J.J. questioned.

"Oh, no," laughed the skunk. "But it does cover about 14000 acres. People come here to ride their dune buggies."

"Great place for it," beamed the little one as she continued to look out over rippling sand. "Bet they have a lot of fun."

"Sure do," Soddy affirmed.

For an hour the three plodded through the sand, exploring the dunes and the many campsites that bordered them. In the distance they could see one lone buggy driver bouncing up and down over the rises.

"Glad this isn't a weekend," J.J. buzzed.

"We wouldn't be walking through here if it was," hooted the skunk. "We'd be dodging traffic."

The Kids laughed and then all three turned to head back to their cart. Soon they were off again. Within minutes they came to the Cimarron bridge and crossed the river.

"Do you know where we're going?" Angel asked as she looked to the skunk.

"Woodward's up ahead," he informed her. "We'll go there and then swing south."

"What's around here?" J.J. quizzed as she gave the handle a hard pump.

"Two more nice parks," Soddy replied. "Alabaster Caverns is just upstream; great cave to explore. And Boiling Springs is just east of the town; has nice trees and some great springs. It's a good place to take on water if you need it."

That suggestion prompted Angel to pull a bottle from the pack and pass it around. All were thirsty. In an hour they reached Highway 412 where the tracks turned due west to follow it toward Woodward. Near the end of the day they reached Boiling Springs where they decided to stop for the night.

"Back to the North Canadian," J.J. mused as she looked south to the river. "Looks like there's good water in it."

"Rivers out here are strange," counseled the skunk as he jumped to the ground. "Water sometimes and then it goes dry as a bone."

"Why is that?" questioned the little one as she followed the others.

"Sometimes the water goes underground and runs a long way before it resurfaces," Soddy explained. "Don't ask me why but it just does."

"Strange," mused J.J. "Must be a reason for it."

"What was that big word we once heard?" Angel chirped. "You know, someone who studies water?"

"Hydrologist!" J.J. nearly shouted, proud of herself for remembering. "He'd be the one to explain it."

"Know where we can find one?" laughed the skunk as he tried to repeat the word.

"Not off hand," giggled J.J.

"I wonder if there's a school in Oklahoma that teaches it?" mused Angel.

"Probably," reckoned the skunk. "It'd be a good field to be in."

J.J. jumped back to the cart and pulled the pack to the ground where Angel helped her strap it on. Then the three cautiously approached the park. They soon found a good place to enter and slipped through the fence. All was quiet.

"There's the headquarters," Angel whispered as she pointed ahead. "Maybe we can find some information.

"Good idea," praised J.J. "Let's go."

Quickly the three skipped to the spot and pulled a flier from the rack. After dashing behind a tree Angel looked it over in the fading light.

"More than 800 acres," she read. "And here's one of the springs you were talking about, Soddy," she finished as she pointed to the park map.

"Right close by," squeaked the skunk. "Let's go see."

The trio skipped to the spring and filled the water bottles before exploring some more. They soon found a nice tree covered table and decided to make it their campsite for the night. In the distance they could see a lone man moving about. Otherwise the park was empty.

"Nice to have it all to ourselves," J.J. yapped as she shed the pack and plopped to the ground.

"A weekday and kind of chilly," the skunk offered as he sprawled out next to the dogs. "But I bet this place hops in warm weather."

"No doubt," chirped the little one as she moved to the pack and pulled out the book. "I think I'll check out Woodward."

"What's it say?" J.J. quizzed as her sister found the spot.

"Looks to be about the biggest town anywhere near here," she read, "about 12, 000 people. There's a Plains Indians and Pioneers Museum and just to the north is an old frontier army post; Fort Supply. It looks pretty neat."

"Do you know how far to Antelope Hills?" J.J. asked the skunk as the little one reached for the map.

"Not too far," Soddy replied. "But you two have one more place to see before we go there."

"What's that?" Angel asked.

"Black Kettle National Grasslands and the Washita Battlefield," the skunk explained. "The hills are just to the north of there."

"We should get there tomorrow without any trouble," the little one chirped.

"One little problem," Soddy cautioned.

"What's that?" J.J. barked.

"I don't think the tracks run there. We might have to do some walking," he sighed.

"Oh," Angel frowned. "Are you sure."

"Pretty sure," confirmed the skunk. "If I remember it right the tracks go straight west to Texas while we need to go south."

"Back on foot," huffed J.J. "Oh, well; nothing new."

"Nope," chirped the little one as she brightened a little. "We've walked all over creation."

"Good dogs," praised Soddy as he gave each a gentle nuzzle.

Darkness soon settled in over Boiling Springs as the Kids and Soddy made ready for sleep. Angel pulled out the sweaters and the dogs helped each other put them on. As was by now his custom, Soddy took a warm spot between them. That night the stars were dazzlingly bright as the three took turns pointing to ones that caught their attention. After hours of stargazing the three drifted off into the heavens of sleep with J.J. being the last to fall.

Dawn brought a soggy warmth as moist Gulf currents blew in from the south. Angel stirred first, yawning loudly enough to wake the others. All three stretched and rose.

"Warm front," peeped the skunk as he turned his face to the wind. "Might mean rain."

"I'm about to burn up," joked J.J. as she tugged at her sweater to get it off.

"Same here," chirped the little one as she helped her sister who then returned the favor.

The trio skipped to the springs for a drink and then began their short walk back to the cart. Reaching it , J.J. hopped to the floor and dropped the pack. Angel and Soddy followed.

"Well, let's see where she takes us," the skunk commanded as the girls manned the handle and began to pump.

In minutes they had crossed the North Canadian bridge and swung north of Woodward. Soon they found the tracks running just along Highway 15 and heading almost due west toward Texas. In an hour they were approaching the town of Gage when J.J. looked hard down the tracks.

"Trouble!" she shouted. "Train!"

Angel turned to look while Soddy placed his front feet on the shaft to rise and get a better look. Less than a mile ahead was a full train running hard towards them, its string of cars reaching back to the horizon.

"Strike must be over," J.J. deadpanned as she dropped her end of the handle and quickly grabbed the pack.

"Must be," agreed the little one who vainly looked around for a place to sidetrack their cart.

"No place to hide," Soddy squealed. "Best make a jump."

Swiftly Angel helped J.J. secure the pack and then the three hopped from the cart to the ground and sprinted for a tiny wooden building about fifty yards away. Before they could turn to look they heard the piercing whine of steel on steel as the train braked. But it was too late. In a boom the air exploded as the locomotive smashed the little cart and sent it rolling from the tracks, its wooden frame shattering into a hundred splintery pieces.

"There goes our Sooner Schooner," whined Angel as she watched the train push the wreckage aside and pick up speed again. "I'm gonna miss her."

"She took us a long way," sighed J.J.

"We were going to have to get off soon anyway," Soddy consoled them. "I believe the highway south is just ahead."

"I remember," Angel acknowledged. "I just didn't want to see it all end like this. I'd grown fond of that old crate. It's a piece of history gone for good."

"That's for sure," J.J. concurred. "Well, we might as well get going," she added, never one to let a temporary misfortune turn her from the task.

The three each had a sip of water and then took one more look at the tracks before heading west. Soon they hit Highway 46 which Soddy believed would take them to Antelope Hills. Here they struck south, turning into a stiff but warm wind. Above the skies darkened.

"Rain coming for sure," the skunk observed as he looked up. "Those clouds are full of water."

"Bad for us but good for the land," Angel piped.

"If it's good for the land it's good for us," J.J. countered with a smile.

"Let's look for a place to ride this out," the skunk advised.

The three began to scope the land around them and soon spied a crumbling old barn just off the road and headed toward it.

"About the best we're gonna find," J.J. reckoned as they moved inside.

"Boy does this thing look ancient," the skunk remarked as he studied the rotting wooden trusses holding up the rusted sheet metal roof. "Hope it doesn't cave in."

Just as the three settled into a corner the first drops began to pelt the ground. Within seconds a slow but steady rain was washing the air and nourishing the land.

"Perfect kind of rain," the skunk commented as he looked out the barn door. "A real good soaker."

"Say Soddy," Angel quizzed. "In the whole time we've been together we haven't told you about the Sooner Silver. Do you know about it?"

"Oh sure," piped the skunk. "Edmond filled me in on everything. But I knew about it before he found me."

"That figures," laughed J.J. "Every critter we've met seemed to have the whole story."

"Gossips carries," Soddy chuckled. "And I know why you're so anxious to get to Antelope Hills. I wonder if that Silver fellow knows you're so hard on his tail?" he added with a grin.

"Don't see how he could," the little one squeaked as she pawed at the pouch around her neck.

"You really guard that pouch, don't you," Soddy purred as he gave it a good sniff. "What's in it?"

Angel dropped it to the ground and pulled out the arrowhead for the skunk to see. He examined it carefully before handing it back to her.

"Figured it was something like that," he peeped. "It's taken you a long way, hasn't it."

"All the way here," J.J. barked as Angel closed the pouch and slipped it back around her neck.

"You've done some traveling," hooted the skunk. "I'll bet you know more about Oklahoma than most Oklahomans."

"We've learned an awful lot," admitted J.J.

"And we've had a great time doing it," added the little one. "It's been one fascinating experience after another."

"Of course there's no such thing as knowing everything," cautioned J.J. "We've just scratched the surface. This trip has just made us hungry for more."

"Good attitude," praised the skunk. "My momma used to say that you should find something that really grabs you and latch onto it; learn everything you possibly can about it."

"Sounds smart," agreed J.J.

"Fun, too," chirped Angel.

"Anything in particular that's caught your fancy?" Soddy asked as he looked to J.J.

"Ohhh," pondered J.J. as she put a paw to her chin. "Kind of hard to say; there's so much of interest. But I guess the early explorations; the movements of peoples. I still can't believe the Vikings might have come to Oklahoma. I'd really like to know a lot more about them and the Indian peoples who were here at that time."

"What about you?" the skunk chirped at Angel.

"Civil War," she barked without hesitation. "It was such a sad and complicated affair. I'd like to know a lot more about it, especially here in Oklahoma."

"Good topics," the skunk replied as he nodded his head in approval. "They'll both keep you busy for a lifetime."

"We've got a job to do first," J.J. reminded him.

"I haven't forgotten that," Soddy counseled. "We'll get a move on as soon as this rain stops."

For another hour Soddy and the girls talked about the many different historic and geographic points that made Oklahoma so unique. Finally the the rain tapered off to a light mist and they packed to leave.

The trio resumed their march south down Highway 46 to the little town of Arnett at the Highway 51 intersection. A sharp dogleg left soon brought them to U.S. 283 where they turned south to follow the road. Late afternoon brought them once more to the north bank of the Canadian.

"Canadian again," whooped J.J. as she looked out over the broad riverbed now filling from the morning's rain.

"Let's get over the bridge and then look for something to eat," the skunk advised as he checked the highway for traffic.

"Sounds good," Angel chirped as she did the same. "Nothing coming."

"Then let's go girls," Soddy ordered as the three stepped up their pace and dashed for the other side.

Safely across the three moved down to the bank to scout around. The skunk found a little pool of minnows and ate his fill while the girls scoured the area but found nothing. Dejected they returned to Soddy.

"Anything?" he asked them.

"Nothing," moaned the little one.

"Well, looks like we have a little emergency," the skunk sighed as he rubbed his jaw. "Time to call for Sally."

"Sally?" questioned a baffled J.J.

"Sally Scissortail," Soddy explained. "Last I heard she lives right around here."

"What's a scissortail?" Angel questioned.

"State bird of Oklahoma," the skunk answered. "Scissortail Flycatcher to be exact."

"Oh," perked the little one.

"We've got over an hour of daylight left. Let's just keep walking and maybe she'll show up," Soddy advised.

With that the three resumed their march south down U.S. 283 before coming to a halt near the tiny hamlet of Roll. Here they found a thick stand of brush just off the highway and crawled through the fence to reach it.

"Good hiding place," J.J. barked as they moved behind the cover.

With Angel's help J.J. dropped the pack and took out a water bottle which the three quickly drained. With the sun dropping fast in the west they surveyed the area for a possible meal. Only a lone farmhouse stood far in the distance.

"Not much around here," sighed Angel as she looked around.

"Nope," agreed J.J. as she rubbed her empty stomach.

Suddenly a shrill cry cut the quiet of dusk. The three looked up to see a beautiful bird of light grey and black and red swooping down toward them. Coming to a landing in the brush just above, the bird twitched its long split tail and cocked its head in greeting.

"Well Sally Scissortail," Soddy hooted. "I heard you were around these parts. Last time we met you were way down on the Washita."

"What are you doing out here, you old skunk?" the bird crowed as she grinned at Soddy.

"Guiding these two dogs," Soddy replied.

"Must be the Blacktail Kids," Sally surmised.

"That they be," affirmed the skunk. "Listen, they're a little shy on grub. Think you can help them out?"

"Let me fly over to the house and talk to Henry. Maybe he'll have something," she cawed as she looked back toward the farmhouse.

"Henry?" the Kids inquired together.

"Their dog," explained the bird.

In a whoosh the scissortail went airborne and disappeared into the darkening night. A short while later she returned.

"He's coming," she informed them as she dropped a fat worm at Soddy's feet. "You looked like you could use a little, too," she finished.

"Could stand it," Soddy gushed as he thanked the bird and swallowed the worm.

In a few minutes the four saw the outline of a large dog crossing the road and moving toward them. He easily slid through the fence and approached the brush.

"This is Henry," Sally offered as the Kids patted the ground in greeting.

"Brought you a little something," the mixed-breed hound woofed as he dropped a sack at J.J.'s feet. "It's not much but it'll hold you for a while."

"Thanks, Henry," J.J. barked as she opened the sack to find six packets of dog food.

"Well, gotta go," the dog nearly hollered. "I'm supposed to be guarding the henhouse."

"Henhouse?" the skunk shrieked as his face brightened.

"No, Soddy," warmed the bird with a deep scowl. "You can't have any eggs; his or mine either."

"All right," the skunk sighed. "But I wouldn't deny myself for anyone except you," he added with a loud chuckle.

"You can behave yourself for once," Sally chirped as she grinned down at the skunk.

Quickly Henry dashed back to the house while the Kids helped themselves to a pack of food each. While they ate, the bird guided Soddy to a good dig where he found several more juicy worms. Then they returned to the Kids.

"Soddy says you're heading for the Black Kettle tomorrow and then up to Antelope Hills," the scissortail spoke.

"That's right," Angel squeaked as she took a sip from a water bottle and then offered it to the others.

"Well, you'd better be quick about it," Sally warned.

"Why's that?" J.J. questioned.

"Word's. out you're looking for a guy in a white van; has writing on the side?" the bird asked.

"Sure are," Angel confirmed as J.J. nodded in agreement.

"I saw one yesterday down at Cheyenne. Stranger driving it," the bird explained. "I've never seen the guy before and I know about everybody around here. Might be your man."

"He's due here about now," J.J. offered as she scratched her chin. "But we thought we still had a few days. Thanks for the information. You'd make a good cop," she finished with a chuckle.

"Tough enough just being a good bird," giggled Sally as she looked to the skunk. "Anyway I hope it helps you. Now you'd better get some rest. I have a feeling tomorrow's going to be a big day for you."

"Good chance of that," Angel squeaked.

"Well, best of luck to you," Sally chirped. "You, too, Soddy. Good to see you again."

"Same to you Sally," the skunk replied. "I'll catch you back down on the Washita in the spring."

"Sounds good," Sally answered. "Just stay away from my eggs," she finished with a beaming grin.

With that the bird lifted off and in seconds had disappeared into the now near total darkness. A strong south wind still warmed the air. The sweaters stayed in the pack as the three bedded down for a night. The Kids would sleep little as bolts of excitement peppered their brains.

Well before dawn they stirred; Angel first and J.J. seconds later. The little one gave Soddy a gentle nudge and then wobbled to her feet. J.J. followed, then went to the pack for a water bottle, the map and flashlight. After passing around the bottle she opened the map as the little one held the light.

"The Antelope Hills are almost due west," J.J. read. "Right down 33. Can't we go straight there, Soddy?"

"Not just yet," the skunk stated with a firm shake of his head. "Cheyenne first."

"The town's just down here," she read as she pointed a few miles to the south. "We're back to the Washita River again."

"Where's the battlefield?" Angel asked as she bowed her head to look at the map.

"Right outside town," Soddy interrupted. "Just to the west."

"Want to eat, folks," J.J. asked as she looked to the others.

"Naw," Angel buzzed. "Let's get going."

"Fine by me," the skunk concurred.

With that J.J. folded the map and returned it, the flashlight, and the bottle to the pack. Then they strapped it down tight on her back. The three were off down 283.

They walked quickly through the early morning quiet. The warm southern breeze was still in command. Shortly after dawn they crossed the Washita and reached Cheyennes northern edge. A sign told them it was a town of less than a thousand that sat right on top of huge deposits of natural gas and helium. A quick cut to the west soon brought them to the battlefield where they stopped to read the markers and grab a brochure. For just a moment they forgot about Silver and the Hills.

"Hard to believe a place as pretty and peaceful as this could have been a battlefield," Angel purred as she stared over the riverbottom. "What happened, J.J?"

"It goes back to 1868," J.J. read "It seems George Custer and his seventh cavalry attacked a band of Cheyennes camped here. The Indian leader was a chief named Black Kettle."

"He was a good man," interrupted Soddy. "I don't know of any Indian, at least in these parts, who tried harder to keep the peace than Black Kettle. But old Custer just had to make a name for himself. Yup, Custer won this one but about eight years later he and his whole command were wiped out at the Little Big Horn in Montana. It was all so sad."

"Must have been," agreed Angel. "What about the grassland?"

"Looks like quite a place," read J.J. "Way over 30,000 acres. It runs all the way west into Texas. They named it after the chief."

"You're about to see a big chunk of it," the skunk informed them. "We'll follow the river upstream through the grasslands until we cut north to the hills."

I know we're in a hurry," Angel chirped as she looked to Soddy, "but I'm glad you brought us here first."

"I knew this was a place you had to see," he answered. "Now there's a faucet. Let's fill those water bottles and get going. We should make the hills by this afternoon."

J.J. did as ordered and then the three set off up the Washita. As they moved through the grasslands they saw game of every type; turkey and quail and deer and antelope to name just a few. Each step through the high grass seemed to flush yet another critter. Near noon they stopped for lunch under one of the few trees they had seen. Then the three quickly resumed their journey, coming to Highway

30 in another hour. Here they crossed the bridge to the river's north side. A look at the map told them that the hills were still miles ahead.

"Still have time to make it before dark," J.J. huffed as she checked the sun now just a little to their left.

"Believe we can," seconded the skunk. "33's not too far ahead. Then it's pretty much a straight shot north."

J.J. checked the compass to confirm the direction and then the trio trudged on. Soddy was right as they reached Highway 33 in less than an hour. They soon reached the little settlement of Durham and the main road ended. But just ahead the stunning hills broke the plane of flatness. A sign told them what they could already see; 'Antelope Hills'. From here a gravel track pushed to the north and the three eagerly walked to its side.

"Not far now!" J.J. nearly shouted. "Look!"

"We'll make it by dark for sure," the little one hooted as she looked to the smiling skunk.

As the eagle had warned them before, hills and mountains always looked closer than they really were. Still they knew what they could see they could soon touch. By early evening they had reached the heart of the range in a deep bend of the Canadian River. In places the hills reached to more than 2600 feet.

"Boy is this a pretty place," gushed Angel as she stared at the rocky hills all around.

"I thought you'd like it," Soddy stated. "Haven't seen 'em myself for quite awhile. Brings back some good old memories."

"Sure seem out of place in all this flatness," J.J. mused.

"Nature's always doing crazy things," squeaked the skunk. "Now let's find a place to camp for the night."

After scouting around the three found a nice sheltered gully nestled between two hills. A stand of brush hid them from the nearby road.

"Great spot," barked J.J. as the three found a soft piece of dirt to lie in. "We can see everything that comes by."

"Do you think Silver will still come?" the little one sighed, worrying that they might have missed him.

"Can't say," admitted J.J. "We'll just have to wait and see. By my account we're a day or two early."

"Aren't you glad you got a move on," Soddy quipped. "Never hurts to beat a deadline."

"That's true," chirped Angel as she turned to look at a haunting red sun now shining its last behind them.

"Sunsets out here must be the prettiest in the world," the skunk offered. "I never get tired of them."

"Why do they call these the Antelope Hills?" J.J. asked.

"Remember that critter we scared up in the grasslands? The one that kind of looked like a deer but wasn't?" Soddy reminded them.

"Yup," confirmed the dogs together.

"That was an antelope. There are a bunch of 'em out here, especially over in the Panhandle," he informed them. "You're going to meet one pretty soon; old Andy."

"Andy the antelope," Angel laughed as she helped J.J. with the pack.

"Could stand some water," the skunk mused.

Angel brought out a water bottle and the three each had a deep drink. Then Soddy marched off into the grass to find some dinner while the Kids shared a pack of dog food. He soon returned to inform them he had found a few grasshoppers for dinner.

"Cold made 'em sluggish and easy to catch," he laughed as he spat out a wing. "They're usually long gone by this time of year. These last few warm days must have brought them out again."

"Cold then warm; warm then cold," Angel puzzled. "I guess the cold will move back in pretty quick."

"Anytime now," Soddy warned.

The three talked for a bit before the weariness of the day's long walk finally grabbed them. One by one they drifted off into a sleep which even eager anticipation could not disturb. Just as the skunk had predicted, the winds soon shifted, wrapping the hills in the cutting chill of a new norther.

Dawn brought a shivering stiffness as the three arose nearly together. Angel shook a water bottle to break up the little bits of ice that had formed inside. Then she passed it to the others before drinking herself.

"What now?" she asked as she capped the bottle and placed it back in the pack.

"We wait," J.J. answered as she focused hard on the road just below. "Nothing else to do."

"I guess you're right," agreed Angel as she looked to the skunk.

"I'm gonna get higher," Soddy informed them as he looked to the top of their hill. "If I see anything I'll signal."

"Okay," the Kids replied together. "We'll stay here."

The skunk quickly worked his way up the side of the hill until he found a good spot near its summit. From there he could see the road for miles in either direction. For two hours they waited. Finally the Kids looked up to Soddy who was waving his arms wildly as he tried to get their attention. Then he pointed to the south where a white van was kicking up dust and gravel as it approached. Hearts racing, the dogs strained to see. Soon the van came out from behind the adjoining lower hill and pulled to a stop in a parking area just in front of them. It was Silver.

"Got him!" J.J. whispered loudly.

As they watched, the driver got out of the van, cell phone in hand. Quickly but cautiously the Kids skittered down the gully and approached from his rear, falling in out of sight just behind the van. Poking their heads around they could hear him clearly.

"Next week," he spoke into the phone. "The fifteenth. Meet me at the top."

With that Silver flipped his phone shut and quickly turned to see J.J. staring at him around the side of the van. Angrily he picked up a rock and charged. With no time to run J.J. growled and began to circle while Angel fell in behind her. Silver thought he recognized the dogs from Robbers Cave, but then muttered to himself that it was impossible for them to be here. He chunked one rock at J.J. but missed. Then he grabbed another.

"Oh, boy," the skunk winced as he worked his way down the hill. "Soddy to the rescue."

In a flash he zipped down the hillside to the road and approached Silver from behind. Then he let out a loud squeal, turned and fired.

"Ahgg!" the thief screamed as the scent hit him.

Right on cue the dogs dashed for their hideout while Soddy shot off through another gully, then climbed the slight rise between the two and rejoined the girls. Through the brush they watched, going into hysterics as Silver flailed away, his hands rubbing his face to rawness. Finally he jumped back into his van, gunned the motor, and took off down the road, gravel flying high with every roll of his wheels.

"Good work, Soddy," J.J. howled with laughter as she watched the van disappear over the rise.

"Thought you could use a little help," the skunk chimed. "So that was the guy, huh?"

"One of 'em," affirmed Angel. "Other one's a County Commissioner."

"Did you hear what he said?" Soddy queried between giggles.

"Ya, but he still didn't say anything specific," J.J. responded. "He just said 'meet me at the top'. Can you figure out what it all means?"

"No, but way out west must mean out in the Panhandle," the skunk reasoned remembering the Kids had told him about an earlier conversation Silver had had.

"That's that long, thin strip of land that tops off Texas," Angel chirped, remembering the map.

"Right," confirmed Soddy. "Andy can take you through it. It's his country."

"The antelope," J.J. barked. "Do you know where he is?"

"No," admitted the skunk. "All I can tell you is that he's somewhere out there," he finished as he pointed to the north.

"Well, we have to go north to get to the Panhandle," Angel huffed.

"Ya," confirmed J.J. "And we've always found what we've looked for. Sometimes it just takes awhile."

"Are you coming north with us?" Angel asked as she looked to the skunk, deep down inside already knowing the answer.

"Nope. This is the end of the line for me," he sighed. "Winter's almost here and I want to get back to my den down south."

"We sure have enjoyed your company," J.J. gushed.

"And your help," Angel added.

"It's been a great ride," grinned Soddy. "I can't wait to hear about it when you find that silver and get that new home."

"How will you know?" quizzed J.J.

"Same way I've known everything else," he chuckled. "Remember, every critter out here loves to talk. I'll know it almost before it happens."

The girls could only laugh at the thought of the animal grapevine going full blast. Would any of the friends they'd met along the way really know how it all turned out?

"Well, I'd better get going," the skunk squeaked. "You, too. You don't have much time."

"We know," agreed the dogs together.

Soddy gave the girls a good-bye salute and then shimmied down the hill to near the road. Once there he turned once more and gave a last wave. The Kids answered with two loud hoots in response. Then they set a course north.

"He's quite a character," J.J. chuckled as she studied the land ahead, looking for an easy pass through the hills.

"Yup," seconded Angel. "I'm really gonna miss him."

THE ANTELOPE

The Kids soon reached the Canadian once more and began to scout for a safe way across. A quick check of the map told them that the nearest bridge was miles away.

"Guess we'll just have to walk the bed," J.J. reckoned as she studied the nearly dry bottom before them.

"What about that current on the far north side?" Angel chirped. "That could be a problem."

"Well, let's find a good, long stick to check the depth," J.J. countered.

"And poke for quicksand," the little one suggested with a wry smile.

"And that," agreed J.J.

Quickly the girls scoured the bank and soon found a thin but stout piece of driftwood about six feet in length. After breaking off the smaller branches from the trunk, they returned to a path that led to the riverbed.

"This should do it," J.J. barked as she tested the stick in the sand. "Let's go."

Side by side the girls poked their way across the wide Canadian, finding nothing but firm sand and a little mud where currents had run after the last rain. Finally reaching the far side, they poked their stick into the ten feet wide channel of rusty colored water and found it to be less than a foot deep.

"No problem," J.J. hooted.

Slowly dropping into the cold water the Kids quickly waded to the opposite shore and then climbed the steep bank back to flat prairie above. After shaking dry they dropped next to a grassy rise for a drink and a bite. Angel unzipped the pack and pulled out a bottle and one pack of food.

"Here you go," she piped as she popped the cap and passed the water to J.J.

"How we doing on water?" J.J. asked as she took a sip.

"Two full bottles," Angel answered. "Maybe we should fill the other two with river water."

"Looks too muddy to drink," J.J. hissed.

"Better than nothing," the little one countered. "I'm gonna fill 'em. It might be all we can find for a while."

"I guess you're right," nodded J.J. "Maybe the mud will settle to the bottom."

"Might," concurred Angel as she took a drink, then grabbed an empty from the pack and skipped back down to the river to fill them both.

Returning to her sister she placed the now full bottles in the pack and then sat to eat. Just as she took her first bite a voice rang out from just over the rise behind them.

"Good job crossing the river," the voice praised. "Pretty smart."

The Kids quickly whirled around in the direction of the sound and sprang to their feet. Looking at them through the noonday sun was a horned creature of white and black and reddish-brown.

"Andy!" the Kids whooped together as they eyed the large but sleek critter with twinkling eyes.

"Andy the pronghorn," he confirmed as he dug a hoof into the dirt. "You have to be those dogs all the critter's are buzzing about."

"Sure are," Angel replied proudly. "I'm Angel and this is my big sister J.J. We're from Texas and we're looking for the Sooner Silver."

"That's what I heard," the antelope answered. "Texas is just a quick trot from here. I've got a lot of family there."

"We want to find a new family, too," J.J. offered. "But first we have to find that silver. Do you know where it is?"

"Nope," confessed Andy. "What clues do you have?"

"All we know is to go way to the west," Angel squeaked. "We figure it must mean the Panhandle. Do you know it?"

"Oh, ya," affirmed the antelope. "I know it well. Just go about another thirty miles north and take a hard left and then you're there. I'll show you."

"Really?" gushed the two together.

"Sure thing," Andy bleated.

"Oh, I forgot," the little one chimed, ashamed at forgetting her manners. "Would you like a drink or something to eat?"

"No thanks," the critter assured them. "I just had a drink from the river and what you have I can't eat," he finished with a chuckle. "I'm not like that old skunk; eats anything that comes along."

"Soddy said he knew you," J.J. barked.

"Soddy knows everyone," Andy cackled. "He's a great guy, at least from a distance. You two about ready to go?" he finished.

"Soon as we pack up," Angel answered.

The Kids quickly filled the pack and zipped it, then fell in behind the critter as he turned to the north. Through the afternoon they talked about their journey and all they had learned about Oklahoma. Near dusk Andy led them to a nice sheltered valley just west of U.S. 283 where they stopped for the night.

"This is a good place," J.J. woofed as she looked to the little draw that ran through it. "Any water there?"

"Enough for drinking," Andy advised. "It's good and clean."

"Great," hooted Angel as she pulled the bottles and drained out the muddy river water. "I'll fill these there."

Bottles brimming she returned to the camp where J.J. had already shed the pack. Then they sprawled out in the cool prairie grass.

"You're pretty good with that pack," Andy observed.

"Helps to have a hand but I can manage alone if I have to," she answered. "Had a lot of practice."

"Well you two have your dinner and I'm going to graze for a bit," the antelope chimed. "I'll be back shortly."

The Kids watched the critter drift off into the falling darkness as they shared the food and watered down. Only the rumble of an occasional truck on the nearby highway broke the still silence of the plains. After dinner Angel grabbed the book, map, and flashlight from the pack and began to study.

"Somewhere along the line we crossed from Cheyenne and Arapaho country back into the old Cherokee Outlet," she stated as she looked at an old map in the book. "And we missed a region. We just left the Gypsum Hills and now we're on the High Plains."

"What's it say about water," J.J. quizzed.

"Not much rain," the little one replied as she turned to a climate map. "Just a little over twenty inches right around here and even less in the Panhandle. But there's a huge aquifer just beneath us; the Ogalla. That's where the water comes from."

"What do the people do?" J.J. queried.

"Cattle and wheat mostly," Angel answered as she flipped to another page. "Wheat and other grains."

"Any towns?" J.J. questioned.

"Not many," the little one continued. "Woodward's the biggest. We've already seen that. And a few others like Buffalo up near the Kansas border.There are a few more in the Panhandle but it's pretty much empty."

"Sure is different from the east," J.J. buzzed. "Back there you can't go more than a few miles without hitting another town."

"It's a whole different world out here," laughed Angel. "Kind of nice though."

"Sure is," agreed the big dog. "What's it say about the Panhandle?"

"Long and narrow," the little one answered as she read on. "About 170 miles long but only around 30 miles wide. And just three counties; Beaver, Texas, and Cimarron. It says that the Panhandle wasn't a part of the original Indian Territory. Texas used to claim it but gave it up when she entered the U.S. and the government assigned it to Oklahoma."

"Beaver County," chuckled J.J. "Remember Bobby the Beaver telling us about his county. Now we know where it is."

"Not just a county but a river," Angel added. "Up here the North Canadian is called the Beaver River, or sometimes Beaver Creek."

"What are you two talking about," Andy piped as he stalked back into the camp, now just a faint shadow in the prairie darkness..

"Just reading about this region," J.J. replied with a grin. "Here and the Panhandle."

"Well you'll see that before lunch tomorrow," the antelope crowed. "As long as this good weather holds."

"Think it will?" the little one asked.

"Hard to say," Andy replied. "November can be fickle. But I don't smell anything in the air that indicates trouble."

"That's good to hear," woofed J.J. as she pulled the sweaters from the pack.

"It will be cold, though," he added.

"Already is," grinned Angel, who took a sweater from J.J. and wrapped herself in it.

"Well, let's get some rest," the antelope ordered. "I like to get an early start."

Instantly the Kids curled up together while Andy bedded down beside them. In minutes all were sound asleep. Only the antelope's husky breathing broke the night's silence.

All awoke just as the sun's first flashes splashed over the eastern horizon. Quickly they rose and ambled to the draw for a drink. Then Andy took a hasty graze in a stand of short brush while the girls split a pack of food. Breakfast done, they stripped their sweaters and stuffed and zipped the pack before loading it on J.J.'s strong shoulders. Soon the antelope returned and they were off into the stiff but pleasant north wind.

"Bit chilly," J.J. coughed before the walking had time to warm her.

"Just right," answered Andy with a smile. "Wonderful walking weather."

Shortly they passed the railroad tracks that they had left just outside Woodward. Angel looked down them as if hoping to find another cart.

"Heard you took quite a railroad journey," the antelope chuckled as he looked to the little one.

"You know about that, huh?" J.J. queried with a shake of her head.

"Old Soddy had a good time; said he'd never done that before," Andy cackled. "Wish I could take a ride like that."

"Find a cart and we'll show you how," chortled J.J.

"Wouldn't matter," remarked the antelope. "Tracks around here don't go the way we need them to. None of them run straight across the Panhandle; at least not east to west."

"So we walk," giggled the little one.

"So we walk," Andy confirmed.

Through the brilliant morning the three continued north just to the west of U.S. 283. They kept a rapid pace. Just before noon Andy stopped and pointed.

"Start of the Panhandle; just a few miles," he informed them as he motioned to their left. "We'll catch 412 just up ahead and make the turn."

"412 covers a lot of ground," J.J. remarked, remembering how many times they had crossed it on their journey.

"All the way across the state," Andy answered. "It's a long one."

In another hour they reached the highway and made the turn, soon passing outside the tiny village of Slapout.

"What a name," laughed J.J. as she read the sign. "It's great."

"Old dog lives around here," Andy informed them. "They call him Slappy. He chases us over the plains to get his exercise."

"Ever catch you?" Angel mused.

"Hahhh!" spat the antelope. "Nowhere even close. We can run almost sixty miles an hour. That old mutt's lucky to make twenty."

"We'd like to meet him," J.J. stated.

"Just hang on," advised Andy. "He'll be along."

Right on cue the three looked out over the grassland to see a good sized blue tick hound heading straight their way. In less than a minute he stood before them.

Well hello, Andy," the dog barked. "Smelled you coming. Ready for a chase."

"Not today, Slappy," the antelope sniffed. "Got work to do. I'm trying to get these two through the Panhandle. They're a little short of food. Got anything?"

"I can probably scrounge up some nuggets," he answered as he eyed the Kids. "Are these the ones who've been traipsing all over the state trying to find that silver?"

"That's us," beamed the little one as she patted the ground in greeting. "I'm Angel and this is my big sister J.J."

"Pleased to meet you," the hound replied with his own tail twirl and a wave of his paw. "Just stay put and I'll see what I can find."

"Thanks," J.J. offered as she watched Slappy turn and zip back toward the little town.

For ten minutes the trio waited in a high stand of grass which shielded them from the light 412 traffic. A few minutes more and the hound made his return, a small sack in his mouth bouncing up and down as he ran. When he reached them he dropped the sack on the ground.

"Should hold you for a few days," he barked. "Nothing fancy but it'll do."

"Yes it will," confirmed Angel as she picked up the sack and stuffed it in the pack on J.J.'s back. "We really appreciate it."

"No problem," huffed the hound. "Sure you don't want a little chase, Andy?" he pleaded as he looked once more to the antelope and smiled, a look of eagerness on his face.

"Next time, Slappy. I promise," Andy answered.

"Okay," the dog sighed. "But I'm going to hold you to that," he finished with a laugh.

"I know you will," chuckled the antelope. "Now we've got to move."

Slappy pawed the ground in a farewell salute as the Kids did the same. Then they resumed their march to the west. After another hour they stopped at a windmill to rest and have a late lunch.

"Forgot how hungry I was," J.J. moaned as she dropped the pack to the ground.

"I'm starving," the little one seconded as she pulled out a pack of food and the sack of nuggets that Slappy had brought them.

As they ate Andy grazed in a nearby little gully, finding a few healthy green shoots to munch on. Dinner done, Angel reloaded the pack and the girls sat to wait for Andy.

"Get enough?" Angel asked as the antelope returned.

"Enough to hold me for a bit," Andy grinned.

"Say, I just noticed something," J.J. noted as she looked to their friend and then pointed to a lone tree on the roadside. "Look at the way that tree's bent," she offered. "Seems that just about all the trees in this part of the state all bend toward the north. Why is that?"

"Wind," explained the antelope. "This is one of the windiest parts of the country. And most of the time the winds are out of the south, so the trees just bend with the breeze from the time they're just little saplings. It becomes a permanent state before long."

"How neat," gushed the little one. "The forces of nature are something."

"That they are," agreed Andy. "Ready?"

"Yep," the Kids replied together as they snapped to their feet.

Angel helped J.J with the pack and then the three walked west once more. Late in the day they came to the Highway 270/ 23 intersection. A sign told them that the county seat of Beaver was just to the north and beyond the town was Beaver Dunes State Park along the Beaver River.

"Wish we could see the park," Angel sighed as she peered up the road.

"No time now," counseled J.J.

"Guess not," agreed the little one as she looked to Andy.

"The day's about done," he bleated as he gazed at the sun now sinking slowly in the west. "I guess we'll make camp here."

"Good place," stated J.J., noting that he had found the one tree within eye shot. "We'll just park it right under this old elm."

"They must have planted this one a long, long time ago," chuckled the antelope as he studied the tree's now leafless limbs.

"Don't trees grow naturally here?" quizzed J.J. as she followed their friends lead.

"Not hardly," Andy answered. "Maybe along a waterway like the Beaver."

J.J. dropped the pack and the little one latched on to a water bottle and passed it around. After drinking Andy excused himself to go forage while the girls ate. Dinner done, Angel retrieved the book, map, and flashlight and sat down next to her sister for a little study.

"What are you looking for now?" buzzed J.J.

"I don't know," confessed Angel. "I just thought I'd look for something interesting."

She flipped through the pages until she came to a section called the Dawes Act. Andy returned just as she began to read.

"This looks good," chimed Angel as the antelope sprawled out on the ground. "The Dawes Act; sometimes called the General Allotment Act."

"What's it about?" barked J.J. as she inched a little closer.

"Well, it goes back to 1887," the little one began. "Basically what it was was the breakup of the old reservation system. Up to then each tribe held its land in common."

"What's that mean?" insisted J.J.

"It means that everybody owned everything together," explained the little one. "But the Dawes Act meant that each tribal member was given title to a certain amount of land; 160 acres for a head of household. Of course after assigning each member his plot, there was still a lot of land left over and you can guess what happened next."

"Other folks moved in," J.J. stated.

"Yup," Angel continued. "What was left were called 'Unassigned or Surplus Lands' and opening those to settlement set off some of the land runs."

"We've heard that term before," J.J. quipped as she thought back to their earlier readings and talks. "Remember the Cherokee Outlet?"

"Did the act apply to all of Indian Territory?" Andy asked as he peered over Angel's shoulder.

"No," the little one replied. "At least not at first. In the beginning it was pretty much a western thing. But later the act was amended to include the eastern tribes as well. Oh, and the act didn't apply to just Oklahoma. It had effect in other parts of the country, too."

"I wonder if it was good or bad?" J.J. mused.

"I guess it all depends on how you look at it," Angel reckoned. "It probably helped some and hurt others. But I guess the Indians would be the best ones to judge that."

"The Panhandle wasn't part of it all, was it?" Andy quizzed.

"Nope. Back then this was all called 'No Man's Land'," Angel cited. "It was pretty much ignored until statehood."

"Lot of land to ignore," laughed J.J. as Angel closed the book and returned it to the pack.

"I wonder how long they've farmed this land?" Angel wondered as she sat down again.

"Quite awhile now," Andy answered. "You should see this place in the spring; mile after mile of golden wheat all ripening in the warm sun. It's a beautiful sight."

"Bet that grain feeds a lot of people," J.J. reckoned.

"Millions," Andy affirmed. "Oh, and lots of antelope, too," he added with a toothy grin.

The three had a good laugh as they pictured Andy and his friends getting fat on the grain fields and having the farmers chase them off. Then Angel suddenly had a thought.

"I wonder why they call this the 'Panhandle'?" she wondered as she looked to the others.

"Because if you'll pay attention to the map you'd see that the state looks just like a frying pan and this part is the handle," J.J. explained as she bopped the little one lightly on the nose and snickered.

"Oh,ya," Angel exclaimed, a little embarrassed to have not noticed it before. "I see what you mean."

"Lesson over," bleated the antelope. "Let's get some sleep."

Angel folded the map and put it away. Then the three reclined under the tree and talked for a bit before slipping quickly into a deep sleep.

The next morning the trio set out once more. After a hard days march they stopped for the night at the Optima Wildlife Refuge, an oasis of wetlands on the dry, open plains nearly right in the middle of the Oklahoma Panhandle. They were astounded to see large stands of cottonwoods and other trees ringing the small Optima Lake. Lush prairie grasses grew thick all through the more than 4000 acre refuge. J.J. found a brochure that told them the place was a haven for migratory birds as well as deer and countless other creatures. Andy told them he always made it a point to stop here when in the area.

"Do you have relatives here?" Angel asked.

"All over," he affirmed.

The three spent the night at Optima and then set out again the next morning. Just after noon they passed around Guymon, a city just below the Beaver River in Texas County. The largest town in the region at over 10,000 people, they learned that Guymon was an important farming, ranching and natural gas center. A large state university, Oklahoma Panhandle State, was just down the road.

For the next two days the three worked their way along 412. West of Guymon 412 is also highway 64 and Highway 3 and the only east/ west road through the region. At the end of the second day they came to the outskirts of Boise City, the only town of any size they had seen since they left Guymon. Along the way they had crossed into Cimarron County, the last county in Oklahoma.

"Didn't think we'd ever see another town," joked J.J. as she peered out over the plains.

"Not many out here," Andy quipped. "I'm glad to say," he added with a slight chuckle.

"I guess we stay here tonight," Angel reckoned as she looked around for a spot with a little cover. "See anyplace that looks good?"

"A little draw over there," Andy bleated as he pointed his horns to a slight dip in the ground just south of the road. "Let's have a look."

The three ambled to the spot and found it a shallow, grass-lined gully. It looked nice and soft and at least a little sheltered.

"Guess this'll have to do," J.J. barked as she slid down the bank.

"Not bad," Angel and Andy stated together.

"Good thing we filled the bottles in the Beaver back at Guymon," J.J. quipped as Angel helped her drop the pack. "I haven't seen a drop of water since."

"It's out here," counseled Andy. "You just have to know how to find it. And it's not always easy," he added with a loud huff and a hard shake of his curling black horns.

"Have you kept track of the days?" J.J. asked the little one as they spread out on the ground and drained half a water bottle.

"I think this was day four," Angel figured as she watched the antelope leave to do his customary grazing. "Four or five. I'm not quite sure."

"Whatever it is it doesn't leave us much time," worried J.J. as she stroked her chin.

"Nope," agreed her sister. "Two or three days at most. I wonder where we go from here."

"I don't know," J.J. confessed. "We'll just go where Andy takes us."

"I guess you're right," squeaked Angel. "We don't have much choice."

The Kids finished eating just as the antelope returned. Together the three were once more treated to an awesome western sunset. As they watched the orange retreat behind the veil of darkness they asked Andy where they would go tomorrow.

"Southwest to the Rita Blanca," he informed them.

"What's that?" Angel quizzed.

"Rita Blanca National Grassland," Andy answered. "It's a place you need to see."

"We're worried about the time," J.J. woofed.

"I know you are," the antelope acknowledged. "But you'll make it."

"Do you know exactly where we're supposed to go?" the little one whined.

"Nope," Andy replied.

"Even though we're almost out of the state what's left is still a bunch to explore," J.J. barked. "That silver could be just about anywhere."

"Ya, but it's not anywhere it's somewhere and that somewhere is what you've got to find," the antelope stated solemnly. "That's your job."

"We know," Angel sighed.

"Cheer up," Andy ordered. "You've done great so far and you'll do fine the rest of the way. One last discovery; one last bit of all out effort and you'll wrap this thing up. I promise."

The Kids shook their heads and grinned, knowing that this amazing critter was on their side all the way. Angel went to the pack and pulled out the map, wanting to see if she could find the Rita Blanca.

"Here it is," she chimed. "Just down the road."

"I guess you've been there?" J.J. quizzed as she looked to the antelope.

"Many, many times," he answered. "Great antelope country. I've got family all over it."

"What's it like?" the little one asked.

"Miles and miles of sweet grass," Andy responded with a smile. "The whole place is over 200,000 acres. And it's not just in Oklahoma. It spills south into Texas and on into New Mexico, only there it's called the Kiowa Grassland."

"Boy that is big," J.J. nearly shouted as she waved the flashlight around.

"We should get there late tomorrow," Angel squeaked as she checked the scale and measured the distance.

"Not if we don't get a good night's sleep and get an early start," warned the antelope.

"Yup," agreed the little one as she folded the map and put it away.

"Grab those sweaters," J.J. commanded with a laugh. "I feel a real chill coming tonight."

Angel offered no protest. She pulled out the wraps and tossed one to J.J. Then they slipped them on while Andy dug out a little dirt with his sharp hoof to make his bed.

"Nice and comfy," he chuckled as he dropped to the ground between them and carefully stretched all four legs before curling them back against his body. "Good night."

"Night, Andy," the Kids purred together as their friends eyelids snapped shut.

"Boy can he sleep," J.J. laughed lightly as she looked to her sister.

"He doesn't seem to worry about much," Angel agreed as she laid her head on his gently heaving side and smiled.

"Not much," yawned J.J. as she buried her head in Andy's soft stomach.

All three drifted in dreamland until nature's clock stirred them with a soft burst of brightness. Angel's eyes fluttered first; then Andy's then J.J.'s. Each rose, stretched, and shook hard against the morning's deep chill. Angel popped a bottle and passed it around. All drank deeply, the cold water washing away sleep's dryness. Surrounding them was an ocean of grass, heavy, wet and glistening with an autumn morning's frost.

"Time to march," Andy ordered as he poked his nose in the air.

Once more the trio set a course west and a little south. The highway was quiet. People and cars were few. Noon brought them to another crossing of the Beaver just east of the tiny village of Felt and their first touch of the grasslands.

"The Rita Blanca's right there," Andy smiled as he pointed south.

"Starts right here?" Angel quizzed as she followed his point.

"No, actually it begins back to the east on U.S. 385," he answered. "That's the main road from Texas into Boise City.

"How far are we going into it?" J.J. asked.

"New Mexico state line," replied the antelope.

"And then what?" questioned the little one as she pulled out the last packet of dog food and ripped it open.

"Then you go north," Andy bleated.

"But not you?" J.J. barked in a tone that was more statement than question.

"Nope," the antelope answered, his eyes showing great sadness. "It's the end of the line for me. I'm heading into New Mexico to find some of my cousins."

"Where to the north?" demanded the little one as she passed a pawful of food to her sister.

"That I can't say," Andy confessed. "You'll just have to follow your noses."

The dogs both let out a deep sigh and looked to their friend. They were sorry to lose him but knew that the climax of their adventure was drawing near.

After a brief rest they set out once more through the Rita Blanca. Through the day they said little, stopping occasionally to rest, water, and admire the scenery. Late in the afternoon a highway sign told them that the New Mexico state line was but a mile ahead. Here Andy stopped them.

"Okay, girls, this is where we turn," he advised. "I know a good campsite close by and we can stay there for the night."

"Can't we go to the border?" Angel pleaded, not wanting to get so close without touching it.

"Why not," bleated the antelope as he checked the sun. "It won't take long."

The trio hopped down the road to cover the last mile, reaching the state line in about fifteen minutes. Here both dogs made a jump forward and stood for a moment.

"First time we've ever been in New Mexico," joked J.J. as she and Angel did a little dance in the Land of Enchantment before crossing back.

"Well, now you have," laughed Andy as he turned to lead the girls north.

The Kids fell in alongside the antelope and quickly covered the ground to their campsite, a nice sheltered spot along Cienequilla Creek.

"This must feed the Beaver," J.J. reckoned as she studied the streambed.

"Yup," Andy confirmed. "Ties in pretty close to here. Lucky for us it's got some water in it. It's dry more often than not," he finished as he slid down the bank to have a drink as the girls followed. Returning to the high ground, Angel helped J.J. with the pack, pulled out the water bottles, and returned to the creek to fill them.

"We're glad you're staying tonight," the little one purred as she smiled at the antelope.

"I thought maybe you'd read me a little more Oklahoma history," Andy hooted. "I want to learn as much as I can."

"Well, I can probably arrange that," Angel laughed as she reached for the pack and grabbed the book. "Lucky for us we still have a little light."

Angel flipped through the book until she came to a section on Oklahoma statehood. She quickly scanned a few pages and then began to read.

"This is interesting," she began. "It says that by the turn of the century Oklahoma had more people than a lot of existing states. And of course of lot of those folks thought that Oklahoma should became a state, too. Now at the time the old Indian Territory had been split, with roughly the eastern half staying Indian Territory and the western part being called Oklahoma Territory. The entire region was called the 'Twin Territories'. When it looked like statehood was coming, the tribes in the east wanted to keep the split and form their own state called The State of Sequoya. The west would be the State of Oklahoma."

"What happened then?" quizzed J.J. and Andy together as they moved in closer.

"Well, the native peoples in the east had an election and voted heavily in favor of separate statehood. But the westerners and the U.S. government wanted one, single State of Oklahoma and that's the way it finally worked out. On November 16, 1907 President Theodore Roosevelt signed the bill that made Oklahoma the 46th state. That act also made the Indian peoples United States citizens."

"No more Indian Territory," J.J. mused as she thought about all the interesting history of the region before statehood.

"Nope, no more," stated the little one as she closed the book.

"Hard to believe that was exactly one hundred years ago," bleated the antelope as he looked out over the darkening land.

"Seems like a long time to us," quipped Angel. "But in history that's just the blink of an eye."

"Ya; I guess you're right," agreed J.J. as she cocked her head in thought. "That's nothing compared to the thousands of years people have been living here."

"Nothing at all," seconded Andy with a grin and a shake of his horns.

Angel paced to the pack and put away the book, then the three curled up to sleep on their last night together. Andy gave each girl one last pat. With the dawn he was gone.

J.J. yawned loudly as she rolled to her feet and stood. Then she gave her sister a little nudge and looked to the antelope's empty space.

"Andy left," she sighed as the morning's first light began its slow crawl over the land.

"I thought he might," Angel reckoned. "He didn't seem the type for long goodbyes."

"Look!" J.J. nearly hollered as she looked to the ground near the pack. "A message."

The girls quickly stepped to the spot and read. In the dirt was scratched an arrow pointing north. Beneath the arrow were the words:

Good Luck to Two Super Dogs.

Your friend, Andy.

"That was nice," puffed the little one as her eyes clouded.

"Sure was," coughed J.J., her throat tightening in disappointment. "Well, at least his message is clear. Go north," she stated as she took a quick compass check.

"But I wonder where," puzzled Angel as she peered out over the empty plain. "The north's a big place," she added with a worried look.

"Like he said," J.J. reminded. "We follow our noses. Let's get going."

THE WHITE BUFFALO

"Is there such a thing as a white buffalo?" Amy asked her mother as she sat down to breakfast.

"Why, yes," Linda answered. "They're extremely rare. Some Indian peoples consider them to be sacred animals. Why do you ask?"

"I saw one in a dream last night," Amy explained with a bright smile. "She was standing in a snowy field with J.J. and Angel.

Linda Russell said nothing, simply stared out the kitchen window and rolled her eyes in distress. In a moment Jack Russell entered and took his seat at the table.

"Morning Precious," he beamed as he looked to his daughter. "You seem awfully cheerful this morning."

Amy said nothing, only grinned widely and then ate quickly. Breakfast done, she left the kitchen with little Max the badger nipping at her heels. Jack Russell looked to his wife who was leaning against the countertop.

"Why so gloomy?" he asked as he poured himself some coffee.

"It's Amy again and another one of those dreams," she sighed. "This time the dogs were with a buffalo. I know she's young but even kids have to learn to accept reality. It's part of the growing process."

"I know," nodded Mr. Russell. "But just give it time."

"Six months isn't long enough?" countered Mrs. Russell as she dropped a pan into the sink.

"Okay," Jack replied. "We'll have another talk with her this evening. If that's not enough we'll take her in to see a specialist. Fair enough?"

"Fair enough," agreed Linda. "But I don't think we should wait much longer."

"Looks like another creek just ahead," Angel ventured as she noticed a narrow furrow in the land.

"Yup," concurred J.J. as she studied the gash that marked Corrumpa Creek, the Beaver's main tributary. "I wonder what it's called?"

The dogs reached the creek bank and dropped down for a brief rest. Angel pulled out the map to identify the stream and look at the land ahead.

"Corrumpa Creek," she read.

"Corrumpa?" laughed J.J.

"Indian word that means 'wild' or 'isolated'," the little one explained.

"Good name for it," joked J.J. as she bent down to a shallow pool for a drink.

PERRYMAN RANCH   PHOTO BY BARBARA FADLER

"Ya," confirmed the little one as she looked to the map. "Hills and the Cimarron River again."

"That looks interesting," J.J. commented as she looked to a spot named Black Mesa just north of the river and south of the Colorado state line.

"And there's a park near it," Angel cooed. "Black Mesa State Park."

"Maybe we'll get to see it," pondered J.J. as the girls resumed their march.

"Hope so," the little one chirped.

Through the day the Kids plowed through the plains. Each step nurtured their respect for those who had come before. For this land in all its vastness tested all comers and swallowed all but the hardiest.

Midafternoon brought them to a spot on the Old Santa Fe trail, perhaps the region's, if not the nation's, most historic trading route. Connecting the U.S. interior with Spanish New Mexico, the road was a magnet for commerce and quite often a hot spot of both political and cultural friction. Reading the plaques and studying the maps, the dogs came to better understand the role a few rutted tracks in an empty land could play in shaping a nation's destiny.

Late in the day they reached the edge of Black Mesa State Park and what was supposed to be Lake Etling. But the water was gone, in its place but a bed of grass now stunted by the season's chill.

"Some lake," scoffed Angel as she peered out over the now empty reservoir.

"Nature can't give what she doesn't have," woofed J.J. "Let's find a campsite."

As the sun began its daily dive the Kids settled down in the little draw that was meant to feed the lake. Confused and dejected Angel helped her sister with the pack and then they plopped to the ground.

"No clue of any kind today," moaned the little one as she passed a bottle to J.J. "And we're almost out of Oklahoma. Where are we supposed to go?"

"I don't know," confessed J.J. with a soft shake of her head. "Say, she brightened. "What was that place on the map; Black Mesa?"

"Ya," affirmed the little one. "Same name as the park."

J.J. scratched her jaw and said nothing for a minute, then slapped herself on the side of her head. Quickly she reached inside the pack and pulled out the little pad and pencil that they always carried.

"I just thought of something," she bellowed. "Let's make a list of all the animals we've met."

"What for?" shrugged Angel.

"Just write," commanded J.J. as she began to name them.

Starting with the antelope, J.J. spouted off the names of each species they had talked to and traveled with along the way. Then in the fading light she looked at the paper.

"I can't see," she popped. "Get the light."

Angel flipped on the flashlight and held it as her sister read. After arranging the names according to letter, she stopped to study the results.

"Let's put them in the order we met them," the little one suggested, beginning to see her sister's logic.

"Badger, beaver and bear.
Loon and longhorn.
Armadillo.
Coyote." "Don't forget the cottonmouth," teased J.J.
"I'll never forget that thing," Angel winced as she continued.
"Kit fox.
Matthew the mule.
Eagle.
Skunk and Scissortail.
And the Antelope."
"Look down the column," J.J. exploded. "What's that spell?"

"BLACKMESA."

"Black Mesa!" the little one exclaimed. "That must be the spot!"

"Has to be!" J.J. howled. "Let's see if the book says anything!"

Angel quickly whipped out the book and nervously pawed through the pages. Finally she came to a section on the Panhandle and scoured the pages.

"Here it is!" she yelled. "Black Mesa; the highest point in Oklahoma at nearly 5000 feet."

"Now it all makes sense," blurted J.J. as she looked at the page. "Remember what the old badger said; something about starting at the bottom and working your way to the top. Now I see what he meant! We started out around the lowest part of the state in Idabell and now we're almost to the highest. Boy was he pulling our tails!" she finished with a loud laugh.

"Ya!" yowled the little one. "Silver said something like that, too. Remember, see you at the top,".

"Sure did!" confirmed J.J. "It's up there! That's where he buried it!"

"Now we have to get there before he does!" Angel shouted. "What did he say; the fifteenth?"

"I believe so," J.J. affirmed. "I wonder what today is?"

"Don't know for sure," confessed the little one. "I've lost track. But it's got to be close."

"Has to be," agreed J.J.

"We still have a little light left," observed Angel. "Let's try to get a little closer before dark."

"Good idea," agreed J.J. as she moved to the pack. "Every second counts."

Hurriedly the girls began a march toward Black Mesa, still barely visible in the twilight. Near the town of Kenton total darkness finally forced a halt.

"Can't see a thing," J.J. complained as she looked to her sister.

"I guess we'll have to stop for the night," Angel sighed as she pursed her lips into a deep frown.

"No choice," agreed J.J. "I guess we'll just stay right here until morning."

Just as she was about to drop the pack she saw a shining set of eyes staring at them from around a big rock. She barked loudly but the creature didn't budge. Finally she approached the eyes and assumed her most threatening stance.

"Come out from behind there," she insisted with a low growl.

"Coming," replied a soft, timid voice. "I don't want trouble?"

"Neither do we," promised J.J. as she relaxed a little. "Who are you?"

"Kenny," the voice responded. "Kenny the Kenton Cave dog."

" A dog!" shouted Angel who had moved in just behind her sister.

"Uh, huh," assured the critter as he moved closer.

"Well come on in," the little one purred.

As the girls' eyes began to adjust to the darkness the visitor's outlines became visible. Tall but scrawny thin, he limped toward the girls and sat.

"Hurt yourself?" J.J. questioned as she noticed the limp.

"Nope," he answered. "I've been like this for a long time."

"What did you say about a cave?" Angel asked.

"Kenton Caves," he replied. "My friends and I live in one."

"Haven't heard of them," confessed the girls together. "Tell us more."

"They were home to native peoples for thousands of years," Kenny explained. Now the whole area is an important archeological site. We stay in one of the caves that they're not exploring just now. What are you two doing here all alone?"

The girls explained their situation and this time were surprised to find that Kenny had never heard of them. When finished he smiled and suggested they follow him to his cave and spend the night.

"It's just over there," he advised them as he pointed a paw to the spot.

"Thanks," the girls offered as they fell in behind him.

The dog led the Kids down a narrow path and in minutes reached the cave entrance. Once inside Angel pulled out the flashlight and shined it around. To their astonishment they found over twenty dogs of all types and sizes sitting or lying on the cave's floor. All looked sad and worn and hungry.

"Do you all live here?" Angel exclaimed.

"It's our home," Kenny answered, "the only one we have. All the dogs here are strays, most of us abandoned by our people a long time ago. One by one we met and finally set up a little colony here. We help each other out as much as we can."

J.J. dropped the pack and Angel opened it, pulling out the food sack and dropping it to the ground. Though hungry themselves, she offered what little there was to the other dogs. Each moved forward to take just a little until all was gone. Angry at the sight of so many starving dogs, J.J. promised to get them help as soon as their job was done.

"We have to climb Black Mesa in the morning," she explained. "Then we'll be back."

Kenny thanked her for himself and the others and then suggested he lead them to the top tomorrow. He knew it well.

"Does anybody know the date?" the little one asked. "We've lost track of time and we're not sure."

"Fourteenth," advised a dog from the back of the pack. "I was trying to filch some food in the park and I heard a car radio," she informed them.

"Then tomorrow's the day," murmured J.J. as her mouth tightened.

"Yup," seconded Angel who turned to look outside. "We'd better go early; first light."

J.J. said nothing, just acknowledged Angel's warning with a firm shake of her head. Kenny showed the dogs to their sleeping spot and told them he'd be ready to go at dawn. The Kids thanked him and then splayed out on the cool floor to rest if they could. But sleep abandoned them that night as nervous anticipation took command. Months of work came down to a final sprint, a hard climb, and a lot of hope.

Fidgeting to alertness just before dawn, the Kids looked outside to see the skies bleeding a heavy white that had already covered the ground to several inches. As they looked out at the snow Kenny rose and fell in behind them.

"First snow of the year," he informed them as they watched the large, wet flakes flurry down. "Pretty, isn't it," he added.

"Yes it is," the Kids agreed together.

"I just hope it doesn't cover signs of the digging. That silver's buried," Angel huffed.

"Well, we can't find it here," J.J. advised. "Ready?"

"Ready," Angel and Kenny both replied.

J.J. strapped on the pack and then the three left the cave while the other dogs watched and wished them good luck. Just outside Kenny led them to the right trail. To the north they could barely make out Black Mesa's silhouette in the first burst of light.

"There it is," barked J.J. as she stopped for just a second. "Let's go!"

Quickly the three picked up the pace. Kenny led. Soon he brought them to the main road leading to Oklahoma's highest point on the fringe of the Rocky Mountains. Plodding briskly through the snow they soon reached the Cimarron

River bridge and crossed. In a short time they reached Black Mesa's summit trail.

"Got a good climb now," Kenny informed them as he turned up the path.

"Let's go," hooted the Kids.

Slowly the trio worked their way up the rugged trail. In two hours they reached the top where they stopped briefly to admire the blanket of white that covered the land. Below all was still.

"Now what?" shot Angel as she looked around, desperately trying to find a sign of where the treasure might be buried.

"Got to be around here somewhere," J.J. spat as she began to poke the snowy ground. "Let's fan out and look for a clue."

Quickly and quietly the three split up, each taking a different direction. For fifteen minutes they probed Black Mesa's summit. Finally Angel came to three large boulders, each lying in a circle about four feet apart. On one rock was a faint scratch mark that looked fairly new. Swiftly she turned and shouted to the others who sprinted toward her.

"Might have something," she shouted almost breathlessly. "Look!"

J.J. and Kenny came and examined the mark while Angel shot between two of the rocks to the space between them. The others quickly followed. Frantically the little one began to dig away at the snow until she reached the ground below. The wet weather had softened the ground and the digging was easy. Inch by inch and dog by dog they dug. Finally J.J.'s nail made a slight thumping sound as she hit an object neither dirt nor rock. Chest heaving with excitement, she clawed furiously while the others pushed away the dug-up dirt. In minutes she had uncovered four square feet of earth to a depth of nearly eighteen inches. The top of a wide wooden box showed clearly.

"This is it!" she hollered as she continued digging.

Angel lowered her head, grabbed the lid's edge in her teeth, and jerked hard upward. The top creaked open. Inside under several layers of cloth was their prize. Crying with joy the Kids turned to Kenny and rubbed his face with their paws. The new dog just blushed and smiled.

"What do we do now?" J.J. barked. "We can't carry all this stuff."

"Oh, ya," agreed the little one as her smile washed away.

Quickly the Kids realized they faced a major challenge. As they pondered their next move Kenny looked down from Black Mesa to the road below.

"Van and a car; heading this way," he shouted back to the girls.

"White van?" J.J. hollered back.

"Yup," their companion confirmed with a hard nod of his head.

"We need to find a cop," Angel advised, "and fast."

"Where?" J.J. shrugged as Kenny rejoined them.

"There's a deputy sheriff who sometimes patrols around here this time of day," Kenny stated. "Maybe he'll be out today."

"Worth a try," Angel bleated. "Maybe we should cover it up before we leave. That might slow 'em down some."

"Good idea," praised J.J. "We'll take one piece to show the cop. Maybe he'll figure it all out."

Angel then pulled out a little polished wooden box from the big chest and opened it. Inside was a gleaming 1907 silver dollar and a card noting the Oklahoma centennial celebration.

"This will do," she chirped as she showed it to J.J. and Kenny.

"Should," they agreed.

Swiftly the Kids closed the top and then all three rapidly scraped the dirt back into the hole. They hoped the snow would cover their tracks. When finished Kenny led them down a back trail that ran to the road. Behind them in the parking area the van and car had stopped.

"It'll take 'em awhile to make that climb," J.J. reckoned.

"And even longer to come back down with that heavy chest," Angel added.

"Yep," concurred J.J. "We just might make it."

The three worked their way back over the Cimarron to Highway 325 just outside of Kenton. Here they waited and paced, paced and waited. After two hours not one car had passed. The snow still fell, covering the land but melting when it hit the still warm road. Finally a lone vehicle approached from the east.

"That's the cop!" shouted Kenny. "See the lights on top?"

"Ya!" blurted J.J. "Let's get in the road!"

The three sped to the highway and positioned themselves abreast in its middle. The police car slowed and then stopped just before them. Hurriedly Angel retrieved the little box from the pack as the bewildered deputy got out of his car and walked toward the snow covered canines. Holding the box in her mouth, Angel stepped out to meet him.

"What you got there, girl," the officer asked as he gave her a pat, then took the box from her mouth and opened it.

"Huh," he laughed. "What's a dog doing with this," he chuckled as he looked at the coin and read the card.

Suddenly his eyes widened as he read the inscription. In an instant he zipped back to his car and grabbed the radio, pulling its cord outside as he stood in the road. The dogs watched.

You won't believe this!" he yelled to the dispatcher. "I'm out here just east of Kenton on 325. There are three dogs standing in the road. One of them was carrying a mint condition 1907 silver dollar. I think it's part of the stolen silver collection."

"That's nuts," screamed a voice from the other end. "Where would a dumb dog get that."

"Just get some guys out here," he shouted as he slammed down the receiver.

The deputy looked back to the dogs who were still standing in front of his car. Then he turned to open one of the car's back doors.

"Okay folks," he cooed softly. "How'd you like to have a ride in a police car?"

With a little whistle he motioned for the dogs to get in the back seat. Kenny balked. His only ride in a car had been to be dumped by the side of the road. Angel nosed his ear in assurance as J.J. hopped up on the seat. Then Angel and

Kenny followed. The deputy climbed in behind the wheel and turned to the dogs.

"Now where did you get this?" he asked.

"Woof!" J.J. answered as she looked toward Black Mesa.

"There?" the cop asked as he pointed to the site.

"Woof!" J.J. snapped again, only this time even louder.

Still uncertain the deputy turned down the county road that led to Black Mesa and slowly approached. Suddenly the radio screeched.

"I'm heading for Black Mesa," he announced. "Back up coming?"

"Ya, a deputy and a state trooper," the voice on the other end informed him. "But I'll tell you, the sheriff's not too happy about sending men on something that sounds so stupid."

"I'll answer to the boss," the deputy spat. "You just get those men here!"

Slowly the officer worked his way down the road, keeping a sharp eye out for any other vehicles. Then he approached the curve leading to the parking lot at Black Mesa's base. Rounding it he threw on his brakes. In front of him was a small herd of bison blocking the road. Behind the bison were the van and the county commissioner's car, both trapped in the lot, each laying on their horns in an attempt to get the bison to move. In his rearview mirror the deputy looked to see two more police cars rapidly coming up behind him. When they reached him he left the car and went back to talk. Then he returned and all three cars slowly rolled to the front of the buffalo herd and lined up abreast.

The deputy exited his car and opened the back door for the dogs who jumped out quickly. Then the other officers joined him. As they moved forward the buffalo began to peel away one by one, each shuffling off toward the hills. Soon but one remained.

"Look!" shouted Angel silently as she turned to J.J. and then to Kenny.

Trembling with excitement, first Angel then J.J. and then the cave dog slowly walked toward the last bison. The cops were right behind.

"Look at that!" the deputy gushed in amazement, for the moment forgetting all about his job. "A white one!"

"First I've ever seen!" another astonished trooper gasped. "Get a camera!"

Angel took another step forward and then pawed at the pouch around her neck. When she did, the magnificent creature snorted loudly and stared straight into her eyes. The little one moved closer. As she did, the van's engine gunned. With lightning speed the buffalo turned and thrust at a front tire with her lance-like horn. A whoosh of air sounded. Then she looked back to Angel as J.J. moved up as well.

"Thanks," they whispered softly as she lowered her head to hear them.

The slightest of smiles seemed to pass her lips. Then she bolted for a nearby hill. At its crest she turned once more to look at the dogs before disappearing over the rise.

"Guess they just never talk," shrugged J.J.

"She said a lot without talking," countered the little one.

"Guess she did at that," agreed J.J.

"Got some great shots," hooted the cop with the camera.

"Now to business," the dogs' deputy bellowed as he approached the van and motioned for Silver to get out.

"You, too," yelled the state trooper as he pointed to the man inside the car.

"What's going on, boys," the deputy smirked as he asked Silver for identification.

"Just taking a hike," Silver answered nervously.

"In the snow?" the cop chuckled.

"What about you?" another officer asked the commissioner. "You're a little off your range aren't you?"

"Little vacation," he mumbled.

"400 miles from home in a county car?" laughed the cop. "How nice."

"You two boys wouldn't mind if we took a look inside your vehicles, would you?" the third officer asked politely but sarcastically.

"Well, uh, I don't know," Silver answered, his voice cracking.

"Well I do know," barked the cop who grabbed the keys from the ignition and moved to unlock the van's back door. "Put your hands on the hood and don't so much as twitch."

Silver stood glaring at the dogs as the deputy searched his van. Only now was he sure that these were the same ones he had seen at Robbers Cave and Antelope Hills. Shaking his head in amazement, he still couldn't fathom how or why they had dogged him all the way around the state.

"Now what do we have here?" the officer growled as he pulled a cover off the treasure box and lifted the top. "I suppose this is your mother's silver service?" he added as he studied the box's contents.

"Uh, ya," Silver mumbled sheepishly.

"My friend, you're under arrest," the deputy stated as he moved back to Silver and slapped on the handcuffs. "The people of Oklahoma want to have a long talk with you."

"And of course you didn't know anything about this, did you?" the trooper snapped at the commissioner.

"Uh, no," he answered. "I don't even know this guy."

"That so," spat the officer. "Then what's this?" he continued as he reached into the man's shirt pocket and pulled out an eighteenth century Spanish coin.

"Had that for years," the commissioner protested. "Carry it for good luck."

"That's one thing you're gonna need," laughed the cop as he snapped the cuffs tightly around the culprit's wrists.

"Better radio in," the searching officer advised as he moved to his car.

After placing the thieves in separate cars, the dog's deputy put them and Kenny in his. The radio soon crackled.

"Did you find the whole loot?" came a voice from the other end.

"Sure looks like it," the deputy answered. "It's a pretty big old box."

"Good work!" shouted the sheriff over the radio. "I'm going to notify the governor and the press right now."

"It'll be a good birthday present," the officer answered. "And tomorrow's the day. Now I'm going to take these dogs into town and get them something to eat. More people coming?"

"Detectives are on their way," cracked the sheriff. "Should be there within the hour."

"Good enough," replied the deputy as he signed off. "Now folks," he stated as he looked to the dogs. "Let's see what we can do for you."

The officer slammed his squad car into gear, turned around, and slowly began rolling down the road. In a short while J.J. gave a loud bark and began to scratch as the side window.

"You need out, girl?" the cop asked as he slowed to a stop.

"Woof!" answered J.J. as the officer got out and opened the back door.

Instantly all three dogs jumped to the ground and ran to a large rock. Behind it was the pack that they had stashed earlier that morning in the interest of speed. Grabbing a strap, J.J. shook it hard to knock off the snow, then with Angel's help carried it back to the car.

"Boy you've got some sniffers," the deputy laughed as he gave it a hard look. "What's in that thing?"

Taking the pack from the Kids the officer unzipped it and examined the contents. Then he closed it and threw it in the back seat.

"School kid must have lost it," he reckoned as he looked back at the dogs who had now jumped back in.

Farther down the road Kenny began to wail as they approached the road to the Kenton Caves.

"Now you need out, too?" the cop shrugged as he again pulled to a stop, got out, and opened the door.

All three dogs hopped to the ground and moved a few yards down the road before turning to the deputy. Kenny gave a loud bark, turned and looked, then yelped again.

"You want me to come with you?" the officer asked.

Another shrill woof convinced him that that's what the dog meant so he fell in behind the three and began walking. In a short while they came to Kenny's cave and went inside.

"Oh, boy," the cop sighed as he looked at all the dogs who were now swarming Kenny and the Kids. "We have a problem."

Quickly he pulled out his cell phone and put in a call to headquarters.

"I know you have enough on your hands right now," he spoke. "But make a call to the Humane Society. I just found about twenty, maybe twenty-five starving dogs living in one of the Kenton Caves. See if they can get somebody out here to pick them up.

"Will do," barked the voice on the other end. "Save one for me."

"No problem," the deputy answered. "I believe this big skinny one's just what I've been looking for," he finished as he looked to Kenny. "And I have a feeling somebody's going to be looking for you," he added as he smiled at the Kids. "Now let's get back to the car. There's going to be a bunch of folks wanting to see you and talk to me."

The deputy loaded the dogs and then stopped in at Kenton to get a little dog food and a bite for himself. Then he hit 325 and headed for Boise City, the county seat. When he got there he found the place swarming with news people wanting to get a glimpse of the thieves now held in the county jail and an interview with the officer. Slowly he worked his car through the throng to his parking space and then emerged with the dogs. Cameras flashed as all four posed for pictures. The sheriff and two deputies then brought out the chest of silver to show the media, placing it on the ground in front of the dogs.

"Mom, Dad!" screamed Amy from the den. "Come look!"

"We're busy right now. What is it? Linda Russell shouted back.

"Now!" insisted Amy as she turned once more to the television.

"I'll see what she wants," Jack laughed as he turned toward the den.

Amy grabbed Max, the badger, and pulled him close as her father entered the room. She said nothing, just pointed to the TV.

'This just in from KDOG television in Oklahoma City. This morning three dogs helped a Cimarron County sheriff's deputy crack the case of the stolen Centennial Silver. The thieves were caught in possession of the loot at the base of Black Mesa, just one day before Oklahoma's 100th birthday.'

"That's great; they found the silver," Jack Russell remarked. "Must have had some pretty good police dogs working up there."

"No!" Amy hollered. "Wait for the picture."

As Jack and Amy waited for more film footage Linda entered the room. As she did, the network cut back to the live feed from Boise City.

"Ohhh!" shrieked Linda as she collapsed into a chair.

"Can't be!" Jack exploded as he grabbed a countertop for balance.

"I told you," Amy stated softly as she watched the Kids and Kenny paw at the chest of silver.

"Call up there!" Linda demanded as she handed the phone to Jack. "I'll start packing."

After several tries Jack Russell finally got through to the Cimarron County Sheriff's Office and told them his story about losing the dogs. Though he took some convincing, the deputy taking the call finally agreed to keep the girls until the Russell's arrival.

"I guess you're telling the truth," the officer offered. "But when I call those dogs by name, they'd better respond."

"They will," Jack assured him.

"What's the quickest way there?" Linda asked as Jack hung up the phone. "Fly to Amarillo and then rent a car?"

"Yup," he answered."Everything packed?"

"Ready to go," Linda replied. "I'll take Max to the neighbor's."

"I'll book a flight while you do that," Jack nearly shouted as he picked up the phone.

"Hey Angel," a cop hooted as he looked to the dogs. "Looks like you and big sister there are going home. Are you going to keep that other one?" the officer added as he looked to the deputy.

"Sure am," he barked. "Never seen a dog that needed a home more than this one, except maybe those others in the cave."

"Are those shelter people going to pick them up in the morning?" the first cop asked.

"Yup," came the answer.

"I'm gonna take at least one," the officer continued. "What are you going to name that mutt," he added as he looked to Kenny.

"I don't know," the deputy shrugged. "Any ideas?"

"Why not Kenton?" the officer suggested. "That's where he comes from."

"That's not bad," the deputy smiled. "Kenton it is."

"Pretty close, Kenny," J.J. laughed as she whispered in their friends ear.

"It'll do," Kenny answered ever so softly.

The Russell's flight touched down in Amarillo at 10:00 P.M. They booked a hotel room for the night and left instructions for a wake-up call at 5:00 the next morning. After reserving a car they had a late dinner and returned to their room. Though all tried, no one slept.

"Restless night," Linda huffed as her husband eased onto U.S. 287. "How far's Boise City?"

"Little over a hundred miles," Jack answered. "Should be there around dawn."

"Good," shouted Amy from the back seat.

Just before daybreak the Russells pulled into town. After stopping to gas up and get directions, they quickly found their way to the county courthouse. The deputy was waiting on the steps.

"You must be the Russells," he stated with a broad smile.

"Yes we are," Jack answered as he introduced himself, Linda, and Amy.

"Bill Terrier," the deputy replied as he shook hands. "I'll bet a little girl wants to see a couple of dogs," he grinned as he looked to a beaming Amy.

"Where are they?" gushed Amy excitedly as she looked behind him.

"Right this way, baby."

Deputy Terrier walked the Russells through the hallway until they came to the Sheriff's Office. Opening the door he let them in.

"They just had a good breakfast," the deputy informed them. "They're out in the courtyard. I'll let them in."

As the Russells waited Bill Terrier opened an outer door and called for the dogs to come. "J.J. Angel. Someone here to see you."

In an instant the Kids flew through the door. Tails twirling they pounced on the

Russells as Kenny, now Kenton, watched and smiled. Tears rolled down Amy's cheeks as she hugged them hard.

"I always knew you were alive," she blubbered.

"Oh," Deputy Terrier spoke as Kenton moved in. "This is Kenton. He was with them."

Kenton moved forward and gave each of the Russells a hard poke with his nose as each knelt to pet him. The officer then told them the whole story about how he had found them and how they had led him to the thieves.

"What's that leather pouch around Angel's neck?" Jack asked.

"Don't know," the officer answered. "She won't let anyone touch it. And I still can't figure out where they got that silver dollar," he laughed as he shook his head.

"We'll probably never know," joked Jack as he readied the family to leave.

"Say," remarked Terrier. "You probably don't know it but Governor Shepherd has made the dogs honorary citizens of Oklahoma. And there's a big reward for finding that silver. I guess it belongs to you seeing as your dogs found it."

"We've got what we want," Linda smiled. "Will you see to it that that money goes to the Oklahoma Humane Society. Set aside a good bit for those Kenton Cave dogs that you told us about."

"I'll do it," promised the deputy as he turned to show the family out.

Bill Terrier walked the Russells to their car and helped them in. Just as they had said their last goodbyes and were about to leave he asked them to wait just a minute. Soon he returned carrying the backpack.

"J.J. found this behind a rock," the officer offered. "She seems to be kind of attached to it. I have no idea who it belongs to so you might as well keep it as a souvenir."

"Thanks," laughed Jack as he started the car.

Deputy Terrier and Kenton watched as the Russells disappeared down the road. Then they went back inside.

"Well, Kenton. Looks like we're going to have to find you some new friends," the officer chuckled as he gave the dog a tap on the head. "Let's go to work."

The Russells drove to a nearby cafe for breakfast. As they were getting out of the car Amy looked to the dogs.

"I can't wait for you to see our new home," she gushed.

"They should like it," Linda offered. "Lot bigger yard to play in."

The Kids looked at each other for a minute and then laughed.

"The Indian woman tricked us," hooted a smiling J.J. as she shook her head. "Same family just a different house.

"She just didn't want to spoil things for us," Angel chuckled.

"Guess so," agreed J.J.

"Open that bag, Amy," Linda suggested as they rolled down the highway. "Let's see what's in there."

"Bunch of stuff," Amy piped as she fished through the pack. "History books and maps, a compass, water bottles, a rope, and two baseball caps."

"Must have belonged to a student," Jack reasoned.

"Well, let's put it to use," Linda ordered.

"Why not," answered Jack. "Let's just take this week off and go on the grand tour. We'll finally give Amy and the dogs a chance to see Oklahoma."

"Uh, oh," J.J. whispered in the little one's ear.

Angel's eyes rolled as she gently pawed the pouch.

In memory of J.J., May 29, 2007 and

Angel, June 6, 2007.

EPILOGUE

The Blacktail Kids have completed another exciting journey. I hope you've enjoyed reading about their travels around your fascinating state. I certainly had a great time doing the research and exploration necessary to write this book. In closing please allow me to make a few points.

1. Trying to cover in detail the history and geography of a state as diverse as Oklahoma in such a short work is an impossible task and was not my objective. My purpose was merely to give a broad overview of many of the significant geographic features and historical events that shaped Oklahoma's development. My hope is that the reader will find a certain topic or topics exciting and "run with it", so to speak, by undertaking a far more detailed analysis. For example, I found the Civil War period in Oklahoma to be a fascinating study, however superficial it was. What I did learn merely made me anxious for more; a lot more. (As you may have guessed, I'm a Civil War buff anyway.)

2. For the most part I portrayed man made geographic features accurately. However in a few instances the locations of some rail lines were invented to fit the story.

3. This book has three central themes: the first is obviously the study of Oklahoma history and geography. The second is more subtle: the need for cooperation in achieving goals. Throughout the book the dogs have to work with each other, as well as the animals they meet along the way, to reach their objective. The same is true for people. Most of you will find that success in life depends in large part of your ability to work harmoniously with others in pursuit of a common goal. Few people can do it all alone. Team sports is perhaps the best example I can think of to illustrate the point. The third central theme is the plight of stray and abused animals. In real life J.J. and Angel were my two dogs, both starving strays I picked up in the country long ago. I hope my readers will always keep in mind the terrible situation we have with unwanted animals and do whatever possible to help with the problem. Make sure your pets are spayed or neutered and take in a stray whenever you can. Also, I wrote the dog fighting scene well before the Michael Vick story surfaced. I personally can't think of a more disgusting practice than animal fighting of any kind. Should you, the reader, ever hear of such behavior please report it immediately to the proper authorities.

4. I found Oklahoma to have a wonderful state park system and I made reference to many of the parks in the book. While I didn't get to visit them all, I did go to quite a few. I would urge the reader to do his or her best to see as many as possible. You can find the entire list on the Parks Department website.

5. Throughout the book I make numerous references to the importance of water. Recent record rainfall should not lull the reader into thinking that the severe drought of the past few years in both Oklahoma and Texas was a passing occurrence. Rest assured that more dry spells are on the way and an ever increasing population will make dealing with them even more difficult. It would do us all well to remember the lessons of Spiro Mounds.

6. Maps-Several maps in the book can be found on the United States Geological Survey website. It's an excellent source for thousands of fascinating maps difficult to find elsewhere and a site I urge you to visit. Simply google USGS.

OKLAHOMA FUN FACTS

1. Called the "Bunion Derby". Andy Payne, 21 year old son of a Foyil farmer, won the 84 day 1928 foot race from Los Angeles to Madison Square Garden in NYC. Out of 250 runners only 55 finished the race of 3423 miles.

2. Tulsa's Philbrook Museum Garden has its own version of Rodin's famous "The Thinker". It's a six feet tall 2800 pound bronze rabbit by Welsh artist Brian Flanigan titled "Thinker on a rock".

3. Tulsa's Spartan College of Aeronautics Technology founded in 1928 is one of the nation's oldest and largest aviation colleges. It has produced over 80,000 pilots and technicians from around the world.

4. In the 1930's parking meters were invented by Carl McGee, an Oklahoma City newspaper editor.

5. The state's oldest town, Salina, was picked as a trading post site by French trader Major Jean Pierre Choteau in 1796 when George Washington was U.S. President.

6. Famous movie and television actor, Oklahoma native James Garner was asked where he lived in Norman. He answered, "I lived in a lot of houses. Every time the rent came due we moved. But everyone was poor. It was all I knew."

7. Oklahoma is a big draw for movie makers. It has eleven different ecosystems, from the Little Sahara in the west to the eastern swamp lands. The only land form not found in the state is the snow capped mountain peaks.

8. Oklahoma's attraction as a movie locale can be traced back to 1908 and the earliest silent movies, often starring Oklahoma western actor Tom Mix.

9. Sparsely settled Oklahoma has had six Miss Americas.

10. Tulsa World headline--"Oklahoma, where the crooks come sweeping down the plains." World famous early outlaws looking for easy money: Belle Star, The Doolin-Dalton gang, Ma Barker and sons, Public Enemy #1 Pretty Boy Floyd, Machine Gun Kelly, and Bonnie and Clyde.

11. Oil was the reason Tulsa had the busiest airport in the world in the 1930's, a 490 acre former wheat field.

12. The state of Oklahoma is ranked fourth in the U.S. in terms of total Indian gaming revenue.

13. A Boston Marathon qualifying event in Tulsa is appropriately called "The Route 66 Marathon" normally attracting around 4000 runners.

14. In other cities the old Route 66 has been paved over by new interstates. In Tulsa the original road still runs right through the center of town.

15. In 1924 Tulsa solved its water shortage problem by building Lake Spavinaw some 60 miles away. A song was written to commemorate the occasion:
    "Clear and cold, pure as gold-nothing like the Arkansas.
    In the tub, no more mud! At the sink, take a drink.

16. Opened in 1953, the 88 mile Tulsa Oklahoma City Turnpike, later named for governor John Turner, was the first of its kind in the Midwest.

17. Oklahoma lists five Heisman Trophy winners: Billy Vessels, Steve Owens, Billy Sims, Barry Sanders, and Jason White.

18. In 1913, 3000 Tulsans awaited the start of a Major League Baseball exhibition game between the Chicago White Sox and the New York Giants when suddenly the right field bleachers collapsed injuring 52 and killing one. The crowd waited for the game to be played as Oklahoma's own Jim Thorpe was playing for the Giants.

19. At one point in the 1920's it was reported that Tulsa had the highest per capita income in the nation.

20. Alcohol was against the law in Indian Territory. In the early 1900's when Tulsey Town was bustling with a contingent of cowboys, coal miners, and newly arrived oil workers. The custom was to hide your whiskey bottle in your boot. Thus the term "Bootlegger" was coined.

21. At 52 stories Tulsa's Bank of Oklahoma building is the tallest in the state.

22. In 1906 more than five million barrels of oil were produced on the Osage Reservation making it at the time the wealthiest nation per capita in the world.

23. Tulsa's American Indian population is second only to Los Angeles.

24. Fourteen flags have flown over what is now Oklahoma.

25. Oklahoma is the nation's third largest producer of natural gas.

26. In 1959, Oklahoma became the last state to repeal prohibition.

27. Bartlesville's annual spring Mozart Festival, an eight day event, has gained an international reputation for excellence, drawing participants from around the world.

28. Pistol Pete, Oklahoma State's famous football team mascot, really existed. One of Oklahoma's most colorful characters, Frank Eaton was an Indian scout, stagecoach driver, a deputy U.S. marshall, a cattle herder on the Chisholm Trail, an Oklahoma land run participant in 1899, and a blacksmith. At age 15 he won shooting contest against Fort Gibson soldiers and the fort commander gave him the name Pistol Pete.

29. Large wind farms now dot the landscape around both Weatherford and Lawton, making Oklahoma number five in the nation in wind power capacity.

30. Oklahoma is capable of producing 111,000 tires a day, more than any other state.

31. Canada, Mexico, Japan, and Saudi Arabia are the current top Oklahoma export markets.

32. "The Oklahoma Hills", by Okemah native Woody Guthrie is the state's official folk song.

33. In the late 1800's, Oklahoma coal mine representatives traveled to Italy to recruit workers. As a result several ethnic communities developed which still feature and the flavor and food delicacies of southern Italy.

34. Tulsa's first opera house, more affectionately known as "Old Lady Brady", was built in 1914 north of the railroad tracks. Most performances were interrupted once of twice by the blasts of the train whistles, much to the chagrin of the famous artists who played there.

35. The Tulsa trolley system which operated until 1936 cost five cents, but policemen, firemen and postmen rode free.

36. Sapulpa, called the "Crossroads of America", has five major highways converging in the town.

37. Fort Gibson, established in April of 1824, served as a home for a time for U.S. president Zachary Taylor, Confederate President Jefferson Davis, and Republic of Texas president Sam Houston.

38. 105 Civil War battles were fought in Indian Territory.

List compiled by Mary Lou Martin

Can you add to it?